FRESHMAN

FRESHMAN

A NOVEL BY

MICHAEL GERBER

HYPERION PAPERBACKS

NEW YORK

Text copyright ©2006 Michael Gerber

All rights reserved. No part of this book may be reproduced or transmitted in any form or by any means, electronic or mechanical, including photocopying, recording, or by any information storage and retrieval system, without written permission from the publisher. For information address Hyperion Books for Children, 114 Fifth Avenue, New York, New York 10011-5690.

First Hyperion Paperbacks edition, 2007

1 3 5 7 9 10 8 6 4 2

Printed in the United States of America

This book is set in 12-point Garamond 3.

Cover design by Michael Farmer

Library of Congress Cataloging-in-Publication Data on file.

ISBN-13: 978-0-7868-3851-6

ISBN-10: 0-7868-3851-5

Visit www.hyperionteens.com

To my parents,
and the tuition for which they stood

Stutts University (and Downtown Great Littleton)

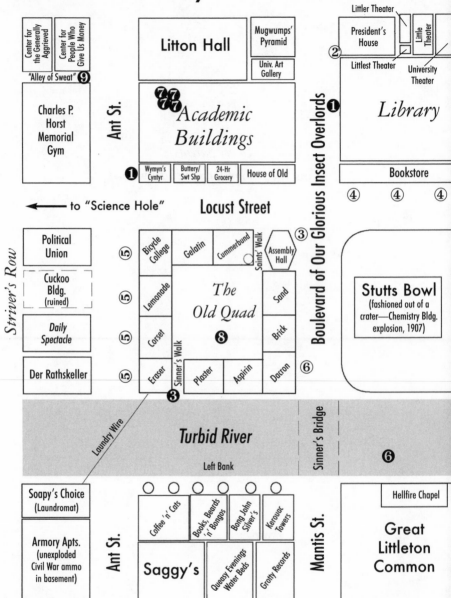

Center for the Generally Aggrieved

Center for People Who Give Us Money

"Alley of Sweat" ❾

Litton Hall

Mugwumps' Pyramid

Univ. Art Gallery

President's House

Littler Theater

Little Theater

Littlest Theater

University Theater

❷

❶

Library

Charles P. Horst Memorial Gym

Ant St.

❼❼❼❼ *Academic Buildings*

❶

Wymyn's Cyntyr

Buttery/ Swt Shp

24-Hr Grocery

House of Old

Boulevard of Our Glorious Insect Overlords

❶

Bookstore

④ ④ ④

← to "Science Hole"

Locust Street

Political Union

⑤

Cuckoo Bldg. (ruined)

⑤

Daily Spectacle

⑤

Der Rathskeller

⑤

Striver's Row

Bicycle College

Gelatin

Cummerbund

Saints' Walk

③

Assembly Hall

Lemonade

The Old Quad

Sand

Corset

❽

Brick

Sinner's Walk

Eraser

Plaster

Aspirin

Dacron

⑥

③

Stutts Bowl (fashioned out of a crater—Chemistry Bldg. explosion, 1907)

Turbid River

Laundry Wire

Sinner's Bridge

Left Bank

⑥

Soapy's Choice (Laundromat)

Armory Apts. (unexploded Civil War ammo in basement)

Ant St.

○ ○ ○ ○ ○

Coffee 'n' Cats

Books, Beards 'n' Bongos

Bong John Silver's

Kerouac Towers

Saggy's

Queasy Evenings Water Beds

Grotty Records

Mantis St.

Hellfire Chapel

Great Littleton Common

Points of Interest

❶ Panhandler
❷ Guy peeing
❸ Rastaman selling oregano to freshmen
❹ Cult members

❺ Roving pack of feral grad students
❻ Lost alum
❼ Student having anxiety attack
❽ Alma Mater statue (w/shaving cream)

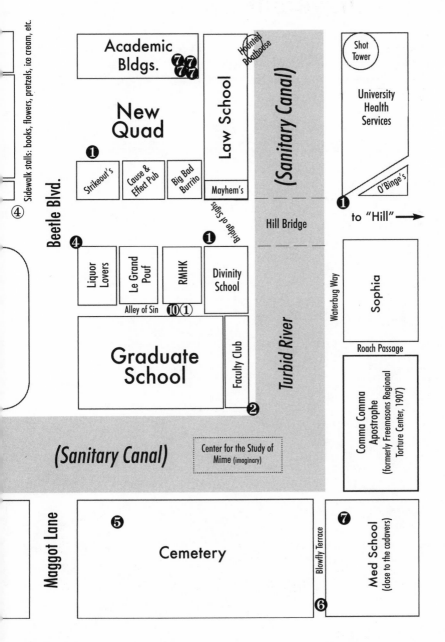

⑨ Visiting high school senior (passed out)
⑩ Visiting foreign dignitary
① Armed robber
② President Whitbread's cat
③ Huge-ass hole they keep digging, then filling up, at 3 am in the goddamn morning
④ More road work
⑤ Car alarm (every 15 min.)
⑥ Mysterious siren outside Hart's window

. . . {T}he unspeakable in full pursuit of the uneatable.
—Oscar Wilde, on fox hunting

PROLOGUE

SLEEPY WITH BOREDOM and gassy from lunch, Hart Fox sat in the hard plastic chair outside his dean's office. A kid walked in the door, pink detention slip in hand, bobbing his head a little so that the purple spikes of his Mohawk didn't get bent on the transom. He slumped down next to Hart. Hart nodded—he remembered this joker from sophomore American History, constantly arguing in favor of anarcho-syndicalism. Was his name Henry? Henry (if that was his name) was sporting a fresh bruise under one eye.

A minute later, a kid with a shaved head—clearly Henry's opponent in the fight—walked into the waiting room, a wad of bloody Kleenex stuffed up his nose. He dumped his stocky body into a chair as far away from Henry as possible. Hart didn't know the bald kid's name, but recognized him, too. He was always sticking his arm inside the vending machine in the cafeteria trying to steal Cokes.

Pretty soon a door opened, and a delicate student smelling vaguely of lilac shuffled out of Dean Gold's office; it was Maximilian, poet, actor, and varsity aesthete. Maximilian always looked sort of green, but today he was a deeper hue than usual. He was clutching a coveted yellow slip.[1]

"Show the slip to the security guard, Max. That'll teach you to keep caviar in your locker . . . Hi, Hart." Dean Gold wasn't Hart's dean, that was Dean Grubbman, but Hart knew everybody and everybody knew Hart; that was one of the perks of being a senior.

"You guys again?" Dean Gold said, exasperated. "I told you two to stay out of my office until spring break."

"But, *Dean*," Henry said, in the plaintive rumble of grievance Hart remembered so well, "Simon called Mikhail Bakunin a douche!"

"Well, he *was*," Simon said. Simon was rebelling against his ex-hippie parents by espousing politics just to the right of the Third Reich. (His sister Garfunkel took it even further. She was in jail for spray painting a whale.)

"Who's Mikhail what's-his-name? Is he gonna show up in my office, too?"

"No," Henry said sullenly. There was something about Henry's manner that made you want to disagree, even when he was right. "He's a Russian revolutionary—"

Dean Gold held up a hand. "I thought as much. Get in here." The dean rolled his eyes at Hart, then closed the door. Hart heard him carp, "Hitler and Stalin signed a nonaggression pact, but you two can't even get through home ec . . ."

Hart looked at his watch. Shit, five minutes until study hall. He needed study hall to finish his physics homework before class. He'd already been waiting for a half-hour; he'd better start now.

---

[1] Pink was for detention, yellow for early dismissal, and black was for putting a M-80 down the girls' toilet.

Just as Hart flipped open his textbook, Dean Prist's door opened. "I don't think you have a thing to worry about," the dean was cooing. "That's one of the finest Stutts application essays I've ever seen."

Hart's ears pricked up at the mention of his first-choice college. Stutts University was everybody's first choice; it was the best school in the country, by far. Philo T. Farnsworth High was a "feeder," which meant one person a year got admitted—except for the years when nobody made it.

Doreen Breith walked out of Dean Prist's office, wearing the uniform, of course: fake pearls over kelly green sweater, pink turtleneck poking out from underneath; lots of hair product and Kissable Conch lipstick. It all added up to one thing: Guys like Hart shouldn't even try. Not like he'd ever been attracted to cyborgs (Doreen was *that* perfect).

Hart was convinced that Doreen Breith had been sent from the future, Terminator-like, to dominate the academic world of Sandy Dunes, Michigan. Naturally, the honor of the human race demanded that he stop her. They had been battling it out, quarter by quarter, test by test, since second grade, when Hart had moved there from Chicago. Stutts promised to settle the matter once and for all. Hart had been the front-runner for the past year; he'd gotten a humor column in the school paper, and that, along with four years of bench-warming for the lacrosse team, made him excruciatingly well-rounded. But last week, Doreen had vaulted him, winning an award from the Association of Frustrated Poets. Her poem was as cunning as it was atrocious: a morbid, all-lowercase, totally calculated hunk of treacle about a dead kid looking down at a car wreck. Even worse, the last six AFP winners had all been accepted by Stutts, with financial aid. Enraged, Hart immediately dashed off a

3

parody of Doreen's poem—but while "too stupid to live" caused much milk to shoot out of many noses during its brief circuit around the cafeteria, the fact remained that Hart was now definitely number two.

Back in the office, Dean Prist asked Doreen, "Would you mind too terribly if I showed your essay to a friend of mine? He was Stutts's local interviewer for several years. It gives him such pleasure to discover that rare student who can *truly* write. . . . Who knows? He might be able to put our application over the top," Dean Prist said.

"That would be great, Jeanette," Doreen burbled—they were on a first-name basis. They also had the same haircut. Gak, Hart thought.

"Excellent." Over–made-up eyes glittering, Dean Prist patted Doreen on the back. "Onward, champion!" she said confidently.

Doreen headed toward the door. "Hi, Hart," she said, slipping him a smile like a stiletto as she passed.

"Onward, Doreen-bot," Hart teased in a low voice. Doreen mouthed a swear word at him and left.

After Doreen had gone, Dean Prist noticed Hart. "Hi, Hart." Giving him the same sneaky-lethal smile, she closed the door.

Dean Grubbman's door finally swung open. "No, no—I had the procedure, I just want the test results! I've been waiting two weeks and I'm going crazy!" Yelling into the phone, he stuck his head out and looked around. He waved Hart in. "No—please don't put me on hold again. All I want is—" He sighed and hung up.

Hart took a seat.

"Doctors!" the dean said wearily, mopping his brow. He

slung his feet up onto the corner of his desk; they barely reached. "Why didn't you say you were waiting? Anyway, I'm probably going to die within the week, so make it quick." The dean was a notorious hypochondriac.

"It's about my Stutts application. It's almost totally done," Hart lied. "You said you'd write me a recommendation, do you have it? The application's due Thursday."

"In six days? Crap!" Hart knew Dean Grubbman only swore around students he liked. And why shouldn't he like Hart? Hart was an academic star, a good kid, a feather in Grubbman's cap—and might even win the dean some serious money, if the rumors about the office pool were true.[2] "I'll do it over the weekend, okay? Is that soon enough? I've got a doctor's appointment on Saturday, but I don't think they're planning on doping me too heavily. If they do, well, it'll just be a little . . . free-form." The dean chuckled nervously. When Hart didn't laugh, he added, "It'll be good, I promise!"

"Okay," Hart said. He liked Dean Grubbman, but sometimes he wished his dean were a little less of an oddball. More no-nonsense, like Dean Gold—or even nakedly ambitious, like Dean Prist. Having Dean Grubbman made him feel even more like a long shot. No Grubbman kid had made it into Stutts in a decade; lately people had been transferring to Dean Prist. Hart had stayed out of loyalty and pity, but sometimes he wondered.

"Is that it?" the dean said, flopping his legs to the floor with a clomp.

---

[2] It was said that everybody on the faculty put fifty dollars on whichever senior they thought was going to get admitted to Stutts. On the rare occasion that Stutts took no students from the school, the kitty rolled over. Nobody had been accepted for two years running, so the faculty was positively smoldering with greed.

"Yep," Hart said, standing up.

The dean offered Hart a moist palm. "Fox, if I had two hundred kids like you, I'd be a well man." They walked out into the hall. "I'll get that rec to you by Monday," he said as the bell rang. "Not like you need it, but—" Smiling, the dean crossed his fingers. Hart did the same, then ran out the door to study hall.

Dean Prist sauntered over. "Jasper, have I showed you Doreen Breith's Stutts essay? It's—I was going to say 'good' but I think 'inspiring' is more accurate. It's a testament to—are you feeling all right? You don't look well . . ."

"I'll look better after Fox wins me the pool!" Dean Grubbman fired back, and slammed his door.

Monday came and went without anything from the dean. On Tuesday, after checking Dean Grubbman's out-box several times, Hart was really beginning to worry—should he forge one? But by midafternoon the letter was there, with a Post-it attached. The handwriting was extremely loose and erratic; "colonoscopy" had been misspelled, and there were several messy cross-outs. Hart prayed Dean Grubbman had been lucid when he wrote the recommendation. The letter was sealed. Hart just had to hope for the best.

That night after dinner, Hart sat at his desk, checking and rechecking the application. The forms were all there; all three essays; all three recommendations; the handwriting analysis; the credit check . . . Hart hoped that his ex-SDS history teacher, Mr. Ashram, hadn't taken his wisecracks about the Weather Underground personally. Maybe he should've asked the newspaper adviser instead? Oh well, what the hell, like Mom always said. Speaking of his mom, why did she have to use a Mickey

Mouse check for the application fee? Why did she have to use Mickey Mouse checks at all? She was as bad as Dean Grubbman!

All of Hart's life seemed like that—ramshackle and cheesy, unique in the worst way. Other kids didn't live in a huge, falling-down mansion where they had to rent rooms out. Other kids' fathers weren't on the lam from Interpol. Other kids' little cousins didn't go around claiming to be CIA-trained assassins. He couldn't even have friends over anymore; there was no telling what his frankness-crazed mother would say. Last time, she'd cornered Hart's friend Steve. "I hear you've gotten a new girlfriend," she had said brightly.

"Yes, Mrs. Fox," Steve had said. He was Hart's editor on the school paper, and massively shy.

"Well, is it serious?" There was an uncomfortable silence. Steve didn't know what to say.

"What I'm asking is, have you engaged in intercourse?"

"Oh, God!" Steve blushed crimson and looked like he was going to throw up.

"Jesus, Mom, can't you act normal just for—"

Mrs. Fox waved Hart off. "It's all right, Hart—we're all adults here," she said. "I just want to make sure Steve's taking care of her needs as well as his own. Steve," Mrs. Fox continued, putting a hand on the terrified boy's shoulder, *The Joy of Sex* was written for a reason. My generation fought the entire sixties so that you could be free."

"Mom," Hart croaked, "we don't want to be free. We want you to leave us alone. Please change the subject before I dump a bucket of water on you."

"Oh, don't be so repressed," Mrs. Fox said. "Would you like me to heat up a frozen pizza?"

Steve wouldn't come over after that, and Hart didn't blame him. How could anybody be expected to be popular under these conditions?

Hart wasn't a total pariah—six extracurriculars helped with that—but looking vaguely familiar wasn't the same as being popular. He didn't have a girlfriend, for obvious reasons. He'd had a one-night thing with a girl from Austria during an orchestra trip last year. The language barrier had made it very confusing; he hadn't realized what was happening until it was almost over. Nobody believed him, and they hadn't kept in touch—Hart misheard her address and wrote it down wrong.

Hart was signing the application, musing grimly as to the doubtlessly overwhelming percentage of Stutts applicants who had girlfriends, when there was a sharp knock on the door. Hart jumped. He was easily startled.

Great, Hart thought—now my signature looks like I had a stroke. Actually, maybe that would help him get in.[3] "Who is it?" he yelled.

"Me," Mrs. Jenkins yelled back. She was a boarder. There were five, and they all tended to blend together in Hart's mind. Mrs. Jenkins was the one obsessed with air flow. "I need you to open my window. I'm suffocating."

Hart opened the door. "Mrs. Jenkins, it's January. Besides, we've put caulk and plastic sheets over all the windows." Hart's mom considered drafts to be a slur against her character, and put up so much clear plastic Hart suspected that some of it had become load-bearing. Every year, Hart spent the entire week-

---

[3] Stutts had scholarships for all sorts of students, turning everything from dyslexia to spontaneous combustion into a definite advantage. Hart sort of had his eye on the one for "high school seniors who have demonstrated talent in journalism while suffering from stigmata." He figured he'd get in first, then work out some scam later.

end before Halloween pointing hair dryers at windows. Again: who could be popular under these conditions?

"Then cut a hole in it," Mrs. Jenkins said desperately. "I need *circulation*."

"But . . ." The word died in Hart's mouth. He knew from long experience that arguments were futile. "Okay." Hart tried to stay out of the boarders' rooms, not only out of respect but also to protect his guttering vision of a pleasant old age. The last time he'd been in Mrs. Jenkins' quarters, he'd noticed that she'd put up tiny streamers so she could monitor air currents. She even had a notebook where she recorded all sorts of readings. Ah, the golden years. Hart tried not to think about them—being young was hard enough.

The first thing I'm gonna do after I get out of Stutts and start making money, Hart thought as he trudged through the snow later that night, is pay off the taxes, kick out the boarders, and convince Mom to sell that goddamned house. It wouldn't be easy—the house had been Grandpa's. The last time Hart brought it up, his mom had said, "Why stop there? Why not flush Paw-Paw's ashes down the toilet while we're at it?"

Hart had loved the house as a kid, when they'd come to visit—but owning it was another thing. And as soon as Dr. Fox had quit his practice and started hawking No-Preg,[4] it had

---

[4] No-Preg was Dr. Fox's invention, a liqueur with birth-control hormones in it. "Alcohol has caused unwanted pregnancies for centuries—why can't it prevent a few as well?" That sounded fine, until a bunch of male customers suddenly developed female sex characteristics. Now Mr. Fox is under indictment in so many countries around the world that the only way he could avoid the slammer was constant air travel; by the time any authorities realized he was in their airspace, he would be out of their jurisdiction. As a result, Hart hadn't seen his father in over four years. They did have a regular Sunday dinner-by-speakerphone, however.

become financially ruinous. But his mother was sentimental, so that was that. Hart realized that the only way he'd ever pry that house away from her was with dynamite.

Hart saw the mailbox up ahead. His plan was to overnight the application to Stutts, then check on it tomorrow. If they hadn't gotten it, he'd still have a day to fill out a duplicate application online, and round up replacement recommendations. That was Hart—plans in depth, every eventuality covered. He'd had to be that way if he wanted anything to be done right. God knows his parents were . . . preoccupied. That was the nicest way to put it.

Saying a prayer, Hart dropped the application in the box. He checked the pickup schedule four times, and made sure he heard the package drop. He could've just e-mailed the application, but there was something satisfying about filling out the form in pen. If Hart got into Stutts, it would be like his own personal Declaration of Independence, the founding document of the new him.

Hart started back to the house. The wind was against him now, blowing hard. The light from the streetlamps bounced off the snow and made it seem earlier than it was, well past midnight. It was cold, but Hart had always liked walking around late at night; he felt like he was stealing time. He had finished the application hours ago, but couldn't stand to wait until morning to drop it off. It was either lie awake in bed, or work off the nervous energy with a long walk.

Sniffing, his face numb, Hart rounded the corner. He paused for a moment, looking at the big old houses on his street. Hearing Lake Michigan's surf, under a black sky speckled with stars, Hart thought: how beautiful. Then: I can't wait to get out of here.

CHAPTER ONE

Hart took a lot of late-night walks over the next few months. His safety schools[5] admitted Hart immediately, but he didn't want to go to any of those places. He wanted to go to Stutts, and Stutts was notorious for taking its time. Hart's interviewer, a pompous, flatulent attorney, told him that the Stutts experience began with waiting to see if you had gotten in. "Anything that excruciating," the interviewer said with a wan smile, "has got to build character."

Hart's midnight strolls yielded a surprising amount of entertainment: people strolling past picture windows buck-naked, classmates making out in lurching, steamed-up cars. Things got nutty late at night. So he wasn't too shocked when a big black limousine gave a short honk and pulled up beside him.

---

[5] *Safety school*—Someplace you'd rather kill yourself than attend, but your parents make you apply to anyway. Hart's safeties were State, and the college his parents attended, which was so hard up for students it was putting pop-up ads on porn sites. Not that Hart would know anything about those, oh no.

Hart turned off his headphones and prepared to give directions. A tinted window slid down, revealing a pudgy guy with a salt-and-pepper mustache and a toothpick in his mouth. He looked like the Buddha gone bad. "Hart Fox?"

"Yeah?"

"Lean down so I can look at you." The driver checked Hart against a blowup of his yearbook photo.

It was a terrible picture. Not only was Hart wearing his emergency glasses (he'd ripped a contact that morning), but there was a bright-red constellation of pimples sprayed across his forehead. And his hair looked like he'd combed it with an eggbeater. "Let me guess: you're scheduling retakes."

"They told me you liked to talk nonsense," the driver said, "but you can quit, 'cause I ain't listenin'." He unlocked the doors. "Get in."

Stranger danger! Hart's hindbrain flashed, and he found himself on the horns of a dilemma. On the one hand, Hart was naturally friendly, almost pathologically so. On the other, he firmly believed that things like serial killers, cannibalism, and human sacrifice were more common than everybody supposed. Resigned to become a statistic, he got in; he'd been trained to respect his elders, and like all ambitious people, Hart had a strong attraction to limousines.

"Who told you I liked to talk nonsense?" When the driver didn't answer, Hart checked out the bar compartment. "Where's the booze?"

"Up here with me," the driver said. "You're underage."

"I thought limousines were like international waters or something." The only answer that came was the sound of the driver taking a swig.

As they drove, Hart got more and more anxious. Not

only was he in a car driven by a complete stranger, but that stranger wouldn't answer any of his questions! And was drinking. And wouldn't give him any!

"This is outrageous," Hart said indignantly. "I would like, in fact I demand, a beer."

"No beer up here. Just hard stuff. And you're not getting any."

"It's totally illogical that I can fight and even die for my country, but some creep who picks me up in a limo, can't give me a—"

"Kid: shut up," the driver explained.

"But in Europe—"

"I'm not listening. Shut up and go to sleep."

Hart saw his point. It was 1:30 in the morning, and he was sleepy. He got sleepy every time he was anxious—how was that for an idiotic evolutionary mechanism? To zonk out whenever the saber-toothed tigers showed up? True to his ancestors, Hart drifted off. Sometime later, from far, far away, Hart heard a voice say: "Wake up, kid. We're almost there."

Hart shifted position, a spindle of drool dropping from his lip.

"Hey! Don't you drool on my upholstery!" The driver shook his head bitterly. "You're annoying even when you're asleep."

Hart sat up. "I wasn't sleeping. I was just resting my eyes," he mumbled, sitting up. No one in Hart's family ever admitted falling asleep. Farting, sure—masturbation, even. But falling asleep, never. It was a point of honor.

Hart groggily rubbed the condensation off his window. It was still pitch-black, and a heavy snow had begun to fall. Great, Hart thought. Now it'll be easy to hide my body. *Why had he gotten into the car?* Idiot, idiot, idiot, idiot, Hart repeated his silent mantra. *What had he been thinking?* Self-laceration was also a Fox family tradition—winners don't avoid criticism, they beat everyone else to it. This strategy took constant vigilance . . . and still he screwed things up. Hart looked down at his jeans. At least he didn't have morning wood; the Erection Fairy was still asleep. Good. It would suck to die with a boner.

Hart miserably scanned the predawn murk for other cars, but all he saw was an armadillo crouched on the shoulder of the road. Hart conjured up a whole story involving a pet armadillo trying to find its way from Indiana to Texas—with a winning lottery ticket in its mouth, and just forty-eight hours to cash it—when he blinked and saw that it was just a curled scrap of blown-out tire. Too bad, Hart thought. He liked the armadillo better.

This happened all the time; faulty vision[6] and a strong imagination conspired to keep Hart trapped in a very different, often alarming world. It always—or almost always—resolved into boring normalcy after a squint, but this constant double-taking kept Hart willing to accept the bizarre, and go along with it, too. Like getting into mysterious limos, for example.

As a hawk attempted to land on the hood of the car (no, wait, it was just a plastic bag) they turned off the expressway and into a bleak, urban neighborhood. Hart smelled the stench of death in the air, not realizing that Gary, Indiana, always smells like that.

---

[6] Thanks to an extremely rare birth defect, Hart's left eye was in his right socket, and vice versa. He had learned to compensate, but Hart looked slightly walleyed occasionally, when his brain was preoccupied and his eyes were left to their own devices. The condition was nearly invisible—and certainly no advantage when it came to getting into college. At least Hart didn't think so. He hoped not. Oh, maybe it had been, and he wouldn't be able to hack it! Hart tried not to think that way.

Hart racked his brain for who might want to kill him. Nobody came to mind; with all the AP-level classes and college-attracting extracurriculars, there simply wasn't much time to make enemies. Abduction/murder wasn't Doreen's style—much too "tacky," to use her favorite put-down. Weird Abigail had a crush on him, and she'd be just the kind to go all *Fatal Attraction* without them ever having dated. But Hart knew her parents had told her to stop playing "Magic" for money, so it was highly doubtful she could've scraped together the cash for a hit man and a limousine.

The only real possibility was Steve of Weed, the guy who sold pot under the football bleachers during lunch.[7] Steve of Weed had hated Hart ever since Hart had made a crack about his shirt in front of some girls. Now that he was about to pay for the joke with his life, Hart was bitter; it wasn't *his* fault that Led Zeppelin was a cliché. Steve of Weed—the guy too baked to wear shoes with laces—was a drug lord. You *do* learn something new every day, Hart concluded glumly. The trick is to keep it from killing you.

The limo turned at the next light, into an even more ruined part of town. Hart's money was on his head, hands, and torso being dumped in three separate locations, to delay identification. There'd be one piece in Lake Michigan, one in a vacant lot somewhere, and one back home (in his locker maybe?), to serve as a warning to others. Hart knew how it was done; he'd seen the cop shows.

They slowed and cruised down a side street. This is it, Hart

---

[7] "Steve of Weed" was the kid's nickname for himself, and he scrawled it all over his notebooks in Olde English letters. "It's my brand identity," Steve of Weed said. "One day, when they legalize pot—and they will, my friend—I'll be the richest dude in America." "Maybe then you'll buy a new shirt," Hart had said.

thought, lying back on the seat and placing the sole of his sneaker on the window, getting ready to break it out. Then he saw the sign:

DARLING CONSTRUCTION WELCOMES YOU!

THE REV. DR. MARTIN LUTHER KING, JR.

GOLF AND COUNTRY CLUB

OPENING 2008—APPLICATIONS BEING ACCEPTED

WE HAVE A DREAM . . .

THE FINEST GOLF COURSE IN AMERICA

Relief poured over Hart like a sponge bath from God. The car ride suddenly made sense. It was something about the Darlings' stupid lawn.

This golf course was the latest scheme of Burlington Darling, a prominent local businessman/asshole. Cutting his absurdly huge lawn had been Hart's main source of income throughout high school. Dealing with Mr. Darling was annoying, but at least Hart wouldn't die. He might want to, but he wouldn't.

Hart wondered what Mr. Darling needed to talk with him about at three in the morning. It could be anything; Mr. Darling had a thing about his lawn like Quasimodo had a thing about bells. Every blade in the rolling two acres had to be perfect. Hart always got an analysis of the previous week's job, short, oddly emotional notes saying things like, "Edging *is* part of the job!" or "Loose matter *must* be swept!" Every quarter, Mr. Darling issued a typed report with a letter grade. Hart pulled straight A's at school, but could barely manage a C- on Mr. Darling's lawn.

The limo pulled up to a sentry station at the entrance to the building site. The driver rolled down his window.

"Morning, Angelo. Where's Stones[8] at?"

"He's on the front nine," a man in a policelike uniform said, not moving his eyes from a mini-TV in front of him.

The driver's response was blotted out by a far-off explosion. Every so often, there were flashes, followed by echoing booms, as another building came down. As the limo jostled over gravel and bits of concrete, Hart looked around, grateful to be alive. Some of the buildings were floodlit, the ones next on the list to be imploded. Buildings interested him; maybe he would be an architect. That seemed like a good job. But the best job was living off the fat of your ancestors, like Mr. Darling did.

The Darlings were one of the city's oldest families, and certainly the richest. The great-great grandfather—"who," Mr. Darling was always quick to point out, "was an immigrant"[9]— had founded *Daily Money*, a huge financial newspaper with editions all over the world. The Darlings had since diversified in a million different directions, including building top-of-the-line golf courses. Now, out of boredom more than anything else, Mr. Darling was running for governor.

Hart's dad had been especially keen on Hart cutting Mr. Darling's lawn. "Money is like an STD," Dr. Fox had told his son. "Get close enough to somebody who's got it, and chances are good you'll get it, too."

---

[8] "Stones" was the nickname Mr. Darling had earned from his staff. It came from the question he asked every job applicant: "If you're going to work with me, you've gotta have stones. Do you have stones?" Of course, prodigious testicles matter very little in most professions, but Mr. Darling was a gangster-movie addict. Like most men too dainty to change a tire, Burlington Darling fancied himself a real tough guy, and peppered his conversation with gangster talk, hoping that it scared others into agreeing with him. It didn't.

[9] From England, where people knew him as Lord Starvelington, the richest man north of Liverpool.

But three years later, all Hart had to show for his troubles was $2,112 in the bank, and golden memories of Trip Darling and his stupid friends—the other seniors at Farnsworth who joined Trip at the lowest end of the bell curve—throwing piss balloons at him whenever he got close enough to the mansion.

At least the end was in sight; the Darlings would look a lot less annoying from a dorm room at Stutts . . . if he got in. Mr. Darling himself had studied there. Not very diligently, judging by the grammar in his notes—but then again, he hadn't needed to. Back in those days, Stutts was a private club for the right sort of person.

Now, after years of tumult followed by decades of self-congratulation, Stutts was a meritocracy. No matter how poor you were, or where you lived, you could get in. And a Stutts degree was a ticket to any career one desired—even President of the United States. Hell, *especially* President. Hart had wanted to go there ever since he was twelve: sleeping over at a friend's house, he'd seen a cheesy teen sex comedy called *Party Dorm* that had been set there. Young Hart had decided: wherever America's best minds gather together to drill holes into the girls' shower with impunity, that was the place for him.

Stutts played a role in this golf course, too. The mayor and Mr. Darling had roomed together there, twenty-five years ago, so the Darling Company won a no-bid contract to turn a swath of public housing into an eighteen-hole masterpiece. In a concession to the city's black leaders, the course was going to be named after Martin Luther King, Jr. Then, the city's Latino leaders started complaining, so the mayor announced that the clubhouse would have a restaurant named Cesar's 19th Hole, after Cesar Chavez. These concessions made the blacks and Latinos even angrier. The mayor was genuinely puzzled—both his Mexican landscaper and his Jamaican nanny had been nothing but smiles when he had mentioned the project. So he chalked it up to a few bad apples.

"Unlike the so-called 'public housing' it is replacing," the mayor had announced, "this club will be open to all—provided they can afford it, of course. That's the American way, and any class warriors drunk on sour grapes should take that up with the Constitution, not with me."

Sensing an opportunity for a time-consuming, utterly vacant gesture, the opposition started a petition. Mr. Ashram brought it into history class, hoping to rekindle the spirit of the Sixties without the benefit of pot, free love, or Beatles records. After appeals to democracy and equality elicted yawns, he offered his students one point of extra credit for every ten signatures. *This* spoke to them: good grades led to good colleges, which led to good jobs and good bank accounts. Within days, a beaming Mr. Ashram delivered a thick stack of signatures to the campaign, never noticing that "Terry Dactil," "J.V. Futbal," "Hugh G. Rection," and all the others weren't enrolled at Farnsworth.

Hart didn't participate in the scam; he didn't need the extra credit. Besides, after all that lawn-cutting, he felt a certain connection with the Darlings. He and Trip Darling— Mr. Darling's son, Burlington Barington Darling III, V—were friends. Well, no, they weren't—friends don't throw piss balloons at you—but they were on the lacrosse team together.

But back to the petition: eventually Mr. Darling decided that there'd been quite enough free speech around here, thank you, and wheeled out the big gun. The op-ed page of *Daily Money* bellowed incessantly, broadcasting the standoff nationwide. Finally, Mr. Darling himself had written an editorial (via ghostwriter, of course): "Prejudice against the wealthy is the new racism . . . Dr. King, that venture capitalist of the human spirit, knew better. If he were alive today, Martin Luther King would be the first one to reserve a tee time. And if he were to birdie our picturesque ninth hole, he would most certainly cry out, 'Three at last, three at last, thank God almighty, I shot a three at last!' "

The limo turned a corner, and Hart saw it, a puddle of glorious July purchased from miserly February. He'd seen similar things many times at the Darlings' mansion—that's why they needed him to cut the lawn year round. But seeing it here, in the middle of a bomb zone, took Hart's breath away.

In the middle of an impossibly green, brightly lit fairway, a short-sleeved Mr. Darling was teeing up golf balls and whacking them into the dark. Enormous heaters blew hot air on the fresh sod, keeping the snow at bay. Solar-spectrum floodlights carved a corridor of afternoon out of the eggplant-colored sky. On either side, slabs of crumbling buildings shook and fell, exhaling death rattles of dust. But even that couldn't penetrate the fairway, an oasis protected by magic.

"Too much money drives you crazy," the driver grumbled. He turned to Hart. "Come back after you're done and I'll take you home. If you behave."

Hart opened the door and got out. He was so mesmerized by the fairway that he forgot his jacket—then a blast of cold air reminded him it wasn't eternal summer for everybody.

Hart's foot crunched over snow, then sank into grass, and the temperature jumped fifty degrees. Twenty feet away, Mr. Darling continued to swing; next to him, a butler in formal attire held a silver champagne bucket full of golf balls. After every shot, the butler expressed his admiration.

"Nicely struck, sir," the butler said in an English accent (even though he was from Cleveland).

"Thank you, Galbraith. I made it an offer it couldn't refuse," Mr. Darling said, his last word obscured by a nearby blast. Some rubble danced into the fairway, and Mr. Darling gave it a dirty look.

The teenager got within ten feet of the mogul and stopped. No one had acknowledged Hart yet, so he considered it best to wait silently. He had never actually seen Mr. Darling this close before—Mrs. Darling's personal assistant usually left an envelope with seventy-five dollars (and the critique) in the lawn shed.

Hart's first impression was: boy, what a terrible golfer. Sure, he *looked* perfect doing it, all graying temples and deep tan, but he stunk. An elemental form of clumsiness not known to mere mortals was on display here. Trip was the same way, looking like the ultimate lacrosse stud until he smacked himself in the sack with his own stick. But it was the laws of physics that were wrong, not the Darlings. They were Greek gods, only with preppy wardrobes and more expensive haircuts.

Hart thought he would be safe if he stayed behind Mr. Darling, but this turned out to be overly optimistic: one particularly troubled whack went straight up, and when it hit the ground, kicked backward daffily. Hart flung himself to the turf, and the ball missed his temple by inches. On the other hand, this finally got Mr. Darling's attention.

"Hello, Bart." Like most successful businessmen, Mr. Darling assiduously ignored unimportant information.

"It's Hart, sir."

Another ball whizzed off in a non-Euclidean fashion.

"Charming one, sir," Galbraith murmured, handing over another ball.

"I bet you're wondering why I brought you out here."

"I thought I was being kidnapped."

"Why would anyone want to kidnap a nobody like you?" Mr. Darling said, swinging mightily. The ball hopped perhaps two feet. "Any idea why I called you here?"

"The lawn?"

"You're obsessed," Mr. Darling said. "Natural servant." He took another swing, but a nearby explosion made him miss the ball entirely. "I need to talk to you about Trip."

Hart, feeling more and more insulted, stayed quiet.

"Bart, my son is an imbecile," Mr. Darling said. "I'm sure you're aware of this. I've seen your transcripts, you're quite book smart. Trip, on the other hand, has other gifts. In hopes of uncovering them, I've gotten him into Stutts."

"That's great," Hart lied. If Trip had taken up the only spot from Farnsworth . . .

"I assume Stutts is your first choice," Mr. Darling said.

"Of course!" Hart said. "It's the best."

"Well, you didn't make it."

Hart suddenly felt the cold. "How do you know?"

"I just spent three days negotiating with the admissions office to get Trip in, that's how I know." Mr. Darling said tersely. "It was going to be you, but I threw in a new boathouse for the crew team. Cost me an arm and a leg . . . Oh, well. Nobody ever said"—Mr. Darling hooked a ball, plunking a passing construction worker—"life was fair."

Hart plunged into his own personal hell. He'd beaten Doreen only to be thwarted by . . . Trip? It was obscene. It made a mockery of every test he'd been given since kindergarten. Trip had taken the SATs drunk, stoned, and with a hamster down his pants (on a bet). Now he was going to Stutts University. What could possibly be worse? Trip as President?

Hart silently swore to devote the next ten years to ninja training, in order to kill all the Darlings, one by one. The last two to die would be Trip and his dad, their naked bodies arranged in a way that gave new meaning to the phrase "bad touch."

"Aren't you disappointed?"

"I'll be more disappointed once I get some sleep. Can I go?"

"No. Seeing your name on the acceptance list got me thinking," Mr. Darling said. "Trip doesn't test well, and if he's anything like I was at school, he'll raise holy hell. Normally I wouldn't care, but these next months are going to be . . . sensitive."

"Why?" Hart asked, not really caring what the answer was. Four years of going the extra mile—working the extra hour, taking the extra class, kissing the extra butt—whisked away by the whims of a well-bred moron! Could he be a Communist *and* a ninja?

"Because I'm running for governor, idiot," Mr. Darling said, as another building went down with a crash. "I can't have Trip embarrassing me during the campaign. I would like you to accompany Trip to Stutts this fall and, in exchange for a reasonable stipend, make sure he doesn't flunk out."

"You want me to tutor Trip?"

Mr. Darling laughed. "No! I don't care if he learns a damn thing. I just want him enrolled—and out of the newspapers. You'll take notes for him, take his tests. Keep him out of trouble. Keep him from falling in with the wrong crowd."

Hart was so out of there, his shoes were already pointed toward the limo. "I'd love to help you, Mr. Darling," he said, "but I'll be at another school, since I didn't get into Stutts."

Mr. Darling frowned; he took complications personally. "There are things more important than a college education, Hart." He stopped swinging and turned around. "Are you telling me you won't do it? After all I've done for you? After all your sloppy edging?"

"Not unless I'm a student there, too."

"Impossible," Mr. Darling said. "They won't admit you."

"Why not? They were going to, until you got involved," Hart said. "The days of Stutts being just for rich kids is over."

"Tell me, do you believe *everything* you read?" Mr. Darling snapped. "They were happy to substitute Trip for you. They know you'll probably end up as some . . . inner-city school-teacher who gives twenty-five dollars to the alumni fund every other year." The tycoon looked back at Hart coldly. "Just being in Great Littleton should be enough for a nobody like you."

"Well, it's not," Hart said. "The weather there sucks."

Mr. Darling swung and turned, sizing the boy up. Hart wasn't backing down. "You've got me by the stones, son, and you're squeezing," Mr. Darling rumbled, low and angry. "I don't appreciate it."

"Sorry," Hart said, not sorry.

"I'll see what I can do," Mr. Darling said. "If I can get you in—"

"—and pay my way—"

"Okay, okay! Why don't you take my house while you're at it!"

"If you can get me in, and pay my bills, I'll try to keep Trip on the straight and narrow."

"Try?" Mr. Darling asked. "For that kind of money, you'll make sure of it, you little punk."

"You got a deal." Hart extended a hand. "Tha—"

"Get out of here before I change my mind," Mr. Darling barked.

As Hart walked away, he could hear Mr. Darling complaining to his butler. "'I never fucked over anyone in my life who didn't have it coming to him.'"

"So you've said, sir."

"Galbraith, that punk's got something coming to him."

CHAPTER TWO

JUST WHEN HART thought Mr. Darling might be welshing on their deal, a thick acceptance letter appeared. Hart's whoops brought several boarders scurrying downstairs, pets in arms.

"Is there a fire?" one asked.

"Is he having a seizure?" Mrs. Jenkins asked hopefully.

"No," Mrs. Fox said. "He just got into college."

Under normal circumstances, Hart would've been levitating with joy, but the attachment from Mr. Darling's lawyer brought him down to earth. "This agreement must be kept absolutely confidential, as it violates many state and federal laws, contravenes the Geneva Convention, is absolutely prohibited under Stutts' academic regulations, and would result in embarrassment for my client." The penalties were harsh, and involved several of Hart's most essential internal organs.

"Dad, do you know any lawyers?" Hart asked during their weekly phone call.

"Too many," Mr. Fox said. He had a clown-car's worth of lawyers, at least ten. Unfortunately, he faced a veritable United Nations of them, one or more from each of the 130 countries where men had (in the words of the court brief) "suffered spontaneous, explosive breast growth as a result of consuming this irresponsible, dangerous product." Every time he landed at an airport, Mr. Fox had to sprint to the first gate he saw, eluding the writ-wavers by only a few steps. It was exhausting.

"Can I have one of them look at this?"

"You don't want to antagonize Mr. Darling," Mr. Fox said. "He may decide that Trip doesn't have to stay in school for him to win the election.[10] Definitely do a spectacular job on his lawn this summer."

It took seven minutes for the news of Hart's acceptance to saturate Farnsworth High—exactly six minutes and thirty seconds after he had told Dean Grubbman.

"Hart, that's wonderful!" the dean said, calculating his winnings. (Since nobody had picked Trip Darling, the entire pool went to everybody who'd put money on Hart.) "Can you hold on a second while I make a quick phone call?" Hart got up to leave, but the dean waved him back down. "No, sit. I want you to be here for this." He dialed Dean Prist's office next door. "Jeanette, it's Jasper. Hart Fox got into Stutts!"

Hart heard her cry of anguish through the phone *and* the

---

[10] According to the polls, Mr. Darling was currently leading fifty-seven percent to forty-nine percent. (Some undecided voters had answered "both.") The former governor had died while in office, and a paperwork error had resulted in his dog being chosen to run for re-election. Mr. Darling entered the race thinking that it would be a slam dunk, but the dog, a Boston terrier, was awfully cute. It had taken forty million dollars in TV ads to build Mr. Darling his current lead. Hart loved to mimic the ads, asking people in a ominous voice, "Do you want your Governor to . . . *lick himself in public?*"

wall. Dean Grubbman winked at Hart. "That's right, you and your precious Darleen can eat shit. Bye!" For a while, the pair just listened to the profanity and sounds of expensive objects breaking. Occasionally, they giggled.

After it had quieted down, Dean Grubbman said, "You better go before she comes out. I couldn't guarantee your safety." Hart gave him five. "I feel *great!*" the dean said, chortling.

"So do I," Hart said, deciding not to tell him about the deal with Mr. Darling.

Victory was sweet, but came at a price. Teachers who had lost money took revenge by marking him devilishly hard; the newspaper adviser even kicked him off, claiming that a humor column Hart wrote contained a secret code predicting the time and place of Armageddon, ". . . which is, of course, against school regulations."

Hart didn't care; he'd already gotten into college. To retaliate, he did an anonymous spoof of the newspaper, and spent a few hundred of his lawn-mowing money to print some up. He dumped copies all around the school, in the same places that the real paper usually was. It was a sensation, especially after the women's gym coach admitted that she actually was a *male* transvestite. Hart got detention, but Dean Grubbman was a firm believer in the First Amendment—at least in the case of students who'd given him a new swimming pool.

Suddenly, everybody had an opinion about Hart Fox. The spoof—and Stutts' magical thick envelope—did something that the honor roll, the school paper, lacrosse, Aged Mentor Club, Helping Hands, and Hugs-for-Tots couldn't do: it made people notice him. Flying under the radar wasn't bad, exactly; Hart had kept himself nice and bland, so he could win bunches of awards and not be surrounded by enemies. But after almost four years of relative anonymity (the only thing under Hart's yearbook picture was "Sit behind him if you want to get an A") it was strange to have a social profile.

Among the other smart seniors, years of friendship strengthened or dissolved, depending on the person's own college situation. If you had gotten into your first-choice school, Hart's success confirmed your good taste, and suggested that Hart would be a good person to know in the future. If you had missed the boat, the very sight of Hart was a knife in the heart, and you joined the chorus of whisperers. "He only got in because . . ."

The *becauses* were myriad, and invariably unflattering— ". . . because he doesn't really have a father and they felt sorry" or ". . . because his eyes are backward—next time you see him, look! It's so weird!" or ". . . because he went down on the interviewer, Trip Darling told me." Trip naturally resented needing an academic nanny, and rather than blaming crappy genes or a brain shriveled by alcohol, he took it out on Hart.

That thick envelope hadn't changed Hart much yet, but people sure treated him differently. The deep crowd suddenly thought he was deeper; the artsy crowd, artsier; the popular crowd invited him to join the clandestine revelry that had been raging since junior high (Hart suddenly understood why certain kids looked like shit every Monday morning). With the full faith and trust of the Stutts Admissions Department behind Hart, everybody else fell into line. Hart realized just how much people love a winner.

The one bad thing about Hart's becoming a minor deity— and it wasn't really that bad—was how people stopped seeing *him*, and started seeing their idea of a Stutts student. Seventy percent of the people he met assumed he was a genius, and the rest assumed he was a rich snob. Hart, being neither, tried to avoid egregiously stupid behavior, and poured on the humility. He never mentioned Stutts unless pressed. If somebody asked where he was going to college, he would look down bashfully, jab the dirt with his toe and mumble, "In Great Littleton."[11]

Becoming what people expected him to be wasn't terrible—but it wasn't him, either. Still, to do otherwise seemed obstinate and ungrateful. He wanted to tell everybody that it wasn't *such* a big deal, but the more people insisted it was, the more Hart began to think that maybe they were right. During that in-between summer, Hart wanted it both ways: he wanted to be celebrated, and he wanted to be himself again. What he really wanted, of course, was to be celebrated for himself—but almost none of us get that. While being profiled in the local *Pennysaver* was great, pretending to be the ultimate Stutts student was like hopping on one foot; it wasn't difficult, but it did get tiring. I'll be able to drop the act when I get to school, Hart thought. We all got in—what else could we possibly need to prove?

Even his parents treated him differently, introducing him as, "This-is-my-son-he's-going-to-Stutts." Thanks to the thickness of an envelope, they saw their son in a new light; who were they to disagree with the admissions department? Dad told him more details about the court battles, Mom extended his curfew. In arguments, they started respecting his opinion more—Hart was suddenly vouched for by Stutts University.

Mr. and Mrs. Fox considered Stutts an unqualified stamp

---

[11] When he got to school, he found out every Stutts student did this while at home—not realizing that false modesty is just as irritating as snobbery, and a lot less honest.

of approval on their parenting skills. Anybody who chalked it up to a happy combination of luck and Hart's knack for standardized tests was cruising for a punch in the nose. "She's just mad because Doreen will have to go to Keasbey University instead," Mrs. Fox sniffed, after almost coming to blows with Mrs. Breith in the frozen foods section of Food Mammoth. "There's no shame in coming in second. Some people just have 'it,' that's all. . . . Honestly, after she acted like that, I can understand why Stutts didn't want her daughter."

Putting Hart into a category worked for everybody, Hart included. Months before he'd ever stepped on campus, Hart had become a Stutts student. And he could never go back. To lose that now—or ever—would turn him into a nothing.

By far the biggest fringe benefit was that girls started paying attention to Hart. Well, sort of; they didn't date him, but they acknowledged his existence. You might be surprised at how much of an improvement that was.

From the moment Hart entered high school, he felt like he was traveling in a foreign country. No matter how closely he listened, trying to catch every cue, he only understood about sixty percent of what was going on. Overnight, everybody else seemed to be able to communicate using a frequency Hart didn't receive. It had been incredibly frustrating, frequently embarrassing, and occasionally downright humiliating.

So when the attention finally came, Hart didn't care that it was shallow; he'd felt misunderstood and lonely even before his pubic hair had crept onto the scene, and anything was better than invisibility. The class hotties could now see why somebody *might* sleep with Hart (even though they themselves would have to be very drunk to do so).

31

Hart learned to flirt—it was easy, once he learned to stop caring. That thick envelope made everyone in his high school the oldest of old news. His dreams were now fixated on the hordes of beautiful, sophisticated, fascinating women waiting for him at college. For Hart, Stutts was going to be half salon, half harem; not only would women there understand him, they would truly *appreciate* him. How could they not? They both went to Stutts, they would have so much in common.

But before that, there was the summer to get through. Hart kept to himself, mostly. Every aspect of his life conjured morbid thoughts of finality. "This is the last time I'll smell my mildewy gym locker"; "This the last time I'll walk across the baseball field"; "This is the last time I'll make fun of 𝔊𝔱𝔢𝔳𝔢 𝔬𝔣 𝔚𝔢𝔢𝔡." He tried to remember to remember everything, but he forgot so often that he decided to quit.

It was uncomfortable to hang out with people already in your rearview mirror. And because they were all leaving soon, their interactions were nerve-wracking. After the third tearful heart-to-heart with someone he hadn't been that close with in the first place, Hart had had enough. He read, tried to teach himself guitar, helped his mom with the boarders, slept.

Hart's monastic summer had one notable exception. Every Fourth of July, his lacrosse teammate Bill Lombardi threw a party at his parents' beach cottage on Lake Michigan. It was a major event, partly because Farnsworth High kids led fairly boring lives, but also because Mr. Lombardi didn't mind if people drank.[12] In addition to booze, there were plenty of

---

[12] Mrs. Lombardi lived someplace else—nobody knew the details, but from the things Bill let slip whenever he got *really* hammered, they were probably pretty hairy. Most people pass out at the far edge of intoxication, but Bill Lombardi cried; a party wasn't over until Bill started blubbering.

undercooked hamburgers, fistfuls of fireworks, and lots of tipsy, possibly willing ladies. Or so Hart surmised; he'd never been invited. So he was shocked to hear from Bill one afternoon. "Hey, Hart. I'm just calling to make sure you're coming to my Fourth party this year."

"I didn't think I was invited. I haven't been before." It was amazing how honest you could be when you knew a person's expiration date.

"Come on," Bill said. "'Course you're invited . . ."

Now that I've gotten into Stutts, Hart added silently.

"And it's not just 'cause you got into Stutts or anything. We couldn't have a party without The Whirlwind!" Bill said, invoking Hart's lacrosse nickname. "You *gotta* come!"

"Sure," Hart said, ignoring the warning siren in his head. As the date approached, his feelings remained mixed. On the one hand, it was flattering. If Trip's stories could be trusted, Bill's party was a notorious sexual crossroads, and the last-summer-before-college vibe would only increase the random hookups. Hart had lusted after quite a few girls in high school, and Bill's party seemed like his last, best chance.

On the other hand, maybe none of that would happen, and he'd feel extra shitty for blowing this best-of-all opportunity. He'd seen *Carrie*, and suddenly being invited after three years of being the only guy on the lacrosse team not invited, made him wonder if some sort of Pig's Blood Spectacular was in store. But as with eighteen-year-old boys throughout history, Hart's lust was more powerful than his fear.

As Hart drove over to the Lombardis' cottage—not really a cottage at all: Bill's dad was a flack for a drug company and the place was huge—he thought about the last four years. Hart's theory was that the most popular people in high school were the ones who fell into preexisting categories: jocks, for example, or bandies. Hart's problem was that he always tried to mix and match. Hart liked science fiction, worked on the newspaper, and played sports. But he wasn't a geek, or a journalism nerd, or a jock. People didn't know what to do with Hart—he was hard to quantify, and that made people suspicious. Now they'd finally found a cubbyhole for Hart: he was the guy going to Stutts.

Hart rang the doorbell. There was loud music playing, so he rang it several times. Finally Bill came to the door, in a Hawaiian shirt, madras Bermuda shorts, and a red-and-white striped Cat in the Hat stovepipe. He was holding a plastic cup filled with beer, which he sloshed when he talked, for emphasis. "*Dude (slosh)*," he said, "not necessary. It's a party—just come on in!"

"Sorry," Hart said, already knee-deep in that horrible I-don't-speak-English feeling. Blushing, he walked into a front room swarming with well-dressed teenagers. Some of them looked at Hart—was he anybody they wanted to talk to? Apparently not. Hart employed a defensive "fuck them," the first of the evening.

In a far corner, Trip was holding court; he and some friends were playing foosball with a raw meatball filched from the grill. They were shoving each other and laughing—some guy had let the ball ricochet into the goal, and now he had to eat it. Instead, he threw it at Bill.

"Nice hat Dr. Seuss," Hart kidded Bill, just before he was hit by the meatball.

Bill laughed, and said, "You guys better watch it—Hart's gonna be your boss one day!"

"Fuck him, I'm going to Stutts, too," Trip bellowed, then emitted a chunky belch.

Bill led Hart into the kitchen. "Chips and junk on the table, more burgers and stuff being grilled. There's beer here in the fridge." Bill opened it up and handed Hart an expensive Ukrainian brew. "And when you get tired of the high-class stuff, there's a keg of Punk on the beach." Punk was the local super-cheapo malt liquor.

"Tired of?" Hart opened his beer. "Too drunk to tell the difference, you mean."

Bill looked at him for a moment—was Hart cracking on him? Then he laughed. "Salty. That's what I like about you, Hart," he said. "You say what you think. That's what *everybody* likes about you."

"I'm sure," Hart said dubiously. Being told he was popular made him wary. It was like having another Miss America contestant say that you had nice boobs, right before she leaked the *Hustler* photos to the press. The knives came out, sooner or later.

"No, it's true," Bill said, without conviction. "Everybody loves you . . . Have fun." He left.

Hart had no idea what "have fun" could possibly mean in a situation like this. First, he grazed a bit—that was a logical solo activity. For a while, he stared fixedly out the window. It was pretty—a beach sunset. He recognized a lot of the people cavorting around. Unfortunately, he didn't like any of them, and was sure that the feeling was mostly mutual. But every time one of them would walk in the back door, they'd give Hart a smile and say "Hi!" warmly, as if they and Hart had been pals for years. It was amazing—completely indistinguishable from a genuine emotion.

After the ninth or tenth example of exemplary android behavior, Hart was weirded out enough to leave the kitchen. But what to do next? There were no other forlorn floating singles to make sardonic jokes with; everyone seemed to be bonded into impenetrable, laughing clumps of "fun." Could he leave already? Clearly he was in no shape to charm any person of the female persuasion, not when he couldn't even wedge himself into a conversation.

The self-laceration began: this was such a stupid idea. These people weren't like him, they were well-adjusted and happy . . . He wanted to go—every fiber of his being screamed for it. "There's the door! Use it! Before something happens to make tonight really horrible!" But he couldn't leave yet, Bill might notice, plus everybody seeing him slink out early would be the lamest outcome of all, lamer even than not being invited in the first place.

He could use the bathroom; that was plausible, nobody would suspect that he was confused and miserable. Unfortunately, Bill's dad spotted him leaving the kitchen. "Hart!" he yelled, too loudly for Hart to feign deafness. "Come here for a second."

They shook hands. "Hi, Mr. Lombardi."

"Enjoying yourself? Good. Looking forward to going to Stutts? I bet. Your parents must be proud of you. Bill got rejected, but we never had much hope—the admissions people . . . I mean, we told Bill, 'Why apply? If you're not a radical lesbian, there's no point.'" Mr. Lombardi took a drink from the tumbler in his fleshy paw. He was wearing a golf shirt and his go-to-hell pants—blue slacks with little dollar bills on them. "If you're not the illegitimate son of a Chinaman and a black, you might as well flush the app fee down the toilet. But, as usual, Bill didn't listen."

Not listening was a family trait. The few times Hart had talked to Mr. Lombardi on the sidelines after a lacrosse match, he'd gotten the impression that Mr. Lombardi spent life making brash statements, then agreeing with himself even more loudly.

"Anyway, Hart, listen: since you're going out there, I've got some free advice for you. And this is just for you, because you have a really golden opportunity here. You don't see me wasting my time talking to any of Bill's other friends. I made sure Bill invited you specifically." Mr. Lombardi put his hand on Hart's shoulder, pinning the boy against the wall. "Life is . . ." Mr. Lombardi paused, then started again. "The key to life is . . ." He stopped again and seemed to deflate slightly— then he found the starting point he was looking for. "Try to make lots of money," he said.

"Okay," Hart said. "Is that it?"

"No, no, wait! Hart, in life there's a lot of little bullshit decisions but basically only one big decision: which side are you on? Understand?"

"I . . . think so," Hart said.

"Really—do you *understand* what I'm saying to you?"

"Yes." He suddenly realized that Mr. Lombardi was very drunk. Drunken adults made him nervous, so he was extra polite. "Yes, sir."

"Good. I hope you do, for your sake." Mr. Lombardi let go of Hart's shoulder to scratch his chest, then reapplied the vise. "Get on the *right* side. If you do, everything else will be easy. If you don't, nothing else will matter."

This didn't sound like life, it sounded like dodgeball. Hart was utterly confused, but when an adult spoke, his default setting was to agree. That's how he'd been raised. "Okay, I will," Hart said.

"Good," Mr. Lombardi said. "Bill gets it, thank God—he's

pre-pledged a frat. But you've got to choose now. The future waits for nobody, not even a Stutts student. In fact, that makes the choice even more important. You could really make something of yourself. Or piss it away with moonbeams and fairy tales, your choice."

Moonbeams? Fairy tales? Was this guy serious? "But Mr. Lombardi—"

"Gil."

"But Gil," Hart asked, picking at the label on his beer, "how can I tell which side is the right one for me?"

"For *you*? For everyone, unless they're idiots." Mr. Lombardi said. "I hope you're not an idiot. Your parents are paying a fortune to send you to school. Bill's pissed away everything we've given him. This frat is probably his last chance."

Hart suddenly realized why Bill smoked so much pot.

"I'm thinking of starting a support group: 'Parents of Ungrateful Idiots.'"

Hart smiled, because Mr. Lombardi clearly wanted him to, but as soon as he did, he felt like he'd betrayed Bill. He wanted to say, "Bill is a good guy, he's just figuring himself out," but instead he said, "I don't *think* I'm an idiot."

"We'll see. It all depends on which side you pick. Going to Stutts will make it clearer." Mr. Lombardi extracted something from the booze-fogged recesses of his brain. "It's basic economics: one percent of the people own ninety-nine percent of everything. . . . It's the same in the animal kingdom—they've proved it with gorillas. One side gets all the bananas . . ." Mr. Lombardi got a wolfish smirk. ". . . and all the females, too."

Hart smiled thinly. Mr. Lombardi's breath stank. Hart wanted to go home. He didn't know whether this guy was pontificating to him, to his own son, or to his younger self.

Frankly, Hart didn't care. He just wanted Mr. Lombardi to shut up.

"The other side knows they've got nothing to offer, so they'll try to convert you with a bunch of idealistic bullshit. Don't you believe it!" He gripped Hart's shoulder extra tight with this last bit, as if he were trying to embed the advice with his fingertips. "Tell me you won't."

"I won't," Hart said.

"Say 'I won't, Gil.'"

"I won't, Gil."

"Good boy." Lombardi took another slurp. "I'm rich, and I sleep just fine!" he said loudly, and disengaged his hand.

Nodding politely, Hart resisted the urge to rub his throbbing shoulder. Temporarily free of Lombardi's clutches, he vainly searched for a means of escape; Bill's dad seemed to be generating a lot of . . . something, and the alcohol seemed to be increasing it. Hart tensed up, ready to sprint just in case Lombardi exploded.

The vise descended again. "That's the great thing about America."

"Right." Disagreeing at this point could be fatal.

"*You* choose. *You're* totally responsible for what happens to you. A lot of people don't like that; they want to blame everybody else, when it's really their own fault for doing stupid things, lollygagging around—when you're your age, you think that you have time to try things . . ."

"Yeah," Hart said.

He'd agreed one time too many; Mr. Lombardi went off the deep end. "Hart, since you're a smart kid, I'm gonna tell you something that I really wish I knew when I was your age . . . You ready?"

"Sure," Hart said, not at all sure.

"The feel of rain on your balls—there's nothing like it."

Hart was speechless. Bill ran up, saving the day. "Dad, the grill's on fire!"

Mr. Lombardi crunched some ice. "It's supposed to be, moron."

"No, Dad. Really! Like, this high!" Bill put his hand to the level of his waist. Hart noticed that his eyes were red, and his pupils were dilated.

Mr. Lombardi grumbled something unintelligible, and put his nearly empty tumbler down. "Will you excuse me for a second? My idiot son . . ."

"Certainly." Hart saw his chance to escape—he would slip out the front door and get away before Mr. Lombardi came back to claim his glass.

Hart wound his way through the crowd to the front door. As he opened it, he caught Trip looking at him from the end of the room. Trip saw him bailing, and there was a nasty little smile on his blunt, pink face. Whatever side he's on, Hart thought, I'll take the other one.

As Hart walked out into the yard, he heard his name.

"Hart! Over here—in the bushes!"

Trying to be nonchalant, Hart leaned over and looked into the cup-filled shrubbery. There, crouching in the dirt, was Weird Abigail. A fellow member of the sci-fi club, Abigail was a year behind Hart. She had carried a very public—and very unrequited—torch for him since she was in seventh grade.

"Hi, Abigail," Hart said. "Come out of there, if you're going to talk to me. I feel stupid yelling into a plant."

"I can't," Weird Abigail said quietly, brushing a leaf out of her hair. "I wasn't invited." Although she was cute enough, in a frizzed, underage Yeti sort of way, Weird Abigail wasn't popular. That was because she liked weird things, and wasn't shy about saying it. She made her own clothes, wrote free-verse poetry, and had been seen more than once wandering through the halls of the school pretending to be an elk (this was her "totem animal"). Like Hart, Weird Abigail was her own category. "I dug a hole under the fence," she said, pointing. She was covered in dirt.

"Why?" Hart asked, genuinely perplexed—W.A. had better taste in friends than Trip Darling. "These people are assholes."

"Because I thought you might be here."

Hart looked down. As usual, W.A. had brought her huge backpack, which Hart could see was filled with sourdough pretzels and Mountain Dew. This had been a stakeout.

"So," W.A. exhaled, nervous but trying not to show it. "Would you want to go out some time? Before you head off to school?" This struck her as too revealing, so she immediately pared it back: "Just for coffee or something. I've been scoping out this new role-playing game based on *Space Pram* that I think you might like."

Hart froze at the mention of such a dorky pursuit. He was just climbing out of the Pit of the Unpopular and now . . . He liked W.A. as a friend; she was smart and nice, and they'd always had interesting conversations about the BBC show *Space Pram* or Schrödinger's cat, or whatever outlandish cultural flotsam preoccupied her at the moment. But people thought she was crazy, and maybe they were right: in addition to the gigantic backpack filled with "essentials for living," W.A. carried

41

around a piece of putty that she worked with her fingers constantly.

People would definitely think he was weird, too, if they saw him hanging out with W.A. One date—one hour at coffee—would undo all the progress he'd made. Then his conscience weighed in: she's smart, and nice, too. What do you care what people think?

"Okay, sure," Hart said.

"Great!" Abigail said, happily and loudly. She clearly hadn't been expecting that answer. "I'll call you later to—"

"Hey, Hart! Why're you talking to a bush?" Bill asked.

"Because that's the closest he can get to some," Trip said, to the delight of his pea-brained retinue. They were walking over to the garage, to pee into the backseat of Bill's convertible. It was a tradition.

Hart's confidence crumbled. "I'm sorry, Ab. I can't." He walked away without looking at her.

Weird Abigail stood up and climbed out of the bush, trying to follow him. "Hart, don't listen to those jerks. . . ." Abigail said bravely, trying to salvage their date.

Bill ran out of the house; he'd seen Trip gathering his troops. "You assholes better not be peeing in my car!" he yelled uselessly. Angry, Bill turned and saw Abigail. "Excuse me, but were you invited?"

"Fuck you," Abigail said. "I'm leaving."

Hart didn't hear. He was already halfway to his car, walking fast and angry. He felt terrible, and now Abigail did, too. He passed the misery along—that was high school in a nutshell.

What did he care what other people thought? Why did he let other people determine who he was? Hart didn't *know* why, and always got angry at himself when it happened. But college would be different, wouldn't it? He'd be a better person, wouldn't he? Of course, Hart said to himself. He'd be a Stutts student.

CHAPTER THREE

THE DRIVE from Michigan to Stutts had been excruciating.

"Mom, I swear I'll puke if you use that word again," Hart said.

"Which one? Vagina? Clitoris?" Mrs. Fox said. "I don't see why. You wouldn't puke if I said 'arm' or 'nose.'"

Hart stared bleakly at some passing cows. "I *hate* the sixties," he grumbled.

"The human body is a beautiful thing, Hart." Mrs. Fox took a swig of bottled water. "Honestly, I had no idea you were so uptight."

"I'm not uptight! I just don't want to talk about sex with my mother!"

"I would be a bad parent if I let you head off to school without going over everything."

Ever since Hart had been in seventh grade and she'd happened to catch a documentary on Sweden's educational system, Hart's mother had been anxious to have an "open, frank discussion about sex" with her son. For all that time, Hart had been equally determined to avoid the subject. He usually ran out of the room, or called his home phone with his cell phone whenever she brought it up. (Once, he'd fired a starter's pistol into the air.) Now, for eighteen hours, Hart was completely trapped. He'd been forced to sprint to his "happy place," go fetal, and hope he survived.

Things hit their nadir on the Pennsylvania Turnpike, as his mother finished up a long, exuberant discourse on fisting. "Oh, Hart, don't make that face," she said. "Even plants do it. I heard it on NPR."

"I swear to God, Mom, I'll throw myself out of the car," Hart said, hand on the door handle.

"Always so dramatic," Mrs. Fox said. "Are you gay?"

"That's stereotyping, and I for one resent it." If Hart could only provoke a nice, distracting argument . . .

"That's not why I asked," Mrs. Fox said. "You haven't exactly been a ladies' man in high school."

"Well, I'm straight," Hart said. "At least I was before this conversation."

"Very funny. Get me a banana out of the cooler."

He handed it to her, then pulled back. "Wait—what are you going to do with it?"

"Nothing. I'm going to eat it," she said. "Thank you. Now hold the wheel, I want to show you how to put on a condom."

"AHHHHH!"

Hart had surely been scarred for life by the time the swaybacked, lightly smoking station wagon rolled onto the faux-ancient campus of Stutts University.[13] And not a moment

---

[13] This "faux-ancient" deserves a little explanation. Stutts, like everything else in the United States, wasn't very old. Several hundred years is something for a Twinkie, but nothing special for a college. In Oxford, Heidelberg, or Bologna, the parking lots are

too soon: Mrs. Fox had been ignoring the Oil light under the dash for at least fifty miles. For every inch of those miles, Hart had been fighting visions of avoidable catastrophe. They'd peter out on the expressway; the car would be totaled; Mom would have to spend the night in his dorm . . .

"Mom, you're going to burn out the engine," Hart said. "We should stop."

"Shh, you worry too much," Mrs. Fox said. "Look at the school! Isn't it cute?"

"Cute?" Hart's first impression of the place was one of imminent collapse—if he was going to make a name for himself here, he'd better do it quickly. They passed a building, and Hart saw it unapologetically spit out a brick.

"Mom, get over into the right-hand lane. I think this building's going to collapse."

"Why?"

"I just saw a brick fall out of it."

"It's just settling. Every house does it. Our house back home—" A larger chunk of masonry hit the sidewalk, narrowly missing a loitering seagull. A group of students hauling dorm crap cheered anarchically. Mrs. Fox switched lanes, cutting off another driver, with her usual wave and smile.

---

three hundred years old. This rankles a certain sort of American tremendously.

The solution was obvious: mass time travel. However, after the head of Stutts' theoretical physics department was declared "missing, presumed successful" in 1934, the nervous trustees decided on Plan B—faking it. They spared no expense, crafting a brand-new campus that looked hundreds of years old. This was a towering, utterly pointless achievement in the history of architecture, but it came at a price: millions were spent on acid baths and burying the roof tiles and paying immigrants to hold small pieces of brick in their mouths for a year. The only downside to this triumph of Potemkinism was that with faux age comes real decay; and so the campus was constantly falling apart. It was actually kind of charming, if it didn't kill you somehow.

The campus was compact; it had filled in the spaces of Great Littleton's warrenish downtown like crabgrass on an oddly angled lawn.[14] The chockablock density of Stutts' campus—as well as the uniformity of its architecture (a mixture of High Gothic and Colonial, dubbed "High Colonic" by the students) made it nearly impossible for newcomers to navigate.

"Oh dear," Mrs. Fox said, "there's Nit Terrace again."

Hart was beginning to lose his temper. "We're on the wrong side of the river. Go toward the river! *Follow the smell!*" It was sweltering, and the wagon's air-conditioning had conked out two hours ago, just outside of Manhattan. Hart struggled with a map.

"We don't need that," Mrs. Fox said. "I have a natural sense of direction."

Hart rattled the map angrily. "Here! Turn *here*—left on Locust."

"Where's Waterbug Way? I remember . . ."

"Left, *left*! Just turn left!"

"Okay . . ." After the crisis had passed, Mrs. Fox asked, "I wonder why every street is named after a bug?"

"Let me look it up in the guidebook."

"Don't do that, I need you to point out the dorm."

"Mom, look in front of us. We aren't going any-where." The narrow streets were crammed with cars just like theirs (actually, most of them were a lot newer). They were double- and triple-parked as they disgorged all manner of belongings.

---

[14] Not that Great Littleton had thrived as a result; quite the opposite. It was the only town in the history of New England that had failed as a fishing village, a mill town, a Union prisoner-of-war camp, and a depot for the state's insane.

"Look at that guy with a candelabra," Mrs. Fox said. "Who brings a candelabra to college?"

Hart ignored his mother, searching the index of *Stutts: Jewel in the Bog*.

"Aren't you glad I bought that?" Mrs. Fox said. She'd ordered it the day Hart got in. "I wish you'd let me buy you a Stutts bucket hat—those are cute."

"Mom, I don't need a hat. I *go* here," Hart said. He was really looking forward to his mom's departure. "Here it is: 'The origin of Great Littleton's street names is a fine example of how the school and the city around it have always shared a common destiny. The plan for the downtown area was created by Ebekenezekiel Cramp, who became President after Stutts' founder had been killed by hostile Indians.[15] . . . For reasons known only to himself, Reverend Cramp believed that the moon was home to a race of giant insects poised to take over the earth. Every Sunday, he hectored his congregation at Great Littleton Confrontational Church; these street names, though ungainly, would curry favor with the insect overlords and perhaps even save his beloved university from their terrible death rays.'" Hart closed the book. "Not really an advertisement for higher education."

"What do you care?" Mrs. Fox said. "Mr. Darling's paying for it all."

"Look at these idiots," Hart said. The candelabra was only the beginning: a group of students were carrying a grand piano across the street. They tried to force their way through the ornate gate, bashing and scarring the instrument, finally making it through. As the students cheered their achievement, Hart

---

[15] Some scholars believe these were students dressed as Indians.

felt a bit of gloom. That piano probably cost 20,000 bucks, and yet they were treating it like someone's nasty-ass futon. Was this really the place for him? Could he ever *belong* here?

The traffic moved again, and Hart tried to think about something else.

Fatigue is a wonderful icebreaker. After six nearly identical farewell scenes (which could be summed up as "kid awkward, parents teary"), the six boys of 102 Dacron[16] were slumped around the common room, getting to know each other.

"Who smells?" The limitations of Stutts' computerized roommate-matching system became immediately clear.

"We all do," Hart said. "Who brought the couch?" he asked, flopping a leg over the arm of a worn, scratchy monstrosity.

"I got it from my brother," a boy named Andy said. "He just graduated. I broke all his records back in high school. Swimming."

"Really." Hart said, without interest. Every ninety seconds Andy's internal clock chimed, and he was compelled to reveal some new accomplishment. Hart could tell how impressive Andrew thought an achievement was by how much nonchalance he forced into the delivery.

The room fell silent. Quick, somebody say something, Hart thought, before Andy—

---

[16] For easier handling, Stutts' 5,000 undergraduates were broken up into twelve dormitories, where students lived, worked, and ate. Stutts being ruthlessly Anglophilic, they weren't called "dorms," but "Colleges." (Unfortunately, the food and plumbing owed much to England, as well.) Each college had been bankrolled by a captain of industry. Rather than name it after the donor—how gauche—each one was titled after the product that had made the alum wealthy. Hart's college was Dacron; others were Brick, Steel, Tonic Water, and Cummerbund.

"Did I ever tell you about—"

"Yeah, White, you probably did," a boy named Peter said curtly. You could always tell the prep school kids; they always used last names. Peter was from Connecticut, liked engineering and sports, and used a wheelchair. Must suck, Hart thought, but at least he got a first-floor room (disabled students got first crack at this coveted commodity).

A tall, handsome kid named Travis went over to the window, and sat on the sill. He waved at some girls walking by. "Are you going to RMHX tonight?" he asked the girls. "The more you show, the less you owe."

"See you there!" a girl said enthusiastically.

Now, that is impressive, Hart thought. This guy hasn't been on campus for six hours, and he already knows where the parties are. Travis was really smooth, the kind of guy who ends up being president one day. "Hey, Mr. President, what's RMXH?" Hart asked.

"RMHX," a kid named Xanthan corrected. His family was worth slightly more than the small, sweaty country they governed. "Random Meaningless Hookup Experience. It's a club. Underage Tuesdays are great, I highly recommend them."

"There's a free shuttle service to the drunk tank," Peter joked.

"Not necessary. I've got diplomatic immunity." Xanthan had been invulnerable throughout a very rambunctious high school career; knowing that this would continue at Stutts, he had hit the ground running. Foreign students got a special orientation the week before school started. Some used it to get a head start on schoolwork, others started building cadres they hoped would propel them to leadership of student groups like East Somalians at Stutts, or StuttsBosnians, or whatever. More than once, a strong organization at Stutts had matured into a political force back home; when you realized how most foreign Stutts students were the sons and daughters of Maximum Leaders, it made sense. Hart knew that Xanthan's mom was a horrifically repressive dictator nicknamed "Madame Blood," but Xanthan seemed like a nice enough guy. "Three shots of mystery booze for a dollar," Xanthan said. "But we have to get there before ten. Anybody else game?"

"Fuck that," a kid named Rudy announced forcefully. "I'm waiting for a call from Pickles. That's my girlfriend back home. We're engaged."

Hart tried not to wince. If Rudy was convinced that he and Pickles were going to last, Hart was prepared to smile and nod. After all, he'd have to live with these guys for a year. College roommates are like an arranged marriage, but with all the morning breath and none of the convenient sex.

Each of the roommates liked *one* of their fellows immediately; in Hart's case this was Peter. The rest of the guys, he could see becoming really annoying—and they felt the same way about him. Far from being a mismatch, Stutts' computers had worked perfectly. The secret school policy was to match up each student with the absolute worst combination the incoming class could provide, based on his likes and dislikes. This was done to build "character." In addition to a possible insect invasion, the founders of the University had been obsessed with building character.[17] However, like firework-making, character development is an

---

[17]What is "character"? It's hard to define, but seems to have something to do with cheerfully enduring something you absolutely hate. So character is different for different people. For some, it's bearing up under a lifetime of backbreaking, badly paid, tedious labor. For others, it's not cheating during the regatta. Well, at least not *blatantly.*

inexact science, and about once per year, dislike matured into homicide. Those lucky enough to live in the suite of rooms touched by murder would receive an automatic "pass" for the entire semester. So it was not uncommon for Stutts students to subtly egg each other on, in hopes that a person would snap, sending one of them to Heaven and the rest to Margaritaville. Hart had heard of this ghoulish tradition over the summer, but hadn't taken it seriously. Then Anton walked out of his room and handed each of his roommates a sheet of paper.

"In the interest of inter-suite harmony," the paper read, "I have compiled the following guidelines for the conduct of my roommates. If each of them is followed at all times"—this last part was underlined savagely in red felt-tip—"I am sure our year together will be acceptable. Needless to say, I am available to answer questions at any time."

"What the hell is this?" Xanthan asked.

"I'm sorry, can you not read?" Anton said snidely, tossing his head to move a flop of hair away from his eyes.

Hart briefly considered going to the suite's communal bathroom, dipping a cup in the toilet, coming back, and dumping it on Anton, but didn't want to make an enemy just yet. So he read quietly, trying not to snicker and developing more character by the second.

1. I require at least *nine* hours of sleep. Each evening, I will place a blue tie around my doorknob to signal that I have retired for the night. Please respect my need for absolute silence. My *health* is more important than your *music*.

2. Any food that I bring into the suite is *mine*, and will be initialed whenever possible. Anyone found consuming my food *will* be charged the purchase

price of the item(s), with any outstanding debts charged ten percent interest *daily*.

3. I have a medical condition (doctor's note on file at the Dacron College Master's Office) which makes it *impossible* for me to urinate in the presence of others. Please leave 3 (three) minutes before I urinate, and do not return until three (3) minutes after I have finished. The signal for urination will be indicated on this stoplight installed in the common room. GREEN means that my bladder is empty, and you may go about your business normally. YELLOW means that urination is imminent, and you *must* vacate the premises. RED means that urination is occurring. During this time, loud noises are prohibited as they may *constrict my urethra*.

4. If I have a guest, I will expect everyone to respect the ambience I am attempting to create. Profanity, drunkenness, or any other coarse behavior will *not* be tolerated. In the case of female guests, a supplemental list of guidelines will be issued to each suitemate, as well as posted prominently in the common room. (During any romantic interludes—doubtless a frequent occurrence—the stoplight will flash RED.)

5. I receive many important phone calls. If I happen to be away from the suite, *please* use the message pads provided. Needless to say, any messages not on official pads will be considered *untaken* and *disregarded*.

Hart thought the bold-ital-underline combo was a nice touch, all the emphasis modern computing can provide. Nothing says "psycho" like nonstandard typography. Hart looked up. Anton was holding up spiral-bound, carbon copy "While You Were Out" pads.

"I've written your name on each one," Anton said, handing them out. "Does any one have any questions?"

"Stop the bullshit, I want to get off," Peter said.

Anton gave him a disdainful look. "My mother says that in any social group larger than four people, there's one who's out of step—the Malcontent. Malcs are forty times more likely to be arrested, eighty times more likely to be sexual deviants, and a thousand times more likely to be killed by a vigilante mob."

"How does she know this?" Peter asked. "Besides giving birth to you, of course."

"My mother is one of the leading psychiatrists in the country," Anton said haughtily.

"She does you for free, right?" Peter asked.

"Think you're funny, Malc? We'll see who's laughing when you're in prison." Anton left and went into his room. Seconds later, they heard loud opera music, and Anton baying along with it, part Brunehilde, part basset hound.

The stunned roommates looked at each other with disbelieving smiles until Hart broke the silence. "Anyone up for a vigilante mob?"

Anton's behavior actually had a benefit: in addition to identifying the suite's Malc, it showed them that they weren't all going to be best friends, and furthermore, didn't have to be. Mr. President went to RMHX to start building his political base; Xanthan accompanied him, for more visceral, short-term reasons. Rudy was in his room, murmuring blandishments to Pickles. Anton, according to the tie around his doorknob, was asleep.

Faced with their first night of collegiate freedom, Peter and Hart were undecided. They tossed a Nerf ball back and forth. Though he'd never admit it, Hart was actually feeling a little homesick. In the background, the college radio announcer stumbled along uncertainly—it was cool to hear the voice of somebody your own age coming out of a speaker, even if they got the names of the bands and songs slightly wrong.

"Three shots of mystery booze sounds tempting," Hart said.

Peter shrugged. "Ehh—I only drink the good stuff."

This was a new attitude; Hart's friends back home drank anything that didn't blind you, and sometimes even that rule was bent. Trip and his pals had been caught breaking into a local brewery and drinking wort straight out of the vats.

"Well, what are you going to do instead? We could make up a drinking game involving the radio—every time they screw up a piece of copy, you drink."

"Nah . . ." Peter said. "Wanna sit out on the Old Quad and make fun of drunks?"

"Sure," Hart said. "Let's come up with a point system: five points if they stumble into a tree . . ."

"If they hit a statue, ten," Peter added.

Moments later the two were in position, Peter next to the Fence, Hart perched atop it. The Fence—an inexplicably beloved campus landmark—wound around the inside edge of the Old Quad, separating the flagstones from the already patchy grass.

"What the hell's wrong with the grass?" Hart said. "The school year just started."

Peter opened the small cooler attached to his wheelchair, and handed Hart a rare Belgian beer. Then Peter pointed with his bottle. "Them," he said. "The golf team."

Halfway across the quad, seven guys in red, white, and blue Stutts sweatshirts and matching plaid pants were practicing their pitches in the dark. Back and forth they windmilled; every time a club swept the ground, it brought a large chunk of grass up with it.

"They're ripping up the lawn," Hart said, then drew breath to yell a profanity.

Peter stopped him. "Don't. You don't need that kind of trouble."

"Huh?" Hart was flabbergasted. "It's the golf team! Everybody should harass them, simply out of principle. Look at their pants! There's this rich guy back home who—"

Peter cut him off. "Mugwumps, dork. The golf team is a feeder for Mugwumps."

"Oh," Hart said. "The secret society. I read an article about them."

"*Senior* society," Peter corrected. "Nothing very secret about Mugwumps. Everybody knows about it."

"The President of the United States was in it, right?"

"*Is* in it. And the Vice President, and the Secretary of Defense, and, and, and. What people don't know is what they *do*," Peter said darkly.

"What do you mean, 'what they do'?" Hart said.

"They run things. Rig elections. Control the birds . . ."

"What do you mean, 'control the birds'?"

Peter didn't answer the question. "Crop circles, cattle mutilation . . ."

". . . and golf?"

"Especially golf," Peter said. "These are really good berries."

"Thank you." Hart's mother had insisted on getting him some at the farmer's market on their way out of town—"so you can remember where you come from." Arggh, Hart had thought then. But he was glad to have them now. His stomach

56

was nearly empty, and this beer was strong. (It also tasted vaguely like garbanzo beans.)

"They're like Satan's Boy Scouts," Peter continued. "Loyal, brave, clean, reverent—and utterly obsessed with world domination."

"I never liked the Boy Scouts," Hart said. "I lasted four days."

"I lasted a week, but that was only because my brother Ted was an Eagle Scout and they gave me the benefit of the doubt," Peter said. "Teddy's a Wumpsman. So's my dad. One of my uncles lost a ball during his initiation."

"A ball as in a nut? A testicle?"

Peter nodded. "At least that's what the story was—I think he found something out that he didn't like, refused to go along, and they . . ."

"Come on."

"They're serious people, Hart."

"No, they're not," Hart said. "They're the frigging golf team!"

Peter belched. "That's what they *want* you to believe."

Hart didn't know whether Peter was putting him on or not. "After President Whitbread's welcome speech, I walked by the Pyramid and there was a cat in the bushes. Somebody opened a little door in the side and let the cat in," Hart said.

"That's Whitbread's cat," Peter muttered darkly. "The Mugwumps pay him to spy on the president."

"Pete," Hart asked, "do you spend a lot of time on the Internet?"

"As a matter of fact, I do."

Hart couldn't tell whether Pete was offended or not, so he

threw him a compliment. "With all those relatives in the group, the Mugwumps'll probably pick you, too."

"It's called 'pinching.' They come up to you and pinch you, that's how you know," Peter said. "I don't know, Mugwumps probably will pinch me. I'm trying not to think about that until junior year."

"Are you going to do it?"

"No!" Peter said. "If half of the shit on the Web is true—"

"Which it probably isn't."

"Even so"—Peter took another swig—"who needs it?"

"People whose dads weren't in it," Hart said with a laugh. "Nobodies from nowhere, like me."

"You're not a nobody, I can tell that already," Peter said. "Anyway, the Midwest isn't nowhere."

"Ever been there?"

"No."

"That should tell you something," Hart said, resting his case.

Peter laughed. "Everybody feels that way about where they grew up. Hey, look!" One of Stutts' student mime troupes was returning from another inexplicably sold-out performance. They were walking against the wind, and it took them five minutes to get twenty feet.[18]

"Oh!" Hart said, relieved. He had thought it was a humongous swarm of moths. He could tell Peter about his eyes some other time.

---

[18] Out of all Stutts' hoary traditions, perhaps the strangest was its student mime troupes. The campus was divided into two factions: those in one of the thirteen mime troupes, and those who bore up under their antics with as much grace as possible. The troupes were incestuous, cultlike, and incredibly annoying. On the other hand, you could kick the mimes in the shin and they wouldn't yell.

"Mimes make me thirsty," Peter said, popping open the cooler. "Want another?"

"Thanks. I've never seen a cooler on a wheelchair before."

"After I got over feeling sorry for myself, I thought, 'What would Jesus do?' And the answer was: 'customize the shit out of his wheelchair.' Watch." Peter flipped open the armrest and hit a few buttons. The chair hopped and shimmied like a tricked-out lowrider. He hit another button and the underside of the chair was flooded with blacklight; then whoomping bass came out of a hidden speaker.

"Wow!" Hart yelled.

"What?"

"I said, 'Wow!'"

Peter shut off the sound system. "I'm sorry, I couldn't hear you."

"I said, 'Shit, that's loud!'" Hart said, ears still ringing. Then a delicious thought occurred to him. "I wonder if we woke up Anton?"

Pete mimicked a cheesy disc jockey: "This one's going out to Anton, from his roommates, love and kisses." He flipped the switch again. It was even louder this time; Hart's vision was blurry from the vibrations. The boys couldn't even hear themselves laughing.

"I'm entering Drunkville," Hart slurred giddily, "population: me."

"Me, too," Peter said. "Constellations are totally Fascist. Know why? There's all those stars up there. I could look at 'em and see anything. I could say, 'Look, there's Piskus, the Pickle.' But just because some historical a-pirate decided that it looked like a dipper . . ."

"Instead of a baseball cap," Hart said.

"Right! I knew you'd understand. My dad tried to teach me all the constellations when I was a kid, but I kept making up my own," Peter said. "We don't get along too well."

"He must've been proud of you getting into Stutts."

"Not really," Peter said. "Everybody in my family goes here. Of course, if I hadn't gotten in, I would've been a bum. All of the expectations, none of the pride." Peter took a swig. "*That's* why I drink."

Wow, Hart thought, a world where all this was no big deal. It blew his mind a little—or perhaps that was the beer. "Peter, can I ask you something?"

"What?"

"How did you end up in a wheelchair?"

"Football," Peter said. "Unlucky break. Did you play sports in high school?"

"Yeah," Hart said. "Lacrosse."

"Then you know—freaky stuff happens," Peter said. "You gonna play for Stutts?"

Hart finished off his beer, his third. This Belgian stuff was strong, and the bottles were humongous. "No—I was never any good."

"I was," Peter said, without shame. "I made varsity as a sophomore. Before the injury, I'd already broke a shitload of records."

"Set by your brother. And your SATs were perfect, you already told us, Andy."

Peter laughed. "Isn't that guy priceless? I feel sorry for him—around here it's only a matter of time before Andy meets somebody who whips his ass, achievement for achievement. And then where will he be?"

"Yeah," Hart said. "I'm sorry. About the wheelchair."

"I'm not," Peter said, with a trace of defiance, then stopped himself. "I mean, I am, but it saved me from a lot of stuff, too."

Hart was puzzled. "Like what?"

"From doing what my dad and brother and uncles did," Peter said. "From being a football hero and homecoming king . . . And then, off to Stutts, with a degree in something businessy—but not too difficult, so I have enough time to go to all the right parties, and meet all the right people, the ones who can help me later—maybe even a girl just like dear old Mom. Then crowning the whole thing with the obligatory Mugwump victory lap." Peter shook out the dregs of his final beer on to the grass. "And they all lived happily ever after. Or not."

"Sounds pretty good to me," Hart said.

"You should come to Thanksgiving at my house," Peter said. "Not so good then."

"Why is that?" Hart asked sincerely. "People with every advantage in life—I can understand why somebody poor is miserable, but a person like that . . ."

"They took it too seriously—" Peter said. Suddenly he seemed quite drunk. "—all this ooky-spooky, rat-race, king-of-the-pile shit. When they finally realized that there's a big difference between a good résumé and a good life, they got bitter."

Hart sprang to the defense of his new college. "Stutts is a great place, Pete. You just take it for granted, 'cause your whole family . . . You can get a great education here."

"True. But most people don't," Peter said forcefully. "Oh, they're learning all right—all the time, in fact. But they're learning all the wrong things."

As if on cue, a group of boys dressed in black, wearing red, white, and blue propeller beanies over monklike hoods, trooped out of a nearby dorm. Single file, they each had their arm placed on the shoulder of the person in front of them. The boys shuffled down the flagstone path, making a circuit around the Old Quad. They seemed to be chanting something. When they got close enough, Hart could make it out: "I am nothing without the brotherhood; I do not deserve to exist. I am worthless. Take me in, make me a man." In the gloom of the lamps, they looked like a line of floating beanies.

There were two older boys, dressed normally, one in front and one in back. The one in front beat a drum and shouted abuse; the one in back applied a paddle, presumably to keep the line moving fast enough. "C'mon, you pukes![19] Straighten up! *{slap}* Double time! *{slap}*" It sounded like movie drill-sergeant talk. "If shit shitted and ate nothing but shit, that shit would *still* be better than all of you! Wrap your head around that one, pussies!" They walked right by Peter and Hart, and Hart recognized the telltale stumble of Trip Darling, third in line. He resisted the urge to stick out his foot.

After they had shuffled out of earshot, Peter continued. "Hart, I'm gonna give you a piece of advice, which you're probably not gonna take, but screw it, I'm drunk and you're my new best friend."

"Let me guess," Hart said. "'Rain on your balls . . .'"

"What? No," Peter said. He looked at Hart with the earnest intensity of the intoxicated. "Don't ever trade yourself for something. Whatever this place says it can give you, you can get on your own, and a lot cheaper."

"What about the Mugwumps, Peter?" Hart said. "That

---

[19] A "puke" was the group's charming name for an initiant. Graduates were known as "Old Pukes."

trade sure as hell gets you something. The last four presidents of the United States have been Wumpmen."

Peter pointed at the line of stumbling, chanting idiots. "And members of that, too." A puke fell down, then scrambled to his feet under a torrent of kicks. "I rest my case."

"Who *are* those guys?" Hart asked. "If anybody talked to me like that, I'd—"

"—get kicked out of the fraternity," Peter said. "It's Comma Comma Apostrophe. Meathead frat. Rush week is totally—"

Hart cut him off. "Do you smell smoke?"

"Yeah, I do. Where's it coming from?"

"Down there." Hart pointed to the other end of the Old Quad.

"If something's on fire," Peter said, "I wanna see it." They booked in the direction of the smoke. "I think it's by the gym," Peter said, when they got to the Locust Street gate. Hart, not motorized and already out of breath, just nodded. A string of firecrackers went off.

Two blocks later, they stood in front of a massive pile of flame. A crowd had gathered, mostly weenies already living in the library and desperate for a study break.

"What's on fire?" Peter asked a perky-looking girl standing next to him.

"A magazine!" she said, tossing her pen into the flames, just to see if it would explode. As at any scene of wanton destruction, a festive atmosphere reigned—the flames were all sorts of weird colors from the ink, which produced awful-smelling smoke. "Some guys from the student newspaper stole the whole print run and set it on fire."

"How'd they do that?" Tales of skullduggery fascinated Hart, especially when he was drunk.

"Showed up at the printer's, pretending to be the editors," the girl said. "Then they took 'em back here, dumped them in a pile, and—flame on! No more—"

"—*Cuckoo*," an upperclassman said. "The magazine's called *The Cuckoo*. It prints cartoons or jokes or something. I've never seen one. *The Daily Spectacle* always finds some way to destroy it before it comes out. "

"Why?" Peter asked.

"Who cares?" the perky girl bubbled. "Isn't college *great*?"

"Competiton for ads, probably," the upperclassman said. "It's been going on for years and years. Whenever the *Spec* reports on it—which isn't often—the paper blames 'rogue elements of a shadowy campus group, Students for Propriety.'" The upperclassman smiled. "That's code for 'the *Spec* editorial board.'"

"Well, you can't expect the *Spec* to rat on themselves," the girl said, in a Southern drawl. "I'd do it too, if I were them."

"So much for freedom of the press," Hart grumbled. He was trying to stay well away from the flames; after the beers, his breath was probably combustible. The pile of magazines sat in front of a ruined building—Hart remembered *Stutts: Jewel in the Bog* saying that the decaying structure was a piece of conceptual art.

Two glum-looking students, one male and one female, stood much closer to the pile than anybody else. Hart wondered if the girl's long hair would catch on fire.

The perky girl was watching them, too. "Those two losers are the *Cuckoo* editors," she said, pointing and laughing. "Look at them—it's like they don't even care everybody thinks they're lame!"

Hart suddenly liked them, in direct proportion to how

much he disliked the girl. They looked nice, calmly waiting for the fire to burn out. The guy was blowing bubbles from a wand and the girl was shaking some pills into her palm.

"Ooo! Do you think she's committing suicide?" the perky girl said hopefully.

Peter said, "I hate to disappoint you, but they look like vitamins."

"Too bad!" She gave a braying laugh, then went back to the library.

CHAPTER FOUR

THE NEXT DAY, Peter and Hart went to breakfast together—they both needed moral support. Drinking on the quad had been fun, but now the boys were feeling a little rough around the edges. Those Belgian beers were like jet fuel.[20]

"Watch and learn." Peter unscrewed the top of a pepper grinder and popped some aspirin in. Grinding the pills, he coated his eggs until they were white with painkiller. Nobody noticed—the Dacron dining hall offered up torrid kisses, shattering breakups, nervous breakdowns, and moments of triumph, all within the same meal. Peter choked down a mouthful. "Got me through prep school," he croaked.

Hart's food seemed to be scowling at him. He stuck his tongue out at it. "Let's not make this a habit," he said.

"The drinking, or the breakfast?" Peter asked.

"Both," Hart said grumpily. The portrait nearest him seemed to be scowling, too.

---

[20] The monks who came up with the original recipe had named it "the celibate's friend."

"Most important meal of the day," Peter said.

"Not if you can't keep it down."

Peter laughed. He flipped open that morning's *Spec*. The tabloid cover screamed, "Magazine of DEATH!"

"They're calling the fire 'a printing accident,'" Peter said. He read aloud: "'*The Cuckoo*, a little-known campus humor magazine desperate for publicity, used an extremely flammable metallic ink on its cover. Stacking the issues caused the pressure to build up. This, plus the ink fumes, meant a deadly explosion was only a matter of time.'"

Hart snorted. "Nobody believes that, do they?"

"Nah, it's the *Spec*," Peter said. "'An unnamed University source expressed gratitude that the explosion happened when it did, and called *The Cuckoo*'s actions "dangerous and irresponsible."' Oh look," Peter said. "A guest editorial from Students for Propriety: '*Cuckoo* Eds Should Be Expelled.'"

Not sure whether it was the yellow journalism or his greasy egg-and-sausage sandwich, Hart stopped chewing and dropped his fork in disgust.

Fifteen minutes later, Hart passed Peter in the common room. Peter had Anton's pink memo pad, and was filling each page with profane couplets. "What's the point of rhyming dictionaries if they don't have the *interesting* words in them?" he complained.

"I'm heading over to Trip's room," Hart said. "Wanna come?"

"What're you shopping this morning?" Peter asked.[21]

---

[21] The first week of each semester, Stutts students "shopped"—that is, attended all the classes they were considering. Along with lessening buyer's remorse, shopping classes was a great way for first-years to ease into college without hyperventilating from anxiety.

"Pokington." This was Percival Pokington, Stutts' world-famous history professor.

"Solid choice, if conventional. Who's Trip?"

"Burlington Darling the Third, the Fifth."

"Huh?"

"He's the fifth-straight the Third." Peter showed complete befuddlement. "Look, it's not important. He's just a jerk from my high school."

"There must've been mercury in my cereal this morning," Peter said. "College—unlike high school—is a time to hang out with people you actually *like*."

Hart laughed and rolled his eyes. If Peter only knew.

"I think I'll pass," Peter said, flipping the pages of the notepad. "I've got five more of these to fill out, then I'm shopping The Lighter Side of the Laffer Curve."

"You're going to take econ? I thought you weren't going to be businessy."

"The goal of this shopping period is to increase my tolerance for boredom." Hart had only known Peter for a day, but he'd already figured out that setting slightly absurd, strangely useful goals seemed to be Peter's preferred way of getting through life. "I've been training hard since July. I can read five whole pages of Kierkegaard before blacking out."

"Don't hurt yourself."

"I know. I wake up with a terrible headache." Peter took two dime-size pieces of metal from a slot in his chair. "Let's stay in touch—I may need you to keep me awake. Put one button in your ear, and clip the other one to your collar. They're wireless."

Hart examined the shiny green buttons. "Did you make this?" Peter nodded yes. "Tell me now: are you a super genius?

'Cause if I find out later from somebody else, I'm going to feel like a retard."

"Wily E. Coyote, su-uper genius!" Peter chuckled. "When you're as bored as I am, nothing is impossible."

"For you, maybe," Hart said. "Tell me all the things you've done to your chair. Just so I can feel really pea-brained for my first morning of classes."

"Well, there's the cooler, which you saw, and the communicators . . ." Peter began ticking things off on his fingers. "There's a sonic air purifier, a GPS system, a camera, a hibachi . . ."

"Nice!"

". . . a spotlight, a massager, a grappling hook, a winch, an eyeglass cleaner, a nose hair clipper, a shaving mirror . . . and a few secret projects I'm working on."

"Amazing," Hart said. He looked at his watch. "Shit, I've gotta go."

Though this often surprised incoming students—and outraged their cash-hemorrhaging parents—the dorms at Stutts were decorated in prep-school shabby. Flaking paint, peeling plaster, gouged woodwork, knocking radiators, boarded-up fireplaces, all faded glory and cold-bath "character." It was Sparta by way of Brooks Brothers.

However!

As befit the scion of one of America's best-connected families, Burlington Darling III, V didn't live in just any dorm. First of all, Trip's college, Cummerbund, was head and shoulders above the rest. It was beautiful—where all the movies were filmed—and had the best food, too. But Trip didn't just live in the tip-top college; another delectable piece of Trip's lucky sperm jackpot was living in the most coveted rooms on the Old Quad.

About a century ago, the original Burlington Darling III decided to spite his striking mine workers by bankrolling The Darling Suite, a collection of lavish rooms reserved for the use of any future Darlings attending Stutts. The result was the last word in pre-income tax opulence. Or so it was said; few people were favored enough to see inside. Rumors abounded: it was filled with priceless art, it had its own cooking staff, it had its own waterfall. Trotsky himself had denounced it, shortly before his death.[22]

On the other hand, Trotsky would've loved where Hart was living. Hart wasn't picky, he would've taken the lowest of the low—and that's exactly what he got. Dacron College was where admissions dumped all the long shots, all the charity cases, all the geeks and eccentrics with a bit too much talent for Stutts to take the chance that some other college might nurture them into wealthy alumni. Occasionally somebody like Mr. President, popular and hygienic, sneaked into Dacron somehow; but those types quickly found friends in other, better colleges, and transferred.

This disdain made 'Cronics (as Dacron residents called themselves) stick together. They reveled in their geekiness, flaunting it whenever possible. Even the college's unfortunate appearance became a point of pride: Dacron looked like it had been made from factory-second peanut brittle. It also didn't have any ninety-degree angles; apparently that counted for something in the 1960s, when the college was built and architects were heavily into drugs.

Hart gave Trip's door a few raps with the gilded knocker.

[22] For this reason, Internet conspiracy theorists whispered that the Darlings had paid for Trotsky's assassination, then received lucrative Caspian Sea oil contracts as a thank-you from Stalin.

It was useless—Trip was utterly unable to listen to music at a normal volume; it had to be loud enough to fill his empty head. Already annoyed, Hart called Trip's cell phone.

"Yo!"

"Open up, fuckhead," Hart said, "I'm here to take you to class."

When Trip opened the door, Hart noticed that he had shaved off his left eyebrow. Instinctively, Hart knew this was not good.

"Guess what?" Trip said. "I'm rushing a frat!"

Hart groaned and walked into the suite. "I saw you on the Old Quad last night."

"Don't remind me about last night! I had a frozen hot dog up my butt the whole time."

"Classy. What are your new best friends called, again?"

"Comma Comma Apostrophe," Trip said. "And they *are* my friends. They just make pledges do stuff, to prove their love for the organization and stuff. We have to prove that we are the best Stutts has to offer."

"By sticking a hot dog in your butt."

"You wouldn't understand. That's what Stutts is about. It's a tradition."

"So was not admitting black people," Hart said. Up until two years ago, CCA had been all-white. It was all over the newspapers.

"What are you talking about?" Trip had missed it; he'd been in a news blackout since birth. "Hart, I'm saying this to you as a friend"—the meathead wrenched open a Louis Quatorze desk and rummaged through it like a robber—"people might like you if you didn't say things that didn't make sense."

71

"Grackle dron!" Hart had never tried to talk nonsense before, but it felt good.

Trip didn't respond—he hadn't been listening. "You know what I worry about? What if people meet you, know *I* know you, and think *I'm* a dick, too? That's not fair."

"Vreebl, vreebl." Hart said thoughtfully. He wandered over to the massive fireplace; Trip's, unlike Hart's, still worked. "What have you been burning in here?"

"Styrofoam, and a couple of rubbers. You know what those are, don't you?"

"Yeah, and I also know that plastic fumes give you brain damage."

"Where'd you read that, a book?"

As Trip tried to find a pen that worked, Hart became more and more bitter. Not only was the place seriously gilded—"Victorian whorehouse" was the phrase that sprung to mind—Trip had already begun its systematic annihilation. Hart couldn't decide what made him madder, that Trip had been given so much, or that Trip felt entitled to destroy it. Drawing a mustache on one cherub could be chalked up to high spirits—or just plain spirits—but doing all five the first night implied a deeply felt commitment to vandalism.

On the suite's upper level, a man in a morning coat appeared. He dangled a rubber tube down to where Trip was standing. Trip, pen finally in hand, put the tube in his mouth. The butler inserted a funnel into the end he was holding, popped open a can of beer, and poured it in. Trip slurped it down at top speed, then gave a rafter-shaking belch.

"Throw the other one down, I'll drink it on the way," Trip commanded.

The butler did so. It hit Trip in the head, but he caught it on the carom. "Sorry, Master Darling. Shall I instruct Cook to prepare you a filet for lunch?"

A butler? Filet mignon? Hart could no longer trust himself not to start swinging. "I'll wait for you outside," he growled.

The walk to Pokington's class was blessedly short. Even so, Trip tinged it with unpleasantness by scrawling a coarse word on the door of the Wymyn's Cyntyr.

"What is your *problem?*" Hart said, grabbing the pen from Trip. "Are you drunk?"

"Yeah, isn't it awesome? I love college!" he yelled.

"I'll give your pen back when we get to class."

"Ahh, keep it," Trip said. "You'll be the one taking notes." He pulled out yet another beer hidden somewhere on his person, opened it, and started to chug. Finished, he threw it in the bushes. "Gotta fill up the tank."

The bell tower pealed the hour, then the theme from *The Simpsons*.[23]

"Shit," Hart said, "we're late."

Trip began to trot after Hart, then stopped. "Wait."

"Come on!" Hart said, pulling at Trip's shirt. Trip held a finger up.

"Bragggp," he belched. "Now, we can go." Hart had a thought: if these are the leaders of tomorrow, the world is fucked.

Every professor had been forced by the bitch-goddess Academia to devote his entire life to the study of one subject.

---

[23] Playing irreverent tunes on the campus carillon was common. Campus legend held that, for twenty years, a grad student had been living up there trying to finish his dissertation, subsisting on black coffee and library paste.

73

Naturally, if only to stave off the inevitable psychological breakdown, the professor considered that subject to be the most important facet of human existence—and his continued fragile pas-de-deux with reality insisted that all his students did, too. Woe to any frosh who let slip that the ups and downs of medieval Flemish textile guilds did not occupy her every waking moment.

At the same time, one of the unquestionable joys of Stutts was listening to its professors. The most lucid and fascinating of these were called the Pantheon. Listening to one of the Pantheon, one *could* care about medieval Flemish textile guilds. (Almost.)

One of the world's foremost experts on China, Professor Pokington was part of this roster of academic immortals. At Stutts, being in the Pantheon wasn't simply a turn of phrase; the ceiling of Muggeridge Hall (where Pokington lectured) was painted with a mural. Each member of the Pantheon was depicted interacting with giants of scholarship past and present in a School of Athens-type toga-clad confab.

Hart and Trip slipped into the balcony. The room was packed—professors made the shopping period editions of their classes as interesting as possible, to keep enrollment high. Professor Pokington stood behind his lectern, expounding vigorously on the topic of Mao Tse-tung's sex life.

As they settled into their seats, Trip pointed at some scaffolding above them. "What's that?" he said loudly.

There was a large, flimsy, window-washer style scaffold, suspended from behind the balcony to above the stage. "Shh! I guess they're adding to the painting on the ceiling," Hart whispered. Pokington had just achieved Pantheon status; he stood between Newton and Aristotle, but since it wasn't finished, it looked a bit like Pokington was flipping Newton the bird.

Hart looked at it, smiled, then didn't think of it again—the lecture was fascinating, except for the parts that reminded him of the drive east with Mom. Trip was less spellbound; he was snoring immediately. Through trial and error, Hart discovered that a sharp elbow between the fourth and fifth rib would shut Trip up without actually waking him. If Trip wanted to sleep through all four years, that was okay with Hart. From his teenaged babysitting days, Hart knew that the more Trip was asleep, the happier he, Hart, would be. Hart grew unhappy, however, when Trip began to release great, billowing, sulphurous beer-farts. Hart breathed through his mouth and tried to concentrate on learning.

Finally Hart had to slip out for a bathroom break—and some air. "If my friend snores, could you elbow him?" he asked the student on the other side of Trip.

"Is *he* the one doing it?" The whole row leaned over and made various silent signals of disgust.

"Sorry," Hart said. "Feel free to draw on him." He left, creeping up the aisle and out the balcony doors. To his left, Hart suddenly saw a giant gray spider, and jumped a mile. Then he looked again: it was only the tubular metal ladder that led to the scaffold. In his fright Hart had narrowly missed bringing the whole rickety contraption down. As visions of crushed students danced neurotically in Hart's head, he took a moment to calm down and curse his switcheroo eyes.

On his way back from the bathroom, Hart remembered Peter's communicator. He pulled the two buttons out of his pocket and turned them on—Pete would want to hear the juicier tidbits. Waiting for a big laugh from the crowd, Hart opened the balcony door and slipped back in.

Trip wasn't there. "Did you see my . . ." Hart caught himself before he said "friend." "Where did he go?"

"I don't know. Believe me, we didn't stop him."

Hart looked around and found his answer: while Hart had been peeing, Trip had walked out of the balcony into the corridor outside, and climbed up the ladder. Now he was crawling unsteadily down the catwalk to the scaffolding which hung in the middle of the auditorium. Trip really was like a big, drunken toddler.

"Jesus, it's fifty feet to the stage," the guy sitting next to Hart said. "I hope he doesn't fall." A quick search of his heart found Hart agnostic on the matter. A Trip-less universe would be heavenly, but Mr. Darling would stop the checks in the event of his son's death. Self-interest kindled, Hart scrambled up the aisle and out the doors, then clambered up the ladder. Trip was twenty feet ahead, balancing on his knees and waving. There was a rustle as people in the balcony below noticed the husky idiot crawling above them.

"Trip!" Hart hissed from the top of the ladder. "What the hell are you doing?"

"I'm going to piss on the professor," Trip slurred resolutely.

Had Trip actually gotten drunker somehow? Had years of binge drinking mutated him so that he could draw alcohol via air alone? "You're going to what on the who?"

"Piss on the prof," Trip said louder. "I gotta do it to get into the frat." He turned and resumed his slow, weaving crawl towards destiny.

Swearing, Hart tapped the "connect" switch on the communicator. "Pete, are you there?" Hart was so scared of heights, just looking at Trip made him queasy.

"Yeah," Peter said tinnily. "What's up? You sound crazed."

76

"You gotta get over here! Trip's climbed up on a catwalk, and he's going to piss on Professor Pokington!"

Pete laughed. "For a meathead, he's very dynamic," he said. "What do you want me to do about it? Let him get expelled. Take pictures, I want to see them."

"No!" Hart pleaded. He saw that Trip had stopped, and was resting his head on the cool metal. "It's a long story, but I can't let him be expelled."

"Okay," Peter said. "But what can I do?"

"You'll think of something, you're a genius!"

Pete couldn't resist the challenge. "I'll be over in two "minutes—stall him."

"*Stall* him? Hello? Come in, Pete—" The communicator was dead. With misgivings and a heaving stomach, Hart started out on the catwalk.

Up ahead, Trip had made it to the part of the scaffold where the painters had been working. Fifty feet above the unsuspecting professor, he stood up—and teetered.

"Whoa-oa," Trip said, laughing.

Hart gasped and doubled his speed, fighting the urge to stop, hug the scaffold, and whimper. Trip, overflowing with liquid courage, had no such problem. Down below, Professor Pokington was equally carefree, unspooling an anecdote involving Mao, Andy Warhol, Jackie Onassis, and two Mongolian "fun girls."

When Hart got to the painters' perch, Trip was unzipped and ready for action. Trip squinted over the side of the scaffold, trying to line himself up.

Hart crawled over and grabbed the railing. "Trip, what the *hell* are you doing? What would your dad say?"

"He'd laugh. He had to piss on the President of Bulgaria,"

Trip said. "Now shut up, I'm trying to concentrate." Trip was suddenly pee-shy; he rocked back and forth, thinking of waterfalls. "C'mon, c'mon, c'mon . . ."

"Trip I swear, if I see *one drop*—" Hart did, and made a grab at the offending organ.

"Hey!" Trip said, shimmying away. "What are you, some sort of fag?"

Hart retreated several feet to plot his next move. This sucked. This really, really sucked.

"Turn around," Trip said. "I can't pee when you're looking at me, fag."

Hart got an idea. "Hey, everybody!" he yelled. "Look at the guy trying to pee on the professor!"

The room turned as one. Some began to point and laugh.

"Thanks a lot, asshole!" Trip said. Not even zipping up, he stumbled over to where Hart was clutching the railing. "Dick!" he declared, punching Hart in the chest.

Far below, blinking out at the audience, Professor Pokington noticed the commotion. "People, please settle . . . Is there anything . . . ?" Audience members pointed up at the scaffold. Pokington turned to watch the contest. Everybody had.

Hart got mad. Forgetting his fear, he launched himself at Trip. A small cheer went up from the balcony. "Five bucks on Stinky!" "Ten on the other kid!"

The two grappled; they were evenly matched. Hart pinned Trip's arms; Trip elbowed Hart in the stomach. Determined to stop the pee at its source, Hart grabbed Trip's penis and twisted. With a yelp of pain and outrage, Trip scrambled away, then bit Hart's ankle. As the boys fought, the scaffold lurched dangerously. Hart took a moment to look down, which was a mistake; Trip punched him in the gut and he went down, hard.

Trip walked over to the edge; using his chest as a sight, he began to recalibrate his wang. "You bent it, you asshole!"

"I say, you two up there," Professor Pokington said. "I don't know if you're planning to take this class or not, but you need to come down right now!"

"Stay right there, Limey," Trip mumbled.

"He's Welsh," Hart said, still winded but defiant.

"Shut up," Trip commanded, spitting to get himself started. "Visualize a urinal," he said softly . . . then he let 'er rip.

As the urine began its sinuous journey earthward, the main doors to the auditorium burst open. "Professor Pokington!" Peter yelled into his chair-mounted bullhorn.

"Yes?" The professor took a step to his left, and the urine fell harmlessly to the stage.

"Goddammit!" Trip yelled, and took aim again. "Short bursts, short bursts . . ."

"There's been a problem with the, uh, Yangtze River!" Peter said. "CNN needs you to comment immediately—please follow me!"

"Right!" Pokington barked, like the RAF man he had been. "Class dismissed!" The professor left the podium, crossing the stage with a stream of urine trailing behind him. Unaware, he strode up the aisle with dignity and purpose, not even stopping to collect his papers. A graduate assistant mounted the stage; sneaking glances upward, she gathered the lecture notes and stuffed them into Professor Pokington's battered briefcase.

"I gotta get *somebody* . . ." Trip muttered. Coolly, with the dispassionate manner of an assassin, he squeezed off a stream above the grad student. The glinting urine caught her eye, and she stepped sideways with a small scream. Trip chased her round and round the stage, until he ran dry. Thwarted, Trip zipped up. Giving a bellow, he shook the railing. The catwalk shimmied dangerously.

"Trip!" Hart said, holding on for his life. Suddenly, he heard a crack and one corner of the scaffold came loose. The boys slid to the end of the scaffold, and dangled there. A few feet away from Hart, Trip griped, "I *told* Dad you'd ruin my undergraduate experience!"

"There's always grad school," Hart said.

The boys yelled for help. Below, the audience was filing out nonchalantly. Two freaks hanging from the ceiling was none of their business—they had classes to shop. Here and there, scattered groups were chanting "Jump! Jump! Jump!"

Trip continued to spit bile. "You don't belong here—you'll never belong here! If it wasn't for my dad, you'd be—"

"Insult me when we're on the ground, okay?" Hart saw a group of boys fighting their way through the crowd, trying to move down the aisle to the stage. They were all wearing beige sweatshirts with punctuation on the front.

Trip hadn't noticed; he was too busy scowling at Hart. Then a dim, small light went on somewhere inside his cavernous skull. "If I die," he said, "you'll have to go back home! Have fun working at McDonald's, you loser!" Wearing a 'gotcha' smile, Trip let go.

"Brother Trip," a frat boy called from the stage. "When we say 'let go,' you —SHIT!" They opened the blanket just in time.

Hart watched Trip stumble to his feet. There were scattered cheers, and a few CCA guys bowed. The auditorium was almost empty. When the last CCA guy walked off the stage, Hart yelled as loud as he could. "What about me?"

The CCA guy turned. He looked so much like Trip they could've been related. Hell, they probably were. "What *about* you?" he said.

Hart's shoulders were really starting to hurt. "Aren't you going to save me, too?"

"Excuse me—have we met?" the frat boy said.

"No," Hart said, "but I'm gonna die!"

"Well, you should've joined a fraternity." He turned and walked up the aisle.

"Wait! *Help me!*" Hart yelled, but the boy was gone. Now the room was empty. Hart hung there, listening to his shoulders slowly separate from their sockets. Suddenly, a boy ran down the aisle. Hart yelled for all he was worth. "You, with the camera! Go get help! I don't know how much longer I can hang here!"

"Great!" The boy stopped about ten feet from the stage, raised his camera, and started taking pictures. "Do you have anything to say? I'm Miles Monaghan from the *Daily Spectacle*."

"For Christ's sake, get help!"

The boy wrote it down. "We'll have to edit out the profanity, but I'll try to keep the spirit of the quote. Listen," he continued, "are you planning on falling? 'Cause that would be a great picture. No rush—I can wait."

Hearing this galvanized Hart; he was damned if he would make anybody's career but his own! Summoning up his last reserves of strength, he pulled himself up onto the broken scaffold. Then he slowly crawled to safety. The boy snapped pictures all the way. "Excellent, excellent! Make love to the camera!"

"Hey," Hart said when he got back to his seat in the balcony, "somebody stole my notes!"

CHAPTER FIVE

THE NEXT MORNING, Hart was still in bed when Peter knocked on his bedroom door.

"Come in," he said grumpily. Hart liked to sleep; he considered it something he was good at, and always resented having to stop.

"I brought you breakfast," Peter said, wheeling in and handing over a paper bag.

Hart looked inside: there was a carton of orange juice and a bagel. "Thanks. I thought you were kidding. Is this just part of the full-service roommate experience?"

"You might want to avoid the dining hall today." Peter tossed the *Daily Spectacle* on Hart's bed. There Hart was on the cover, hanging from the catwalk. Next to the grainy photo, in two-inch-high letters, was the headline: "Rain of Terror!"

"Oh, no . . ." This was not how Hart had hoped to start his Stutts career. With mounting horror, Hart read the article (it was nestled in the back, among the escort-service ads). Every important fact was wrong.

"Trip isn't even mentioned! And they got the professor's

name wrong: 'Reached for comment, Professor Stokington said "Blorg!"' "Blorg isn't even a word," Hart fumed. Nevertheless he filed it away for his next nonsense war with Trip.

"Student journalism is a blunt instrument," Peter said sadly. "Maybe 'Blorg!' is Welsh slang for something. Or maybe the writer couldn't read his notes."

"They call me 'The Mad Pisser'! *I am not a 'execreto-terrorist'!*"

"Keep your voice down," Peter said. "Look on the bright side: nobody could possibly recognize you. The photo is too crappy. Like that blob there—for all I know, that could be Bigfoot."

"It's Trip," Hart said. "Same difference."

Peter assumed teasing position. "This 'Trip'—are you sure he's not imaginary?"

"I wish," Hart said, burying his head in his hands. He decided to tell Peter about the arrangement he had with Mr. Darling. "Could you close the door, please?"

Five minutes later, Peter whistled. "What an asshole! Yesterday makes a lot more sense now."

"It would've been a lot worse if you hadn't shown up," Hart said. "I should've told you before."

"Don't mention it," Peter said. "It was fun leading Professor Pokington all over campus 'looking for the CNN truck.'"

"That sounds dirty," Hart said, opening the juice. "'Son, what were you doing with that girl?' 'We were looking for the CNN truck.'"

Peter laughed. "Pokington called me 'a star-spangled nincompoop,'" Peter said. "I think American college students disappoint him."

"They disappoint me, too."

"Don't be embarrassed about this thing with Mr. Darling," Peter said seriously.

"Why not?" Hart asked, through a mouthful of bagel. He swiped ineffectually at the crumbs, which were already worming their way deep into his bedclothes. "I got in through the back door."

". . . and if you can't hack it, you'll get kicked out the front one."

"Don't joke."

Peter laughed. "God, relax. The only way to feel you belong is to decide you do. Keep your ears open in the dining hall—everybody sits around thinking that *they're* the one that shouldn't be here, that the admissions office made some mistake. Athletes think they got in 'just' because they're athletes; legacies 'just' because their parents went here; poor black kids 'just' because they're poor and black."

"Maybe they did."

"But *who cares*? None of us deserved such a lucky break. And the sad thing is, some people waste the rest of their lives trying to prove they did. 'See how brilliant I am?'"

"I see," Hart said, finishing off his breakfast. "So now isn't a good time to tell you I'm going to try to write a column for the *Spectacle*?"

"Oh, sweet Mother of God." Peter said. "Promise me you'll destroy them from within." He backed out of the room, noting that the walls were bare. "Aren't you ever going to decorate this place?"

Hart thought for the first time that day how broke he was. There would be hundreds more times.

* * *

84

Hart gave himself a week's deadline to write two funny columns and submit them to the *Spec*. He got an idea immediately: he would opine on the campus and its inhabitants from the vantage point of Mau-Mau, President Whitbread's cat.

Even with an idea, it was hard to find the time. In the mornings, Hart had to shop, not only for himself, but for Trip, too. Now that he'd gotten into CCA,[24] Trip didn't care what classes Hart took on his behalf. So Hart picked ones that *he* liked—and ones he hoped would be easy, too, since he was taking two students' worth at once. When he'd picked them all, he called Trip, so their stories would match, if it ever came to that.

"Trip, it's Hart."

"Spit it out, Mad Pisser. I'm busy." The brothers were over for a game of Texas Hold 'em—rather, one game had been going for forty-seven hours. The Darling suite was heaven, compared to the CCA house. Really anyplace was nicer than the CCA house, which was infested with fifteen boys, hordes of cockroaches, numberless rats, a squadron of mice, three distinct nests of termites, a few bitchy squirrels, and even the occasional deer.[25]

"I just wanted to let you know that you're an archaeology major," Hart said.

"Sounds faggy." Trip gnawed on a pretzel—it was stale, so he threw it at a Tiffany lamp. "What's that mean?"

Hart grabbed for the simplest explanation he could find. "The study of old stuff. I picked it because I figure, once you

---

[24] Though he had missed the mark, "golden shower"-wise, it was the effort that counted, especially when your name was Darling.

[25] It was sometimes seen in the attic. Nobody knew how it could've gotten there. They fed it beer, and occasionally hard drugs.

know the basics, you can probably fake it pretty good. I mean, they can't make more."

"Sounds boring . . . I've already gotten laid six times," Trip said brightly.

"What does that have to do with archeology?"

"Nothing. I just wanted you to know what I've been doing while you've been taking my classes." Trip inspected a bruise on his forehead. People said he'd fallen down last night; he'd have to take their word for it.

Through the phone, Hart heard a crescendo of calls from his frat brothers: "Trip, quit talking to your girlfriend!" "It's your deal, fartknocker!" "If you're not back here in three seconds, I'm lookin' at your cards!"

"Hey! *Shut it!*" Trip yelled back. "And quit pickin' the jewels off that thing—I wanna do it." Then, to Hart: "Bye, fag."

Hart was glad he didn't tell Trip what major *he'd* decided on: Study of Things. It was supposed to be really demanding, but the class he'd shopped, Intro to Things, had been fascinating. And how hard could it be? With something like that, weren't you *always* studying, kinda-sorta? Anyway, if it was too difficult or the people were annoying, he could always change later. That was the beauty of being a freshman.

The only thing more fascinating than his classes was Hart's new hometown. Buildings in Great Littleton seemed to slump, an attitude shared by most of its inhabitants.[26] Stutts, on the other

---

[26] In the 1970s, school geologists had finally solved the mystery: Great Littleton had been sited atop an aquifer. As the groundwater percolated up, it passed through a selection of sediments that, when combined, produced a powerful depressant.

hand, threw off a buzz of upward striving that visitors found almost intolerable. These two opposing weather fronts had been mixing since 1691, when a group of local ministers drained a pestilential seaside bog and erected a few rude huts for scholars to cower in.

Ever since, the townies had acted like the citizens of an occupied nation; resentments had been nurtured, then passed down for at least thirteen generations. While there hadn't been a true town-gown bloodbath since before World War II (the notorious "Snowball Fracas," which took its name from a hastily convened congressional report), there was still a distinct crackle of dislike.

"Coming through, nerd!"

"Sorry," Hart said, and stepped off the sidewalk as a group of Great Littleton toughs on Big Wheels rumbled sullenly past. Knees to chin, the last one flipped him the bird. "Sorry," Hart said, again, and felt stupid for it.

Still, under the right circumstances, and for a limited time, the two sides could come together. The always-sweltering beginning of term was one of those times. There was money to be made. The sidewalks were full; students swarmed in and out of stores, spreading prosperity like preppy fairies. The windows were full of cool displays; some stores even had barkers, trying to pull students in with jokey prattle.

Hart had to fight the urge to stop and take it all in—if he did, he'd be shoved aside by the herd of people buying posters and paint, bedsheets and bongs (for tobacco, of course). He passed the school bookstore—the place to get textbooks, and everything else as well, since the bill could be sent home to your parents. Hart looked in the front window; things were just barely under control. If it were possible to explode from raw commerce, this place might. He felt a sharp jab in the small of his back.

"Hey, watch where you're going," Xanthan said. "You just ran into Hart."

"Sorry," Mr. President said. "I was just talking to my girl-friend."

Mr. President had a girlfriend already? *Jesus!* Mr. President and Xanthan were both loaded down with pieces of ugly particle-board furniture. Don't ask me to help you carry that shit, Hart thought. Don't, don't, don't. "Hey, guys. Looks like the last copter out of Saigon in there—no offense, Xan."

"None taken," Xanthan said. Xanthan's precise ethnicity had been a topic of much conversation among the roommates, but it seemed rude to ask.[27]

"Gotten all your dorm stuff, Hart?" Mr. President asked.

"Haven't even started." . . . because I have no money, Hart thought. "I'm waiting until November."

"Smart," Mr. President said. "What about textbooks?"

Hart's blood pressure spiked: yeah, what about textbooks? He needed to change the subject. "What are you guys carry-ing?"

"Bookshelves," Xanthan said. "I bought a thousand bucks' worth of books yesterday. I barely have room for my bed."

"What major are you going to pick?" Hart asked.

"Investigations in Popular Culture," Xanthan said. "The reading lists are humongous." IPC majors used the tools of aca-

---

[27] In an effort to expunge racism on campus, a person's race was factored into every-thing. This made everyone slightly anxious, which was the natural state of a Stutts student anyway.

demic discourse to make all the things people enjoy talking about (TV shows, movies, pole-dancing) just as stultifying as all the things they don't (covalent bonds, Kant, Restoration drama). The major was staggeringly popular—once you learned the lingo, it was four years of pompous pronouncements and sitcoms for credit. Harmless enough . . . unless the actual creators heard that they were being studied. Then whatever they were doing invariably went to shit. Hart knew the tragedy well; it had happened to his favorite comic book.

"IPC is bullshit—try poli sci with a minor in econ," Mr. President bragged. "I've got ten books for Ruining Third World Economies alone!" He spotted some friends coming down the street behind Hart. "Hi, Teresa. Hey Gavin! Marcello, ciao! Could you guys help us with these bookshelves?" Mr. President's popularity did have its advantages.

They left, and Hart continued to wander down the street. He stopped and browsed at the used-book stall on the corner of Locust and Beetle, until Sneezing Peckham got mad because Hart wasn't buying anything. Sneezing Peckham—no one knew if that was his real name or not—was the hay fever–wracked, stringy-haired, strangely implacable man who owned the stall. How long he'd let you browse before screaming at you was one of the university's many unique markers of status. Only one student within living memory had ever been granted unlimited time.[28] Everybody else was chased away sooner or later—and Hart, as a new arrival, suffered sooner.

"The library's next door!" Peckham yelled hoarsely,

---

[28] That guy, who had been an NFL star, then a Supreme Court Justice, then finally vice-president of the United States, was generally considered an overachieving suck-up.

throwing a pamphlet at him. Sneezing Peckham was such a well-loved piece of Stutts lore that even someone as shy as Hart knew not to take it personally.

Sweating freely—Great Littleton was notorious for working your pores—Hart walked down Locust Street in a dream of contentment. He stepped out of the stream and into a doorway, to savor the moment and take in the scene. Enveloped in a cloud of clove cigarettes, a scruffy black-clad art student loped by, looking serious and ignoring his twittering acolytes. Behind him a group of barrel-shaped athletes were ineptly shepherding a half-keg from the liquor store to the scene of tonight's intoxiganza. A man wearing eye makeup and a toque sat on a bench writing in his journal, as two shockingly thin girls next to him ate frozen yogurt and gossiped.

This was college! Hart exulted. He'd finally found something that was actually better than the movies made it appear. After spending the first eighteen years of life as an adjunct to his parents, an extraneous bit of mewling protoplasm, *here* was a place—an entire world—designed for his amusement. There were cheap restaurants serving every cuisine. There were clubs to find love in, book and record stores to browse, coffee shops to plot and opine in—to Hart, Great Littleton was heaven. He let it wash all over him.

A cute woman in a concert T-shirt tapped on the glass door behind Hart.

"Yeah?" Hart said. Wow! She was pretty; and she was talking to him! Here he was, just standing here, and cute girls *were* irresistibly drawn to him. College romance was just like he'd always dreamed. Women *were* different here. They weren't shallow, or hung up on looks. They were attracted to people for who they really were. They—

"You're leaning on the doorbell," the girl said.

"Oh, sorry," Hart said.

"No problem," she said, and left.

Talking to his roommates about textbooks had enlarged the only dark cloud on Hart's horizon: to get back at him, Mr. Darling had wiggled out of paying for books or supplies. When Hart had gotten his first check, he had written Mr. Darling's accountant asking about this.

"Mr. Fox:" the accountant's reply began. "Regarding the matter referenced in your e-mail of 9/2, I have been instructed to pass along the following message: 'Tough titty.'"

Hart's Plan B—reading as much as he could while standing in the aisles of the school bookstore—was obviously not going to work. Painful as it was, there was only one solution: Hart had to get a job.

"Maybe Mayhem's is hiring?" Peter asked that evening after dinner, as they both shot little plastic discs at a beer-can pyramid in the corner of the common room. They'd bought the disc guns at Mayhem's, a comic-and-toy shop on the first floor of the Stutts Law School building. "I think we're going to need a lot more of these little plastic dudes, and an employee discount would really help."

Hart aimed and fired; the disk curved out the window into the Old Quad, hitting a nonplussed junior. There was really no telling where these little bastards would go—which was part of the fun. "I asked," Hart said. "No dice."

Peter grunted his disapproval, and kept shooting at the beer cans. Hart opened the *Spec*. Peter pumped five quick shots into the newspaper, which produced a series of distracting smacks.

91

"Quit," Hart said. "Don't make the excruciating job-hunting process even worse."

Peter's only response was to shoot again. "All right, you asked for it," Hart yelled, and the firefight began. It lasted, off and on, for several minutes, until they ran out of ammo. Peter tried putting dimes in the gun. He test-fired at Anton's stoplight, and the red lens cracked on impact.

"Excellent!" Peter yelled, with berserker glee. "Now we can do real damage!" He and Hart shot a couple dollars' worth of dimes at Rudy's bedroom door. Eventually Rudy put down the phone and came out.

"What are you assholes—"

"Aim for the feet." Peter said.

"Ow! Shit!" The door slammed shut again. Peter was right—dimes *were* excellent!

"That one was for Pickles!" Hart shouted.

After they ran out of dimes, the evening then turned into a quest for water balloons. "The girl upstairs has stuffed animals," Peter said. "Balloons are a natural extension. Go ask her." By midnight that night, Peter and Hart had gained a reputation as Dacron's most immature duo. "It's something to build on," Peter said. Hart had to agree.

At the end of an utterly pleasant—that is, wasted—evening, Hart sat in bed, circling ads in the back of the *Spec*. Twelve hours later, he presented himself at the library. A day after that (after they'd made sure Hart was a citizen and didn't have an outrageous criminal record), he had a job as an accessor.

Hart loved Harriman Library from the moment he saw it. Back home, librarians were busily trying to siphon knowledge into computerized form, but Harriman had books, millions of books, on every topic imaginable. Enough books to lose a life in.

Harriman was part museum, part repository, and part temple; its collections were so immense, diverse, and chaotic, that no one knew exactly what they contained. That's where Hart came in.

"Our charter insists that we take any object donated to the university by an alum. As a result, we are constantly cataloguing, storing, or discarding massive amounts of material," said Mr. Charivaria, Hart's new boss. "Your job, Mr. Fox, will be to open packages, examine the contents, and pass them on to processing, where a team of people will ready them for eventual accession into the collections." A short, dapper man with a tendency to overuse cologne, Mr. Charivaria sat behind his desk, fingers steepled.

"How many people will I be working with?" Hart asked.

"No one, unfortunately. I'd hire twenty students, but there are budget restrictions. So if you're not willing to work," Mr. Charivaria said severely, "please go bother the glamour boys over at the University Museum. Here at Harriman, we work."

"How much material is there, about?" Hart said.

"You'll be starting on the year 1966." Mr. Charivaria said. He stood up and they shook hands. "Glad to have you aboard. I'll show you the way to your work space."

Hart followed Mr. Charivaria out into the library, to the catalog room. Stutts had recently computerized their collection but, typically, had kept the paper card catalog as well. Hart asked why.

"If there's a loss of power—say, a hurricane or stray electromagnetic burst from those fools over at the Department of Modern Religions[29]—we want our students to be able to access

---

[29] The Department of Modern Religions was where Stutts conducted its most secret research projects for the U.S. government. The building was originally called "Not-a-Secret-Government-Project Hall," but that didn't fool anyone.

the collections," Mr. Charivaria said. "Our motto is, 'Until the End of Time.' And that goes for fines, too."

The card catalog projected out of the room's walls like bay windows. Hart counted twenty-four separate "sides," each with a rack of twenty-four drawers; the catalog was duplicated on the other side as well. "Two catalogs, no waiting," Hart quipped. Mr. Charivaria didn't respond; library science was not a joking matter.

"Here we are." Mr. Charivaria stood in front of the last rack of drawers on the last bay. Looking to see that no one was watching, he leaned down and grabbed the last drawer, which was unmarked. He pulled the drawer out halfway, then shoved it back.

Then he put his shoulder against the rack and pushed; it didn't budge. He repeated the operation with the drawer and tried again. No luck. "Sticks sometimes—humidity," he said, straining. Still nothing. Mr. Charivaria started to mumble, something Hart would come to recognize as steam before the eruption of a volcano. "Goddamn piece of crap nineteenth century secret passages . . . Those architecture department idiots couldn't just build a door, that would be too easy . . ." (Hart suspected that, in Charivaria's opinion, anyone not affiliated with the library was a sub-moron.) Finally, the mechanism worked—the panel of drawers pivoted inward and revealed a passageway down. "After you," Mr. Charivaria said.

They walked down a narrow hallway a long while, and the air grew cooler. After three minutes of walking, Hart asked, "How far down are we?"

"About a hundred feet, I think," Mr. Charivaria said. "The original builders of the library excavated a network of storage chambers—we call them 'The Catacombs.'"

"Wow." Hart stepped on something crunchy, and tried not to think about it.

"Before refrigeration, the university needed a place to store perishables," Mr. Charivaria said. "Nowadays, it's used for items that require preservation—and general storage." They had reached a door with a pebbled-glass window marked ACCESSION. Mr. Charivaria opened it. "This is where you'll be working." It was a tiny room, with just enough space for an antique wooden desk. There were open chutes behind and in front of the desk; the side walls were covered with pneumatic tubes.

"Sit down," Mr. Charivaria said. "Is the chair comfortable? I'll get you another one if necessary."

"No, it's fine," Hart said, working his butt around in the chair a bit.

"Don't be hasty," Mr. Charivaria said. "You'll be sitting for hours at a stretch."

"What are the tubes and chutes for?" Hart asked.

"The old campus mail system. There's a tube-end in almost every room—you'll notice them, once you know to look."

"And the same with the chutes?"

"No, they're a big part of your job. It's simple, really; just grab a package from the full chute behind you—"

Full? Hart thought. More like overflowing.

"—then you unwrap it, catalog it and send it down the appropriate chute on the other side of the room."

"Sounds like fun," Hart said.

"Glad you think so," Mr. Charivaria said. Every year, he watched this job drive students mad. They started out enthusiastic, but in a matter of months they became babbling shells, their spirits broken by an unending stream of crap.

"Remember, everything you receive here is University property. You may not, under any circumstances, take anything for your own use, even if you plan to return it. Is that clear?"

"Yes," Hart said.

"The in-chute is hundreds of feet long. Whenever the university gets a gift, the postman just chucks it into an opening on the first floor. The chute's packed solid—"

"Constipated."

"Er, yes, that's one way of looking at it. We—you—slowly dig it out from this end. Throw the wrapping in this chute—it goes to the incinerator. Then write down what the gift is, and which of the chutes in front you'll put it in." Each chute in front of Hart's desk had a label: To Archives; To Auction; To Incinerator; For Professional Review.

"Things that you know have historical interest, send to the Harriman Archives. Items that look valuable but not rare, send to our auction house. Worthless items go to the incinerator. Things you aren't sure about, place in the chute for professional review," Mr. Charivaria said. "Simple enough?"

"What if I make a mistake—put something valuable down the incinerator?"

"Don't worry about that," Mr. Charivaria said. "Just as long as you don't send it to the University Museum. Understand?"

Hart didn't understand, but the look on his boss' face told him to drop the subject.

Secret, middle-of-the-night doubts about their worthiness aside, every Stutts student considered him/herself pretty hot fudge. Outside of the Mugwumps, the pulsing epicenter of self-regard on campus was unquestionably the offices of *The Daily*

96

Spectacle. Sure, the paper itself was a grab bag of murky photos, garbled half-truths, and dubious assertions, but the paper wasn't the point—it was the careers of the students running it that mattered. Only a freshman or a fool thought that journalism had anything to do with it. At the job it considered important—being a launcher of flaks, pundits, and high-level functionaries—the *Spec* was superb.

It had been that way since Howard Sproul '24 had begun his relentless march to fame and fortune nearly a century ago. The son of missionaries, Sproul had inherited their zealotry, but avoided their principles; consequently he was a great success, at college and beyond. Sproul had gone directly from Stutts— where he'd supervised the *Spec*'s changeover from a dreary, ponderous broadsheet to the shrieking semi-factual tabloid it still was today—to the founding of the magazine, *Flag.*

For the next fifty years, *Flag* (subtitled "A Living Record of Our Glorious American Way of Life") hadn't just reported on world events. That was for lesser papers—and lesser men. Sproul took facts by the scruff of the neck and shook them until they fell into line. Sentimental, simplistic, commercial, patriotic, and above all Sproul-promoting, *Flag* was a testament to how much trouble one guy can cause, if enough people listen to him. According to Sproul, Marie Antoinette was a wet-eyed bleeding heart. "The only law is Strength," Sproul was fond of saying. "The rest is bunk." He'd even had it inscribed on his tombstone.

Famously called "God's bushy-browed sledgehammer," Sproul was an adviser to presidents, a shaper of world opinion, every Stutts student's wet dream. Throughout his long life, Sproul had been proved incorrect almost as often as he'd expressed an opinion. But that didn't stop him from being worshipped inside the building he'd built for the *Spec*. Nor did it stop every *Spec* editor-in-chief from trying to rule as Sproul did, by divine right.

Below the editor-in-chief, various other high holies carved out and maintained spheres of influence: the publisher, managing editors, and so forth. At the bottom were, of course, the wretches who actually put out the paper. And woe to that student who ignored politicking in favor of journalism; the shifting alliances and intrigue were like the court of the Borgias, only more ruthless.

This was common knowledge: joining the *Spec* was signing up for two years of indentured servitude unknown since the comparatively carefree days of the Black Death. Hart hoped that by becoming a columnist, he could get into the paper without having to go through the hell. So, armed with two humor columns (another bit of gamesmanship: humor didn't require any checkable facts), Hart walked into the *Spec* building.

The smell of old newsprint mixed with deadline sweat hit Hart like a weather front. People sat at computers, typing hell-for-leather (Hart suddenly realized where misquotes like "Blorg!" came from). Others were yammering on phones, or designing the next day's issue. The computer screens were twice the size of the ones at Hart's high-school paper.

He saw something out of the corner of his eye and jumped—there was a snake hanging from that coat-tree! . . . No, it was just a green scarf. Obviously. A snake, how ridiculous. Hart thought he must be getting comfortable in his new surroundings; he still saw things, but he was recovering more quickly than before.

The staffer next to the coat-tree saw him looking, and

rested a phone against his shoulder. "You the guy from The Frottage Barn?" he barked.

"Excuse me?" Hart was still a little shaken up.

"Are you the guy who called about the ad?"

"No, I'm not him," Hart said.

"Good, he said he was coming over here to kick my ass," the staffer said. "Apparently two-for-one canings ended last week. So, why are you here?"

"I wanted to submit some humor columns," Hart said, then had a moment of blinding clarity: the scraps in his sweaty paw were perhaps the two least funny things ever to slink from a pen. The only reason he wasn't *sure*, was that they would have to compete for the title against each other. "This first one's a guide to getting along with your new roommates, and the second one's about a cat . . . Should I give them to Hayley?"

The student put the phone to his mouth and said, "You'll never guess what this freshman just asked me. He asked if he should give his stuff directly to Hayley!" He returned to his conversation with Hart. "You're kidding, right? Tell me you were kidding."

"Sorry—I just thought—"

"Hayley Talbot has way more important things to do than read your shit. She's the 'My Generation' reporter for the effing *Times,* I assume you've heard of that?"

"I know," Hart said. "I read her piece last week—"

"Hayley *summers* with the effing editor. She's made the "Twenty Under Twenty" hot list five years running. She's . . ." The staffer sighed at the impossibility of expressing the majesty of Hayley's achievements to someone who was so clearly a rube. He gestured impatiently. "Hand 'em over. Somebody'll read 'em."

Hart put them on his desk. The staffer didn't move.

"Why are you still standing there? I told you somebody would read them."

"Okay, sorry."

"If we use them, we'll call you," the staffer said as Hart turned to go. "But don't get your hopes up. Now go call Mommy and Daddy back in Podunk and tell them to cross their fingers."

CHAPTER SIX

HART NEVER heard from the *Spec*. Two weeks later, he found out why.

It ruined his brunch, which was an accomplishment. Sunday brunch in the Dacron dining hall was rapidly becoming Hart's favorite time at school. There, under the glassy stares of various unfortunate ex-animals, too-dark portraits of long-dead administrators, and the occasional dinged-up intramural trophy, 'Cronics let their hair down. But quietly—most of them were hung over.

Brunch was the only moment during the week where people's workload eased up enough for them to show a glimmer of their true, non-stressed selves. The rest of Stutts was a headlong rush. The school song, hardly a place one would expect gritty realism, owned up to "four years fleeting." Every hour spent at Stutts seemed slightly smaller, like European sodas.

Peter's theory regarding this was Einsteinian. "The faster you go," Peter said, "the faster time passes. Back home, it's already the twenty-fourth century. When I go home for break, I fully expect the apes to have taken over."

"So what can we do about it?" Hart had asked.

"As little as possible. Slow down—stretch it out for as long as you can."

Hart thought this was very sensible. Though he was taking classes for two, he tried to keep his other commitments down to a bare minimum. But every weekend his discipline crumbled and he crammed the days to bursting, just like everybody else. The weekends were stolen time, filled with a manic, almost compulsory pursuit of fun. Students packed themselves into clubs and bars and movie theaters and improv shows, all to distract themselves from the schoolwork constantly threatening to bury them .

"Whenever I'm having a conversation with somebody," Hart admitted to Peter, "I wonder if this five minutes of wasted time is the pebble that will cause the avalanche."

"You worry too much," Peter said. He studied, sure, but always seemed to have time to improve the design of a water-balloon launcher. Hart envied that.

But Sunday brunch was a few blessed hours poised between fun and duty, a time for reflection (and occasionally regret). The workweek began at 2 P.M. on Sunday, as the library filled up with sullen scholars. But from waking until then, everything was ease, and pure pleasure.

Hart looked at his watch: only three hours of grace left. He chewed a bagel—slowly—and tried not to think about it. Everybody else in the dining hall seemed to be in the same frame of mind, moving languidly, talking softly. Hart heard shouting and the sounds of a chase from outside; some people were playing touch football on the Old Quad. The thought of physical activity this early in the morning (11:57 A.M.) made him nauseous. "Are those people *crazy*? I can't even *look* at them without throwing up into my mouth."

"Vitality is wasted on the stupid," Peter said over his newspaper. Peter always got the Sunday *Times*, and read it from cover to cover. He'd been doing this—or so he claimed—since age eleven. If anybody else had dangled this factoid (Andy, for example) Hart would've dismissed it. Mumble as they might at home, at school Stutts students were always lobbing self-compliments into conversation; it was PsyOps for the campus rat race. But Peter didn't play those games, and attacked the paper with the precision and relish of a hardened addict. He even read the wedding announcements.

Hart was desultorily picking his way through the sports section when Peter looked up. "What was your humor column about? The one you submitted to the *Spec*?"

"How lame all of us look from the point of view of President Whitbread's cat." Hart flipped a page. "I guess it sucked, they never called me."

"I don't think that's the reason . . ." Peter said, and handed Hart a section. "Bottom third, left-hand side."

"'Contents Under Pressure,'" Hart read. "'Day after day, I see them trudge past. Loaded like pack animals under book sacks bulging with words and woe, eyes cast down on the chipped flagstone paths, the Leaders of Tomorrow doggedly pursue their Destinies. Some are going to class, others to work—or perhaps a hurried meal with friends gulped under the reproachful eye of commitments unfulfilled. None of them notice the beautiful Indian summer, last gift of the sultry season. Nor do they notice that they are young, and it is the right of youth everywhere to be carefree. And they certainly don't notice me, the cat lurking in the dirt under a hedge. But I see them all . . .'"

It's just like what I wrote, except pretentious and not funny, Hart thought, then looked at the byline: "My

Generation—Essays On Tomorrow's Newsmakers by H. R. Talbot."

"SON OF A BITCH!" Hart yelled, shattering brunch's mellow mood. A girl digging through the salad bar was startled, and banged her head on the sneeze guard.

"Breathe deeply," Peter said quietly.

"She stole my idea!" Hart yelled.

"Shut up!" some people hollered from across the room.

"I don't like the look of that vein in your forehead. It's too big."

"Gurrh! Gurrh!" Hart was too angry to use words. He threw the paper down and stamped on it. "Bas-tard! Bas-tard! Bas-tard!"

"Good. Let it all out," Peter said, dipping his fingers into his water and flicking it on Hart. "Cool down."

"Quit flicking your spitty water at me." Hart said, momentarily spent. Then the anger came back. "Why? Why steal an idea from some freshman?"

"Precisely. You're just a freshman, so why not?"

"But isn't the whole point of writing to express yourself? Your own ideas, not somebody else's?"

"Yeah," Peter said, "but apparently the whole point of being Hayley Talbot is to be a giant butt hole. Can I have that section back?"

Hart picked it up and tried to smooth it out. "Sorry."

"What do you think they teach people over at the *Spec*, Mr. Mad Pisser? They teach 'em how to climb to the top of the heap by any means necessary. Hayley's a pro."

"I guess," Hart said. "But I'm still fucking irritated."

"Understandably," Peter said, unspooling a small, penlike laser from the armrest of his chair. He traced around a picture, cutting it out. Peter was creating a floor-to-ceiling collage in his bedroom. "I think we should join *The Cuckoo*. Let's help 'em get out an issue, just to fuck with the *Spec*."

Hart looked doubtful. "Everybody thinks they're lame . . ."

"Which is exactly why you should be there instead of swimming with the sharks," Peter said. He plucked a table tent from the center of the table.[30] "Look at this. They meet every Wednesday night, in Lytton Hall."

Hart looked at the sheet of paper, which had a big, demented-looking bird on it. There was a spelling mistake roughly every four words.

"We should go—you could write for them, and I could do art."

"You can draw?" Hart asked.

"It's amazing what you can learn when you're flat on your back for a year."

"What if they're losers?" Hart had spent high school branded as an oddball. Stutts was his chance to do things right, not a second tour through social purgatory.

"Then we can wander around looking for an honest man. Do you mind living in a jar? Well, two jars, I need my personal space," Peter said. "*The Cuckoo* used to be quite a big deal."

"Before or after the Revolutionary War?" Hart asked.

"You know that abandoned building next to the *Spec*, over on Ant Street? That used to be the old *Cuckoo* offices. My grandpa told me when FDR came to visit the campus once, they stole the braces right off his legs."

---

[30] A "table tent" was campus slang for a folded sheet of 8.5x11 paper, placed on tables in the dining hall. It was Stutts *samizdat*, a cheap way to promote your campus event. Each table had a Lucite holder in the middle to keep the tents from spilling everywhere, which they always did anyway.

"You're kidding!" Hart burst out laughing. His interest was kindled—stuff like that got on the national news. Maybe *The Cuckoo* could get him somewhere. After all, the *Spec* was no longer an option. "Did the Secret Service arrest them?"

"Almost. The circulation manager was an engineering whiz. He improved 'em, then gave the braces back," Peter said. "FDR hired him on the spot. My Grandpa knew the guy, said he designed the P-51 Mustang."

Hart didn't follow. "So you're saying we should join *The Cuckoo* because we might end up swiping embarrassing personal loot from the president?"

"No, I'm saying if the magazine's boring, we can do pranks. Win-win."

Hart put the table tent back, then the pariah-fear hit him again. He picked up his food tray. "After that thing with Trip, I think I've had enough of pranks."

"Tell me you'll think about it!" Peter shouted as Hart walked away.

"I'll think about it!" Hart passed his tray through a little window into a steamy hole. "Shit, Hart," said the shock-haired student in charge of washing-up, "I could've *told* you: never order the ziti." The boys laughed over the crash of silverware. When he wasn't slaving in the dining hall, this guy created the most amazing paintings. Only at Stutts would a beautiful mutant like that spend twenty hours a week elbow-deep in half-eaten ziti. Couldn't they find a job that harnessed his talent? They didn't want to, they wanted to teach him a lesson: "Art's all right, son, but you'll never make a living from it."

That was what worried him about Pete's *Cuckoo* plan. Irreverent *and* creative—at Stutts there was no quicker way to find yourself on the outside. Creativity was fine, when it helped to make money. And irreverence could be excused when caused by strong drink. But those who habitually combined the two ran afoul of Stutts' angry inner-Puritan.

In areas like art and literature where individuality was unavoidable, Stutts usually let time drain away any threat. The faculty was littered with retired *enfant terribles*, once-important characters now put out to stud in New England's manicured wilderness. Whenever Stutts did lose its head and embrace a fad, pride insisted that they become the international center for it, and keep practicing it long after its moment had passed.

Stutts students were even more conventional. Their history boasted no Byron or Oscar Wilde; decadence simply wasn't in Stutts' DNA. Of course, now that the risk of censure had passed, every student the least bit bi-curious considered himself a sexual revolutionary. Then went to work for a big New York law firm.

You didn't go to Stutts to be an individual—you went to tear off a chunk of mainstream success, and that's exactly what Hart had in mind. Was *The Cuckoo* worth imperiling that? Was anything?

Still . . . it *did* sound like fun. There was power in irreverence. Maybe he could be the one who could make it *without* having to follow the rules—simultaneously work the system, and show he was above it. To succeed on his own terms, that was the grand slam. And why *couldn't* he do it? He was bright, he worked hard; anything could happen—this was college.

Several days later, Hart was sitting in Abnormal Psychology ("Crazies for Lazies") listening to a lecture by Ernst Yttrium. Doughy, ill-clothed, vaguely Mitteleuropean, Dr. Yttrium was the genius inventor of "therapeutic dating." In this controversial procedure, the doctor paired one student with another for one or both students' psychological benefit.

Interesting idea, Hart thought. Maybe if I get desperate, I'll show up during his office hours. The boy was drowsy—the room was overheated, and the professor spoke in a quiet monotone. When Hart let his eyes go slack, the water-stained plaster above Yttrium sort of looked like a leering, obese Cupid.

Today Yttrium was explaining to the class the principles of his newest invention, the computerized mental health professional. "People are essentially the same," Dr. Yttrium said, "and so, the mental problems that they manifest are inherently similar. Shoes are standardized to fit the normal range of customers, why not mental health solutions? 'Work less,' 'Get more exercise,' 'God is *not* telling you to punch a hole in your skull to give your brain more air'—this is common advice and can be standardized. Furthermore, much of the therapist's function is passive, simply listening and supplying the appropriate verbal cues. Voice-recognition technology can monitor the patient's speech for appropriate lacunae, and insert any number of meaningless, encouraging phrases."

"I AM SO BORED," Hart wrote, underlining it twice. Glumly, he decided he had to stay awake; this class wasn't big enough to hide in. He drew a little cartoon of a psychiatrist telling a patient, "Now, I could be nuts, but . . ."

Yttrium was bored, too—he hated teaching undergrads. Stutts had a fetish about that, and Yttrium resented it. His passive-aggressive response was to make his class as stultifying as possible.

Dr. Yttrium inscribed a triangle on the blackboard. Just as he was labeling one vertex "Crazy Person," a young man with curly hair stood up and walked purposefully up the aisle. Dr.

Yttrium still had his back turned when the young man began to speak. Pointing at the teacher, his voice quaking, the young man boomed, "I'll see you in HELL!"

The professor whirled around, dropping his chalk. There were several moments of shocked silence; nobody moved. The tension mounted, then the student turned and ran up the aisle as fast as he could, emitting a low, whirring moan. Just as he got to the exit, the young man veered into the doorjamb at full speed. He sprawled, then staggered to his feet. Clutching his broken nose, he yelled, "*Cuckoo* organizational meeting Wednesday! Free pizza!" Then he ran out, leaving a trail of blood.

Now *that's* commitment to a prank, Hart thought. The CCA guys could learn a thing or two. As if on cue, a CCA brother slumped in the last row voiced his opinion: "What a bufu, he ran into the door!" (There were a lot of CCA brothers in Crazies for Lazies.)

Whenever he was agitated, Professor Yttrium pulled on the hair in the front of his head. "Hate . . . undergrads . . ." he mumbled, tugging his hair into a forward-pointing cone. Year after year, these students were demonstrating the virtues of large conscript armies.

A student raised her hand. "Professor, what was that supposed to demonstrate?"

"What do you mean?" Dr. Yttrium said, still shaken.

"You clearly hired that guy to do that, to demonstrate a psychological theory. What were you trying to prove?"

"I didn't hire him," the professor said. A draft, *that's* what they needed . . .

"Nobody would just wham into a wall like that—unless they were crazy. Is that what you were getting at?"

Drills with live ammo, Yttrium thought. Right out on the Old Quad. Weed out the dim ones. "I had nothing to . . ." The class gave a grumble of disbelief. "Honestly, I didn't," the professor said. "I was as surprised as you were."

"Denying it is part of the theory," another student chimed in. "My roommate took this class last year."

"No!" the professor said, starting to lose his composure.

"Mass hypnosis," Hart called out, just to add fuel to the fire.

"Mob psychology!" someone else said.

"Role of violence in propaganda!"

"Infant attachment!"

"Oedipal transference!" The class was spinning out of control.

"The next person who talks will be penalized!" Yttrium yelled, but punishing college students was like shoveling the ocean. The class continued to offer more and more outlandish possibilities, until Yttrium was forced to admit defeat and declared the class over.

The Cuckoo[31] became an idée fixe with Peter. He kept up the pressure for several days, slipping masses of notes under Hart's bedroom door. Retrieving someone's broken inkjet printer, Peter made a small voice-controlled 'bot that clipped to the bottom of the door and slipped a new note every five minutes. After over six hundred notes, most containing profanity, Hart gave in.

---

[31] In a choice that was to influence thousands of schools after it, Stutts University's mascot was the eagle. In a choice that was to influence absolutely nobody, the humor magazine was *The Cuckoo*.

On the way to Lytton Hall, they passed the bell tower. "Do you think it's true?" Hart asked.

"Probably," Peter said. Stutts students were very open-minded. "Do I think what's true?"

"That there's somebody up there living on black coffee and library paste."

"I don't believe it," Peter said. "There are limits, even for grad students."

It took them a while to find *The Cuckoo*'s office—they had to follow about twenty handwritten signs, each spelled as poorly as the table tent. When they got to the subbasement of Lytton Hall, they smelled pizza. They followed the smell to a door with a sign that read, "Homemade Fireworks Club." A sign underneath that one read, "Danger—Testing in Process."

Hart and Peter looked at each other. They moved a little way down the hall, to shield themselves from any blast, then Peter took out his disc gun, and squeezed off three rapid shots at the door.

"Come in!" several voices yelled.

They opened the door. Hart and Peter's first impulse was to turn and run, and looking back, perhaps they should have. *The Cuckoo*'s office was a Sargasso Sea of immaturity and pop culture. There, once-promising college careers got mired, lost forever in junk food and bad horror movies, Rubik's Cubes and rotisserie baseball.

For Hart, it was love at first sight. The décor was Modern Overstimulated. For once, the crazy things Hart thought he saw were actually there. That *was* a life-sized stuffed tiger that nodded when you petted it; that *was* a half a mannequin sticking out of a toilet. Action-figures of Beethoven and Christ were locked in tiny, hand-to-hand combat atop an upended ET wastebasket. A model volcano oozing red goo went *blurp, blurp, blurp*. The walls were covered in layers of posters: a water-stained Travolta next to Freddy Krueger next to a '70s-era Farrah next to a picture of Elvis shaking hands with Richard Nixon (whose head had been replaced by that of a gray alien). Freddy had a wipeable vinyl speech balloon taped over his head; in it, someone had written, "Jason Voorhees squats to pee."

Where there wasn't a poster there was a corkboard loaded down with funny news clippings (and angry letters from printers looking for money). Strands of blinking, chasing Christmas lights rimmed the ceiling and gave the room some vaguely Vegas-inflected good cheer. In the corner, there was an inflatable sex doll, apparently a souvenir from a long-ago staff trip: it was wearing a tacky beaded sombrero and a T-shirt with "One Tequila, Two Tequila, Three Tequila, Floor—Playa del Carmen" on it.

There were few signs that this was a magazine office and not, say, the lair of a VH1-obsessed serial killer. There was a phone; the wall next to it was black with years of obscene doodles and scribbled numbers. In one corner, there was an ancient Macintosh on which someone had written, "This machine annoys fascists" in gold glitter pen. Next to the Mac was a small altar, where things could be burned as an offering to the computer gods.[32] There were several long tables along each side, and one at the back; under each table were boxes labeled "Back Issues." The few stray chairs scattered about the room were all broken, Dumpster salvage jobs.

---

[32] This machine had such a tendency to crash, the staff joked it was a gift from the *Spec*. Actually it was the fact that all the software was at least five years out of date, and pirated besides.

Two students, obviously the editors, were talking passionately about their plans for the magazine, but no one seemed to be listening. The new recruits were lined up in front of a table, eating and drinking lustily, backs turned. One young woman sat behind the desk at the front of the room, squirt gun in her lap. The other—the curly haired gent who had pulled the prank in Hart's psychology class—paced about nervously.

"Did you guys come to eat, or join a magazine?" the woman yelled. When this got no response, she raked the line of grazing students with the squirt gun. The students paid no attention; they wouldn't realize the gun had bleach in it until the meeting was long over.

Peter cleared his throat. "Is this *The Cuckoo* meeting?"

"Hi!" the girl behind the desk said, pushing her glasses up. "We just started. There's pizza and stuff over there, where the feeding frenzy is." Grunting and smacking, the students were jamming pizza down their gullets, folding it for greater speed. Food was being consumed so quickly that bits were actually flying into the air.

"We're hoping they eat each other," the pacing prankster said. He stuck out his hand. "I'm Reed Rodriguez. Co-editor."

"Hi," Hart said, trying not to stare at the nasty-looking bandage on Reed's nose. "I saw your prank Monday. Impressive commitment."

"Oh, don't make me blush," Reed said, shaking Hart's and Peter's hands. "I bleed more. That's Ellen Pokorny. She's also co-editor."

Ellen said, "I hope you didn't have too much trouble finding us."

"It was kinda difficult," Peter said.

"You see! You see!" Ellen said to Reed. "I told you the

113

reason nobody's here is because they couldn't find us!"

"Nobody's here because Stutts is full of career-obsessed automatons," Reed said.

Ellen wasn't convinced. She was the type of person who couldn't imagine other people *not* being interested in anything she found fascinating. "They'll come. It's just a matter of time."

"You've been saying that for years," Reed said.

"It's just below the surface," Ellen said. "I can *feel* it."

"That's the ziti," Reed said, rolling his eyes. Ellen was convinced that the magazine was about to become staggeringly popular, so they should keep doing it. Reed was convinced that it wasn't, and *that's* why they should keep doing it.

Ellen turned to Hart and Peter. "We have to function under an assumed name—"

"Humor guerrillas!" Reed interrupted passionately. "Hiding in the tree line! Setting traps! Making jokes! Being ferried by armored train through Germany, then doing standup to topple the Czar!"

"Actually it would be the Kerensky government," Hart said. "By the time Lenin returned, the Czar had already abdicated . . . Sorry, I just saw a documentary."

"I like this guy!" Reed said. "He's a logic Nazi, just like me!"

Ellen paid no attention. "As I was saying, we have to function under an assumed name, otherwise people from the *Spec* will break in and steal our stuff. They've stolen our last three issues. Sometimes they steal it before we print it," she said wearily. "Sometimes after. Once, *during*—still don't know how they did that."

"Sometimes, just to screw with them, we fill up a bunch of cardboard boxes with bricks, and trick them into stealing those. And last month, we did a fake cover, which we wrapped around a bunch of old *Spec* back issues," Reed said with glee. "We tricked them into burning their own back issues!"

"We saw that fire," Peter said, impressed. "Nicely done."

"In this job, you have to take your fun wherever you can get it," Ellen said.

"Wait," Reed said, "you guys aren't *Spec* plants, are you?"

"No!" Peter said. "We hate the *Spec*—him especially." He pointed at Hart.

"Why do you hate the *Spec*?" Ellen asked Hart.

"Hayley Talbot stole my column idea."

"Join the club," Ellen said. "I'm responsible for her first book."

"Hayley's published a book?" Hart said. Now he really hated her.

"You may also know him as The Mad Pisser," Peter said proudly.

"Total fabrication," Hart said. "Didn't pee a drop."

"Not a drop," Peter echoed. "They ruined his life, and now he wants to get even."

Reed was still suspicious. "And what's your story?" he asked Peter.

"I'm his roommate. I saw what they did to Hart. And there's that whole 'career-obsessed-automaton' thing you said. I thought, what's the least useful way I can spend my Stutts career? When I saw your table tent, the answer was obvious."

"Fair enough," Reed said. "But you two better not be turn-coats, or else we'll—"

"—do nothing," Ellen said. "I'm going to assume you guys aren't assholes until you prove otherwise. Anyway, we won't have to worry about the *Spec* much longer. Can you keep a secret?" Ellen's face shone with crazed exuberance. "We're going to print our issue on a microdot on one of my teeth, one of the ones in the back I don't really need. Then the printer will pull the tooth out, enlarge the document using Cold War–era photographic equipment presently in hock at The House of Old, and—"

More eye-rolling from Reed.

"It will work, you goob!" Ellen said. "What do you care? It's my tooth!"

"I didn't say anything," Reed sighed. "Sit anywhere, guys."

Hart looked around. There were no useable seats. Reed saw his quandary. "Just clear some shit off a desk. Or sit on the floor, I don't care. Here, lemme move some stuff around for . . . ?"

"Peter," Peter said, already halfway to the pizza table.

Hart moved a menagerie of wax souvenirs, then hefted the stack of old humor magazines underneath. As he dropped them onto the floor, Reed said, "Careful, that's Ellen's swipe file."

"When in doubt, steal," Ellen said. She turned back to the grazing students, who were still hard at work. "Anyway, dick-heads, as I was saying: *The Cuckoo*'s really old, even older then Stutts. Some people believe it dates back to Roman times. How come it's lasted so long? Because people love to laugh—"

"And eat," Reed muttered glumly. "Hundred bucks right down the crapper."

Ellen continued. *"The Cuckoo* has lasted because—and I'm obligated by law to tell you this—it's a whole new method of perceiving reality. It's like dropping acid—"

"—except with more chromosomal damage," Reed added.

"—once you join *The Cuckoo*, you'll look at life differently. You'll care about different things. And the things that every-body else thinks are important won't matter to you. They may even strike you as ridiculous. Maybe that makes some of you

116

uncomfortable . . . maybe some of you infants, some of you *little babies* want to keep working for The Man—"

"Ellen, babies don't work," Reed said quietly.

Ellen paid no attention. "Do you want the red pill or the
blue pill?" she raved.

"Uh, Ellen, that's copyrighted material," Reed said.

"Any of you that wants to keep snoozing, snug in your
cozy cocoon of lies," Ellen said, "you can just leave right now!"

Everybody but Hart and Peter left, some chewing, others
wrapping the final pieces of pizza in napkins. Reed watched
impassively. "Happens every year," he said. One particularly
brazen character had a full bottle of soda under his arm. Reed
blocked the door. "Hand it over," he said.

"Never gets any easier to watch," Ellen sighed, "but it's
necessary. *The Cuckoo* isn't for dilettantes—it asks too much.
Better to have them show their true colors now, rather then
halfway up the side of the Mugwumps temple with a power
painter."

"Was that *you guys*? I read about that in high school!" Peter
exclaimed. Several years ago, someone had painted an all-seeing
eye on the top of the Mugwumps pyramid. It had made all the
wire services (then was mysteriously removed from their
archives).

"Yeah," Reed said. "Us, and the Invisible Army."

"That's *Cuckoo* slang for our alumni," Ellen said. "Have you
seen the magazine? Let me show you some." She pulled out a
flat box; inside were a bunch of scraps. "This was last May's
commencement issue. The *Spec* poured acid all over 'em. Reed
saved this one copy."

"Ruined my jeans, too!" Reed said ruefully.

* * *

Later, the four students repaired to The Cause and Effect, a rationality-themed pub on Locust Street. Its dark-wood paneling studded with pictures of the world's great secular humanists—Einstein, Sagan, Asimov—the C&E was a great favorite among Stutts students. Through a quirk of nineteenth-century international relations, it was legally part of the United Kingdom; thus the United States drinking age did not apply.

"That's a cool wheelchair," Ellen said. "Did you customize it yourself? My brother has cerebral palsy, so I'm a bit of a connoisseur. Vitamin?" There were no takers. "Fine, *don't* live to be two hundred, see if I care." She threw a handful of multicolored tablets into her mouth, then washed them down with a long drink from her yard of beer.[33]

"Ellen's a health nut," Reed said.

"I prefer 'wellness freak,'" she said. "Anyway, big bro went to Stutts a couple of years before me."

"Was he on *The Cuckoo*, too?"

"Yeah," Ellen said. "He ran our political action committee."

"Ellen's too modest to tell you this," Reed said, "but her brother single-handedly made Stutts drop Physical Requirements.[34]"

"No more rope climbing! I'll drink to that," Peter said.

"So," Hart said, "was that stuff you said in the office bullshit? About the magazine stretching back to Roman times?"

"It may be bullshit, but I choose to believe it," Ellen said,

---

[33] The glass was actually 3.1415 feet long. It was a specialty of the house.

[34] "Phys Rec" had been one of Stutts' least endearing quirks, a set of meaningless skills accrued over the centuries that each student had to achieve before being awarded a diploma. They included swimming, climbing a rope, milking a cow, catching a greased marmot, and measuring lengths of string by eye.

digging a mathematical formula into the wooden table with a key. Prior generations had made sure that every wooden surface had been covered with similar formulae and intellectual aperçus.

"It makes sense, if you think about it," Reed said. "Julius Caesar started the first newspaper; something making fun of that was bound to follow."

"When's the next issue coming out?" Hart asked.

There was an uncomfortable silence. "Uh . . ." Ellen said. "In addition to the stealing problem, we're a little short on funds at the moment."

"And people, too, when you get right down to it," Reed said. "No offense."

Hart said, "I wrote a humor column for my high-school paper. And Peter can do art. Peter can do anything he puts his mind to."

"Is that true?" Ellen asked. Peter was burning calligraphy into the table with a laser. "That's a nice piece of tech—do that yourself?"

"Yeah," Peter said, blowing away some ash. "I heard you're working with Master Wilkinson." In addition to being the titular head of Dacron College, Master Wilkinson was the Pantheon's entrant from the engineering department. "That's impressive."

"He's off his rocker," Ellen said.

"All the best people are," Reed said.

Ellen smiled. "Anyway, you guys are on, if you want to be."

"Yeah, welcome aboard," Reed said.

"Is there any sort of initiation thing we have to do?" Ever since Hart had arrived, the campus had been crawling with people humiliating themselves in public for the right to join one group or another. Even the Wymyn's Cyntyr had initiates standing on the corner of Locust and Ant, dressed up like Elizabeth Cady Stanton, sucking helium and reciting the Seneca Falls Declaration.

Reed and Ellen laughed. "We don't do things to humiliate people," Reed said. "Our public appearances always have a purpose. That prank in Yttrium's class was designed to test the limits of peer pressure. I wanted to see what would happen if one person did something utterly outrageous within a larger group. Would the larger group act to stop the individual? Or would they look to the authority within the situation, to determine what was outrageous? I thought they'd look to the authority—"

"Which is exactly what we did," Hart said, smiling. "Everybody thought the professor had staged it."

"The urge to follow the leader is powerful," Reed said.

"You'll find out just how powerful, if you hang around the office at night," Ellen said.

"Why is that?" Peter asked, looking up for a moment. He was hard at work with his laser. He'd moved on from formulas to something much bigger.

"This office was the site of some very famous experiments," Ellen said. "A psych professor posed as a researcher interested in the effect of aversion therapy on learning. A volunteer was shown into a room with a person—an actor hired by the researcher—hooked up to a machine that appeared to deliver electric shocks. The researcher read a series of questions, and with every wrong answer, the volunteer was instructed to give the actor a bigger and bigger 'shock.' The actor pretended to be in excruciating pain, begging for the volunteer to stop, but the researcher kept urging the volunteer to continue, not to pay attention to the screams."

Reed jumped in. "That this was important research, that they'd agreed to do it, all that."

Ellen continued. "The vast majority of people kept giving shocks until the researcher told him to stop. Even though they thought they were frying some poor person. The desire to follow authority, their fear of stepping out of line, overrode their qualms over torturing someone."

"These were normal people," Reed said, "right after World War Two, with all the Nazis saying 'I was just following orders.'"

"These weren't Stutts students giving the shocks, right?" Hart asked idealistically.

Peter snorted. "You'll have to forgive Hart; the scales are still falling from his eyes."

"Some students, some townies," Reed said. "Didn't matter, they acted the same."

"Anyway, if you're working down there late at night, sometimes you hear buzzers and screams. Just tell them to 'Shut up!' in an authoritative voice. They'll be quiet."

"Voilà." Peter blew away the last ashes from the table and sat back, admiring his work. There, in swoopy Coca Cola–style letters eight inches high, Peter had burned "The Cuckoo." When you couldn't publish a magazine, you had to get the name out somehow.

In the tiny, damp-smelling room deep below the library, Hart was enjoying his job immensely. There were no ghosts (that he knew of), and the flood of things he sorted through was always interesting. On an average afternoon, Hart might unwrap a postcard from Sarah Bernhardt, a set of pornographic napkin rings once used by the last emperor of China, and a skeleton that purported to be the missing link between chickens and people.

Sometimes what Hart found was even a little sad. *Since graduating in 1893, I have devoted my life to collecting bottle caps*, a letter read. *To some it might appear a useless hobby, but I assure you that it has given me years of enjoyment (and a small measure of prominence in my community). I have recently been diagnosed with an incurable disease. As I do not have any money or property to bequeath Stutts, I am sending the crown jewels of my collection: the only four caps ever produced for a short-lived, foul-tasting beverage named Rhutastic.*

Hart turned the cap over in his hand—there was a big-eyed stalk of rhubarb on it, made humanoid in the style of 1930s cartoons. What was the value of this? Was it saleable? Or did it belong in a museum? Or—and this seemed to be the case with a great number of the things sent in—was it only valuable to the person sending it? About once a week, Hart would unwrap a stack of love letters; the recipient had sent them to the University in a vain attempt to preserve something of their lives. Though Hart had never been in love, he understood that these letters represented the finest, rarest thing that the sender had experienced. It was right to want to preserve that, Hart felt, and it pained him to throw them in the incinerator. He asked Mr. Charivaria what he should do.

"The only time you should save personal correspondence," Mr. Charivaria said, "is when one or both parties is famous." Hart found the answer depressing but typical; becoming notable was Stutts' unofficial religion. There was a guy in one of Hart's classes who spent every lecture signing his name on one- and five-dollar bills, "to build name recognition."

After that, Hart sorted with a hard heart; he couldn't afford to get fired. He spent hours of each workday trying to figure out the relative fame of strangers. Was the neighbor "Will Rogers" mentioned in a letter *the* "Will Rogers" or just *a* "Will Rogers"?

One afternoon in October, as he tried to figure out whether Arturo Toscanini's nickname really was "A-Train" or whether the person in a letter was just some nobody from Brooklyn, Hart heard a commotion outside. It sounded like animals—many animals—tearing down the hall. The library's just settling, Hart thought, hearing his mom's voice inside his head. He looked up at the clock; it was almost time to go. He hoped that whatever was out there would be gone before he wanted to leave. The key to ziti-avoidance was getting to the dining hall early.

The sound died away. Hart thought that he might *still* be hearing something, but the sound was too faint to place, like a TV set to "mute." He realized he was clutching his staple remover like a weapon. "Quit freaking yourself out," Hart said aloud. After a bit, he calmed down—the sound of his own voice seemed to help. "Last one of the day."

As he slit the envelope, the door opened and a jostling, squeaking mass of sewer rats gushed into the office like a furry, sharp-toothed tidal wave. Each one seemed to be wearing a pastel ribbon. Hart laughed to himself. *What will my eyes think up next?*

Unfortunately, the rodents were all too real, as Hart realized when he felt little paws scrabble against his bare ankle, Hart shrieked and kicked, and scrambled onto his desk. He bumped the hanging lamp; as it swung drunkenly, Hart looked around and realized there was no escape. Rats covered the floor, and more were pouring in by the second.

Determined to die bravely, Hart clicked the staple remover menacingly. "All right, you bastards—who's first?"

123

CHAPTER SEVEN

THE STAPLE REMOVER proved to be a very poor weapon. The one time Hart got close enough to pinch a rat, it had leaped aside nimbly, then danced halfway up his arm. It took a grand-mal freak-out to shake the rat off, something Hart was all too able to supply.

Perched atop his desk, Hart watched the pulsing, chittering mass of rodent flesh with horror. It wasn't that he had a rat phobia, but there were hundreds of them, maybe a thousand, crawling all over each other, covering every surface. Hart knew that the death of a thousand nips would be slow, bloody, and painful.

Hart was considering diving into a chute and hoping he didn't get stuck, when the second wave of insanity hit.

Creepy music poured into Hart's brain, pushing out all rational thought.[35] Hart clapped his hands over his ears. A rat

---

[35] If you must know, it was Mozart's *Requiem*, played on a creepy organ, with just enough notes changed to avoid having to pay royalties.

dropped from the ceiling onto his head, but he couldn't even hear himself scream. He felt his strength ebbing away . . . If he could just get to the For Professional Review chute . . .

Suddenly, the music stopped. Hart lifted his head slightly (the rat fell off) and saw a girl in an oversize sweater walk in. When she saw Hart, she gave a little yelp.

"Oh, gosh! I am *so* embarrassed!" she said. The girl began shooing the rats out of the room. "Don't look at me like that, I'll play with you later."

Hart lay on the desk in a fetal position. If his brain had been functioning, he would've noticed that she was a cute red-head.

"Here, let me help you," she said, taking Hart's hand. "That was really thoughtless of me. I assumed you'd be gone by now."

"The music—the rats—" Hart gibbered. When he tried to stand, his legs gave way.

The girl caught him. "Easy . . . The rats are gone, I sent them home." She dumped him back in his chair, then extended a hand. "I'm Tabitha Twombly," she said, extending a hand. "You can call me Tab."

"Hart . . . Fox," Hart slurred. "That crazy music . . . Did you hear it?"

Tab smiled. "Do you like it? I just downloaded it off the Internet. Or do you like this, instead?"

Hart sat up. "The Girl from Ipanema" was playing softly in his head. "How did you do that?"

"I'm a vampire," Tab said. "Theme music is part of the package."

"Vampire . . . ?" Hart suddenly needed a very large, very strong drink.

"Yep," Tab said lightly. "I hope you're not prejudiced."

"No . . ." Hart had never thought about it. Under normal circumstances Hart might've challenged her, but in his weakened mental state he was willing to believe anything. "Don't bite me, okay?"

"Oh, T.T.F.W.!" she said sibilantly. (She was wearing a retainer.)

Hart looked confused.

"Too tacky for words." Tab adjusted her hairband. "Mumsy drilled it into me: 'Never bite anybody unless they ask.' Vampires who go around biting everyone are super *rude*. Do you want a glass of water? You look a little fainty."

"No, thanks."

"I work the night shift here," Tab continued. "Didn't expect to see you. I guess I was so busy changing my theme music, I forgot to look at the clock. . . ."

"It's okay. I'm just glad I didn't wet myself."

There was an awkward silence. Tab resorted to the questions all Stutts students used when they couldn't think of anything to say but didn't dare stop talking, "So where are you from? What college are you in? What's your major?"

So vampires have social anxieties too, Hart thought. This made him feel better for some reason. "Michigan, Dacron, and I don't know yet. Study of Things, I think."

"Mine's sociology," Tab said, picking at a pill on her sweater. "Going for the big money. I was going to do pre-med, but I'm not particularly good at bio, and I hate the sight of blood, but I've done almost every other major! Well, not calc, that's too hard." She seemed nervous. "Sorry, I'm just a little flustered. I don't usually . . . Having somebody see my rats is really majorly embarrassing. "

As Tabitha squirmed, Hart edged toward the door. "I have to go," Hart said, then bolted. He sprinted to the surface, tap-dancing through the rats still loitering in the corridor. A vampire who hates the sight of blood? What could be more ridiculous than that? Besides taking sociology to make money, that is.

After that, Hart saw Tabitha every few days, when his shift ended and she took over. She was pretty nice, once you got past the obvious insanity. This was hardly rare; Stutts students said strange things all the time. And strange things happened there, too, even adjusting for the *Spec's* tendency toward hyperbole. Last Wednesday, the math department had discovered that the number nine didn't really exist.[36] An English prof had just proven that Shakespeare's plays had been penned by a Vietnamese potbellied pig. And down in Science Hole, a team of worried grad students were chasing an escaped black hole. And that was just this week! After a few months in Great Littleton, the unexpected simply *wasn't* anymore. So his coworker said she was a vampire and kept hundreds of pet rats—big deal. The rats never reappeared, but Hart couldn't explain the music that played in his head whenever Tab was around. Still, as long as she kept it to a reasonable volume, he saw no reason to complain.

Most days, Tabitha would show up a little early and they'd talk for the last ten minutes of Hart's shift. Hart began looking forward to their chats. It was nice to have someone to complain about work with, and she was pretty and funny, if a little

---

[36] They were still figuring out how to announce it this to the public without caus-ing mass hysteria, especially among eight-year-olds about to have a birthday.

preppy. One day, as he was cataloguing his last few items, Hart asked her, "Do you ever worry you're going to throw away something hideously valuable?"

"Oh, sure, at first," she said, playing with a tie tack from the Grand Order of Skunk Catchers. "Then I thought, in a hundred years, who'll care? And if anybody does, I'll suck out all their blood." Tabitha thought this was screamingly funny. Hart didn't see the humor. "*Kidding*, Hart! God, you take everything totally seriously. I haven't bitten anybody for years—well, there was that one time, but I was drunk. Anywho, it's not the vampires you have to worry about, it's the reverse-vampires."

"*Reverse*-vampires?"

"Yeah," Tabitha said. "They go around putting blood *into* people. Ick. Total jerks, shouldn't have even brought them up . . . All I'm saying is: being one hundred and seventy-three helps put things in perspective."

"If you're one hundred and seventy-three," Hart said, setting a trap of purest logic, "how come I saw your picture in the Frosh Facebook?"[37]

"Because I'm a first-year, duh," she said.

"A 'Lifetime Learner,' eh?" This was a program where older people from Great Littleton could take classes at Stutts and make the students feel weird and self-conscious.

"I'm not," Tabitha said. "My girlish figure allows me to keep enrolling and graduating, enrolling and graduating." She opened a long envelope, and looked at a copy of *Flag* from 1967. "Look," Tab said, holding up the magazine. There was a

[37] The Frosh Facebook, aka "The Scammer's Bible," was published every August and allowed members of the class to circumvent the time-consuming process of getting to know each other as people.

big photo of Jimi Hendrix, with the headline, "Pot Turned This Paratrooper Into Psychedelia's Pied Piper."

Hart laughed, then said, "How Sisyphyean—your college career, I mean."

"Before I got a Philosophy degree, I wouldn't have gotten that," Tabitha said. "Last June I graduated for the thirty-eighth time. Every time I say it's the last—then I start thinking about having a real job . . ." Tabitha shuddered. "And today my adviser told me that sociology majors don't make any money. How could I know? It sounded sciencey." She sighed, and flipped through Hart's logbook aimlessly. "You have cool handwriting."

"Thanks. But why do undergrad over and over?"

"Have you *seen* what grad students look like? Overworked, underfed, and suicidal. I may be overeducated, but I'm not stupid." Tabitha laughed. "The biggest problem with being immortal is what to do with yourself—I just love to learn things. I want to be the first vampire ever to win *Jeopardy!*"

"That's a noble goal," Hart said.

"Tell that to my parents. They want me to get married and settle down . . ."

". . . bite a few kids," Hart teased. "Castle with a white picket fence, husband with a good job at the local blood bank."

"*Exactly*," Tabitha said. It wasn't a joke to her. "They want me to move back to Rhode Island. That's where I grew up." She anticipated Hart's question. "They're vampires, too."

"Are there a lot of vampires in Rhode Island?" Hart asked.

"Not as many as there used to be," Tabitha said. "Most of the old-timers have moved down to Palm Beach. But there's still a few of us up here, the traditionalists." A rat wearing a pink ribbon embroidered with green whales appeared at the door. "No, Tippi, I'm busy." Tabitha turned back to Hart. "Sorry. Tippi's needy."

Hart nodded. "Are those, like, your pets?"

"Yes and no," Tabitha said. "They just sorta come with the vampire thing, like the music. I remember being really freaked out—is that still the lingo?—before I figured out what was happening."

"Sure, 'freaked out' works."

"Good. I've been young for so long, it's hard to stay current," Tabitha said. "I still wear my raccoon coat, though, I don't care if it's old-fashioned. Do you like the ribbons? Green for boys, pink for girls. Being undead is no excuse not to be kicky. I make little Lilly Pulitzer shifts for them. It's a hobby." Tabitha laughed, a nice free, light sound. "I have a *lot* of hobbies!"

"If preppiness were garlic, Tab, you'd be in trouble," Hart said, pushing away from the desk and grabbing his jacket.

Tabitha slapped him on the shoulder. "You're a stitch and a half, Hart Fox. Say hi to the people food for me." For a nosferatu she certainly was nice company, Hart thought.

Over the next several weeks, Tabitha told Hart all about herself. "Tell me," she asked him one afternoon, "did your copy of the *Spec* have a hole in it this morning?"

"Yeah, as a matter of fact," Hart said.

"Great!" Tabitha opened the door to the hallway and yelled, "Good job, my sweets! Extra petting tonight!" Returning to her chair, she explained. "The *Spec* ran a big article today, outing me as a vampire. Or, they tried to."

"Jerks."

Tabitha nodded. "Hayley Talbot is one of the super-bigots behind the Van Helsing Society. I commanded my little furry friendies to chew the article out of every copy."

"I should introduce you to my buddies on *The Cuckoo*. Could your rats chew up the whole paper?" Hart joked. "Anyway, what do you care if people know you're a vampire? You told me the first time we met."

"Hart, there are only three times that a lady's name should show up in the newspaper: when she's born, when she's married, and when she dies. Notice I did not say 'Whenever the Van Helsing Society wants to stir up cheap anti-vampire sentiment.'"

"The Van Helsing Society is . . . ?"

"A group of Stutts students determined to eradicate vampires. As if." Tabitha picked at her nail polish with annoyance.

Hart wrote another item into the catalog, and tossed it down the Archive chute. "Don't worry about it, Tab. Nobody believes the *Spec*. Did I tell you I'm The Mad Pisser?"

"Get *out*. Really?"

"The one and only," Hart said. "Only I didn't do it." He proceeded to tell her the whole story—minus the backstory about his deal with Mr. Darling.

Tabitha sighed. "That sounds like fun."

"Are you kidding? I almost died!"

"I know," Tabitha said. "Such *drama*. Sometimes I wonder what life would've been like if I'd never gotten bit."

"Sounds like you did it on purpose," Hart said.

"Of course I did! That's the only way it happens!" Tabitha said. "Back when I was a girl, it was expected. Very much 'the done thing.'"

"Really?"

"Really. Newport's whole social scene took place at night. All the debs 'came out' during the Midnight Regatta. *Everybody* was a vampire. The Astors, the Vanderbilts, J.P. Morgan, John D. Rockefeller . . ."

"But I've seen pictures of all those people," Hart said, still trying to trap her. "I thought vampires couldn't be photographed."

"Actors work cheap," she said with a smirk. "The whole no-photo thing is really the only downside I can think of."

"What about sunlight?"

"Right. I always forget that one," Tabitha said. "An hour without sunscreen and I'd look like a kipper. Oh, and we can't have children. And garlic gives us reflux."

Hart thought of vampire reflux. "Yuck."

"No kidding," Tabitha continued. "We play up the inconveniences, because if everybody knew what being a vampire was like—the parties, the connections, the sweet deals on life insurance—we'd have to let *everybody* in."

"Advantages? Just for biting people's necks?"

Tabitha rolled her eyes. "Do you eat spaghetti with your hands?"

"No," Hart said, "but—"

"Then why would I, a gracious and polite young lady who likes to think that she is at least mildly presentable, bite someone's sweaty old neck? What if I hit a necklace? Dentistry isn't any cheaper for us, you know."

"Sorry, I didn't mean anything by it."

"It's okay," Tabitha said. "I blame the movies. As I was saying, there are advantages to being a vampire—why else would people do it? First of all, I can eat anything I want and never gain an ounce," she said. "Secondly, anything that has a 'lifetime guarantee' is like money in the bank to me. Thirdly, I haven't paid for a cell phone call in years, because all my friends and I talk at night. Plus, we can work at night when everybody else is asleep. My father is king of the foreign stock markets."

"Okay, okay, you've made your point. Can I borrow some money?" Hart joked.

"Like I said, they're mad at me," Tabitha said. "Anyway, what do you need money for? You have a job? Granted," Tabitha continued, "if you knew what the library pays me per hour to do your same job, you'd puke. That's why the Van Helsing Society exists—they're just jealous, nasty people."

"So why don't you . . . you know . . . drain them?"

"Hart Fox, what kind of person do you think I am?" Tabitha said. "Would you ask a vegan that question? Vampirism is simply a dietary restriction. I eat blood, that doesn't mean I go around being Sally Suckalot."

Hart being who he was, this choice of words awakened impure thoughts. While he wondered if vampires had sex, Tabitha continued talking.

"I hate Halloween," Tabitha said, taking a long slurp out of a Super Big Gulp. It sounded clotty. "How would you like it if there were a holiday where everyone dressed up as, I don't know, people from the Midwest? As soon as somebody finds out I'm a vampire, they jump to all these conclusions."

"Like what?" Hart asked.

"Once, a guy I was dating asked me if I could turn into a bat."

"Tab, you gotta admit it's a fair question," Hart said.

"Not in the middle of a great big crowd of people waiting

to see *Dracula* on Broadway!" Tabitha made a face. "That's just impolite! I said to him, 'Herbie, if I could, don't you think I'd just fly in through the stage door transom and go get Mr. Lugosi's autograph, instead of waiting here with you to buy a half-price ticket?' I think he was"—Tabitha's voice grew low and conspiratorial— *"sexually obsessed* with me turning into a bat. He was a real perv, and let me tell you, I've dated all kinds," Tabitha said. "So I dumped him. . . ! Aren't you going to ask me what his name was?"

"Why should I care?"

"You might. Try it and see."

"Okay, who was he?" Hart asked.

"Herbert Hoover."

"I think you made the right choice," Hart said. "I don't think the U.S. was ready for a vampire First Lady."

Tabitha continued. "If I had a dollar for every time that somebody asked if I sleep in a coffin . . ."

Hart opened his mouth.

"It's more like a futon that folds into a coffin," she said with annoyance. "I got it from Ikea. We get a special catalog." She took another slurp.

"I don't want to know what's in that cup, please don't tell me," Hart said. "You're not supposed to eat in the library."

"Rules are for tools," Tabitha said. "Nobody cares if I eat down here, they know how hard I'd be to replace. I even have my own keys to the building," she said, taking out a large key ring with a cartoon whale on it. "Isn't he cute? I love whales. I think they're my favorite animal. That's what I'd like to turn into, not a bat."

Hart put his pen away and closed the logbook, through for another day. "Does Mr. Charivaria know you're a vampire?"

Hart had been humoring her for so long, that he found himself beginning to believe it. Maybe she was, that would be cool. Stutts students prided themselves on being open-minded. It tickled Hart to imagine how shocked his parents would be, even his mom.

"Ol' Chari just thinks I'm weird," Tabitha said. "I don't care, I *am* weird. Anyway, I know all the security guards. One of them always walks me home." Tabitha slipped into an impression. "'You don't know what kind of people you'll meet this late,' he says. I try not to laugh—he's very sweet. Once I wasn't paying attention and the music came on in his head for a few seconds. I felt so-o-o bad, but I couldn't even apologize." There was a fly buzzing around, one of the last before the freeze. Quicker than Hart could follow, Tabitha reached out and grabbed it.

"I sincerely hope you're not going to eat that," Hart said.

"*Honestly*," Tabitha said. "I've never met anyone so poisoned with negative images adopted wholesale from our mass media." She walked over to the door, opened it, and let the fly go out into the hallway. "Like that? I heard it in class today."

"Sorry, I didn't mean to be . . . nonbloodsucking-ist," Hart said. He tried to think of a bland question. "Where do you live? Is there a vampire College?"

"I live off campus, over the Turbid," Tabitha said. The Turbid River, also known as the Sanitary Canal, wound through campus to the ocean.[38] "Next to the Common."

"You're kidding me," Hart said. "You live in the cemetary?"

---

[38] The Founders had originally dug this canal to spread cholera more efficiently throughout the town. They thought contracting cholera built character.

"Where else, Mr. Stereotyper?" Tabitha said, smiling sunnily. She dropped the cup into the garbage can. Hart caught a glimpse of the inside, and convinced himself it was cherry. "What about you? What's your deal?"

"Oh, I'm boring," Hart said. "No immortality, no special diet, no coffin/futon."

Tabitha made a face. "You're making fun. I knew I'd regret telling you that."

Hart felt a little sorry for Tabitha. Being a vampire was probably kinda lonely, like being the only person at Stutts from Ecuador or something. (Actually, the one student from Ecuador was so mindbendingly rich he could buy all the friends he needed.) "Sorry, Tab—I didn't mean to hurt your feelings."

"It's all right. I'm just a little sensitive today because of Hayley and that article." Tabitha flipped through the logbook, a habit of hers. "What did you unwrap today? Anything groovy, kicky, or generally peachy-keen?"

"Not unless you like celebrity nutcrackers," Hart said, showing her one from the fifties that looked like Liberace. Things seemed to cluster in the strangest ways. One day, several dolls would pass his desk; other days, it would be medical instruments, or exotic yarn, or Lincolniana. He handed Tabitha the last item of the day, a World War Two–era tin whistle in the shape of Stalin's head. "What do you think of this? Museum or auction?" As she examined it, he said, "The letter says it came from a box of Allied Snaps cereal in 1942."

"Something this small . . ." Tabitha looked up at Hart and said, "I think you ought to sell it yourself."

Hart was deeply shocked. "But—it belongs to the university!"

"The university has more things than it knows what to do with. That's why you have a job."

True, Hart thought, but— "If I get caught, I'd be fired."

"So don't get caught," Tabitha said coolly. "I do it all the time."

"Yes, but you have your vampiring to fall back on. I would be out on the streets."

"No, you wouldn't," Tabitha said. "The worst thing that could happen is you'd get rusticated."

"That sounds painful."

The girl-vampire laughed. "It's just a fancy way of saying, 'forced to live off-campus,'" Tabitha said. "You'd probably like it. I lived in the dorms for the first forty-seven years I was enrolled, but I wouldn't go back now if you paid me."

"Yeah, but if I *did* get kicked out . . ."

"Hart, take it from a student who's been implicated in tens of mysterious deaths—it's really, really hard to get kicked out of Stutts. Now that they've chosen you, the last thing they want is to be proven wrong."

This made sense, but Hart hated to give in so easily. "Yeah, but . . ."

Tabitha bulldozed him. "I do it all the time. My parents cut off my allowance when I turned one-fifty, and my trust fund doesn't kick in until I turn two hundred. I just stick stuff in my pocket and walk out. Nobody will miss it— they don't even know it exists if you don't write it into the logbook. Just don't steal anything too big, and you should be fine."

Pretty girls are so damn convincing, Hart thought. "Where do you sell your stuff?"

"The House of Old," Tabitha said. "Come on, I'll take you there."

"Don't you have to work?"

Tabitha had an answer for everything. "I just won't take a break at midnight."

Hart grabbed his knapsack, and before he could change his mind, Tabitha tossed the whistle into it. "Come on," she said. The two of them walked up the passageway. Hart noticed that Tabitha—who thoughtfully kept the rats at bay—didn't smell like a vampire; she smelled like a girl. The impure thoughts came back but Hart, being an eighteen-year-old boy, was expert at functioning with an erection. As he walked through the metal detector at the library's back entrance, there was a beep. Hart froze. At first he thought the library had installed boner-sensors, but the reality was much worse.

"Open up," the guard said sternly. He was much warmer to Tabitha. "Hi, Tab."

Hart's mouth was dry, and he considered taking off. Tabitha put her hand in the small of his back, which helped a lot. They were coconspirators.

The guard dumped out the backpack. He picked up Hart's notebook and shook it to make sure there was nothing stuck between the pages. Then he pulled out the whistle. "Where'd you get this?"

Hart paused. Tabitha, the hardened criminal, leapt into the breach. "You remember—that toy store down in Greenwich Village. The one next to the naughty bakery."

"Oh, right," Hart whispered, trying not to puke.

The guard paused a long moment, then seemed satisfied. "Can I blow it?"

Hart nodded, and the guard gave a small toot. Smiles all

around. Then the guard pulled out a library book. Hart had forgotten it was in there.

"Here's the culprit," the guard said, looking in to check the date. "Archaeology, huh? Ever heard of King Tut's curse? Mummy running around, killing people . . . "

"You watch too many movies," Hart wisecracked, taking back his pack.

"Bye, Tabitha," the guard said. "You coming back?" he asked her plaintively.

"Only if you walk me home," Tabitha said, batting her eyes almost imperceptibly. After over 150 years of flirting, she was *good*.

"Jesus Christ, I almost booted!" Hart said giddily, as they walked down the steps and across the Boulevard of Our Glorious Insect Overlords. "I can't believe I let you talk me into—" Hart looked around to make sure nobody was near enough to listen—"*stealing*!"

"You worry too much," Tabitha said. "I told you everything would work out. You'll feel better once you sell it to Chauncey. I think he'll pay a tidy little sum for it."

"Chauncey? Who's Chauncey?"

"He runs The House of Old," Tabitha said, steering Hart into a doorway. "Right here." Tabitha tapped on the glass. A tall, gaunt old man with thick glasses and thinning white hair was just flipping the sign from OPEN to CLOSED.

Chauncey opened the door a bit, puffing a scent of dust, mildew, and foxed paper into the chilly night. "Hi, Tabitha," he said through the crack. "Come back tomorrow, all right? *Cow Cop* is on in five minutes."

Cow Cop followed the adventures of a crime-solving

ruminant.[39] All the boarders back home never missed an episode. Hart hadn't thought about it in months. One of the nicest things about Stutts was how you forgot about all the stupid stuff that everybody else paid so much attention to, like TV shows, elections, and wars.

"I can't, Chauncey—the sun fries me like a fritter."

Did Chauncey know? Hart wondered, then reminded himself that he didn't really believe Tabitha was a vampire. Or maybe he did; he wasn't sure anymore. Tabitha seemed truthful, and who was he to dispute the Van Helsing Society, even if the Terrible Talbot was involved? A broken watch was still right twice a day.

Chauncey hesitated.

"You know how delicate my skin is," Tabitha said.

"All right, but make it quick." He opened the door and stepped aside. Hart followed Tabitha in quickly; Chauncey was quite tall—he looked like Robert Frost after a few years on the rack—and his suspenders looked like they could break at any moment. Hart thought they had owls on them, but was afraid to tarry long enough to look.

The House of Old was a pack rat's paradise. Vitrines—there must have been twenty of them, Hart felt it was rude to count—crammed the walls, packed with every type of object. Above each vitrine was shelf after shelf, one atop the other, all the way to the painted tin ceiling. Everything above a certain height was accessed by means of a rolling ladder and/or a metal grasper on a pole. There were thousands of old books; a jumble

---

[39] *Cow Cop* had even spawned a spin-off, *Firefighting Snake*, which was nearly as popular. It was amusing to watch the snake struggle with the hose, but in general Hart didn't see the appeal.

of ancient toys; old signs, painted and neon, winked out from the walls; a rack of vintage watches turned slowly in its motorized display; there were eyeglass frames and fountain pens, furniture and radios, postcards and earrings. The House of Old was ten pounds of stuff in five pounds worth of space, and if it hadn't been so neatly arranged, visitors would've been crushed by toppling curiosa.

Hart was amazed at the sheer amount of stuff Chauncey had crowded into his showroom, and marveled too at the order of it all—certainly necessary when dealing with such a profusion. In the window, sewing dummies modeled ancient gowns; a corner display featured things for Halloween; there was costume jewelry and sunglasses; lunchboxes and comic books; in short, a place for everything old. This went for customers, too: a sign behind the register read, NO ONE UNDER 17 ADMITTED. (Underneath that Chauncey had written "NO Exceptions!" with an infinity sign under the NO, as if that was the ultimate in underlining.)

"What do you have, dear? You always bring in the most interesting items," Chauncey said. "Do you have another mahjongg set like the one you brought in over the summer? I've got a collector who's dying for one."

Tabitha was trying on a pair of sunglasses. "Sorry, Chauncey," she said. "I only had the one . . . What do you think?" Tabitha said, turning to Hart.

"Those glasses really suit you," Chauncey said. "I have it on good authority that they once belonged to Jackie Kennedy."

"Pish," Tabitha said. "Hart, always keep in mind that Chauncey's a born salesman."

"She means 'liar'," the old man said.

"You said it, not me," Tabitha said, putting down the

glasses. "Hart's the one with something for you. Take it out, Hart; let Chauncey see it."

Hart handed the whistle over. Chauncey looked at it, breathing noisily. Hart smelled the slightly curdled odor he remembered from the boarders back home. That must be what living a long time smelled like, he thought.

"Interesting piece," Chauncey said. "Any idea where it came from?"

"A cereal box," Hart said. "It's from nineteen forty-two."

"Can you tell me your source?" Chauncey asked, "Or do you prefer to remain mysterious, like Tabitha here?"

"He prefers to remain mysterious," Tabitha said. "Don't you, Hart? Anyway, when have I ever given you a line of b.s.?" Tabitha said. "Unlike some people—Jackie Kennedy, my caboose," she murmured playfully. Hart realized Tabitha had Chauncey charmed, too.

"What I wouldn't give to know where you get all this stuff." Chauncey looked at his watch, then scratched under his suspenders. "It's a rare piece, no denying that. How about two hundred?"

Hart couldn't believe his ears. "Sure!" he said. Both sides suspected that they were fleecing the other, so money was exchanged quickly before either changed his mind.

The moment he was outside, Hart started to feel guilty.

Tabitha cut him off mid-excoriation. "You're too much. You obviously didn't grow up with money," she said.

"What does that have to do with it?" Hart said defensively.

"You're so scrupulous. It's cute," Tabitha said, grabbing a moth. She looked at Hart, then ate it just to scandalize him. "Roughage," she said. "The University doesn't need the money, and Chauncey's rich."

"That guy?" Hart said with amazement. "He looked like he'd been wearing that same shirt since World War Two."

"Rich people always dress down," Tabitha said. "Really rich people, that is. And Chauncey is really rich—he invented the candy wagon. Have you ever heard of that? It was a sort of cart, with jars of candy on either side, and popcorn in the middle. Peddlers took it around. Back in the thirties and forties, it was like the first franchise business. Chauncey made a mint—I should know, I watched him do it."

"The thirties and forties?" Hart exclaimed. "How old is Chauncey?"

"I don't know, I've never asked."

Bilking a hundred-year-old man, that was even worse! "Are you a bad influence on everybody, Tab, or am I special?" Before Hart could lacerate himself properly, he spotted Trip among a drunken phalanx of students marching purposefully down the sidewalk toward them. The fairest flower of CCA manhood was hauling massive quantities of booze from Liquor Lovers' back to The Darling Suite. The Old Quad would be alive with the sounds of vomiting tonight, Hart thought grimly. It's a good thing they're looking forward to the party, because they certainly won't remember it.

"Let's cross," he said.

"Why? They're just frat boys."

"I went to high school with one of them, and I don't feel like dealing with him right now." Hart crossed against the light, a Stutts tradition. "We'll be safe near the library. They fear scholarship."

Hart may have not felt like dealing with Trip, but that didn't stop Trip and his cronies from heaving not-quite-empty beer cans at him and Tabitha.

"Charming," said Tabitha, once they finally got out of range. "I take it you two were best friends back home?"

Hart took a deep breath and briefly explained his relationship with Trip. He didn't leave anything out.

"Wow," Tabitha said. "Now there's a chump who deserves a biting."

"If you do, be sure to make it really *hurt*."

CHAPTER EIGHT

HART LIVED with an underdog's idea of fate; after getting away with it once, he solemnly decided to limit his sales trips to The House of Old to the fewest absolutely necessary. His resolve lasted thirty-seven minutes—in other words, exactly as long as it took for Peter to find out.

"Dude, this is perfect for our magazine!" Peter said.

"It's our magazine, now, huh?" Hart asked.

Peter paid no attention. "We can sell a bunch of stuff and do loads of issues!"

"But the *Spec*'ll steal whatever we print."

Peter waved him off. "Don't worry about those idiots. "I'm working on some stuff for the office." He looked around and lowered his voice. "Countermeasures."

"Countermeasures?" Hart often wondered what it was like in Peter's brain. He pictured a dank stone aerie full of strobing electrical devices, with a pale, sweaty, lab-coated Peter dancing around his hunchbacked assistant, cackling, "It's alive, it's alive!"

"A taser net that drops from the ceiling, maybe a stinger-'bot or two, nothing too intense. We don't want to kill anybody, just delay their careers with a short trip to the infirmary."

"What's a stinger-'bot?" Hart asked, trying to distract Peter. He really didn't want to push his luck fencing stolen goods.

"Syringe on wheels, basically. Somebody sneaks in, trips the motion detector, and—don't try to distract me, you've stumbled on a gold mine," Peter said. "It's fate. You believe in fate, right?"

"That's exactly why I . . ."

"The University won't miss it. And we've already seen what happens when you get caught by the guard: nothing."

Opposing Peter was like opposing the weather; all it did was make you tired. Hart stole small collectibles for the next week without incident, but *The Cuckoo*'s expenses were enormous. No printer would publish them without cash upfront—and lots of collateral, just in case anything got damaged as a result of *Spec*-related terrorism. The juice on the Mafia loans (not one of Ellen's better ideas), the legal bills from the *Spec*'s nuisance lawsuits, keeping the office fridge stocked with all the gourmet foods Reed needed to "feel funny" . . . it took a lot of baseball cards to make that nut.

Peter added up the figures. "It's not enough. We need to sell more," he said.

"'We' meaning 'me,' and 'sell' meaning 'steal.'"

"This is no time to argue semantics," Peter said. "Fill your backpack. Nobody would touch that thing."

"Hey, I *like* this backpack," Hart said with an injured tone. "It's broken in." Hart's backpack, the same one he'd used through high school, was truly filthy. The suede portion at the bottom still smelled faintly of soured chocolate milk from a lunchroom prank Trip had played on him last year. "If I fill my backpack, somebody's going to get suspicious and mention it to Charivaria. He'll put two and two together."

"All he cares about is that the pile is going down. Hell, he'll probably give you a raise!" Peter shot dimes at Anton's door, a favorite occupation. "Is there any way to (*thunk*) move stuff out of the library (*thunk*) another way? A tunnel (*thunk*) or something?"

"Maybe there's some route through the Catacombs," Hart said. "I took a wrong turn to the men's room once and heard the sound of lapping water. Could there be a river?"

"We could load up a boat!" Peter said, eyes alight. "A treasure barge!"

"No, that won't work either," Hart said. "I can't make *too* much progress with the pile. Mr. Charivaria will suspect. Plus, Tabitha needs a job, too."

"Tabitha?" Peter said. "Who is this Tabitha of which you speak?"

Hart found himself blushing, which was stupid. She was either a creature of the night or nuttier than a squirrel. And anyway, they were just friends. "A girl who works in the library. She does the same job I do, only the graveyard shift."

"It would be a lot easier if she were in on this," Peter said. "Is she cool?"

"She's really preppy—"

"Smile when you say that," Peter joked. He'd never met a piece of madras he didn't like.

"—but on the other hand, she says she's, uh, a vampire," Hart said. "Draw your own conclusions."

"A vampire? Like 'Bleh, bleh, I vant to suck your blood'?"

Hart nodded. "She says it's like being anti-vegan."

"What? Oh, I get it," Peter said. "I *have* to meet this chick."

The next day Peter accompanied Hart to work. Getting his chair through the secret door in the card catalog wasn't easy, but with some muscle and the judicious application of some K-Y jelly Peter had in a secret compartment ("No comment," said Peter) they finally managed it. Descending the passage, Peter had to ride the brakes to keep from gaining too much speed.

"I didn't know they played badminton in seventeen ninety-seven," Peter said, pointing at a framed program. The walls of the passage, like the rest of the library, were festooned with memorabilia, paintings, and gargoyles. Carved from yellow bedrock, the gargoyles in the passage all shared an underground motif: moles, worms, ants, death by cave-in.

"Look at this guy!" Hart said, patting a stone mole wearing dark glasses.

"My ears just popped," Peter said, after they'd walked/rolled for more than five minutes. "I always forget how far Great Littleton goes down."

"It's been going down since the day it was founded," Hart joked. "Do you think it's true, about all the stuff buried under the Common?" There was supposedly a hoard of Pilgrim gold under the Great Littleton Common.

"Maybe," Peter said. "Or maybe the grad student living in the carillon dug it up."

"What is Pilgrim gold, anyway? I bet it's Bibles," Hart said, answering his own question. "That would be just like the Pilgrims."

The boys reached the door to Hart's room. Just as Hart put the key into the lock, Peter shushed him. They listened for a moment—and heard the faintest lap of water.

"Cool!" Peter said. "We'll have to explore down here some time."

"We've got four years," Hart said. "Unless you get me expelled."

"You worry too much." There wasn't enough room for both of them to be in the office with the door closed, so they shoved Hart's desk against the wall. Peter looked around. "Bingo—problem solved." He tapped the metal tubes on the wall. "We could send things from here to any room on campus—if I can get the pneumatic system up and running."

"Look at the labels," Hart said. They were brass and engraved in a slightly antique script. "Lytton Hall, Cheesborough Hall, Truax Auditorium . . . All these go to the Old Quad . . . There's even one to the Mugwumps Pyramid," he said mischievously. Hart turned to Peter, who was pondering something. "We should use the pipes to distribute the magazine. What are you thinking?"

"You should be able to unscrew this part . . ." Peter did so, and peered down the tube. "I have to find out whether it was forced air or vacuum—blowing or sucking, basically—and hook up the appropriate blower or sucker."

"And how will you do that?" Hart asked.

"I'll make 'em. Then"—Peter measured the span of the tube—"make some capsules. If I can get this thing to work, we should be able to move a ton of stuff. You can fill canisters with little things, and send two to me, two to Ellen, two to Reed . . . Anything we can't sell to what's-his-head—"

"Chauncey."

"—we can always sell it on the Internet."

Hart, as usual, began to worry. "You sure it will be safe?"

"Oh, sure," Peter said breezily. "What could go wrong? I'm going to go upstairs to the stacks."

"Don't you want to wait for Tabitha? She's worth it, I promise."

"No," Peter said. When he got excited about a project, nothing else mattered. "The plans for this system have got to be somewhere," Peter said brightly. He was never happier than when investigating a new problem. He rolled to the door and said, "You're lucky we found this, Hart. I was about to insist you start smuggling out extra stuff in your butt."

For the next several days, Peter's bedroom had the DON'T COME IN—SOLDERING sign hanging on it.[40] When Peter came up for air, Hart asked him how things were going.

"You can hook the smoke detectors back up," Pete said, and went back to work. "Steal me a sandwich from the dining hall, would you?"

"Sure," Hart said. In high school, he'd won multiple citizenship awards; now, it seemed that all he did was steal stuff for people. Stutts had destroyed his morals.

By the weekend, he and Hart had returned to Hart's little workroom carrying several small, surprisingly heavy devices. "Blowers," Peter explained. He fitted their flexible rubber ends over the pipes, then switched the blowers on to check the seal. They worked. "Just to be sure, I'll put vacuums on the other end, the receiving points. That should be more than enough." He handed Hart a capsule. "My capsule's a lot lighter than the old ones, and the seal is a lot tighter, so we'll need less pressure. Should go like shot through a goose."

---

[40] Someone—Hart strongly suspected Anton—had crossed out SOLDERING and written in JACKING OFF. Pete's difficulties getting a date pleased Anton no end. (Of course, he couldn't get a date either.)

"What if it gets stuck?" Hart asked.

"It shouldn't if you lube it." Peter raised a forearm-size bottle. It had a pouty dude wearing chaps on the label. Hart laughed. "Don't skimp, really grease it up. Give me a half hour to get back to the room, then send a test item. Something useless."

Hart spent thirty minutes reading a magazine and hiding funny little notes for Tabitha to find. He then drew a cartoon of himself lubing the capsule, with little hearts floating up from the capsule.

It went through. Peter sent back a note: "Now try something heavier." Hart fished around in the donations pile, and sent a cigarette case that used to belong to John Wayne. It worked again. Fascinated with their new toy, the boys sent junk to each other all afternoon. It was e-mail, Victorian-style.

Around 4:45—it was overcast, and the days were getting shorter—Tabitha walked in unexpectedly. "I just forgot my retainer—Hart, what are you doing?" Hart was caught red-handed, dropping the last capsule of the day into the tube.

Hart sang like a canary. Not only was he lousy at keeping secrets—the whole Darling arrangement had maxed out his abilities in this area—but he figured, if Tabitha had already told him about being a vampire, he owed her one. ". . . So please don't say anything, Tab, okay?"

Tab pulled out her Palm Pilot. Hart noticed there were bats drawn on it in pink glitter-pen. "Are the magazine meetings at night?" she asked.

"Yes," Hart said. "Idiocy prefers the modesty of darkness. We could always use more help. The *Spec* is constantly messing with us."

Tabitha tapped her lips with the stylus. "I do hate the *Daily Spectacle*."

"Tab, *The Cuckoo* is totally worthless careerwise. As somebody who has spent the last century and a half in college to avoid getting a real job, you're practically our patron saint," Hart said. "You can always quit later, if you want."

"Okay," Tabitha said. "Consider me joined. Well, rejoined. I discovered Mark Twain when he was but a lowly sophomore with cystic acne and an uneven haircut. Before I showed him the ropes, he was strictly flowery poems and bad limericks . . ."

"Yeah, right," Hart said, not believing her.

"It's true, I swear," Tabitha said. "I'm trying to remember, did I deflower him?"

"Come on," Hart said, blushing. Was Tab flirting with him? Hart had been wrong so often in high school, he kept that thought to himself. "I gotta go . . ." he mumbled. "Don't wanna get stuck with the baked scrod surprise again . . ."

Tabitha saw him blush, and was secretly pleased. One hundred and seventy-three years old, and she still had it.

"I'd like to call this meeting to order." Ellen grabbed her long hair and gathered it into a ponytail.

"Make a noose!" Reed said.

"After the meeting, if you're good. I'm happy to announce," she said, elastic band in her teeth, "that we finally have enough cash to do an issue."

"*And* pay off the last printer we hired?" Reed asked. They'd been forced to use an outfit with Mafia ties, and after the *Spec* had slipped peanut butter sandwiches into the presses, things had turned very ugly for *The Cuckoo*. Several overly intense gentlemen of Sicilian extraction had been seen loitering around Lytton Hall.

"Of course," Ellen said, pushing up her glasses (which she

had to check every morning for bombs). "We owe it to our newest staffers, Hart and Peter."

"Thank you, thank you," Peter said through a mouthful of pizza.

"Don't forget Tabitha," Hart said.

"And Tabitha, who we hope will spread the magazine far and wide throughout the undead community."

"Tabitha, when you told us you had something to tell us but we shouldn't be frightened," Reed said, "I thought you were going to say, 'I'm a libertarian.'"

Everybody laughed, then Ellen got them back down to business. "Peter and I are working with the printer to develop a fire-retardant coating, so if anybody tries to burn a copy, it will give off a tranquilizing smoke."

"The idea is, they'll be incapacitated, so we can take a picture of them doing it, and sue 'em!" Peter said.

The thought of suing the *Spec* for one of their many spare millions was delicious. Ellen continued, "So now that we have the money to do an issue, it's time to consult the Oracle for the issue topic. Reed, would you do the honors?"

"Certainly," Reed said solemnly. He got down on his hands and knees and extracted something from under a table. It was covered with a blanket so musty and beer-soaked that Hart could smell it from where he sat. Reed pulled off the blanket and Hart saw the magazine's Oracle: a bingo cage with the papier-mâché head and tail of a bird. He placed the cage on the table.

Ellen cracked open a bottle of banana-flavored schnapps and tipped it over the Oracle. "An offering," she said, "for a good issue topic."

"Ick," Tab said. "Smells like suntan lotion."

"Round and round she goes," Reed said, turning the

handle. "Tabitha, as our newest Good Egg, you pick." (A "Good Egg" was *Cuckoo* slang for a staff member.)

"Get a good, dirty one," Hart said. He was going to have to write a lot, and wasn't sure he could be funny without swearing. This wasn't his high-school newspaper, this was the—well, he was going to say Big Leagues, but maybe Triple-A was closer. Whatever the metaphor, he wanted to do his part.

Tabitha opened the cage and plucked out a ball; it had a word written on it in marker. "Politics," she read. Everyone groaned—nothing could be more boring.

"Redraw! I demand a redraw!" Peter shouted.

"No, no! The Oracle has spoken, and the Big Bird says we must obey," Reed said. (The Big Bird was the magazine's guardian spirit.)

"I think we'll need some inspiration," Ellen said. "I move that we conduct the rest of this meeting at the C&E." The motion was passed unanimously.

Once the staff began to think about it, they realized that politics wasn't such a bad topic. After all, even though nobody else on campus had seen the issues, Ellen and Reed had three years' worth of practice. On top of that, Hart and Peter had a great topic in Mr. President, who had recently won leadership of the freshman class by the largest margin in Stutts history.[41]

---

[41] For the last several weeks, Mr. President had been involved in a too-close-to-call election for freshman class president. His opponent was a girl whose slogan summed up her appeal: "Jen: Nice Person, Great Rack." Jen was the perfect candidate: women liked her because she was nice, and men liked her—well, it was obvious why men liked her. But Mr. President, in just the sort of audacious move that defines history's winners, dumped his first girlfriend and started dating Jen. This may have seemed harsh to some, but it made perfect sense; Mr. President—like Jen and nearly everybody else at Stutts—was career-sexual. That's what they reserved their tenderest feelings for, and what stirred up the strongest emotions in them.

Armed with this mandate, Mr. President immediately transferred out of Dacron to a much cooler college. Mr. President's bedroom would remain vacant for the rest of the year—so in addition to providing *Cuckoo* fodder, Mr. President's victory bequeathed unto his former roomies a booty suite, if they wanted it.

"Come on, guys," Peter pleaded. "I *need* a home-field advantage." Peter had launched himself kamikaze-like into the Stutts dating scene, and like a kamikaze, gone down in flames. "You!" he shouted, pointing at Rudy. "You need a booty suite just as much as I do!"

Pickles had just given Rudy the ol' heave-ho. Rudy had been drunk for seventy-two hours straight, the first twenty-four of which were spent wailing. Now he was so depressed his heart was averaging three beats a minute. "No . . . use . . . Never love . . . again . . ." he mumbled.

"Now, Rudy, don't be retarded," Peter said, putting his arm around the boy, who hadn't gotten out of his bathrobe in days. "Today's breakup is tomorrow's sympathy-inducing pickup line! Some solid food, (*sniff*) a shower, perhaps a little blues music—and a booty suite—and you'll be rutting like a pirate in no time!" Peter carried the day. Everybody except Anton chipped in a little, and the outfitting began. Some shag carpeting here, a round bed there, and Mr. President's drafty, dinged-up room was transformed into Cupid's dungeon. Peter found some factory-second leopard-print wallpaper on the Internet. Xan contributed a heart-shaped door, made from the old-growth forests of his homeland. Andy hung his mirror on the ceiling, which wasn't very sexy—it only worked if you lay perfectly straight, in the absolute middle of the bed—but it was a nice thought. Rudy contributed a stereo, which he'd bought four months before to provide sonic cover for the moan-a-riffic orgies he and Pickles would surely be having. Now the mocking sound system was no use to him. Hart found the finishing touch: a pair of lava lamps, in the shape of naked women.

"Wow," Peter said, after he'd dimmed the recessed track lighting and flicked on the lamps. "Those make the place." The room looked like the love nest of a dictator.

"House of Old," Hart said. "There is no substitute." He stopped doodling in his notebook and looked up. "Should I do something on Trip's dad for the issue?" Hart said.

"Trip the Dynamic Meathead?" Peter was making the final tweaks on a vending machine he'd converted to dispense mixed drinks.

"Yeah. His dad is running for governor back home in Michigan."

"Of *course* he is," Peter said sardonically. "Sure, do it. Just don't use his name."

"He and the rest of CCA might figure it out, then beat the shit out of me."

"I don't think 'figure out' is in their vocabulary," Peter said. "You'll be safe as long as you're taking all Trip's classes for him. "

"Thanks for reminding me," Hart said, and went off to study for Trip's archaeology midterm.

The next few weeks were a crazy blur of work. The first semester always started slow, to keep the number of suicides down, but by October, Mother Stutts had her wincing charges firmly in hand. Though every undergrad complained incessantly, Hart did have it particularly bad, with two students' worth of classes, exams, and papers—and still no textbooks.[42] He borrowed books and reading packets from other students whenever he could; he got to know the wee hours well, through a haze of caffeine; he even sneak-studied during his three afternoons a week working at the library (their larceny had reduced the pile enough for him to fake it). The approaching *Cuckoo* deadline was the cherry-on-top of this devil's sundae of labor. Hart thought he could feel his brain actually getting bigger; or maybe that was a hallucination brought on by fatigue. One thing was for sure: Hart was working harder than he ever had, or even thought he could.

So when Trip, red-faced and agitated, showed up at Hart's room one afternoon, it was no surprise that Hart wasn't there.

"Are you Trip? I thought you'd be fatter," Peter said.

Like his father, Trip simply ignored information that confused him. "Where's Fart?"

"Oh, good one." Peter fake chuckled. "Couldn't tell you exactly, 'cause he always changes the subject whenever I talk about planting that tracking chip in his scalp."

"Just tell me where he is."

"At work, I guess. Do you know where he works?"

"Somewhere in nerdland, right?" Trip said. (This was witty CCA slang for the library.)

"You have to go to the card catalog and—"

"—look under *G* for gayrod," Trip said, then walked away.

Ten minutes later, Hart felt his phone vibrate. "Hi, Trip,"

---

[42] Actually, one student had it even worse. Through a computer error, a sophomore in Dacron had been enrolled in nothing but five classes' worth of English 327: Punctuation and Its Discontents.

he said, nonplussed. "Was your grade in Runes for Goons acceptable? I shoot for low Bs, just so you know—don't wanna attract attention."

"Whatever," Trip said, deeply uninterested. "I need you to do something for me, homo."

"When you ask like that, how can I refuse? I'll mince right over after dinner."

"No! I've told you before, I don't like being seen with you," Trip snarled. "Besides, tonight's too late. I need you to write me a speech *right now*."

"A what?"

"A speech, a speech, like you read in front of people. My dad wants me to give a speech this weekend, and I need you to write me one quick. It takes me a while to memorize things."

There's a surprise, Hart thought. "Okay. What's it supposed to be about?"

"Can't remember," Trip said. "I wrote it all down when I was talking to Dad, but I was throwing matches at the Gnomes and the paper caught fire."

Gnomes?[43] What the hell was Trip talking about? Hart chalked it up to early-onset d.t.'s.

Oblivious to Hart's witty internal monologue, Trip continued. "Dad hates you, by the way."

---

[43] To remain on the right side of the faculty, CCA had to maintain a certain grade-point average. After too many years of painful study, some geniuses had come up with a plan: admit a person or two into the fraternity who could do everybody else's schoolwork. These academic galley slaves, "the Gnomes," were members in name only. Their squalid basement living quarters were called "the Cage," and torturing them was a CCA pastime.

After buying his son a spot in the freshman class, Mr. Darling's first plan had been to subsidize a team of five Trip-specific Gnomes. But the frat's trustees had worried that doing so would "dilute the brotherhood's unique spirit." And besides, hiring Hart was cheaper.

"Trip, I can't really write you a speech unless I know what it's about . . ."

Trip's habitual disdain sloshed over into anger. "Oh, right," Trip said sarcastically. "It's so typical of people like you that you think it matters. Just write something good that makes my dad look like a good guy."

"Ah, science fiction."

"Shut up, wiseass!" Hart heard somebody shush Trip, and Trip bellow in response, "Fuck you!" Hart chuckled, and Trip continued. "I wanna watch you do it, so I can make sure you don't slip in any stupid jokes or anything. I'm in the card catalog room. Dork-on-wheels told me how to get down to your hole, but his voice gave me a headache, so I stopped listening. Tell me again."

Five minutes later, bitching and moaning about the walk, Trip shambled into Hart's office. "Jesus Christ! Could you work any farther away? Halfway down I had to stop for a whizz."

"Don't you ever knock?" Hart asked.

"What, were you whacking off?"

Restraining himself, Hart wearily opened his notebook. "How long should it be?"

"Five minutes." Trip made himself at home immediately, picking up things and breaking them. "What's this, a dildo?"

"No, it's a—" Trip dropped it; Hart was sure he did it on purpose. "—*was* a Tiffany crystal candlestick. How about this, 'My dad has always been my hero' . . . ?"

"What are these?"

Hart looked up. His piggish eyes bright with malevolent curiosity, Trip was picking at the seal of one of Peter's custom-made blowers. "Trip, don't—"

That was the wrong thing to say. Trip grabbed it in his meaty paw and began to work it over in earnest.

159

"Trip, for *Chrissake*—"

"Tell me why you care, Fox, and maybe I'll quit."

"It's a pneumatic tube system," Hart said, desperate to prevent Trip from ruining all of Peter's good work. "Peter and I use it to send messages back and forth."

"Loverboys can't bear to be apart, can you?"

"Something like that," Hart growled.

Trip had unscrewed the cap and was looking down the tube. "So, what—you put something in here, and it comes out where?"

"In our room," Hart said.

Trip hawked a big phlegmball from the back of his throat, and spat down the pipe.

One week (and three slightly injured members of a *Spec* exploratory team) later, *The Cuckoo*'s politics issue was ready. The campus was buzzing. Not only had the microscopic staff of the magazine been able to get an issue out for the first time since 1978, but Reed had done some important prepublication promotion. He had nominated one of the broken chairs from the office to be sophomore class president. Its slogan was, "I am useless, elect me."

The chair's subsequent victory gave the issue an excellent send-off. To keep the momentum going, Peter and Hart decided that instead of just dumping the issues in piles outside every college dining hall, they would throw a little party in their new booty suite, and hand the issues out there.

Perhaps it was the mood lighting, or the free beer, or perhaps the issue was actually funny: all three thousand copies were snapped up for a buck apiece. When the last one was gone, Reed and Ellen busted out cigars.

"Where'd you get these?" Hart asked, remembering the awful, cheap stogies that the boarder Mr. Murphy used to smoke. Before he died, that is.

"The Skunk Shop," Ellen said, naming a local tobacconist's. "It's our private stock."

Reed smiled. "Cubans, of course."

He might've said they were Martian, for all Hart knew. He didn't like the taste, but downloading a mouthful of carcinogens in such an old-fashioned way made him feel like a real Stutts student.

"It's an old *Cuckoo* tradition," Ellen said. "Back in nineteen sixty-two, a bunch of editors laid in some smokes, and the Skunk Shop's been storing them for us ever since."[44] She exhaled a large cloud of blue smoke. "Now that we're publishing issues again, we might have to buy a new supply."

Hart coughed.

"It's an acquired taste," Tabitha said.

"In other words, something that you have to be addicted to," Hart said. "Ugh—I can feel the lesions forming."

"Hey!" Reed said. "I'll thank you to keep your disgusting but all-too-possible imagery to yourself, at least while I'm wrecking my health." As if on cue, Ellen took a hit from

---

[44] This was one of the greatest pranks in the history of the magazine. In 1962, some *Cuckoo* editors impersonated the Stutts University chess team during a goodwill tournament in Havana (the real team had been bound, gagged, and dropped in the middle of the university forest forty-five miles outside Great Littleton). Even though they played chess at a fourth-grade level, they were somehow able to infiltrate Fidel Castro's private humidor, and make off with its contents down to the last cigarillo. Castro was outraged, but the President of the United States—as usual a Stutts alum—refused to hand over either the pranksters or their stinky treasure. As a result, we had the Cuban Missile Crisis, but the *Cuckoo* staff felt that this was a small price to pay.

her inhaler; it was vitamin C in aerosol form. She believed it counteracted the smoke.

Reed, typically, looked at the issue's sales in the most pessimistic way. "I think it was *Spec* plants, buying up the issues just to burn 'em."

"Good! I hope it was!" Peter said, full of piss and vinegar. "They'll pass out as soon as the cover catches fire. We'll walk around campus later, to see if anybody's unconscious."

There were only a few, whom Peter and Hart arranged in embarrassing ways (after removing their shoes and tossing them over electric wires). Most of the purchasers were real readers, and most of them really liked it. Special delight was taken in Ellen's piece on "How to Fix an Election" and Reed's "Fill-in-the-Blank Campaign Speech." Hart's major contribution was a series of e-mails supposedly between a Stutts student and his father running for office back home. In each e-mail, the son did something more boneheaded and hideously damaging than last time, until the father finally hired a hit squad to silence Junior the week before the election. Hart needn't have worried about it being too obviously Trip and Mr. Darling; so many Stutts students had a parent running for office that there was a mini-eruption of paranoia on campus. (The *Spec* ran a story about how health services was forming a support group for these students, using Dr. Yttrium's computerized therapist prototype.)

But Trip, a true narcissist, swore revenge—without having read the article. "I don't need to read the article to know what that ingrate is trying to do," Trip said to his brothers over vodka and pornographic videos. "He's trying to keep my dad from being elected."

"So what, Trip?" Brother Felch said. "He's a loser, everybody knows that."

"Shut up!" Trip yelled, pounding on the arm of his recliner. "This is about honor!" Trip belched. "Not only did the article make fun of my family, it also made fun of the frat. Who the hell told him about the secret initiation ceremony?" This involved dipping one's private parts in habañero chili sauce.

"Not me," Brother Nipples said.

"Don't look at me," Brother Bentweiner said. "I blacked out. The last thing I remember is smelling like a taco." CCA brothers spent so much of their time utterly wasted that very little of what they did was secret to the rest of the school. In fact, more details were secret to the brothers themselves; frequent blackouts will do that.

Trip gave the other brothers a hard look. "Nobody insults a Darling."

Brother Felch looked confused. "But, Trip, you're always saying what a buttlick your dad is."

"It's not the same!" Trip said.

"So you *don't* want us to send all the postcards addressed to 'Mr. Buttlick'?" Brother Nipples asked. "'Cause I already mailed one."

"So did I," Brother Homoerotic added.

Trip paid no attention to the chatter. He was really wound up. "I'm going to make him pay. All of you—" he pointed at every brother in turn. Brother Scabpicker was asleep. "Somebody wake him up."

Brother Nipples threw a hot piece of pizza at Scabpicker, who ate it, then fell back asleep. Trip pointed at him anyway. "All of you are going to help me restore dignity to my family name and this fraternity, or else . . . uh . . ." Trip searched for a threat with teeth. "Or else you won't get to hang out with the strippers after the Christmas party!"

CHAPTER NINE

EVEN IF HART had known that the not-so-fertile minds of Comma Comma Apostrophe were hard at work cooking up something unpleasant with his name on it, he wouldn't have had time to do anything about it. He went into Trip's final midterm examination (on Halloween, no less) completely unaware that he was about to enter Stutts lore forever.[45]

At the same moment that Hart was nose-deep in a blue book, filling it with a speed-cramped scrawl, a CCA brother had sauntered into Mayhem's, "A Toy Store . . . and *More!*" Walking down the infantilism aisle, Brother Nipples[46] grabbed a small bottle of blowing bubbles, then made his way to the counter.

---

[45] Of course, "forever" has a slightly different meaning at a place where nobody sticks around longer than four years. This, combined with the loveably self-dramatizing aspects of Stutts students, meant that "being famous forever" was pursued relentlessly, and always unsuccessfully.

[46] As you may have noticed, all CCA members were given a humiliating name upon entering the frat. Pledges were told this was to encourage bonding, but really it was something the upperclassmen insisted on. "If I'm going to be called Bootysniffer," the argument went, "next year's group will get it even worse!" Brother Nipples was called this on account of his larger-than-average areolae.

"Can I see the chemist?" (Mayhem's employed a Stutts chemistry major as an on-site consultant.) The cashier went into the back, and presently a strapping young lad appeared.

"Yes?" The student was swooshing brown liquid around in a beaker. For the past several years he had been trying to concoct a fine single malt Scotch out of common household chemicals, working on this between customers. "What can I do for you?"

"I have a special order," Brother Nipples said, digging a crumpled piece of paper from his pocket. "My name is Hart Fox," he lied.

The chemist put the beaker down. "Do you have the order number?"

"Yeah—2948xx." Since special orders were often used for something quasi- (or outright il-) legal, Mayhem's identified them only by a series of numbers and letters.

"Right, the double-x," the chemist said. Double-x was medium security; triple-x had only been used once, back in 1969, when the ever-madcap Stutts marching band had requested a low-yield recreational nuclear bomb. The chemist handed Brother Nipples a small package. "Don't drop this," he said, "and if you do, run. Trust me, Hart, you *don't* want any of it to splash on you."

"Gotcha," Brother Nipples said. "And these bubbles, too." He paid, stuffed the package and bubbles into the front pouch of his sweatshirt, and walked out.

Meanwhile, Trip and a few other brothers were lounging around the library's card catalog room, trying to act nonchalant. They felt out of place among the books and studying students, so when Brother Nipples walked in, Trip threw down his copy of *Thong 'n' Uzi* and bounded over.

"You got it?" Trip asked eagerly. Brother Nipples nodded. "Guys, let's huddle up," Trip said to the four other brothers who were milling about, defacing academic journals. They formed a tight circle, to prevent any outsiders from seeing what they were doing. Trip reached into Brother Nipples' front pouch.

"Fag!" Brother Nipples said, more for appearances than anything else.

"You know you love it," Trip said. Trip slipped the package into the pouch of his own sweatshirt. "Follow me over to the card thingy." With Trip in the middle, hidden from view, the group shuffled to the card catalog. "Form a wall." The brothers did so, and Trip was able to open the secret door. "Now wait," he said. "If anybody wants to use this part of the catalog, punch 'em."

It was dark in the tunnel, and Trip smacked his forehead against a gargoyle more than once. Halfway down the passage, he smelled urine and smiled; he was half tempted to pee again, just to mark his territory. But then he thought: no. I have a job to do.

The frosted glass on Hart's door was dark. Trip breathed a sigh of relief; he had checked his schedule with the registrar's office and knew that Hart was in a midterm—but Hart had mentioned that there was somebody else who worked there too, some girl.

Looking around nervously, Trip got out an immense ring of keys. Over the decades, the brothers of CCA had painstakingly assembled skeleton keys for nearly every door on campus. Hart's door opened easily. Once inside, Trip felt exhilarated in a way he only felt when drunk. It would be cool to be a criminal, he thought. But I'd have to be a white-collar one, 'cause of

166

my family . . . People thought it was easy to grow up rich! Nobody ever talked about all the things you *couldn't* do.

Trip turned on the lights, then took out the bubbles and the package and put them on Hart's desk. The bottle from Mayhem's was really small—he'd *kill* Nipples if he screwed this up! The label checked out with what the Gnomes had written down: ethyl mercaptan. Trip took out a binder clip and put it over his nose, then very carefully unscrewed the bottle.

"Gaah!" Trip yelled. He could still smell it a little through his mouth—the rottenest, nastiest eggs you could imagine. Eyes watering, he poured the thimbleful of evil into the bubbles. Closing the bottle of soap very tightly, he gave it a good shake.

Trip walked over to the entry point of the pneumatic tube and unscrewed it. Then, after a few seconds to steel himself for the smell, he opened the bubbles and poured the froth down the tube as fast as possible.

"Take that, you son of a bitch," Trip said. Tossing the bottle in Hart's trash can, he turned off the lights and began walking back upstairs. That fucker's room will never smell the same, Trip thought as he treated himself to a congratulatory pee in the passageway.

With a light heart and empty bladder, Trip emerged; the catalog room was empty. "Where is everybody?" he yelled. Then it hit him: "Oh, GOD!"

Less than a minute after Trip had poured the foam into the pneumatic tube, the catalog room upstairs had filled with an unbearable stench. No stranger to unsettling smells, Trip's CCA brothers stayed at their post for as long as they could, but were finally forced to run for the exits. No one connected the smell with the bubbles cheerfully blooping from an ancient standpipe behind the attendant's desk.

People were pouring out of the library, coughing, gasping, throwing up. The staircases were a death trap, slick with vomit; those unlucky enough to be on upper floors had been forced to empty their stomachs en route. When he thought he might not make it, Trip heaved himself through an open window into some bushes outside.

The prank had worked perfectly—far too perfectly. Trip had just wanted to stink up Hart's suite in Dacron, but thanks to the vast network of tubes and the power of Peter's little blowers, the smell was being forced into every building at Stutts. The same scene was being reenacted all over campus. Rank and decorum melted away in the face of raw, pulsating discomfort. Students crouched next to professors, deans next to janitors—all were equal in the face of nausea. Gangs of students roamed, nostrils plugged with dry leaves, swearing and looking for something—or someone—to blame.

Hart (writing as Trip Darling) had just turned in his exam when the noxious foam burbled out of the tube at the front of the classroom. Within a minute, two hundred students had cleared out, and Hart was frantically dialing Peter for answers.

"What the fuck is going on?" Hart yelled. "Some awful-smelling shit is coming out of the tubes!"

"No way—I thought it was just here in the room," Peter said. "I stuffed one of your T-shirts in there to block it up."

"Thanks a lot," Hart carped, then leapt out of the way of a woman sprinting to a trash can. "Did you *do* anything?"

"No!" Peter said. "I thought maybe you did!"

"This sucks this sucks this sucks," Hart repeated like a

mantra. Calmed, he took a deep breath—bad idea. After the gagging stopped, he gasped, "What could be causing it?"

"Smells like gas," Peter said.

"But wouldn't there've been an explosion by now?" Hart said. "What the hell do I know, I'm a Things major. Where are the bubbles coming from?"

"I don't know. Where are you?"

"New Quad." Hart looked around at the students lying on the ground, moaning, writhing, scrabbling at their noses. "It's like World War One out here."

"I've turned off the blowers and suckers. It should die down eventually," Peter said. "I wish there was a fucking *wind*."

"This is bad, Pete."

"I know." Peter actually sounded worried, which made Hart feel even worse.

By dinner, the school was crawling with people in hazmat suits, tracing the stench to its source. The Dacron dining hall—and every other place students could huddle around large, open windows—was buzzing with speculation. Nobody had any interest in food, that was for sure.

Peter and Hart picked at their food glumly and went to bed early, certain that the trail would lead to them sooner or later. Early the next morning, after a night of fitful sleep punctuated by a freezing breeze and nightmares of expulsion, Hart was summoned to the Dacron College Master's office. "Soften him up for me," Peter said with gallows bravado as Hart left.

"I suppose you're going to deny everything?" Master Wilkinson asked haughtily. Masters were the administrative heads of each College, selected especially for maximum haughtiness. This Master, an aged bachelor professor in the engineering school,[47] considered the students under his control to be as annoying, unpredictable—and occasionally downright terrifying—as bad weather. Naturally, Master Wilkinson avoided them whenever possible.

In those times when contact was unavoidable, Master Wilkinson awkwardly peppered his conversation with what he believed to be current adolescent lingo. "Eh, dude? Speak up, bro." This last word was pronounced distinctly, like a foreign swear.

"I didn't do anything," Hart said.

"Get real, Mr. Fox. F to the E double-S up. Somebody"—Master Wilkinson paused for a moment, and surreptitiously checked the cheat sheet he'd taped under his desk blotter—"dropped a dime on you while you were grabbing some Z's. We got an anonymous tip . . ."

Effing Trip! Hart thought. It had to be him. Or was it the *Spec*? How the hell did he get so many enemies? He hardly had time to sleep.

"The smell was traced to your workroom in the library, and this bottle"—he held up a sealed baggie—"was found in your trash can."

It *was* Trip; he knew where Hart worked. "I've never seen

---

[47] Master Wilkinson's professional interest was renewable energy, and he was obsessed with taking his College "off the grid." His most ambitious endeavor to date had been the flagstones. All the paths and courtyards in Dacron looked like normal flagstone, but they compressed with every step. The compression forced liquid through tiny channels lined with microturbines. Then they decompressed, forcing the liquid back the other way. This generated some power, but not enough to unhook the College completely. More recently, the Master had been experimenting with a flotilla of helium balloons coated in photovoltaic paint. The entire College was festooned with these balloons, bobbing in the breeze, but Great Littleton's scarce sunlight made them nearly useless.

that before in my life," Hart said. "Have you dusted it for fingerprints?"

"What do you think I'm running here, a crime labizzle?"

"Huh? I just thought that—"

Master Wilkinson cut Hart off. "This was clearly a major operation. Who helped you pull it off?"

"Nobody. Nobody helped me," Hart said. He might go down, but he was determined to protect Peter and the magazine.

"I thought you said you hadn't done anything." The Master smiled with grim satisfaction. "Do you admit to altering the pneumatic tubes?"

"Yes, but—"

"Why?"

Hart shifted in his seat. "Just for fun."

"Was there anybody else involved?"

"No," Hart said.

The Master opened a drawer, took out one of Peter's blowers, and placed it on his desk with a thunk. "Tell me, Mr. Fox, does every Study of Things major possess this kind of mechanical skill?"

"No," Hart said, thinking quickly. "I gave Peter Armbruster some money to do it—I didn't tell him what it was for."

"I'm not sure I believe you, but it really doesn't matter," Master Wilkinson said. "You realize that you no longer have a job at the library, correct?"

"I figured as much," Hart said glumly.

"What, bro?"

"I said, I figured as much."

The Master was displeased; he wanted more contrition.

This first-year had ruined his annual Halloween party—he'd vomited coq au vin all over his Oscar Wilde costume. "I suppose you thought this would be a fun little Halloween prank, eh, Mr. Fox? That everybody would think you were one . . . er, hep cat?"

Knowing that he was screwed, Hart opted for honesty. "I restarted the tube system, but I didn't dump anything into it."

"Then why did you purchase the chemical at Mayhem's?" Master Wilkinson said. "We have the receipt."

"I didn't buy it."

"So it was *another* Hart Fox. Perhaps one not enrolled and just passing through town." The Master was enjoying this; so many hijinks went on, and it was so rare that anybody was caught this red-handed. "If we could only harness your mendacity, Fox—the world's energy problems would be solved."

Hart got exasperated. "Okay, here's the deal: I don't know who did it, but I think it was Trip Darling."

"Of the Winnetka Darlings? 'The Darling Suite' Darlings? I think not! Why would he bother?"

. . . with a nobody like you, Hart finished the Master's thought. "He was trying to get back at me for an article I wrote in *The Cuckoo*."

"Oh, I doubt that," the Master said. "Nobody reads that rag, even when they do publish." (Wilkinson was a *Spec* man from his undergrad days.) "And I happen to know that during the time in question, Trip Darling was taking a midterm exam."

Shit, Hart thought. He was trapped.

"Someday, you'll realize that life isn't all fun and games, Mr. Fox," the Master said, "or should I say Mad Pisser? I suppose Trip Darling did *that*, too."

"Yes he did," Hart said weakly.

The Master shook his head. "Mr. Fox," he said sadly (and haughtily, but that goes without saying), "it's clear you have some animus toward the more fortunate. That may be"—Wikinson checked his cheat-sheet again—"how you roll, but there is no place for class warfare here at Stutts. Here, we are all equal. Your hatred—and your unwillingness to admit your wrongdoing—sickens me. I have no choice but to ask you to leave Dacron College before you infect others with your hate. As of this moment, you are rusticated."

"What does that mean, exactly?" Hart asked with a plummeting stomach. "Will I have to pay for everybody's dry cleaning?"

"What a splendid idea," the Master said. "But thanks to the nineteen-sixties, we Masters no longer have that kind of power. 'Rustication' means that you're still enrolled, but you cannot live in Dacron—or any other college—for the rest of the year."

"Where will I live?"

"That's your problem," the Master said. "Perhaps you should've thought about that before you dumped satan's cologne down the pneumatic tubes. You need to be out of your room by 9:00 A.M. Monday morning. Anything left in the room when the campus marshal changes the locks will become university property."

Hart was silent, feeling the sucking of this in every fiber of his being.

Master Wilkinson wound up for the *coup de grace*. "You know what I think, Mr. Fox? I think you're a 'taker.' A person who is so used to getting everything in life that they feel entitled to destroy it," Master Wilkinson said. "Takers never do well at Stutts. It's against what we stand for here. Do us all a favor and transfer down to Keasbey."

Master Wilkinson threw the blower back into the drawer and closed it with a bang. "Tell Mr. Armbruster that he and I are going to have a little talk. I went to school with his father, and I'd expect a student of his background and promise to have a little better taste in friends." As Hart left, Master Wilkinson twisted the knife. "I hope you're happy with yourself, Mr. Fox. It's taken nearly four hundred years to make Stutts the greatest university in the world, and it only took you one hour to make it smell like shit."

That afternoon, Peter disappeared into the Master's office, and Hart packed until he couldn't take it anymore. Deciding against suicide (for the moment at least), Hart decided to walk out to the Hill, an area next to campus where all the professors and grad students lived. Hart thought it was extremely unlikely—asteroid-hitting-the-earth unlikely—that anything with a roof remained unrented this late in the semester. But he felt he should do something.

At least it would be a pretty walk. The Hill was sprinkled with mansions from the late 1800s, when Great Littleton experienced its sole paroxysm of prosperity. Reality soon realized its mistake and returned Great Littleton to its customary desperation. A few wealthy families still lived there, mostly out of inertia. Hart found that inertia comforting, as well as the beauty, age, and order of the houses. God knew he needed comfort at the moment.

The campus looked gorgeous that Saturday—a morning of excruciating autumn brightness had mellowed into a softer afternoon. Under different circumstances, Hart would've been oozing happiness and gratitude, breathing in the bounty and potential of his life with the cool fall air. As it was, he was glad to lose himself in the throngs pulsing drunkenly out of the belly of the Stutts Bowl.

Hart passed a souvenir booth. "Wanna pennant?"

"No thanks," Hart said, and kept walking.

"You kids got no school spirit." That was unfair—only a masochist or a fool gave their heart to Stutts athletics. The football team had lost—as usual—but since they expected it, the crowd never took it too hard. In the last pitiful moments of every game, as the Stutts Eagles spasmed ineffectually, the students would chant nastily, "That's all right/that's okay/you're gonna work for us someday." This, and liquor, softened the sting of defeat.

Wrapping his Stutts scarf around his neck—there was a wind—Hart lingered on the Hill Bridge. On this damp slab of brick and stone, Stutts' twenty presidents faced an equal number of carved criminals and eccentrics. Stutts' stonemasons were irrepressible and inexplicable; they were always trying to encapsulate some great truth in a lion's head or an idiot's gap-toothed grin ten stories off the ground. The great truth was usually lost, but their work gave the campus' snobbish grasping for grandeur a pleasant cartoony counterpoint.

Firmly on the side of the criminals and eccentrics, Hart fed popcorn to the ducks below. "Hey, don't be a hog," Hart admonished a duck that was scooting around grabbing all the popcorn. Bullies *are* everywhere, Hart thought. Mr. Lombardi would be proud.

As he idly scanned the Turbid, a man tapped Hart on the shoulder. "Excuse me, can I take your picture? It's for the University—we're doing a brochure to send to prospective students."

"Sure," Hart said. It took supreme will to arrange his features into a smile. As the photographer fiddled with Hart's scarf, Hart was making up captions: "Rusticated, roundly despised student mopes on the Hill Bridge."

Click. "Thanks," the photographer said.

"Don't mention it." Hart turned back around. It was a testament to the weather that even "that crapulous, swill-swollen ditch"—what Charles Dickens had famously called the Turbid when he passed through town back in the 1840s—looked positively picturesque.

The crew team was rowing back and forth beneath him, practicing hard. Unlike football, where skill could lead to a payday, crew was an esoteric enough sport for Stutts to actually excel in. Stutts specialized in accumulating people with talents that couldn't be harnessed commercially. It was a point of pride; Stutts students didn't have to worry about making money.

Hart considered gobbing on them. Could he run for it, if necessary? As he pondered, Hart saw a couple in a sailboat, having much too much fun. Idiots! he thought irritably . . . then saw that it was Reed and Ellen.

"Don't jump!" Reed shouted to him playfully.

Hart waved listlessly. Ellen steered the boat over to the bank. Reed moored it and the two scrambled up the cobblestones and onto the bridge.

"What are you guys doing?" Hart said.

"Chicks dig the nautical look," Reed said.

". . . and smelling like dead fish?" Hart was determined not to be cheery.

"Hey, a little respect," Reed said with mock offense. "Is that any way to talk to an admiral in the Stutts Navy?"

"*Rear*-Admiral, no doubt," Hart grumbled.

"The Stutts Navy is an old tradition," Ellen said. "It died when students here started to taking themselves too seriously."

"There's no time for hijinks when you're remaking the world in your own image," Reed said. "The joke was on them, though; turns out the world didn't change, and they didn't get to play around in boats."

"So we resurrected it," Ellen said.

"There's a May regatta," Reed said. "It's gonna be great! People are already building the weirdest stuff—*The Cuckoo*'s gonna have a float, obviously . . . What rank would you like to be?"

"Swabbie," Hart said glumly.

"What's up?" Ellen asked. "Are you worried about what happened yesterday? That's one way to make your mark on Stutts history, even if you didn't do it."

"Peter told us you had a meeting with Master Wilkinson," Reed said.

"Yeah, I—"

Ellen cut Hart off. "You didn't mention the magazine, did you?"

"No," Hart said. "Somebody put a chemical down the pipes, and Pete's blowers blew the bubbles everywhere. I think that asshole from my high school was behind it."

"The CCA jagoff?" Reed asked.

Hart nodded, then threw the last bit of popcorn. The bully duck got it.

"It's good you told us," Ellen said. "We were about to dump bags of quick-setting concrete down all the chimneys of the *Spec* building, in retaliation."

"Oh, you should do it anyway," Hart said, his enthusiasm coming back. "Just . . . I can't help. I'm rusticated."

177

"Didn't they outlaw that in the sixties, along with Biggieball?"[48] Ellen asked.

"If they did, they brought it out of retirement especially for me. I've got until Monday morning to find a place to live. Do you know what happened to Peter?"

"Wilky told him not to associate with the 'wrong sort,'" Reed said. "Which only encourages us, by the way."

"What is the 'wrong sort' doing this afternoon, and would he like some company?" said Ellen.

"I'm going up to the Hill to see if there's a tiny unheated garret with my name on it. You guys are welcome to come."

"Cosigners, character witnesses, whatever you require," Ellen said. "Cuckonians stick together."

"Cuckonians?" Reed said, expecting a long spiel on the history of the magazine.

"Just made it up," Ellen admitted.

Reed looked outraged. "From now on," he said, "whenever Ellen feeds us some tidbit about Stutts history, I insist upon documentation."

"I don't have any more!" Hart told the noisily protesting ducks. "Ellen, did *Cuckoo* staffers really invent the blow job?"

"Absolutely," Ellen said. "I've seen the illuminated manuscript."

Their apartment search was fruitless. Even worse, by the time

---

[48] "Biggieball" was a much-beloved Stutts tradition where teams from all the student organizations would attempt to push a large, inflatable ball all over the Old Quad. Since there were no agreed-upon goals, or field, or rules, games could go on for hours. Once, the ball ended up in Grand Central Terminal. Soon after that, the administration outlawed the game. *The Cuckoo* retired with an undefeated record, just like everyone else.

they had gotten back to campus, Hart's connection to yesterday's mass fumigation had hardened into fact. That the rumor wasn't true only made it spread faster, as person after person was free to add details that made the story more delicious. Ellen fetched Peter at Dacron, then the four of them went to the Cause & Effect.

"Why?" Reed groaned. "The food sucks."

"Precisely," Ellen said. "Nobody will be there now except for your serious alkies. And it's dark."

"Dark sounds good to me," Hart said.

Minutes later, Reed was attempting to choke back a flagrantly inedible Welsh rarebit. He looked at Ellen and said without pity, "I blame you."

Ellen couldn't deny that her food smelled like detergent. "Don't blame me, blame the College system."

"You know, I think you learn all this Stutts history just to annoy me."

"Do you want to hear what I have to say, or are you content to abuse me?" Ellen took the mass grumble as assent. "The College system was originally intended to break the students up into smaller groups, so that they could form friendships more easily. But the smaller groups encourage gossip, rivalries, and cliquishness—there's no place to hide."

"That's true," Peter said. "I don't think Hart would've made it out of the dining hall alive."

"And that's really ironic, because the rich guy who originally gave all the money was a social pariah when he was at Stutts. He gave a ton of money, and everybody at reunions *still* called him 'Webfoot.'"

"People are cruel," Hart said, summing up his day.

". . . Like, whoever cooked this rarebit, for example," Reed

179

said, throwing his fork down in disgust. Just then, a rowdy group of students walked in; it was Ipecac, one of Stutts' fabled eating clubs. Ipecac's mission was to eat the worst food possible, usually locally, but after some robust alumni fund-raising, internationally as well.

"Time for us to go," Hart said, and everybody agreed.

It was decided that Hart would sleep in the *Cuckoo* office until he could find a better place to stay. They stored his stuff in an office down the hall, which hadn't been used in years; the basement of Lytton Hall was where the university sent student organizations to die, and most of them quickly obliged.[49]

Reed's collection of glow-in-the-dark tiki masks aside, the *Cuckoo* office wasn't so uncomfortable; Hart filled a big black trash bag full of wadded-up copies of an old parody of the *New York Times*, and slept on that. About 3 A.M., he was wakened by sounds of buzzing and screams.

"Please stop!" a male voice shouted. It sounded far off.

"Can I stop?" replied another voice, this one female. "He's making terrible faces. Look at how his eyes are bugging out! I don't want to hurt him."

"You must continue," a third voice said. It was followed by another buzz and more screams. Hart was terrified . . . then he remembered Ellen's advice about the ghosts.

"Shut the hell up!" he shouted. "And that's an order!"

It was quiet after that.

---

[49] It was, for example, the headquarters of Migraine, the world's only headache club. Migraine was now blessedly defunct.

CHAPTER TEN

STUDENTS AT STUTTS didn't say "hello," they said, "I have so much work." For once, Hart was grateful for it. Within a week, the Day of the Stink had been pushed out of everyone's minds. It wasn't the creeping fear of final exams that made Hart old news. It was Gotterdammerung.

"G'rung," as every Stutts student inevitably shortened it, was the annual pre-Thanksgiving break football game between Stutts and Keasbey. It had been christened thus by an over-heated *Spectacle* sportswriter, back in the days when games were "tilts," men were "champions," and women went to school someplace else. It seemed amazing to Hart that Stutts students had ever taken such rah-rah stuff seriously—beating Keasbey didn't help you get laid or find a job. Yet back in the old days, students really *cared*. Ellen showed Hart old issues of *The Cuckoo* that proved it. And they weren't the only ones, either; the result was always front page news in the *Times*. For its first forty years, the cavernous Stutts Bowl had never seen an empty bench.

(There were no seats, just wooden benches. It built character.)[50]

Stutts students—as they were quick to tell friends at state schools—had *invented* college football. Four downs, the forward pass, tailgating—all this was pioneered in Great Littleton. But even the most frenzied booster couldn't pretend they still played the game with much skill. Why? There didn't seem to be a point. Similarly, the whole idea of "rooting" for your "school" seemed silly. In a school full of valedictorians, individual achievement was the only kind that counted.

So football seasons came and went without the students taking much notice. Occasionally the *Spec* editorial board would loose a self-righteous bleat of flatulence—"Gridsters Must Pursue Excellence." These editorials, which always seemed to be written by the board member who wore a bow tie, were dutifully reprinted in the *Stutts Alumni Magazine*, and became a time-honored way to grab the attention of future employers. The fact was, the teams *couldn't* improve—for decades, well-heeled alumni from both sides had been bribing the worst high-school players in the nation to go to the other school. Then, these same alumni would bribe each team to throw the game, so what took place wasn't football but a battle of wide-ranging, well-rehearsed ineptitude. No other game was quite like G'rung, and thank God for it.

But G'rung still counted, because it was personal. Every Stutts student had a high school rival who'd ended up at

---

[50] Nowadays, the passion once attached to football and other quaint expressions of school spirit went into political activism. Student activism wasn't about changing anything in particular—after all, if you were going to Stutts, you had it pretty good—as much as pointing out the obvious flaws in other people. The disdain once reserved for opposing teams was now directed at supposed racism, sexism, and homophobia. Strangely, elitism never came in for many licks.

Keasbey. This competition had actually increased with time: G'rung was an excuse for alumni of both schools to convene and compare families and careers, all the while gnawing wheels of brie and slurping bloodies by the gallon.

The current students wandered through the Volvo-strewn parking lots amazed and not a little intimidated; so many rich strangers one-upping each other with such surgical precision. Many had the urge to flee. But college students, like raccoons, are remarkably courageous when free food is on the line. Hart and his pals were no exception.

"Do you think we'll ever be like that?" Hart said, munching on a free-range antibiotic-free, basil-and-sun-dried-tomato chicken bratwurst.

"What do you mean?" Reed asked. "Look out." A few kids were running around with three-dollar bottles of Perrier, shaking them up and shooting them at each other by letting their thumbs off the tops.

"You know, so worried about who's got the most or the best."

"Hart, I hate to break it to you, but we're already like that," Peter said.

"I don't see the harm in it," Ellen said. "Would you rather be doing keg stands at State U.?"

Reed pointed: "CCA is doing keg stands over there."

"Am I the only one who thinks that they might be *ironic*?" Peter postulated. "Like, an Andy Kaufmanesque performance art parody of stereotypical frat guys?"

"If so, Trip's not in on the joke," Hart said, finishing his sausage. "He's really that dumb."

"I think they just like getting shitfaced," Ellen said.

"Speaking of," Hart said, "I could go for a Bloody Mary."

They scanned the parking lot for a generous-looking host.

"Bingo," Reed said, pointing at a fellow leaning against the open tailgate of a black station wagon. He was definitely a Stutts alum; a massive red, white, and blue flag had been mounted on the roof. The boys homed in like booze-seeking missiles.

"At least the alums are honest," Ellen said. "I get so tired of the false modesty here. We're already elitists—"

"Snobs, you mean," Reed said.

"Why else would anybody put up with the place?" Ellen said. "We're obviously convinced that going to Stutts makes us special."

"Doesn't it? Make you special?" Hart asked sincerely, and everybody laughed. As usual, Hart felt that everybody else knew how to go to Stutts *correctly*.

"Hart, the one honest man," Reed said, clapping him on the back. "You'll never be a snob."

"Hi!" Peter said cheerfully. "We were wondering, do you have a few Bloody Marys to spare?"

The man scooping drinks out of the cooler looked over his shoulder, saw Peter's wheelchair, and said, "Sure, if you don't mind a few blades of grass." A toddler wearing a "Stutts Class of" T-shirt sporting an absurdly far-off year was standing by the cooler, preparing to throw another fistful of grass in. "Preston, if you do that, I'll blister your bottom." The man turned to his wife, who was chatting with another well-groomed suburban mother. "Bunny, would you help me here? I have to intoxicate these students."

Drinks in hand, they thanked their host and wandered away. "Nobody says no to the handicapped," Peter whispered triumphantly.

Hart laughed. Ellen and Reed were up ahead, arguing about whether it was better to be an honest snob, or to politely pretend otherwise.

"Is today hard for you?" Hart said.

"Why would today be hard?" Peter asked.

"Because you might be playing in the game—if things had been different."

"You want the honest answer, or the polite one?" Peter said.

"Honest."

"I try not to think about it," Peter said, lifting his Bloody Mary. "Is yours strong? I wonder if it's flammable." Peter unhooked a lighter from the arm of his wheelchair and tried to light the drink. The blades of grass caught—the boys laughed.

Tabitha had been quietly keeping an eye on Hart since the Day of the Stink. Immediately cleared of any involvement, she had read the *Spec*'s four-part "Anatomy of an A-hole" series, which purported to reveal "the mind of Stutts' most destructive anarchist." That had almost made her write a nasty letter to the editor, but when you're part of a misunderstood minority like Tabitha was, you learn to keep your head down. She decided to help Hart in another way, and that's what brought her to the CCA building the night of G'rung.

Walking up to the Comma Comma Apostrophe house, she discovered (of course) a party going on. Stutts had lost lopsidedly, which gave the festivities a sorrow-drowning ferocity. Of course, had Stutts won, the party would've raged just as mightily—after the third or fourth drink, defeat was indistinguishable from victory. And after the tenth, people were splayed around the CCA lawn, in various attitudes of intoxication.

Tabitha slipped around to the back, where Trip's bright yellow Hummer was always parked under its cloth cover. This was Trip's baby—he wouldn't let anybody in the frat touch his car, much less drive it.[51] Taking out the pound of sugar she'd picked up on the way, Tabitha unscrewed the gas cap, unflipped the easy-pour spout, and got to work.

Nobody took any notice of her. CCA affairs were always wild, and the ones where alumni showed up were even more so—the old guys partied with something to prove, desperate to show they could still keep up. As Tabitha finished, a balding man was heaved through a second-story window, landing on the back hedges. He didn't even stop singing. Another bunch of alums were chasing around the house ululating, taking frequent breaks to vomit and pee.

The paltriness of her vandalism in the face of this sea of obnoxiousness suddenly hit Tabitha. "Not enough," she said aloud, stuffing the empty sugar bag into her purse. But what could one lone vampiress (with a somewhat restrictive sense of decorum) possibly do in the face of all this unbridled anarchy?

Tabitha got an idea. She walked around to the front of the house, taking care to avoid suspicious puddles and falling frat brothers. It was late November, but naturally the front door was wide open. She hadn't been back here since her ex-boyfriend Man Ray had washed out, Pledge Week 1908. She had promised him never to go in again, but he was long dead, and besides, it was for a good cause.

In the front room, some alumni were funneling beers.

---

[51] Trip had blackmailed Mr. Darling into buying him the Hummer after catching his dad doing the deed with his mistress.

Tabitha looked around, scanning the room for Trip. On the way to the kitchen, she got her ass pinched four times; the last guy got a judo chop. She threw him onto a pile of coats, which turned out to be a couple making out. "Hey!"

"Sorry!" Tabitha headed upstairs in search of her idiot quarry. She went from room to room, opening doors and surprising couple after couple.

"Hey!"

"Sorry, looking for the bathroom."

Finally, in the last room she looked, there he was. America's moron scion was sprawled out on the bed atop some poor girl, kneading her breast like an angry baker.

"Hey!" Trip yelled.

"Sorry, looking for the bathroom," Tabitha said. Closing the door, she looked both ways, then dissolved into a mist, and seeped through the keyhole.

Trip sat up. "Did you fart?" he asked romantically.

The girl slurred something inaudible, ponytail askew.

"It smells weird in here." Trip began fumbling with his pants.

"Wait," the girl said. "I have to go put in my thing."

"Don't worry about it," Trip said. "I'm not fertile this time of the month."

Oh, my God, Tabitha thought. This girl should thank me for what I'm about to do. The girl squirmed away and headed to the bathroom.

"Hurry, my buzz is almost gone." Trip got undressed. He threw the covers back and flopped heavily back onto the bed. Reaching for a beer on the nightstand, he knocked it over.

"Shit!" Trip said with genuine emotion, as most of the can poured out onto the carpet. He scrambled to pick it up, not to lessen the mess—what did he care?—but to save as much beer as possible. If he drank this, would he be too drunk to bone? Priorities were priorities; Trip finished it off and gave a loud belch. Turning over, he yelled, "Corkie, come on!" Trip closed his eyes and thrashed angrily like a little kid.

Switching off the light, Tabitha reappeared.

"Corkie, you *know* I like it with the light on."

Locking the door, Tabitha tried to approximate Corkie's voice. "I'm shy."

"The Cancun Police Department would be surprised to hear that," Trip mumbled.

Tabitha extracted a small silver case from her purse. Opening it, she took out a syringe and some tubing and assembled them expertly. This was Baron Harteloup's Artificial Leech—Tabitha's blood-removal device of choice since the 1850s. She'd learned on it, and just never gotten the hang of anything else.

"C'mere, Corkie, stop playin'," Trip said.

"I'll be over in a second," Tabitha said, mimicking Corkie's babyish drawl.

"S'matter with your voice?"

"Nothing, stupid!" Tabitha said. "Your ears are drunk!"

"Don't call me stupid, I'm—" With one fluid motion, Tabitha jammed Baron Harteloup's Artificial Leech into Trip's left buttock, and pulled the plunger back savagely.

"Yeeow!" Trip bellowed, trying to get up. Tabitha had to lean on his beer-fed girth for all she was worth.

"You bit me, bitch!" Trip yelled. "Help! Psycho bitch! Help!"

"Trip, baby, what's going on?" Corkie said from behind the door.

"Quit . . . moving around!" Tabitha said with effort. "It will hurt more if you struggle."

Corkie heard Tabitha's voice and went nuts. "You've got someone else in there, you bastard!"

"Corkie? What the fuck?" Trip was totally confused. When angered, he was nobody to trifle with; Tabitha felt like she was riding an alcoholic bronco. The Artificial Leech was finally full. Tabitha disengaged it, and vaporized almost instantly. By the time Trip had turned on the lights, Tabitha had wafted out the open window.

Trip opened the door. "Where is she?" Corkie said, charging past. "You *promised* you weren't going to do this again!" Crying, livid, hair askew, Corkie ripped open a closet. "Come out, you whore! I know you're in here somewhere!"

A heartfelt and completely truthful denial was forming in Trip's brain. But thanks to the booze, all that came out was, "My ass hurts."

Tabitha, though educated in nearly every other subject, still had an 1850s understanding of disease. So it simply never occurred to Tabitha to disinfect her Artificial Leech after every use. She'd just wash it out, scrub the needle with toothpaste, and let the whole apparatus dry on the windowsill. Consequently, it was teeming with over a century's worth of bacteria. That was the only way vampires could kill you—slovenly eating habits. Nowadays, their victims would be schlepped off to the hospital, diagnosed with an infected bug bite, get pumped full of antibiotics, and be as good as new. Eventually.

As much as Trip's discomfort would've pleased Hart, he didn't know about it yet. On the first day of Thanksgiving break, Hart was sitting in the *Cuckoo* offices reading back issues, eating crackers, and feeling himself grow steadily more bummed out. Everybody had gone home, but Hart didn't have the money—now that he was out of work, thanks to Trip's skullduggery. So when Trip called on his cell phone, he was spoiling for a fight.

Trip skipped the salutations. "I freaking *loved* the articles about you in the *Spec*. You're really fitting in," quoth the meat-head acidly.

"You can read?"

"Why don't you just transfer?" Trip sneered. "I told you you didn't belong."

Hart tried to chew into the phone extra loud. "So you're calling from home just to rub it in?"

"Stop feeling sorry for yourself," Trip said. "I'm still here, too. I got a . . . spider bite or something. It felt like a goddamn rattlesnake."

"Where'd it bite you? On your ass, as you were running away?"

"Not important."

"It *was* on your ass! That's excellent," Hart laughed. "I'd like to shake that spider's hands."

"Stow it, buttmunch. I'm in the infirmary. I'm gonna be here for a while, so I need you to pick up some clothes and stuff from my suite."

"Don't you have a manservant for that?"

"He's on vacation," Trip said. "Listen, if you want those tuition checks, you'd better keep working for them."

Hart had a delicious thought. "Wait—does this mean you won't be taking any more classes this semester?"

"Depends on how many different kinds of antibiotics they have to try before one works. Probably not."

Hart whooped into the phone. "I could kiss that bug!" Stutts with only one student's worth of work—that was like paradise. He got out a pen and grabbed a back issue to write on. "What do you want?"

Trip dictated a long list. ". . . Put it all in a box, write 'Darling, Shot Tower Infirmary'—I forget the room number but it'll get to me, they know who I am—and leave it downstairs. I don't want to see you."

"The feeling's way mutual," Hart said, and hung up. He walked over to the Darling Suite. Trip had left it unlocked, and there was a homeless person stretched out on the leather chesterfield. Hart was delighted.

"Don't get up," he said. "Feel free to pee on that if you want."

"Don't mind if I do," the guy said cheerfully. "You live here?"

"Nah," Hart said; he could smell the man's whiskey breath from across the room. "I'm just here to get some stuff for the guy who does. He's in the hospital. You should be fine for at least a week."

The homeless guy sat up and scratched his side. "You guys are on break, right?"

"Yeah."

"Then why are you still here?"

"Because I don't have any money."

The homeless guy burst out laughing. "Whoever heard of a Stutts kid without money!"

Hart smiled weakly and went to the kitchen. He found an empty box—once home to a case of expensive scotch—and started filling it with Trip's list. On the way out, Hart remembered something. He walked out to the living and said to the homeless guy, "There's a credit card number written in chalk on the board next to the phone. Use it." If Trip and his CCA buddies were going to run up Mr. Darling's American Express, it was only fair to extend the privilege to somebody who could really appreciate it.

Hart dropped the box off. When he got back to the *Cuckoo* office, he saw that there was a message on his cell phone. "Where the hell is the hand lotion and porno mags?" Trip's voice said angrily. Hart deleted the message.

Sometime that evening—poring over back issues, Hart had lost track of time—there was a tap on the office door. Who could that be? he wondered. More ghosts?

"Come in," he said.

Tabitha flounced in wetly, some early snow melting in her hair. "Reed told me you were staying here over break, and I thought you might like some company."

"Thanks, Tab," Hart said, glad to see her.

Tab took a small package out of her Coach bag. "I brought you a hamburger." She handed it to him.

"What dining hall is open?" Hart asked.

"Law School," Tabitha said. "There's no rest for the soon-to-be wicked."

"You've got universal privileges?" This meant that Tabitha could eat in any dining hall; it was sort of the opposite of rustication, and much prized. "The food in the Law School is supposed to be really good," Hart said, wolfing down his burger. "The University's afraid of lawsuits."

"If you say so," Tabitha said. "Can't imagine why anyone eats those disgusting things. But I've been saying that for a century, so clearly there's something I don't understand." Tabitha was talking very rapidly and punctuating her sentences with a little laugh.

"Is everything okay, Tab?"

"Sure. Of course. Why wouldn't it be?"

"You just seem . . . nervous."

"Why would I be nervous?" Tabitha said. "We're just down here talking, right? Oh, that reminds me," she said in a sort of abrupt way, "I did you a favor Saturday night."

"A favor?" Hart asked, wiping his mouth. "What was it?"

"Aren't you going to thank me?"

"Thank you," Hart said. "What did you do?"

"Promise you won't get mad?"

"Jesus Christ!" Hart said. "Just tell me, okay?"

"You're mad," Tabitha said.

"I'm not!"

Tabitha looked down sheepishly. "I bit Trip."

"You *bit* Trip?" Hart yelled. This roused the ghosts down the hall, with the buzzing and the yelling. "Shut up!" Hart hollered, then turned back to Tabitha. "You bit him? Why did you do that? Now the shitheel's going to live forever—he's irritating enough as it is!"

"Calm down," Tabitha said. "I didn't *bite him* bite him. I only nibbled him *a little*."

"Nibbled him?" Hart asked, wondering if he was even strong enough to drive a stake through Trip's heart. Maybe his beer gut would be good enough. "What does 'nibbling' mean?"

"I took out some of his blood with my little doohickey"— Tabitha reached into her purse and pulled out the Artificial Leech, which had an embroidered cozy around it—"isn't it cute? I only bite people I really like, and only if they ask me to. I told you that when we first met."

Hart wasn't very reassured. "He called me from the infirmary. Are you *sure* he's not turning into a vampire?"

"Positive," Tabitha said. "He's just got a hangover. He'll be good as new in a week." Then Tabitha remembered how much Trip drank. "Well, maybe a month. Anyway, I did it for you, Hart. I know you couldn't get back at him for doing that stink bomb thing, because of your arrangement, and I had read all the stories in the *Spec* about you, which were totally unfair, and I just got madder and madder. I was going to write a letter to the editor, but then realized that probably wasn't a very good idea . . ." Tabitha sighed. "Mumsy always tells me never to express my emotions through my blood-sucking, but I felt so *awful* for you. Putting sugar in the gas tank of his car just wasn't enough."

"So you decided to . . . nibble him instead?"

"Well, *and*," Tabitha said. "He also needs a new engine for his Hummer." She shifted in her chair. "Can I come sit next to you? There's a spring or something that's poking my—me."

"Sure," Hart said. Tabitha sat down next to him, and he was suddenly aware of . . . something. More ghosts, maybe? "Was it very painful for Trip?" Hart asked with enthusiasm. "Please say yes."

"I think so," Tabitha said. "He certainly jumped around a lot on the bed."

Hart suddenly had a nauseating thought. "Tab, how did you get close enough to . . . ? Don't tell me you and Trip . . . ?"

"Blech!" Tabitha said, hitting Hart playfully on the arm. "Don't make me sick! I snuck in the room while he was sucking face with Corkie."

"Is Corkie that girl he's always with? The one who looks like a Pomeranian?"

"Oh, don't be mean, Hart. From what I saw she has a rough life. He cheats on her, for one thing."

"Yet another reason to stop having sex with Trip," Hart said. His stomach lurched. "We have to change the subject. Do vampires have sex?"

Tabitha blushed and laughed. "You don't beat around the bush, do you, Hart Fox? Just come right out and ask, 'Blah-blah-blah,' and leave the rest of us to deal with the wreckage!"

"What wreckage? I don't see any wreckage," Hart said. "Well, do they?"

Tabitha did a little fluttery thing with her hands, then started to play with her add-a-bead necklace. "Ye-es. It's very private."

"Well, *obviously*," Hart said. "Everything works the same way?"

"I guess," Tabitha said. "I never did it before I was a vampire."

"Oh." There was an awkward silence. Hart suddenly noticed how close Tabitha was sitting next to him.

"We can't have babies," she said. Hart didn't know what to say to that. "I just bring it up. It's just a fact that I thought you might find interesting."

Hart's mouth was suddenly very dry. He cleared his throat. "It *is* interesting."

"Are you getting a cold?" Tabitha said. "I've never been sick a day in my life. We can't get diseases—something about white blood cells."

"I see," Hart said. "Must be nice." Not knowing exactly what to do next, he took a bite of hamburger.

Tabitha watched him chew for a bit, then blurted out, "Hart, you're not actually going to make me *ask*, are you?"

"Ask what?" Hart said, chewing.

Tabitha gave a cry of utter frustration, then threw herself onto Hart, kissing him.

Pinning him down, she started to unbutton his shirt. Hart's brain was out of commission, but his hand somehow found its way to her bottom. Scratchy gray flannel never felt so good.

"Wait," Hart said, sitting up. "Where's your retainer?"

"Are you always this romantic?" Tabitha pushed him down and kissed him again. Hart didn't have any questions after that.

CHAPTER ELEVEN

"... **G**REAT," the university photographer said, snapping a photo from his knees. "That's really great. Trip, how's your bum?"

"Okay," Trip said. They'd spent an hour cutting a hole in the bed so Trip could sit up higher without too much pressure on his wound.

"Excellent. Just a few more," the photographer said. "Shelly, I think we need less flowers. Looks a bit . . . funereal . . ."

An assistant scurried into the frame and removed some of the profusion of baskets that ringed Trip's bed. Trip and his father remained in a hearty get-well handshake.

"Don't take too many flowers away," Mr. Darling hissed through his frozen smile. "I want him to look popular."

"I *am* popular, Dad."

"Quit knocking me in the head with your cast," Mr. Darling said irritably. "I know you're doing it on purpose. What's wrong with your arm? I thought the problem was with your ass."

"My arm's fine," Trip said, "I just like to use the cast as a weapon. I made them put a bottle opener on it . . . Bap!"

"I TOLD YOU, QUIT KNOCKING—"

"Please, gentlemen, just a few more seconds . . ." The photographer writhed around, getting the proper angle. "Good. You can move again."

"You didn't have to crush my hand, you nitwit," Mr. Darling grouched.

"Dad, don't be a pussy," Trip said disdainfully. "You've got girl's hands."

Mr. Darling *did* have small hands, and was self-conscious about them. "Keep disrespecting me, and I'll have you over in Cambodia smelting nine-irons so fast you'll . . ."

"But that wouldn't get you any votes, would it?" Trip said. Mr. Darling looked like he'd need every vote he could get; one of his ads had called dog owners "traitors to their species," and enraged pet-lovers were coming out in force.

The photographer stepped in. "Now, I wonder if we couldn't do the same thing, from the other side? Your father on your left, right?"

"Right?" Mr. Darling asked.

"No, his left."

"But you said, 'right,'" Mr. Darling said.

Like all dysfunctional families, the Darlings loved to join forces against an outsider. It was the only time they actually liked each other. "Dad's right," Trip said, "you did say 'right.'"

"Correct," the photographer agreed, silently calculating his fee. It was soothing. "Your right, his left."

"I know I'm right," Mr. Darling muttered.

"No, Mr. Darling"—the photographer waved with

building annoyance—"your son's left! Trip's *left*!"

"No, he hasn't. He's right here."

"Are you *purposefully* . . . ?" The photographer finally grabbed the pair and positioned them. As he did so, he recalled a documentary he'd seen once about the Roman Empire, and how the upper classes all had brain damage. "Okay—now—Mr. Darling, put your arm around your son. Grip his shoulder. 'I love my son.'"

"Are we going for the fag vote, now?" Trip said through his smile.

Family solidarity still flickered. "Hell, no!" Mr. Darling said.

"Just put your arm *near* him, then." The photographer shuddered inwardly as he framed the pair of lupine grimaces— both of them smiled *angry*. "Smile, Mr. Darling! Step on the tack in your shoe, like we said."

Mr. Darling had run as a one-issue candidate, that issue being the deep human desire to spite friends and relations. "Before he died," Mr. Darling had said, "my opponent called me an 'aberrant, dead-hearted, crony-encrusted dilettante.' Easy for him to say!" The crowd laughed.

"Isn't that just like an English teacher? Lots of big words, but not a lot of common sense." Candidate Darling never missed an opportunity to remind the voters that the former governor had taught high-school English before entering politics. Hating the teacher, of course, made him a man of the people. "We're talking about who can run the state, not take the SATs.

"Now I'm facing a tougher opponent: Widget the beagle . . . or as I like to call him, 'Teacher's Pet.' I have nothing against Widget. In fact, nobody loves dogs as much as I do. But tonight, as you go into that voting booth, I want you to think about something—not whether I'm qualified, or which candidate will do the better job, or what's best for our future. That's for God to decide. I want you to think of all the people you know who support my opponent: the nerds. The know-it-alls. The teacher's pets. Think of how annoying they are, how they're always proving you wrong in arguments and insisting that you have reasons for doing things! You hated them in high school and you hate them now. Why? Because they think they're *better than you*.

"I'm here to say they're not. You're just as good as they are, with all their books and big words and logical thought. None of that stuff matters. Here's how you can prove it, how you can really get back at them: vote for me! Maybe I'll do a good job, maybe I won't—that's not for me to say. But one thing's for sure: it will drive the nerds *nuts*. For the next six years, every time they look in the newspaper they'll see just how much being smart matters! And every day you open the newspaper you can think to yourself, 'Because of my vote, anybody can grow up to be governor.' That's what this country is all about!"

This strategy, interspersed with bald-faced appeals to personal interest, had gotten Mr. Darling through the primaries and into a dead heat with his canine opponent. The race was so close—and so dirty—that the state legislature had decided that there had to be a run-off. And the father/son photos, worth a thousand lies, had pushed him over the top. Amazingly, the university photographer was able to kindle this brief spark of father-son unity into a passable facsimile of affection. The photos put Mr. Darling into the governor's mansion, but that didn't stop him from stiffing the photographer on his fees.[52]

The first phone call Mr. Darling made—after the movers and his mistress—was to Trip. "Trip, I've got some good news."

"You're gonna die of schlong cancer," Trip replied.

"I'll give you one free shot, because you're sedated."

"You wish! I'm not on anything except Pabst Blue Ribbon!" Trip belched loudly.

"You better start showing me some respect," Mr. Darling said. "I just got elected governor of Michigan."

"State troopers can kiss my ASS!" Trip whooped. (His erratic driving had resulted in a long-running battle with the Michigan Highway Patrol. "So, Governor Pudwhack, can I go? My buzz is wearing off."

"No, I've got something to tell you," Mr. Darling said. "Now that I'm elected, it doesn't matter whether you stay in school or not. I'd like to fire that asshole what's-his-name . . . The geeky kid, you know who I'm talking about. Do you have any objections?"

"I dunno, Dad." The prospect of actually doing schoolwork wasn't appealing. "It's really funny watching Hart not fit in."

"Well, I don't want to have to pay for it anymore, so unless you want it to come out of your trust fund . . ." Mr. Darling let that hang in the air until Trip broke down.

"Okay, fire him, but not until after finals, okay?" Trip said. "After that, we can audition a bunch more Gnomes. I don't think anybody has to worry about CCA becoming the nerd frat

---

[52] Mr. Darling never paid any bill that was smaller than one thousand dollars; he knew it would cost them more to take it to court than to simply write it off as a bad debt. He called this "the Darling method," and was constantly threatening to write a book about it.

as long as I'm in it. Did you hear about our G'rung party? There were *three* ambulances!"

"All right—he can take your finals, but after that, it's your problem." Mr. Darling hung up, pleased at making Trip's life more difficult. When he was his age—well, no, he had been just as coddled, but that wasn't the point! Now, to tie up the loose end. Mr. Darling called another number, a private number.

"Hello, Burlington," a deep, dispassionate voice said. "Congratulations."

Mr. Darling was nervous—Hamilcar Barker had always affected him that way. "Amazing, Ham. It was just announced here five minutes ago."

"Fresh information is like fresh meat—there's more life in it."

Mr. Darling suddenly remembered why Ham made him so nervous—and why he had dialed this number, instead of another one. "Ham, I need your help. I have a loose end." A "loose end" was Mugwumps slang for anything inappropriate that needed to be cleaned up. Hamilcar was the head of the Nefarious Cabal Association of America; this was the Mugwumps' shadowy legal face and octopus-like parent organization. There was no loose end that the NCAA couldn't tie up.

"Is it something we can talk about over the phone?"

"Not under *this* presidential administration," Mr. Darling said. The country was going through a period when it was not being led by a Wumpsman. Thankfully, these dark eras were becoming increasingly rare.

"Can it wait two weeks?"

Mr. Darling didn't know what Hamilcar meant by that, and didn't think he wanted to know. "No," he said.

202

"I'll send my jet for you, and we can meet for lunch tomorrow at Der Rathskeller," Hamilcar said. "Be at the airport in two hours."

Doing as he was told unpleasantly reminded Mr. Darling of his and Hamilcar's senior year. As did the chill he felt the next day, when he and Hamilcar shook hands. "Burlington," Hamilcar said in a voice stripped of emotion.

"Ham," Mr. Darling said, withdrawing his hand. He was glad he was up-to-date on his payments to the NCAA; Hamilcar's perpetual deep tan, short, wiry white hair, and icy, unblinking blue eyes combined to create something unsettling, cold-blooded. He radiated well-manicured menace, like a beautiful, powerful reptile you know has acquired the taste for human flesh.

They met at Der Rathskeller. Nestled next to the *Spec* building, Der Rathskeller embodied the power and tradition of Old Stutts, as well as its Puritan suspicion of decent food. There was a riot of Stutts memorabilia on the walls. Even the urinals had a rah-rah aspect to them: someone had embedded pennants from Stutts' nearest academic rivals into the porcelain, so that diners could express their Stutts spirit passively.

In earlier, more romantic times, there were songs written about the "Skeller," and every Hollywood movie dealing with high society had at least one scene there. Nowadays, its profile was lower, but having a meal at Der Rathskeller was still a mandatory stop for all alumni passing through town. As a result, it did a very good business, and also as a result, it was necessary for the Mugwumps to construct a penthouse atop the regular restaurant, so that its members might dine there in the secrecy and comfort they insisted upon.

For once, Mr. Darling left his foul mouth and gangster talk

at home. It was clear who was tougher in this conversation, and it wasn't him. The two men tarried over small talk until Mr. Darling could take it no longer. As the vulcanized veal cutlets arrived, he blurted out, "Say I needed to kill a Stutts student."

Surprised, the waiter dropped a pat of butter into Hamilcar's water glass. He was summarily sacked—not for contaminating the water, but for obviously eavesdropping on a private conversation.

"The quality of service has gone down," Hamilcar said, with more sadness than anger.

"You could say that about the entire world," Mr. Darling said.

Hamilcar returned to the question at hand. "Why do you make this request? Has a member of the group revealed our secrets?"

"No, no," Mr. Darling said. "Nothing as serious as that. There's just a kid . . . Some nobody, a freshman."

"Burlington, you know what the NCAA thinks of violence," Hamilcar said. "There are rules. We're not some tawdry murder-for-hire service. Think of the people we've killed in the past—Kennedys, Rockefellers . . . Both killer and victim are always from the best families."

"I know, I know." Mr. Darling chuckled. "Do you remember that look on Michael Rockefeller's face when we showed up in Papua New Guinea?"

"I liked him. It's a shame he talked to that reporter about the group," Hamilcar said. "Killing someone is a serious thing, especially if they're still enrolled. The university doesn't like us taking money out of its pocket. To you, he's just a freshman, but to them, that's three more years of tuition oozing onto the carpet."

"Goddamn," Burlington said. "*I'm* paying for this kid to come here—I got him accepted in the first place. He's been tutoring Trip."

"I wondered how Trip managed to survive first semester," Hamilcar said. "No offense."

"None taken." Actually, there was, but Mr. Darling knew his place.

"I don't understand—if you went to all this trouble to make this arrangement, why are you so anxious to get rid of this kid after one semester? Won't Trip get booted?"

"I just needed Trip to play the role until I got elected. Now if Trip fails out, he can go chase foreign tail for a few years," Mr. Darling said chummily.

Hamilcar's face stayed impassive, rejecting Mr. Darling's attempt at levity. He was an exquisitely serious man. "Why kill? Someone like that is . . . infinitesimal."

"He's from my home state, and I—"

Hamilcar got a tingle of foreboding. Darling seemed much too invested in this decision. Murder was risky, malevolent neglect much better. "We can't do it."

"Gee, Ham, I'm sorry to hear you say that, seeing as I just got elected to the eighth most populous state in the U.S."

"You took an oath," Hamilcar bristled. "You are bound to help the group whether or not we swat this fly. *The oath is binding* . . . ask Michael Rockefeller."

Mr. Darling knew he'd gone too far, and turned tail. "Sorry," he said. "Of course I'll help the group, whenever, however, and as much as I can." He resolved to send Hamilcar a big fruit basket when he got home. Hamilcar liked apples.

"Of course," Hamilcar said, mildly placated. "Obviously, we won't hinder you. Is the killing business or personal?"

"A little of both."

"Too bad it's not entirely business. Then you could write it off, as miscellaneous expenses," Hamilcar said. "A hit man wouldn't be right for this job anyway—he'd stick out. Football season's over, so he couldn't be 'an alumni booster.'"

"I was thinking that maybe a student could do it?" Mr. Darling said. "Maybe we could make it the delegation's annual project?" Every year's worth of Mugwumps—called "a delegation"—was given a project to complete during its time on campus.

"Afraid it's a bit late for that," Hamilcar said. "They're already trying to destabilize the euro. Anyway, no reason to use a Wumpsman."

"I'd feel better if it were."

"I understand that, but you have to work with what's possible," Hamilcar said. He was determined to shield the larger group from what was feeling more and more like an ill-considered personal vendetta. "What I'd suggest is finding a bright, ambitious young person, and present them an opportunity for career advancement. Post it on the mentor/mentee bulletin board and see what happens. Does Trip know anybody?"

"A lot of people." Mr. Darling was almost as sensitive about his son's popularity as Trip himself was. "But they're all in his frat, and I wouldn't trust those guys to wash a dog."

"Which frat is it?"

"Comma Comma Apostrophe."

"I see what you mean," Hamilcar said. "I thought they'd shut that down."

"No," Mr. Darling said. "It's like smallpox. They could eradicate it, but then they'd be unable to study it. It's different than in our day—no style, just lack of substance. They had to bring in a few weenies to keep the group's grade-point average up."

"This place has really gone downhill," Hamilcar said.

"I've been saying it for years," Mr. Darling said. "Bringing weenies into a group like that is liable to destroy the whole tone of the frat. . . . They do the best they can; they keep them in the basement, don't invite them to parties . . ."

"I just had an idea," Hamilcar said, noting that the sauce made the vegetables taste a little less like wood. "Why not make it a frat-wide contest?"

"Ham, be serious. This kid could make trouble for me."

"I am being serious," Hamilcar said. "Individually, each is almost guaranteed to fail. But if they all attempt to kill the target, the odds of success skyrocket. Well, perhaps 'skyrocket' is a little strong," Hamilcar said, "but you get the picture."

Mr. Darling turned the idea over in his head. "What's the enticement?"

"The experience? We used to do it for all the beer you could drink," Hamilcar said.

"Don't forget the T-shirts. I still have the one we got for Lumumba—or was it the Diem brothers? Anyway, things are different now," Mr. Darling said. "I'd probably have to give the murderer a cushy internship."

"Kids today are such careerists. It's disgusting."

"Ham," Mr. Darling said, "do you think we could admit the winner into Mugwumps? That's a real incentive."

Hamilcar frowned. "Won't that create a connection between our group and the murder?" Hamilcar said. "It's not the killing I mind, but—we have to expect real ineptitude. It could be embarrassing."

"You could always say the student group was freelancing . . ."

This wasn't enough for Hamilcar, so Mr. Darling continued. "Or pin it on a patsy, some townie. Or you could always welch on the deal afterward . . . Disavow all ties, and cut the kid loose—after all, he'd be a criminal. A disgusting, despicable murderer," Mr. Darling smiled. "I'm not telling you anything you don't already know."

Hamilcar looked satisfied. "Deal," he said. "I consider this loose end tied."

"So do I," Mr. Darling said. Time to change the subject. "Those are interesting cuff links," he said. "What are they?"

"Oh, these?" Hamilcar fingered one absently. "Baby teeth. Would you care for dessert?"

"Why punish ourselves?" Mr. Darling said, smiling. He liked his own smile, and sneaked a glance in the back of his soup spoon. In the reflection Hamilcar looked grotesque, while he looked distorted and small.

That night, Mr. Darling paid a surprise visit to the rickety premises of Comma Comma Apostrophe. It was just as squalid as he remembered it, full of burning smells, sticky stains, and broken furniture. The only new addition was a small plane that had crashed through the roof during G'rung weekend. Nobody could be bothered to remove it, so it hung there, creaking ominously in the wind.

The ten Brothers sat in the common room, hanging on Mr. Darling's every word. Trip, sitting on a hemorrhoid doughnut, was ostentatiously bored. "Dad, could you hurry up? We have some porn to watch."

"Trip, I understand if *you're* not interested in what I have to say, but some other brothers might be."

"Yeah, Trip," the frat's President, Brother Crackers, said.

"Mr. Darling is an Old Puke, so according to our constitution, he has a right to address the group. Go ahead, Mr. Darling. Or should I say, Brother—"

"Mr. Darling," Trip's dad said coldly.

"Oh. Sorry," Brother Crackers said, chastened. Then, quickly: "You can sleep here, if you want."

"No, he can't!" Trip said. "He's my dad and he's a dick and a tool." Then, turning to his dad: "Go back home and make Mom's life hell!"

"Thank you, Brother Crackers," Mr. Darling said mildly, "but I have accommodations for the evening. Plus, I'm behind on my shots." Mr. Darling cleared his throat. "I have a proposition for you men. This afternoon, I had lunch with the alumni head of the Mugwumps—"

A whisper shot through the room.

"It's okay, I can say the name, I was a member," Mr. Darling said. (The group circulated the fiction that non-members couldn't speak the word "Mugwumps" without invoking a centuries-old curse. Only simps believed this.) "He was telling me about a student that's come to his attention, a certain freshman."

"Told ya," Trip said loudly, looking around.

"No, Trip, it wasn't you," Mr. Darling said. "Luckily. This student is a no-fit. He's a taker. Not what Stutts is about." Mr. Darling began passing out flyers with Hart's facebook picture on them. "You already know him from your prank: Hart Fox.

"Generally, all you have to do with a student like this is let him alone. The university rusticates him to prevent his bad attitude from spreading to others, and he eventually drops out. But the gentleman from Mugwumps thinks this Fox character is different. More dangerous. Highly virulent."

"Look at this bunghole," Brother Uniball said, twisting his expression into a lampoon of Hart's.

"Why are all his classes and stuff on here?" Brother Crackers said.

"Gentlemen," Mr. Darling said solemnly, "at this point, I'm going to have to invoke CCA's sacred confidentiality clause. Anyone who can't keep the secret I'm about to reveal should leave the room now."

No one left.

"Good. Nice to see that there's still pride in the group." Mr. Darling paused, then said, "The Mugwumps think that Hart Fox is a clear and present danger to Stutts and its traditions. They want him liquidated."

The room was silent. Then, tentatively, Brother Nipples raised his hand. "Mr., uh, Trip's dad?"

"Yes?"

"I don't understand. Do they want to drink him?"

Mr. Darling considered throwing up his hands and leaving, but he held his temper. "No, they want him killed."

"Whoa!" Trip said, with vacant enthusiasm. "Greek life is the *best*!"

"Trip, please. This is a man's life we're talking about," Mr. Darling said.

"Oh come on, Dad!" Trip said. "It's just fucking Hart. You hate him."

Mr. Darling's face darkened. He had been trying to hide his connection with Hart.

"Uh-oh, now I'm in trouble," Trip teased.

"This is not about me, Trip. It's about being a loyal alumnus. Obligation—responsibility—giving back—maybe someday you'll understand." Mr. Darling continued: "The

210

Wumpsman asked if I knew of any group of students brave and resourceful enough to carry out such a sensitive assignment. I immediately thought of you gentlemen. Bold. Capable. Discreet." With every adjective, Mr. Darling had to fight harder to suppress a laugh. He continued: "It can be done. As Michael Corleone said in *The Godfather: Part II*, 'If there's one thing that history has taught us, it's that anyone can be killed.'"

"So what do we do, just grab him off the street and put a plastic grocery bag over his head?" Brother Molepicker asked.

"No," Mr. Darling said. "This must be done secretly, with stealth. No one must know who was responsible."

"We could invite him to a party and give him a Coke with Pop Rocks in it," Brother Nipples said confidently. "That makes your heart explode."

Mr. Darling didn't gratify that remark with a response. Brother Crackers raised his hand. "Yes?"

"But isn't murder, like, illegal?"

"In most cases, yes," Mr. Darling said, preparing to pull something directly out of his ass. "However, due to a bill forced through Congress during the chaos following Abraham Lincoln's assassination, no member of the Mugwumps can be prosecuted for murder."

"So get them to do it," Trip said.

"They would, with pleasure," Mr. Darling said. "But some members are worried that if the public found out about that particular fringe benefit, they might vote differently in the next election."

"So rig the voting machines," Trip said with a shrug.

Mr. Darling paid no attention. "I've arranged that whichever one of you kills Hart Fox will be immediately and

211

irrevocably inducted into the Mugwumps. That is your reward."

"Even if you're not a junior?" Brother Crackers said. He was a junior, and felt a little put out about the possibility of somebody younger than him horning in.

"For the first time in five hundred years, they are willing to admit a candidate early. This is an extraordinary opportunity," Mr. Darling said. "I almost wish I were a student again."

"Let's start now!" Brother Uniball said enthusiastically. "I'll go get a brick!"

"No, no," Mr. Darling said. "Start second semester. You'll need time to formulate plans—winter break is an excellent time to plot. Plus, there are finals."

"But the Gnomes—" Uniball said.

"Don't burn out your Gnomes too early in the year," Mr. Darling said. "This offer is open to them as well. Would somebody go down to The Cage and let them know?"

"Can we form teams?" Nipples asked.

"What about expenses?" said Crackers. "The only place that still takes our checks is Liquor Lovers', and you can't buy bombs there."[53] The room was beginning to get boisterous.

"Quiet down! Gentlemen, *please*. Yes," Mr. Darling said, "you can form teams."

"Behold!" Crackers said, striking a contorted pose. "The ninja!" He was serious.

"Trip will happily pay any expenses. But I must insist that

---

[53] Not anymore, anyway—back in the late sixties and early seventies, you could. You just had to say you were taking American Studies 413a: The Violent Overthrow of the United States Government. Not only did you get college credits, but for many Stutts students it was a great, direct way to get back at their parents.

this errand attract as little attention as possible. It's not good enough to blow up"—Mr. Darling brought his reading glasses out and glanced down at Hart's schedule— "Lytton Hall when you know there's a *Cuckoo* meeting. This must be surgical, precise!" These last few words had to be shouted. All around the table, brothers were lost in fantasy, demonstrating karate chops, and giddily explaining to each other their lethal plans for Hart.

"Gentlemen! Gentlemen!" Mr. Darling yelled, banging his palm on the table. As the frat brothers started to wrestle, he gave up and slipped out of the room.

CHAPTER TWELVE

HART WAS LIVING on borrowed time, but at least he was enjoying himself. He hadn't really had a girlfriend before, and he finally understood what all the ruckus was about. Losing his virginity to that Austrian girl had been completely random—it had only happened because he had never had schnapps before, and her English wasn't very good. Since then, Hart's entire sexual experience had been one half-hearted blow job from a girl he hardly knew. She didn't really like Hart before or after, but had read an article in a magazine and didn't want to miss out on "the craze that's sweeping today's high schools."

Hart and Tabitha spent a lot of time together, the majority of it naked. He finally got to see her apartment, a crypt in the cemetery off Maggot Lane filled with all sorts of cheery knickknacks. It got so Hart would get an erection whenever he saw nautical bric-a-brac.

Most of the time, however, they were holed up at the *Cuckoo* office. Tabitha slipped money to the caretaker to let her live in the cemetery, and there would be no end of trouble if somebody happened to see Hart ducking out of the crypt post-coitally tucking in his shirt. Unfortunately, the *Cuckoo* office began to reek of sex, so Hart had to confess to the other members exactly what was going on.

"Interstaff romance is a recipe for disaster," Ellen said sternly. Peter's concern, voiced in private, was that Tabitha would "eat you, or something." But at Stutts, sexual relations were rare enough—a small miracle, really—so nobody seriously counseled either party against it.

"You only live once," Tabitha said.

"I know what it means when I say that," Hart said, "but what do *you* mean?"

"Oh, I was a real stress case when I got bit," Tabitha said. "It took me fifty years to calm down enough to have my first orgasm."

"Really?"

"Yes," Tabitha said, picking a pill off her Shetland wool sweater. "Nobody told me explicitly, but from the way my mother acted—acts—I guess I felt enjoying sex was a bit N.O.C.D."

"N.O.C.D.?"

"'Not our class, dear,'" Tabitha said. "My first thirty or so boyfriends took it personally, when it wasn't their fault at all. Men always assume that it's all about them. Maybe you're just thinking about shoes or the plot holes in a movie. But now I have the knack, thank God—" Hart raised his hand. "Yes, Hart?"

"Thirty?"

"Please tell me you aren't a counter. I hate counters."

"I'm not . . ." Hart said. ". . . *Thirty?*"

"Over fifty years!"

"The first fifty years," Hart said. He didn't know whether he was teasing or not.

"Don't start thinking I'm some sort of—something, because I'm not," Tabitha said. "I'm very picky."

"Well . . ." Hart wisely let her off the hook. "Anybody I know?"

"Sure," Tabitha said. "Mark Twain, I already told you about him. Man Ray . . ."

"The photographer," Hart said. "I'll bet he was kinky."

Tabitha mimed zipping her mouth shut. "I'll never tell."

"Come on! What's the point of having an immortal girl-friend if she won't spill the juicy details?"

"You might appreciate that trait someday," Tabitha said. "Let's see, there was Enrico Caruso, Jesse Owens—*definitely* a sprinter . . . Jonas Salk, Edison, and Tesla. You know, inventors are surprisingly unimaginative in bed . . . Paul Robeson, Sun Yat-Sen, David Niven, Gertrude Stein—"

Hart looked shocked.

"A worthy experiment," Tabitha said. "And of course, there was my first love, General George Armstrong Custer."

"What?" This was the only truly objectionable choice. "Custer was a total a-hole!"

"Like I'm the first woman to fall in love with one of those," Tabitha sighed. "Classic bad boy. He was handsome, I was young. . . . Anyway, I have no regrets, about Georgie or any-body else—the exact opposite, in fact. If I could stand the sunlight, I'd go around spreading the word. I'd be the Johnny Appleseed of female orgasm."

"And to think I once thought you were a priss," Hart said.

"Cardigans, turtlenecks, and pearls," Tabitha laughed. "I like to travel incognito."

In addition to having his first-ever sex life—as opposed to isolated and somewhat troubling sex events—Hart had his usual double helping of academics to slog through. But just like Tabitha and orgasms, Hart found that there was a knack to Stutts. It got easier the longer you did it. However, when you had a girlfriend who insisted on staying up all night (and made it quite pleasant to do so), the candle inevitably began to burn at both ends.

By the time he was set to fly home for a monthlong Christmas break, Hart was in a fatigue-induced fugue state. The good news was, so was everybody else. The fog of work had cleared to reveal quite a nice place. Stutts looked beautiful, now that Hart had time to notice: for the moment at least, Great Littleton was covered with fluffy snow instead of shoe-invading, foot-deadening slush. People were nicer, too, now that Mother Stutts had lifted her heel from their windpipes.

The holidays were full of parties. Hair combed, dressed in their best, men and women rushed from party to party, carrying packages and/or package goods. Every crenellated corner of the campus was lit for celebration. For most of the year, Stutts was a dour, High Colonic rat's maze, but for the few days after finals and before everyone left for home, the school was positively jolly. There was, for once, more comradeship than competition. Hart felt that he would miss it—how quickly Stutts had become home.

Deranged with holiday spirit, Hart hoped that Trip would invite him to CCA's year-end bash, as a thank you for keeping him painlessly moving toward an unearned degree. He'd decline, of course, just to show how popular he was. But this fantasy was unfulfilled; as a first-year, and a pariah, his holiday schedule was depressingly open.

"It's not like I want to go to the CCA thing . . ." Hart grumped to Peter, who was putting the finishing tugs on a bow tie.

"Relieved to hear that," Peter said. "You can come with me to the Philo Ball. We'd be honored to host someone from your high school." Ellen had nominated Peter for admission into this coterie of Stutts tinkerers, and Peter had accepted. The Philo T. Farnsworth Society was better than secret—it was unintelligible to anybody who wasn't a brilliant engineer. They had weekly dinners and an annual ball at Christmas. "Anybody who doesn't have a date gets an android."

"You're kidding."

"Only way to find out is to come."

Hart picked up a yo-yo from Peter's desk and began playing with it. "No thanks. I like my girlfriends—"

"—undead," Peter teased.

"I hate the CCA guys, it's just that I wanted to be able to say no. I wanted the option." Hart used to be good at yo-yoing, back when he was a kid. This one had Santa's face on one side, and Satan's on the other. The nose of each lit up as it spun. "Where'd you get the yo-yo?"

"Secret Santa present. CCA guys are losers—hiring strippers is so *desperate*," Peter said. "Though, at this point, I wouldn't say no." Peter's death march through the Frosh Facebook was reaching legendary proportions. There was the girl who never showed up, and the girl who left halfway through the movie, and the girl who invited an auxiliary guy to the same dance and decided to dance with him while Peter sat on the sidelines . . . The disasters were legion, and Hart had the sinking feeling that too much of it had to do with Peter's disability.

Hart flicked the yo-yo downward. "You think Tabitha's cute?"

"Sure, if you like *Nosferatu*," Peter said. "Just kidding. Yes, she's cute—but in my condition, so is Grandma."

"In your condition?" Hart let the yo-yo spin at the end of its string.

"I'm swimming in so much excess testosterone, my vision is blurry," Peter said. "Screw the parties—why don't you and Tab cruise Winter Carnival? That's what I'd do, if I had a girlfriend."

"Good idea." The string snapped, and the yo-yo skittered across the room and under Peter's bed.

"Thanks a lot," Peter said.

Winter Carnival was one of the few Stutts traditions that the whole town actually liked. Every year as soon as the Turbid froze, local entrepreneurs hauled out booths, carts, and displays that had been in storage since the summer. For a month Stuttsies and townies alike strolled the surface of the river, eating sausages and fried dough to the sound of Italian music.

"Why Italian music?" Hart asked, as he and Tabitha walked down the river.

"They reuse it from the Feast of St. Anthony's," Tabitha said. Great Littleton had a lot of Italian-Americans, and the Feast of St. Anthony's was their big June celebration. "I want a *zeppole*."

They walked over to a booth. "Okay, since you know everything," Hart said, "do you know why the booths are on the banks of the river, and the people walk on the ice? I know. Do you?" He poked Tabitha playfully. She giggled—at moments like this it was easy to forget that she was older than some countries.

"No, tell me—STOP!" she grabbed his finger. "I'll only listen if you stop."

"It's because the original Winter Carnival was held in memory of a Stutts president's only son who fell through the ice."

"So now the entire town risks falling in?" Tabitha said. "Typical Stutts. When was this supposed to have happened?"

"During the Revolutionary War," Hart said. "He was a Colonial soldier who was trying to escape the British. The Redcoats were camped over there." Hart pointed toward the left bank.

"At Bong John Silver's?" It was the campus head shop. "No wonder the Brits lost the war."

Hart spotted a photo booth with a mammoth prop armchair in it. "Come on, Tab, let's get our picture taken," Hart said.

"But—"

"No buts. I want a photo to show my mom." Hart grabbed her by the hand.

"But, Hart—"

"How much for a picture of me and my girlfriend?" Hart asked the seedy gentleman standing next to the tripod.

"Fi'bucks," the man said, blowing on his hands.

Tabitha wrapped her remaining *zeppole* up in wax paper, as Hart pulled her up on to the platform. "You never listen to me . . ." she mumbled.

"Shh, sourpuss," Hart said. "Smile for the nice man." The flash went off, Hart paid, and they repaired to a nearby bench to watch the instant photo develop.

"Brr," Hart said. "Cast-iron benches."

"Hope our butts don't stick," Tabitha said cheerily. "Isn't it pretty with the lights and the snow?" The merchants had strung red, green, and white lights across the river, and they twinkled as they swung slightly in the breeze. The snow combined with the deep shadows made a black-and-white world, where every splash of color was brilliant. "I wish it would snow."

"It has."

"I mean I wish it would snow *more*," Tabitha said.

"I don't," Hart said. "I have to take a plane tomorrow." He shook the photo impatiently.

"I wouldn't mind you getting stuck here," Tabitha said, squeezing closer. "I'm going to miss you."

"I won't be away too long," Hart said. "But I'm glad I'll have your pict—hey!" The photograph had only one person in it. Hart's arm was encircling air.

"Vampire, remember?"

Meanwhile, fifty feet behind the couple, Gavin Bartels, aka Brother Crackers, was gunning the engine of an ancient Chevy, swigging from a pint of Wild-Eyed Hibernian, and eyeing Hart with evil intent.

The early part of his evening had been filled with beer and poker, laying down a base for the CCA bash to come. Then he'd forced one of the Gnomes—Biff or Beekman, he could never remember which was which—to loan him keys to his car.

Brother Crackers was a junior. Prior to Trip's arrival on campus, he had been the leader of Comma Comma Apostrophe, its titular head as well as its guiding spirit. Now president in name only, he seethed over the attention and respect that had been lavished on Trip Darling. In fact, before Trip joined, Brother Crackers was called by his real name, the highest respect a CCA member could muster. But Trip had insisted that Gavin smelled like saltines smeared with butter, and so "Crackers" he became.

Crackers had fastened on winning Mr. Darling's contest as his path back to power. "I'm gonna walk in there, like nothing," Crackers said to himself between cough-inducing swigs. He gunned the engine. "I'm just gonna smile and wait for somebody to ask me what I'm smiling about, and I'll just say, 'I did it,' and throw the kid's spleen on the table." Emotions welled up in Crackers. "They'll see that, and they'll remember who the *real* leader of the frat is!" he yelled, wiping away a single tear.

Up ahead, oblivious to Crackers' ravings, Hart was telling Tabitha about his proudest moment. It had happened one recess in the spring of fourth grade. "I was pitching, and this kid, Kenneth, came up to bat . . . You know how at that age, some kids grow a lot faster than others? Did that happen in the eighteen-fifties?"

"I vaguely remember that," Tabitha said.

"Well, Kenneth was like, eleven, and three years into puberty at least. Every game we'd play, he'd leave a trail of bodies. Baseball was the worst; he hit line drives *at* kids—whole teams were going to the nurse's office."

The tires on Crackers' car squealed as he let out the clutch. Three tons of metal lurched toward the chatting couple.

" . . . So by then I was good and goddamn fed up," Hart said. "I reared back and threw the ball as hard as I could at Kenneth's head."

"Did you hit him?" Tabitha asked, concerned.

"Nah. I missed him by a mile."

Grinning maniacally from behind the wheel, Crackers judged that his bumper would hit Hart squarely in the back of the head. "It's gonna pop right off like a dandelion!" Crackers yelled, bouncing in his seat and pounding the steering wheel. "C'mon, Christine!" Then: "Oh, you're fucking kidding me! *This pile of shit!*"

Unfortunately for Crackers, "Christine" was the worst junker on campus. The engine sputtered impudently, then died. The forward momentum of the car kept it rolling; with ever decreasing speed, it trundled toward Hart.

"*That* was your proudest moment?" Tabitha asked. "Missing some fat dude in fourth grade?"

"No," Hart said. "My proudest moment is this: so Kenneth charges the mound, and I turn to fall to the ground and cover up—that was my preferred fighting style: I called it 'the Turtle' . . ."

"You can't do this to me!" Crackers raged. Crackers twisted the ignition key and pumped the accelerator savagely. If the engine started, he could exterminate this freshman and get into Mugwumps. Too bad about the girl, she seemed cute. Maybe he could just injure her, then ask her out after she left the hospital. "Do it! Do this one thing for me!"

Out of the corner of his eye, Hart thought he glimpsed a car rolling toward them. He figured his switched peepers were playing their usual tricks, so he kept talking. "As I fell, I raised my left leg to protect my crotch—and kneed Kenneth right in the balls. It was perfect!"

"*That* was your proudest moment?" Tabitha shook her head. "Guys are *so* weird."

"Hey, everybody carried me off the field!" Hart said defensively.

Crackers' blandishments proved worthless—the engine stayed dead. The car slowed, and finally came to a stop—but not before giving Hart the tiniest tap on the back of his head.

"What the hell?" Hart said, turning around.

Tabitha gave a yell and leapt to her feet. The car wasn't moving, but there was a man in the driver's seat, swearing and crying. He got out and walked away, without even shutting the door.

Some street toughs on Big Wheels were crunching down the street. One rolled up to Hart and Tabitha. "That your car?" he asked.

"Nope," Hart said. "Go ahead and take it. Merry Christmas."

The toughs attached bungee cords from their Big Wheels to the car and jubilantly hauled it away.

In a certain way the frat Gnomes, Biff and Beekman, were the most important members of Comma Comma Apostrophe. Without them, everything—the sprawling parties, the raucous tailgating (recently featured on the Travel Channel's *Hungover America*), even the knee injuries suffered on the glass-strewn basketball court behind the house—would screech to a halt.

Usually one Gnome was sufficient, but CCA's current crop of anti-Einsteins required two. The rank and file of the frat had opposed this, fearing that excessive scholarship would somehow infect the group. "I don't want to hang out with a bunch of weenies," Brother Uniball had griped at a meeting. "That's the only reason I let you dudes put a frozen hot dog up my butt in the first place." After the massacre at midterms, however, there was no choice but to admit Biff and Beekman as a matched set.

At CCA, intellect was handled somewhat like the Ebola virus: containment was (to use one of Brother Crackers' favorite words) key. Each Gnome was allowed upstairs only rarely, and never unsupervised. Even more humiliating, they were forced to wear a red cloche hat at all times. Removing this symbol of servitude would result in some unspecified—but much feared—punishment. "Not knowing is the worst part," Beekman often said. He was naturally glum.

Biff and Beekman lived in The Cage, an area of the basement created out of prefab cubicle walls stolen from the local SuperOfficeStopDepotCloseoutExplosion!!!. There was no heat or running water in The Cage, just two rickety desks and one bare bulb hanging above them. They were strongly discouraged from going upstairs, even to use the bathroom. Most of the time, they peed in mason jars. It was awful.

Party nights were the worst, because Biff and Beekman could hear the fun through the floor.

"This sucks!" Biff shouted. He was short and rumpled, and sported a fresh black eye, from where Crackers had just punched him. He was holding a bag of frozen peas on his face.

"Shh! Do you want to get kicked out?" Beekman said, convinced that Trip had been telling the truth when he mentioned the listening devices. Beekman was taller, which gave his wrinkled clothes more room to spread out. Otherwise the two freshmen looked strikingly similar. Systematic deprivation can do that. (Also, the hats.)

"I *want* out!" Biff said, slamming an econ book shut. "I'm sick of taking showers at the gym! I'm sick of having to answer 'secret passwords' to get food—that I *bought*—out of the refrigerator! This morning, Trip ate an entire package of *my* Pop Tarts right in front of me. And it wasn't the first time, either!" He ripped the red felt cloche hat off his head and threw it to the ground. It burned Biff up that he and Beekman had agreed to this. But some geeks want to be popular even more than popular kids do.

"Please put your hat back on," Beekman said. It made him nervous whenever Biff took his off. He suspected Biff knew this and did it partially to torment him. "We've been over this," Beekman said. "We can't leave. Everybody not in CCA already hates us for being in it. If we 'go rogue,' everybody *inside* the group will hate us, too."[54]

Biff couldn't deny Beekman's assessment; after all, Beekman handled the humanities side, while Biff specialized in math and science. There was a muffled cheer from upstairs. "Hear that? Up there, Ms. Candy Cane has just pressed the eject button on her spring-loaded brassiere, and we're down here 'Getting a start on the next semester,'" Biff said bitterly. "Screw next semester, and screw them, too!"

Beekman exhaled calmly. "Tell me again why Crackers punched you?"

"My car[55] died."

"But your car *always* dies," Beekman said. "Other cars are for transportation, yours is for dying."

"I know, I told him that," Biff said. "He was trying to run over that kid, to win the contest."

---

[54] "Going rogue" was the fraternity's term for anybody who resigned from it. Niels Bohr went rogue, as did Hugh Hefner.

[55] Not many Stutts students had cars; the street gangs of Great Littleton could strip one and carry the pieces away on their Big Wheels in seconds. Those few that did have vehicles only used them to passive-aggressively punish their parents through insurance and garaging fees. Biff's family had long ago shed normal interactions in favor of this kind of mutual guerrilla warfare.

Beekman got a thoughtful look. "Why don't we try to win the contest? That way we could get out of this group, and be in a better one, too. The *best* one."

"I bet we could do it—that kid looks pretty weak," Biff said. He scratched himself; some basement-dwelling bug was biting him every night as he slept. "The thing is, I don't wanna go to jail. I don't wanna be anybody's boyfriend."

"Don't be homophobic. It's ugly."

"I'm not. I'm being ass-rape-ophobic."

"Intolerance is intolerance," Beekman said serenely. "Anyway, is jail any worse than this?"

"Good point," Biff said. "But my parents would shit. They sent me here so I could get into law school, not prison."

"We could hire somebody."

"Too expensive," Biff said. "I still have to buy Christmas and Hanukkah presents. Goddamn blended family . . . Plus, what if he messes it up? Then we'd go to jail *and* be out the money."

Beekman got a special look on his face whenever he got a particularly stupid idea, and Biff saw that he was wearing it now. "We could invent a machine to do it," Beekman said. "I see a rope, with a big knife on one end, and a heavy weight on the other. All you'd have to do is sneak up close to him, and then swing it around. If he survived the knife, then the weight would come in." Beekman smacked his palm against his head. "Wham! Introducing, The Kill-inator!"

The Kill-inator failed to impress Biff. "They'd still arrest you."

"Can they get fingerprints off a rope? I don't think so," Beekman said in a "game-set-and-match" way.

"They wouldn't need to!" Biff said with annoyance.

227

"They'd see you! Christ, Beekman, I think being in this frat is rubbing off on you."

"It was just an idea." Biff's rude dismissal of what Beekman considered to be a perfectly good solution stalled the conversation for a bit. Finally Beekman said, "My second choice, obviously, would be a mummy."

"Eat me, I'm serious."

"I'm serious, too."

"Mummies don't exist," Biff said.

"Sure they do," Beekman said. "The University Museum has loads of them."

"First, they're dead," Biff said. "And second, they're all dried up. It'd be like siccing a giant raisin on him."

Beekman shrugged. "Maybe he's allergic."

"To what? Raisins? Mummies?" Biff lost his temper. "I *hate* it when you get like this."

Beekman wore a satisfied smile. "I call it 'creative block-busting.'"

"Whatever the hell you call it, it's freaking *intolerable*," Biff said. "Even if we could reanimate a mummy to kill this kid, how's that different from a machine?"

"No fingerprints," Beekman said, wiggling his fingers. "A mummy is completely untraceable. And since the mummy doesn't know English, it can't tell anyone who's controlling it. 'Who's your master?' 'Unnhhh!' 'What College is he or she in?' 'Unnnhhh!'" Beekman was having fun. "Plus, the mummy doesn't have any weapon."

"So how does it kill you?" Biff asked, wearing down.

"With fear," Beekman said confidently. "You can't get arrested just because somebody else dies of fright. You could say that you were just joking."

228

By now, Beekman was in the realm of pure ideas. Unfortunately for him, Biff was actually warming to the plan. Biff wasn't thinking so clearly; he was tired, and there were spilled alcohol fumes seeping through the ceiling. "Well, how do we get a mummy?" Biff said, as the duo's "man of action."

"You don't get a mummy. You have to raise one from the dead. Then it can go around doing stuff."

"Does it have to do whatever you tell it to? 'Mummy, get me a beer!'" Biff practiced. "'Mummy, sodomize Trip Darling!'"

"I think it has to," Beekman said. "Or maybe it can only do things within its own moral code."

"You're thinking of being hypnotized," Biff said. "Mummies have to be different. Otherwise, all those monster movies would have mummies just going around acting normal instead of killing people."

"I don't claim to be an expert," Beekman said. "I'm an ideas man."

Biff considered this to signal his victory in the argument. Feeling magnanimous, he said to Beekman, "I'll do some research on mummy raising over the break."

There was a loud thunk from above, as if a slightly tipsy, larger-than-average woman had lost her balance and fallen while giving a vigorous lap dance.

"I hate those guys," Biff said. He threw the econ book at the ceiling. It bounced and hit the light, plunging the Gnomes into darkness.

CHAPTER THIRTEEN

TWO WEEKS into winter break, Hart was in heavy Stutts withdrawal. It got so bad that he drove over to the local community college and walked around, just to be on a campus again. The security guard didn't understand what he was doing, and Hart didn't really, either, but in just three months he had become a university addict. He sat in his kitchen, talking to Peter on the phone—this helped take the edge off a little. Peristalsis the box turtle, the latest in his cousin Lulu's nev-erending line of pets, lumbered back and forth across the linoleum with a small package taped to his shell. (Lulu was try-ing to train him to carry explosives.)

Hart stuck his foot out and stymied Peristalsis. "God, I can't wait to get back to school," he said as the turtle strained against his sole.

"Me too," Peter agreed. "Watching public television helps."

"I'm getting shaky—do you get shaky?" Hart asked. "It's 10:00 P.M. and everybody's already in bed. Actually, that's not true, Lulu's watching one of her videos." Hart mimicked the narrator's voice: "*Kill Like a Craftsman.*"

"Who's Lulu, again?"

"My cousin. She goes to the Grade School of the Americas." Hart didn't think it was right for a ten-year-old to watch videos like *The Gentle Art of Strangulation* but Lulu insisted it was schoolwork. "She's staying with us over the holidays, 'cause her parents are survivalists," Hart said. "Why they have to rehearse Armageddon *now* is beyond me. God would never start the final conflict on Christmas."

"I don't know," Peter said, "it does sound like His sense of humor."

Hart laughed—cheerful blasphemy was one of the many things he was missing. Also, being able to sleep past nine. In the Fox household, the earlier you got up, the better a person you were. It didn't matter if you were a mass murderer, as long as you didn't "loll around in bed" before doing your dirty work. "Did you get any cool presents?"

"Apart from Polarfleece swimming trunks?" Peter griped. "That's my crazy aunt with the Polarfleece obsession. Then there's the other one who thinks I have polio. She's ancient. Whenever anybody contradicts her she says, 'It won't do to hide the truth from him.' If she sends me *one* more book about FDR . . . A lifetime of gin is a terrible thing, Hart."

"I'm afraid to ask, but any flickers of high school romance?"

"It's different when you go to boarding school. There's only a few kids from my town, and we figured out years ago we all hated each other. Have you noticed how everybody got Joe College'd up? I was at a party and the school poet—" Peter interrupted himself. "Did you have one of those?"

"Yeah, a guy named Max. I think they extrude them in some factory. Every high school class is issued one. By the way, they're not always gay—sometimes they just fake it, to lure the artsy-craftsy girls into the sack."

"Weasels!" Peter said. "Anyway, he came up and teased me about the Stutts football team—this guy who probably thinks the 'Big Ten' is an enlargement cream." Peter sighed. "If anybody calls about New Year's Eve, I'm faking mono."

"That's a great idea," Hart said. "I went to see a play at my high school—"

"Foolish boy."

"—and got into it with my old English teacher."

"Ex-school poet."

"No doubt. My getting into Stutts cost him a lot of money in the faculty pool."

"I still think you should've gotten a cut," Peter said.

"Wouldn't say no. Every time I see another person I went to high school with, I think, Wait—I killed you!" Hart said. "People who keep living after they leave my life are just plain rude."

Peter laughed. "You know who are the worst? The ones who come up to you like you're best pals—like high school was D-Day or something. 'Dude, all I ever had in common with you was being born in the same year.'"

Hart changed the subject. "I've gotten a lot of good ideas for the magazine."

"Do any of them involve money?" Peter asked. "'Cause that's problem numero uno, now that our pneumatic tube ring is kaput."

"Tabitha would still steal for us," Hart said. "I guess that wouldn't be enough."

"Probably not." Peter exhaled, then continued. "But don't forget the other ideas—Ellen was talking about doing a weekly table tent, just until we have enough for another issue."

"As long as something comes out, that's the important thing." Hart gnawed on a stale Christmas cookie that one of the boarders had made. Having boarders made the holidays particularly depressing. Some had holiday plans, but most just waited like puppies in a pet store, yipping and scrabbling frantically at the glass whenever a car that looked like the one their son or daughter drove sped by. Hart had a new understanding of holiday suicide. He felt bad for the boarders. Great Littleton was the only place he knew where "old" didn't mean "useless." "I can't wait to get back to school—did I say that already?"

"Four or five times, but don't worry. The phone bill is paid with Paternodollars." Paterno- and Maternodollars were a favorite concept of Peter's; it looked like normal money, and spent like it too, but you never owed anything because the bill went straight to Dad or Mom.

"You know what being at home is like?"

"Like being in a land where everybody drives everywhere, goes to bed early, and observes a bizarre custom called 'the weekend'?"

Hart laughed. "It's like when you're walking, and the head of your peen starts rubbing against your underwear every time you take a step. And you can't readjust there in public, so you just have to endure it and try not to go crazy."

Peter laughed. Just then, Lulu padded into the kitchen to complain about the noise. "I gotta run, Pete," Hart said, "Lulu says I'm talking too loud for her to hear 'the distinctive hollow crack of a windpipe.'"

* * *

Earlier that same day, Biff and Beekman met at The Chubby Roach. The Chubby Roach—invariably shortened to "the Chubby"—was a diner down the street from the Ponce School, the tony Manhattan prep school Biff and Beekman had graduated from last May. On any given afternoon, roughly one third of the diner would be filled with Ponce students flirting, cutting classes, or simply rehearsing their newest personality for friends. In a normal diner, the other patrons would've put a stop to this, and possibly, violently; but the only other people who frequented the Chubby were the neighborhood's doormen, maids, and nannies—employees of the parents of the kids acting so annoying. So the Chubby had become Ponce's unofficial school cafeteria.[56]

Though Ponce had produced seven U.S. presidents, its latest claim to fame was as the epicenter of the nation's supposed teen blow job craze. Oral sex would seem to be a perennial favorite of the human species, immune to the sort of ups and downs of, say, strappy sandals. But things that happened at Ponce tended to get media coverage, not least because so many Ponce parents (and Old Ponces) worked in the media. So one particularly slow news week, Ponce became synonymous with spitty privates.

This had made high school difficult for Biff and Beekman. Every day their genitals remained dry, the more unpopular they felt. The two boys did everything they could to kindle affection among their peers—they dressed right, talked right, and guarded against incorrect attitudes and opinions with

---

[56] A clandestine war had smoldered between Ponce kids and the Chubby staff for decades. The condiments had been booby-trapped so relentlessly—shaker caps loosened, cigarette ashes tapped into the pepper—that customers had to sign for them at the counter. Even the silverware was on chains, like pens at the bank.

incredible vigilance. But the most exclusive clubs can't be joined through something as common as trying.

Soon, their quest became an obsession—far more tormented than the total outcast is the person barred from entering that last room. Other students picked up on this and began insinuating that oral sex was taking place everywhere at Ponce, between everyone—except for them.

"The entire Spirit Club, Beekman! Right there on the auditorium stage!" Biff, the more high-strung of the pair, nearly cracked up midway through senior year. "I can't take it!" he said, with a hormone-haunted look. "I'm like a diabetic in a fudge factory!"

"I find drinking heavily helps," Beekman said. Beekman was socially awkward, accepted it, and fervently hoped that college would be somewhat more like the movies than high school had been. "A fine single malt can administer a certain insouciant bludgeoning to life's difficulties. Of course, a warm '40' of malt liquor also works."

Through the persistent application of alcohol—chemical castration, really—Biff kept a lid on his libido until graduation. In the meantime, this shared pain had made Biff and Beekman friends. It also drove them to do a lot of stupid things to move up in the social hierarchy, and the Chubby had been the setting for many of their most ill-fated schemes. There was something in the food that helped spawn life-ruining ideas; joining CCA as Gnomes for example, had seemed brilliant over patty melts. Now, three months later, college was becoming a rerun of high school.

Or so Beekman felt, as he ordered his food. "Burger and giganto-fry."

"Drink?" the waiter asked.

"A beer," Beekman said.

"Coke," the waiter said as he wrote, and walked away.

Oh well, Beekman thought. Life disappoints. Biff and Beekman had expected better. Both had heard gobs of Mozart through the uterine wall, and been given the brainiest toys money could buy. Through micromanagement of their schooling, and a schedule of lessons and playdates extensive enough to require a secretary, Biff and Beekman had been groomed impeccably. They were the best that American education had to offer, and their test scores confirmed this. But so was everybody else at Stutts. As a result, they were being thrown back on their somewhat shriveled personalities. *Something* had to be done, and Biff, as the more impulsive one, was determined to do it.

Beekman, as the more sensible one, sensed that there is such a thing as being too smart. In each other's presence, Biff and Beekman tended to push their brains too far and come back around on the other side, ending up incredibly stupid. Returning to their high school hangout as great big college men added a dash of hubris to the mix. And they had just gotten a bunch of money over the holidays. So the stage was definitely set for some bad idiocy.

Beekman was covering his food with a prophylatic layer of ketchup, then mashing it into a paste—standard operating procedure—when Biff bounced in.

"Niki!" Biff called out, like the cook was an old friend. "A cock-fry with cheese!" (All the Ponce kids called the Chubby's speciality—a wedge of fried potato roughly the length and girth of a penis—a "cock-fry." Beekman had been uncommonly polite by using its proper name, giganto; he thought it sounded like something that fought Godzilla.)

"Don't talk to me like I like you," the cook said forcefully.

236

To him, all Ponce kids looked the same. Like assholes.

Biff chuckled good-naturedly. The idea that any adult would actually dislike him—especially after "getting to know him"—was completely foreign. He waved at Beekman, who was attempting to hide behind his Coke. Biff strutted over to the booth and slid in.

"God, I love this place," Biff said, taking off his Stutts scarf. "It's good to be back. *Damn* good. Do you remember that time we came in after having that big bromthymol blue fight? Do you remember how everybody *stared?*"

"Yeah," Beekman said flatly. He remembered getting some in his eye.

"Have you considered what we talked about?" Biff asked. Then dropping to an excited whisper: "The contest, with that kid?"

"No," Beekman said. Here it comes, he thought, a toboggan ride to hell. Beekman came up with a lot of crazy ideas, he'd be the first to admit it. Talking about crazy ideas was fun. But Biff actually did them—Beekman never remembered that. Then, he had to argue Biff out of doing something he himself had suggested, which was nearly impossible. Once Biff fastened on to a plan, there was no stopping him, there was only triage.

"Well, I have. Check this out, Bubba Ho-Tep." Biff pulled a cellophane envelope out of the pocket of his peacoat and slapped it down on the table.

"Bubba who?" Beekman said, reaching for it. "I've been meaning to tell you: I really don't comprehend most of what you say."

Biff quickly grabbed it back. "Are your hands clean? This is five-thousand years old."

Beekman knew he could be messy, but he didn't appreciate how Biff harped on it. That's why he's not more popular, Beekman thought, covering a napkin with ketchup. He's too critical.

"Show me your hands." For his part, Biff thought that Beekman was so incredibly untidy that his parents should stand trial. After Beekman passed inspection, Biff handed him the envelope. Beekman untied it and removed the document. It was just a scramble of odd figures—he turned it upside down and tried to read it that way, then tried the reflection.

"Is it mirror writing?" Beekman said, covering one eye.

"What are you doing?" Biff snapped, pulling Beekman's arm down. "Do you want everybody to see?" Biff looked around, then whispered, "It's ancient Egyptian instructions on how to raise a mummy from the dead. You convinced me."

Beekman felt really stupid; giving Biff an idea was like giving a three-year-old a blowtorch. "You're kidding," Beekman said. "You got this over the Web or some shit."

"No. Honest to God, it's real."

Beekman felt a small heave of foreboding. Was this how everybody made him feel, or had he just gotten used to it through prolonged exposure to Biff? "I thought you were kidding. I thought all the radon in the basement had gotten to you."

"I've never been more serious in my life," Biff said. "Three and a half more years down in The Cage—I can't face it."

"Where'd you get it? You didn't—" Now it was Beekman's turn to look around and whisper. "You didn't steal it, did you?"

Biff laughed. "Hardly. I called up Cushing Mortimer Paley. They found it."

The waiter dumped Biff's cock-fry on the table with maximum disdain, sending his pickle spear bouncing to the floor. Biff missed the slight entirely. "Thanks," he said brightly. Dipping the heavy fry into the bright yellow cheese sauce, Biff said to Beekman, "I love the people here. They're really picturesque."

"What's Cushing whatever whatever?"

"A knowledge service. My dad uses them all the time." Biff's father was a venture capitalist. "You call them up and ask for everything on, say, bikini waxing in China, and CMP sends over a pile of documents, with a bill."

"Expensive?"

"Not when Dad is paying," Biff smirked. (The Paterno-dollar is truly a universal concept.)

"How is your dad's chain of Beijing waxing shops going?"

"He got out of that," Biff said. "Not enough body hair. He's into drinking-water now. People gotta have it. Anyway, I called CMP and asked them to find out about raising mummies. This is what they sent. It's a spell."

"Wow," Beekman said. "Do you believe it? Can you read it?"

"No, but I can read this." Biff pulled out another piece of paper, and they traded. Beekman dropped the document right into his ketchup-meat-and-potato smashup.

"Shit!" Biff said, grabbing the paper back and blotting it with his napkin. Several words were smeared. "I specifically asked you not to get crap on it, and then you—"

"You just got cheese sauce on it!" Beekman said.

"Immaterial." Biff was always brisk when he was defensive. "This is the phonetic pronunciation of the spell—well, most of it, anyway. When can you go up to school with me to try it out?"

"I don't know . . ." Beekman said, uncertain. He knew this feeling so very well.

"You came up with the idea! It was your suggestion!"

"I know, Biff, but . . .

"You wanna ki—" Biff lowered his voice. "—win the contest, don't you?"

"Yeah, but—"

"You wanna get out of The Cage, don't you?"

"Yeah, but—"

"*This* is the way to do it," Biff said. "I'm sure of it. It can't fail."

Taking all human history as a whole, no three words—not even "I love you"—have launched more disastrous endeavors than the phrase Biff had just used. Beekman sensed this, but he also knew Biff well enough to know that further argument was useless. He could twist and flop like a fish, but eventually Biff would reel him in, so why not save a lot of time and trouble? "Okay."

Biff wasn't satisfied. "You're just saying that. Don't say it if you don't want to do it. This is going to take *total commitment*. Are you totally committed?"

"I think *you* should be totally committed," Beekman said gruffly. "Yeah, sure, let's go raise a mummy. Then, if there's time, we can drive a stake through a vampire."

"Not funny." Biff leaned back. "You don't sound committed," he said, skeptically chewing his cock-fry.

Beekman looked at his watch. School was letting out soon. "Screw this—it's Christmas break," he said. "Let's go scam on the senior girls."

"For God's sake, that's lame."

"Oh, right. Why don't we go raise a mummy instead?"

"Fine," Biff said. "Stay down in The Cage if you want. I'll do it myself. The mummy and I will come by and say hi some night second semester, on our way back home from the Mugwumps' meeting, right before seeing our incredibly hot Brazilian girlfriends. Jerk," Biff sniffed.

This is where it always fell apart for Beekman, when he started to feel like he was being mean. "Don't be like that, Biff. It's just that . . . a lot of your plans don't always work out, that's all."

"They're *your* ideas."

"Yeah, but I don't actually do them. I know they're stupid," Beekman said.

Biff was insulted. "Stupid? Like when?"

"Streaking at that thing with the First Lady."

"Did we or did we not get talked about?" Biff asked. "We got in the damned *New York Post*, what more do you want? It's not my fault you couldn't turn our stardom into poontang. That was *your* job."

"Okay, how about the whole Gnome thing?"

"We both wanted to do that," Biff said defensively. "Okay, say we don't raise a mummy. What's your big plan to bust out of the frat?"

Beekman sat there picking glumly at the glop on his plate. He hated when Biff got like this.

Biff took a final bite of his cock-fry and chewed it piston-like. "I'm waiting."

"Transfer schools?"

"Hmm, let's think about this," Biff said mock-thoughtfully, tapping his finger over his lips. "What an incredibly boring idea. Would it work? Maybe—if I didn't fall asleep." Biff leaned back in his chair. "I really expect better from you, Beekman."

Beekman felt like he was being mean and being bullied at

the same time. "Okay, okay, I already said I'd help you!"

"Grand Central at noon? We'll take the train."

"Fine!" Beekman began to capture water in his straw by putting his thumb over the end. He was doing this to get back at Biff.

"I hate it when you play with your water," Biff said.

"Why does it bother you?" Beekman asked, delighted as usual that it did.

"I don't know, I'm not conehead Yttrium!" Biff snarled. "Just cut it out!"

The next day, Biff was late. Beekman sat in the waiting area of Grand Central Station gnawing a bagel, unfazed. Being Biff's friend always entailed a certain amount of waiting, and besides, Beekman was in no hurry to board the uncomfortable, foul-smelling train.

Presently he saw Biff trotting across the floor, coat open, dropping a glove. He waved at Beekman, yelling his name. As Beekman tried to hide behind his bagel, Biff slammed into a lady leading a small child by the hand. They had a brief shouting match. He really spread joy wherever he went, did Biff. Beekman waited for the nasty scene to dissipate, then walked over to meet Biff.

"Sorry, I overslept," Biff said. "I was up all night hitting on Kiki's lame friends." Biff's sister went to Ponce, as did Beekman's brother, Freemason.

"Did you get anywhere?"

"No," Biff said. "I was too intellectual for them. Freemason wasn't there, just so you know."

"Why would I care?" Beekman said, as they walked toward the platform.

242

"I would care," Biff said. "Are you sure your bro's not gay?"

"What if he is?" Beekman said, annoyed. "Afraid he'll make a pass at you? I'm tired of your casual homophobia."

"Sorry . . ." Biff said, then quietly, ". . . fag." Avoiding Beekman's swipe, Biff skipped away, laughing.

"I *knew* you were going to say something like that! I really need to get some new friends. You're so goddamn depressing."

Biff stopped skipping. "You're being ironic, right?"

"No!" Beekman angrily stuffed the paperback he'd been reading into his bag.

"Oh, let's stop bickering," Biff said. "I hate it when you get oversensitive."

"It's not bickering if you're being a jerk," Beekman said. "And I'm not being oversensitive, you're turning into a frat-rat ass-clown." They walked down a tunnel full of diesel exhaust and ozone; meanwhile, all the things that Beekman didn't like about Biff suddenly crowded into his mind. Biff ate *only* boysenberry Smiling Bacillus yogurt—no other flavor or brand was acceptable. And Biff was scared of the color green. Who the fuck was scared of a color? As they settled into their seats, Beekman took comfort in his friend's myriad failings and neuroses—the only really dependable comfort that this life affords.

Beekman read. Biff tried to sleep but couldn't. He took off his shoe and offered it to Beekman. "Could you knock me unconscious?" he asked. "I feel like I'm riding through a crime scene," Biff said, looking out of the smeary Plexiglas window.

The route juttered through the ruins of ten New England towns, each grimier and more job-free than the last, with Great Littleton squatting at the end like some sort of hobo king. The squalidness of the stops seemed to rub off somehow; the trains themselves were awful, a testament of man's inhumanity to man.

"I think they make these trains shitty on purpose," Beekman said, "just to make the vacation ads on the walls look better." He shifted position fruitlessly—the seats, stick-to-the-flesh vinyl, waged an all-out war against comfort. Every surface was hard plastic or stainless steel. This was done for ease of cleaning, an operation that, as far as any passenger could tell, remained wholly theoretical. Fluorescent lights glared down from the ceilings, advertisements shouted from every corner. The décor was stolen from a flyspecked, off-brand, failing fast-food joint. The bathrooms—especially important for Beekman, who felt every jolt and jostle of the ride in his stomach—were wreathed in noxious fumes, thanks to a chemical originally developed to deforest Southeast Asia.

"Look at that woman," Biff said, pointing at an ad. "She looks like she's coming. It's just Bermuda, for God's sake."

"Can women get orgasms from hammocks? I've heard of that happening on motorcycles."

"You've got to stop reading *Penthouse* Forum," Biff said. He got out a key and began scratching something into the Plexiglas window.

Once, things had been different on the train. Before the line had been modernized, the trains were plusher, the ride more pleasant. Now, commuters were shuttled with all the tender care shown aspirin bottles on a production line. But the train actually took longer than it had before; each little comfort destroyed in the name of efficiency had actually added up to a net loss. So more people drove, and the train grew more and more threadbare. The riders, taking their cue from their surroundings, whiled away the trip with casual vandalism.

"Next time we should drive your car," Beekman said, returning from the men's room.

Biff was finished. "Check it out," he said proudly: school and class year, right where all the commuters would see it. The boys smiled. It wasn't immortality, but it was something.

If the train had been a two-hour lesson in the evils of the modern world, the University Museum showed that the past was no paradise, either. Established in 1803 as "a storehouse of everything wond'rous and useful," the University Museum had immediately degenerated into a mammoth collection of crap. Utterly useless in every other way, it was illuminating from a psychological standpoint, suggesting that the Victorian mania for curios was an organic disorder masquerading as a hobby. As the chute in Hart's office made clear, *every* gentleman who had gone to Stutts before 1900 collected something, and each of them felt entitled to donate it to the University Museum. As a result, Stutts had the world's definitive collection of antimacassars, as well as a wonderful selection of Civil War uniform buttons, decorative beaded snoods, and God knows what else.

One of the things that had been collected by the richer run of Stutts alumni was antiquities. This meant that, in addition to a constant stream of mail from irritated governments asking for their stuff back, the University Museum had a basement full of mummies.[57]

Biff and Beekman walked through the museum, appraising the mummy collection like no visitor had ever done before.

---

[57] Typically, when the collector died, the collector's wife or children shipped the whole lot to the U.M. with a triumphant note saying, "He's finally dead—now *you* find a place for it!"

"How about this one?" Beekman said. "Looks like most of his face is still on."

"Yeah, but look at his arm," Biff said. "The kid we're trying to kill is eighteen—the mummy's going to need both arms. Anyway, don't look at the mummy, look at the label." For each mummy, the museum had used a computer to reconstruct what the individual had looked like in life. "How about this one? He's in better shape."

"Doesn't look very strong," Beekman sniffed. Biff had turned down all of his choices.

"So we'll bulk him up a bit," Biff said. "Send him to the gym, feed him spaghetti . . . "

"What do mummies eat?"

"I don't know—scarabs?" Biff said with irritation. "Do you think there's a handbook? Are you living in a goddamn *fantasy world*? Raising mummies is a strictly do-it-yourself thing," Biff said. "And I don't mind that. It will give me a greater sense of accomplishment."

Beekman walked into the other room, miffed. Fine, he thought. Do it yourself, then. I'll let him pick out the mummy. I'll let him do everything, and then I'll slide in at the end, if the mummy actually kills the kid. Otherwise, Biff can go screw himself. Wait—would Biff sic the mummy on *him*? That'd be totally like Biff, Beekman thought. He'd better make sure that the mummy was somebody he could take in a fight.

Beekman saw a massive sarcophagus in the corner of the room. It was hewn from pink granite, and covered with Plexiglas. There were small handprints all over the Plexiglas: an exitable, caramel-covered school group had come through earlier that day. At the moment, however, the museum was relatively empty, and Beekman was getting the creeps. He wanted to pick the mummy, raise it, and get the hell out of here.

Biff ambled up. He, on the other hand, was enjoying himself.

"How about this one?" Beekman said, trying to move things along.

Biff appraised the figure in the sarcophagus like a housewife picking out a roast. "Looks kinda scrawny."

"He's a kid," Beekman said, pointing to the label. "We can beef him up. Enough protein shakes, and this guy will be ready for the Green Berets."

Biff read the label on the wall. "'Nubhotep, the twelve-year-old son of a Third Dynasty King. The fracture at the back of the skull suggests that Nubhotep died as the result of foul play.'" Biff paused, considering this, then said. "Nah, I hate kids. They're annoying."

"No, you only hate your sister. *She's* annoying."

"What if he's got diseases?"

"I have some antibiotics left over from our trip to Cancun last year," Beekman said. (He'd sorta hoped he'd get an STD, but all he came back with was a bad sunburn.)

"Okay," Biff said. "Let's do him. He'll be younger and easier to control. Come with me."

"Where are we going?"

"To the gift shop," Biff said. "The spell doesn't give him clothes."

Ten minutes later, they returned to the sarcophagus with plastic bags full of clothes in various sizes. "We'll return the stuff we don't need," Biff said. "Go close the doors. Do you have the sign?"

"Yeah," Beekman said. He had swiped a CLOSED FOR

RENOVATION sign from the truly disgusting exhibit[58] next door. Hanging the sign on the outer knob, Beekman closed the doors.

"All right," Biff said, pulling out the spell translation. "Get ready, 'cause you may have to say it with me."

Beekman's good sense kicked in. "Biff, are you sure . . . ?"

"I'm sure, I'm sure," Biff snapped. He cleared his throat and began to read. "Okay. 'Vulture, vulture, kind of like a foot or something, owl, owl, mouth, hand, snake, foot (I don't care, that's what I'm calling it), arm, arm, foot again, then there's the part you ruined . . .'" He shot Beekman a look. "Vulture, sun, rabbit, beer jug . . .'"

"Cool!"

". . . another part you got crap on, hope it's not important . . .'"

This continued for quite a while. When it ended, Biff threw himself on the floor.

"Why did you do that?" Beekman asked.

"I didn't know if there was going to be an explosion," Biff said, getting up and brushing himself off. "I didn't want to get pulled back to ancient Egypt."

"So it's okay for *me* to get sucked into the time-space continuum . . ." Beekman complained. "What do we do now?"

"Wait, I guess."

The pair waited. Beekman laid out a few T-shirts, shorts, and flip-flops, all in different sizes. He occupied the time by comparing various combinations.

"What are you doing?" Biff asked.

"Trying to see which outfit looks best."

Biff started to make a comment, then stopped and said, "I

---

[58] The Dung Pottery of Lake Titicaca.

smell McDonald's. Wanna go get McDonald's? If he's not alive and walking around in ten minutes, we'll go get a burger." To encourage school groups, the museum had put in a McDonald's. Its collections were slowly beginning to smell like grease.

The boys were getting bored. "Don't check your watch so much," Biff said. "It makes the time go slower." Finally, Biff was prepared to throw in the towel.

"Oh, well," Beekman said, secretly very glad. "Back to the drawing board."

They heard a very weird sound. "URK!"

Biff smacked Beekman. "Shh! The guard will come!"

"I didn't say anything," Beekman said.

There was another sound, burbly and guttural. Whoever it was didn't sound well.

"Okay, dicknose, what's the idea with the ventriloquism?"

"It's not me, I swear!" Excited (and a little frightened), the boys peered into the sarcophagus.

Biff gave a whoop, then covered his mouth quickly. "Take the clothes and stick 'em in the crack of the door. We gotta muffle the sound." As Beekman did so, Biff went over to the sarcophagus. Through the Plexiglas he saw a boy sitting up unsteadily, holding his head.

"Shhh!" Beekman had joined him and began miming various symbols of silence.

He didn't need to. With a final moan, the boy toppled over, dead.

Biff and Beekman were silent. Then Beekman said, "Great spell, dude."

"Shut up!" Biff said. "It raised him, it just didn't make him immortal, which is probably a good thing. Do you want to have a mummy following you around for the rest of your life?"

"No," Beekman said, "but I didn't wanna come up here in the first place."

"Too bad," Biff said. "It's your fault for picking a mummy with a hole in its head!"

"How was I supposed to know that's how he died?"

"Read the little card next to the sarcophagus!" Biff said angrily. "I'm outta here." He stomped out of the exhibit and didn't even wait for Beekman to get into the cab to the train station.

Neither boy spoke until they were halfway home. Just as the train pulled out of Stamford, Beekman got that look. "I wonder," he said, "if there's such a thing as a remote-control flame-thrower."

CHAPTER FOURTEEN

BY THE END of winter break, Hart was ready to gnaw his leg off. During the flight back to school, he nearly had to: his bargain airline ticket was on a near-bankrupt carrier known for its excellence in food poisoning. Then, after landing in New York, he had to endure that rolling offense to humanity, the commuter train. The last leg—and final insult—was a beat-up, pee-smelling cab.

"Hallelujah!" Hart shouted at the sight of Stutts' Civil War–era shot tower. "Thank you, Jesus!" he yelled, hands waving like a holy roller. Hart kissed the ground in front of Dacron, then headed directly into the dining hall to make up for a day's worth of missed meals. It's difficult to whistle happily while eating clam chowder, but Hart managed just fine.

Hart's joy wasn't unique. The whole college greeted each other as comrades-in-arms, back where they belonged and anxious to resume writing the next chapter in their triumphant life stories. As trying as it could be, most Stutts students enjoyed their experience (while complaining about it).

The next day, feeling reabsorbed into Greater Stutts, Hart

walked over to his mailbox. Among the usual flurry of credit card applications, Hart recognized a letter from Mr. Darling's lawyer. He breathed a sigh of relief. It was time to deposit next semester's tuition. Hart didn't like to owe anybody money, much less the Stutts University bursar's office. And it was a lot of money, too: $75,000. The bursar's office charged rates of interest that made the local Mafia don shake his head.

Hart tore open the letter and felt for a check—nothing. He looked inside, then shook it. Nothing cashable fluttered to the ground. An icy claw grabbed his heart and squeezed.

"Dear Mr. Fox," the letter began. "My client was highly disturbed to find your name in the Recently Punished column of the *Stutts Alumni Magazine*.[59] Several days later, he was even more dismayed to receive a mailing from the university. They are using your sorry exploits to spearhead an emergency fundraising campaign, 'Stutts Can Smell Good Again.'

"Though President Whitbread may find your antics useful, I assure you that my client does not. Since Mr. Darling's connection to you is well known throughout the university administration, and the purpose of your arrangement with my client was to shield the reputation of the Darling family, these are grave circumstances.

"Furthermore, it has come to my attention that the young Mr. Darling has been injured. As Trip's guardian, academic and otherwise, damage to his buttock represents another failure on your part.

"As a result of this and earlier violations, both in letter

---

[59] This magazine was a monthly chronicle of Stutts' alumni love/pretend-hate relationship with their educational attainment. Recent cover stories had included "Our Burden," "The Mugwumps' Pyramid—Happiest Place on Earth," and "Arrogance: Sin or Social Good?"

and in spirit, my client has decided to terminate the agreement. As of the above date, you will receive no payments, aid, or assistance of any kind from Mr. Darling, his family, or any other subsidiaries. Any questions you have regarding this matter, while useless, should be addressed to my lawyers."

As Hart read, a numbness spread from his heart to his entire body. He slumped against the wall of mailboxes. Then, after his brain rebooted, Hart thought: Wow. A lawyer with lawyers, that's hardcore.

Hart spent the rest of the day in a daze. This turn of events wasn't illogical—Mr. Darling *was* a bastard—but it altered Hart's life so quickly, and in such a basic way that Hart found it hard to think of it as real. When he broke the news that night at the C&E, his fellow Good Eggs were anything but dazed. They were angry.

"He didn't even tell you himself?" Reed asked. "How chickenshit can you get? I've never met a rich guy who wasn't a coward."

"As I recall, nobody's starving at your house," Ellen said.

"I'm talking *rich*-rich," Reed said. "We're just upper middle-class." Everybody at Stutts considered themselves upper middle-class, even the ones whose family homes had helicopter pads.

"Can't you just apply for financial aid?" Ellen asked.

"Not in the middle of the year," Hart said glumly. "And even if I could, my dad would have to reveal the location and amounts of his assets, and the moment he does that, they'd all be seized by Interpol."

"Oh," Ellen said.

"Fuck the lawyers, I say we torment the *shit* out of Trip." Peter said.

"I'll torment him, all right," Tabitha fumed. "I'll fly up his nose, then reconstitute in his skull. Nobody treats my boyfriend like that."

"Wait," Reed said. "I thought Satan was your boyfriend."

"That's just a figure of speech," Tabitha replied.

"Speaking of you and Hart . . ." Ellen paused, trying to put it delicately. "I think Hart should find another place to sleep."

There were cries of protest from the rest of the group. Hart kept silent. It didn't seem appropriate for him to have an opinion.

"Ellen, couldn't this wait? Today's the exact wrong time to talk about this." Turning to the others, Reed said, "You've got to excuse my friend. She's unfamiliar with the ways of carbon-based life-forms."

"He doesn't have anywhere else to go!" Peter said.

"The office reeks of sex," Ellen said bluntly. "I'm just asking for a temporary relocation, so it can . . . dissipate a little."

Reed wasn't convinced. "Don't pin this on Hart and Tab. It's always stunk. Sex is an improvement from sweat and Cheetos."

"Ah, that's it," Hart said. He'd never quite been able to place the smell.

"I had no idea you were such a prude," Tabitha said coldly.

"I'm not!" Ellen was really defensive now. This was the part she didn't like about running the magazine; she was always forced to play the adult. "We need a useable office. The air's so thick in there that any new female staffers would run a very real risk of spontaneous impregnation."

"Oh, bullshit," Reed grumbled.

"Come on, Ellen," Peter said. "Who here votes to keep Hart in the office . . . ?"

Ellen, seeing that she was losing, sighed and said, "Okay, look—I didn't want to get into this, but a friend of mine who works in Whitbread's office says that Hart's on the official watch list."

"What's that mean?" Hart asked. He was feeling more and more like something the body of Stutts was determined to excrete.

"And who's this friend?" Reed said. "It isn't that Dork von Tool from Mugwumps, is it?"

"Yes, it is." Ellen said, a little defiantly. Dirk von Thule had been really friendly to her lately.

"I've been here since the 1850s, and I've never heard of an official watch list," Tabitha said. "It sounds like bullshit to me."

"Maybe, but I'm afraid I'm going to have to insist," Ellen said. "Dirk also saw Hart's rustication order, and it says that any group that allows Hart to use its on-campus facilities to evade the order will be shut down."

"And you believe Dirk?" Reed asked.

"Why would he lie?" Ellen countered.

"Sorry, I forgot—Mugwumps guys are known for their truthfulness," Peter said with heavy irony. It was common knowledge that Wumpsmen took a solemn oath to tell the truth inside the group, but to lie to outsiders whenever doing so might gain the group an advantage.

"So if the university finds out I'm sleeping in the office, they'll close the magazine?" Hart asked.

Ellen nodded.

"Well, then I'll leave," Hart said. "Tab, can I crash at your place for a while?"

"Sure," Tabitha said. "I'll slip the caretaker a little extra this month. But do me a favor: don't come before midnight, just to keep the hassle down to a minimum."

"If somebody sees me, I'll say I'm on a scavenger hunt or something."

That night, after everybody else had left the office, and Hart waited for the clock to strike twelve, he and Peter talked.

"Why does Trip hate me so much?" Hart asked, almost plaintively. "Why do they all hate me? All I do is help them— I cut their lawn, I kept their kid in school . . ."

"The Darlings don't hate you," Peter said blandly. "Hating you would be recognizing you. The Darlings try to pretend you don't even *exist*."

"That famous quote is right," Hart griped. "The very rich *are* different from you and me. They're assholes."

"*Very* rich?" Peter sniffed. "Don't give them so much credit; to the people who really run things, the Darlings are little fish."

"Bigger fish than me."

"For the moment," Peter said. "Look, if you want to hurt them—"

"I do!" Hart said.

"— you have to understand them. Trip and his dad know they're not smart. Money is the only thing they've got. They hate themselves for needing your help, so they push you down, partly as a reflex, but also to reassure themselves that they're not slipping. The boredom and fat living—they know it's taking a toll. They're worried."

Hart didn't say anything. Fully warmed to his subject, Peter continued. "Treating you like dirt isn't personal—it's just the toxic by-product of them being shit-scared. And you *do* scare them, Hart. Make no mistake about that. You're their natural enemy, a striver—a smart, ambitious kid who has wormed into the inside but hasn't been bought off yet. Guys like you are in their nightmares: the lawyer with the class-action suit, the prosecutor that breaks up the monopoly, the general that leads the coup. Bonaparte, Lenin, Franklin Roosevelt—strivers."

"Oh, come on," Hart said. "FDR was rich."

"You come on," Peter said. "He said that not getting into Mugwumps was the biggest disappointment of his life—really rich people either get in, don't care, or both. He was rich like the Darlings are rich, near the top, not at it. To people at the top, you and the Darlings look the same. And the Darlings know that. They know they can be replaced—and people like you are the ones that take their places."

Hart rubbed his temples. "This is making my head hurt. How about if I just hate them and leave it at that?"

"Suit yourself," Peter said.

The Walk of Shame—that is, a lover's early-morning trudge back home—takes a certain kind of fortitude under the best of circumstances. It's even worse sneaking out of a crypt. After the third uncomfortable scene,[60] Hart decided that it was time to get a new job—at least he could pay for a bed somewhere. But with the Day of Stink still lingering in the nostrils of recent history, who would hire the man who launched a thousand lunches?

Like every other undergrad, Hart was totally ignorant of the various cold wars that crackled beneath the civilized surface of the university. But had the Stutts bookstore carried an organizational chart showing who hated whom, Hart would've

---

[60] "Lady, I told you—I'm not a necrophiliac, I'm rushing a frat!"

known that there was one person for whom his supposed pranking made him irresistible: Fanton Mandrake.

Mandrake ran the University Museum. His sworn enemy, administratively speaking, was Mr. Charivaria. The functions of the UM and the archives of the library were simply too close for either man's comfort, and each was constantly trying to knock the other out. While this one-upmanship made for a blizzard of fascinating (and sensationalistic) exhibits on campus, neither organization could whup the other decisively. The University Museum could get on the front page of the *Times* Arts and Leisure section with "Etruscan Pin-Up Art," and two weeks later, the Library would counter with "Sex Toys from the Vatican Collection" and even bigger crowds.

But the Day of Stink—plus the cleanup and the investigation—had brought Mr. Charivaria's department to a standstill. Dr. Mandrake was determined to put some distance between himself and his rival. So he was very grateful to the student he *thought* was responsible.

"We don't usually hire the rusticated," Dr. Mandrake said in the not-quite-Boston-not-quite-Britain mid-Atlantic accent peculiar to all Stutts faculty members. "One bad apple, you know." Dr. Mandrake adjusted his eye patch. (He was giving up smoking.) "But in this case, I think we'll make an exception."

"Thank you, Dr. Mandrake. I won't let you down." Hart was genuinely grateful for the job, but these days, no positive feeling seemed to last very long.

Sure enough, forty-eight hours later, he was *pissed*. Soaked in sleet, Hart stood in the middle of New Quad, dressed as a Hopi medicine woman. He was handing out flyers to promote the museum's newest exhibit, "Drug Abusers of the Old West." "All the peyote you can eat," he yelled listlessly.

Unwittingly, Hart had become the museum's latest "Community Interface Specialist." This job was perennially on the *Spec*'s annual list of the worst student gigs on campus.[61] Others included Research Monkey Neuterer and Pesticide Taster.

"Howdy, ma'am!" Peter hollered that night at dinner. Hart had shown up in his togs.

"Don't go there," Hart said morosely.

"It's a job, right?" Peter said, trying to be cheerful.

Hart refused to be cheered. "Tomorrow I have to wear the giant squid costume." The tentacles trailed forty feet and were constantly getting stuck on stuff.

"Is that for the documentary? I was just reading the table tent," Peter said. "'Giant Squid, Garbo of the Deep, Join the intrepid crew of the research ship *Insipid* as they fail to find one of the ocean's most mysterious creatures.' Sounds somniriffic."

"Just another of Stutts' 'delightful smorgasbord of intellectual opportunities,'" Hart said, ironically quoting the speech President Whitbread gave them the very first weekend they were on campus. September seemed far, far in the past.

Peter smiled at the reference; they had quoted such stuff back and forth all first semester. "I'll come with you, for moral support."

Dr. Mandrake's assistant, Paula, actually looked sorry for Hart as she helped him into the costume. "Try not to let the tentacles get run over," she said, activating the light-up hat. Hart promised he wouldn't, but once he was strapped into the

---

[61] Dr. Mandrake was notorious for covering the CIS employment agreement with a contract for another, much cushier position. However, the uppermost contract was carbon paper, so when the student signed up for "Mummy Duster" or "Amber Arranger" or something easy, his or her signature would be transferred to the CIS contract below. Hart had been the first person in a decade to sign up willingly.

costume, it was difficult; dragging that much tentacle, it was hard to do much of anything. Peter had helped him get into position in front of the theater, where he was supposed to "engage passersby in squid-related small talk." Paula had given him a stack of little slips of paper to pass out.

PUNY HUMAN!!!
THIS is as close as you will get to
the Giant Squid!!!
If you were a fish, you would be DEAD.
Since you aren't a fish, come see the
terrifying new documentary,
TENTACLES
Samuel Insull Auditorium
Tuesday · 8:00 P.M.

"Whoops." An icy gust blew the entire stack out of Hart's freezing hand. He galumphed slowly after the twirling paper, but after four steps, he had to stop to catch his breath.

"Forget it," Peter said. "There's nobody here anyway." He took a sip of coffee.

"Where'd you get the coffee?" Hart asked.

"Flick the Bean," Peter said, naming a new coffee shop/sex toy emporium. "I go there to pick up the ladies. I figure, they're already thinking about sex . . ."

"Yeah, with people they *already* know."

"You might be right," Peter admitted. "I got hit on the head with a Pyrex dildo."

The two freshmen shivered in the deserted New Quad, outside the bunkerlike building where the movie was to be shown. It was a terrible night, cold and icy. Through an unfortunate quirk of meterology, Great Littleton possessed a unique, particularly horrible microclimate: for eight solid months every year, it was able to combine piercing rain with bone-chilling cold to produce a kind of super-sleet. A mile away in Science Hole, defense department contractors were trying to re-create it in the lab, for use as a nonlethal weapon.

Hart's massive costume was just warm enough to keep him extremely uncomfortable. Peter fared better—his chair had a built-in heater.

"I think the sign suits you," Peter joked. Atop Hart's head, a series of tiny lightbulbs blinked "Behold! The squid!"

"What a drag," Hart said, surveying his lot. To fend off sinking spirits, he changed the subject. "What's Ellen doing tonight?"

"She's going to dinner with a bunch of guys from Mugwumps."

"They're looking her over, huh? Makes sense, now that *The Cuckoo* actually publishes issues." Hart couldn't help wondering if he'd be having those same kind of dinners in a couple years. "When's Pinch Day?" Pinch Day was the day when all of Stutts' senior societies—and there were more every year—selected their new members for the following year.

"It's secret, of course. Sometime in late April, before finals," Pete said. You'd be walking around, like it was a normal day, and somebody would pinch you, hard. Then they'd yell, "[Name of society]—will you join?" If you said yes, you were then marched back to the group's temple—if it had one, and formally inducted, which usually included drunken nakedness, incense, and robes. It was all very Stutts.

"Did you give Ellen the same spiel you gave me? About how the Mugwumps are the source of all evil in the universe?"

"No," Pete said.

"No?" Hart said, a little outraged. "How come I get the rant and she doesn't? Christ, it was practically the first thing you said to me. 'Promise not to join Mugwumps.'"

"I never asked you to promise that," Pete protested. "I just said *I* wouldn't. Anyway, it's different with Ellen. She's told me a lot about how she grew up. She was poor, man. If Mugwumps can help her be successful, that might be the first good thing it's ever done."

"Come on," Hart said. "Ellen doesn't need to be in Mugwumps to succeed. How many patents does she have?"

"She doesn't like to talk about that," Peter said.

"Why not?" Hart asked. Some girls walked by, and Hart tried to look ruggedly handsome. This proved to be impossible in a giant squid costume; next time he'd try for pitiful.

"She thinks it will jinx her. There's the one for a building material made of cheese, and another for a genetically engineered spider that excretes soft-serve ice cream instead of silk . . . She told me all of them, once, but I've forgotten," Peter said. "Probably out of jealousy."

"You and Ellen have been hanging out a lot, huh?" Hart asked.

"Yeah," Peter said, then added quickly, "always more *Cuckoo* stuff to do. You know, it's not just that Ellen is poor, she also runs a magazine that makes fun of this place. She's not the kind of person who usually gets into Mugwumps, but she's probably the exact type who should."

Hart chewed this over, then asked, "Is anybody going to pinch Reed?"

"Puff and Tipple, looks like." Puff and Tipple had been founded in the mid-1700s, as a brotherhood of wastrels. Around 1900, it had changed into a collection of campus gour-

262

mands, after it was found that its alumni were dying of cancer and cirrhosis before the age of forty.

"That's a good fit," Hart said. Reed always stocked *The Cuckoo*'s fridge with exotic treats. Hart's thoughts turned to Ellen again. "Can you imagine, Ellen and Hayley Talbot swearing a blood oath to 'support and protect' each other? They'll have to, if they both get into Mugwumps."

"Success makes for strange bedfellows," Peter said. "I'm going to go watch the movie."

"I think you might be the only one in there."

"Call me on my cell if you get bored," Peter said.

Peter went inside. A student straining under the weight of an immense backpack staggered by. For some, the library was an addiction.

"Come see a movie," Hart said, flopping his tentacles without enthusiasm. "It's about a girl who finds love at the bottom of the ocean."

"Don't touch me, freak," the girl said.

Forty feet away, Biff and Beekman were tromping around in the ice and snow, collecting the ends of Hart's costume. Bundling the tentacles into their arms, walking slowly so as not to attract Hart's attention, they walked to a nearby car.

"This car is so damn cool," Beekman said. "Not like all your other pieces of shit."

"Thanks," Biff said. He'd sold all of his dad's golf clubs on eBay[62] and bought a cherry 1937 Buick hearse. It was massive, black, and bulbous, like a steel insect. "I'm thinking of getting

---

[62] Biff told his dad that his mom had done it. He rationalized this to Beekman by saying they were going to get divorced soon anyway.

it painted up. What should I do? You're the humanities guy."

Beekman thought. "How about that girl in a bikini silhouette that you see on the mud flaps of eighteen-wheelers? Or that cartoon character pissing on a Chevy logo?"

"I think that's copyrighted," Biff said. "I don't want to have to pay for it."

"It's not copyrighted, I invented it," Beekman said. The number of things he claimed to have invented were legion. "I came up with that the same day I designed the Star of David."

"You didn't invent the Star of David," Biff said. "You're not even Jewish."

"I did too! You weren't there, how do you know? I drew it in study hall in eighth grade!"

"You saw it somewhere and copied it—just like 'Pub_ic Library.'"

This was a sore spot; Beekman had claimed for years that he'd been the first person to think of this prank. Agreeing to disagree, they threw the tentacles into the open back window, then rolled up the glass so that the tentacles were secure. "Is it tight enough?" Beekman worried. "Will it hold? He probably put on a little weight over break."

"It'll be fine," Biff said, walking to the front seat and getting in. After the mummy debacle, the pair were down in the mouth and resigned to let someone else kill their way into the Mugwumps. But the resilience of youth, plus a few days in The Cage, was all that was necessary to get them to try again.

This time, they were really planning: they were following Hart, learning everything about him that they could. They decided he would be most vulnerable in the giant squid costume, which was essentially a straitjacket with crazy-long arms.

"I wish we had a remote-control blimp," Beekman mused.

"Don't even start," Biff said. He was determined to keep it simple this time around.

Beekman took a swig of peppermint schnapps to steady his nerves, then handed it over, coughing. Biff declined. "I'm driving, dillweed."

Beekman finished it off and threw it into the back. The schnapps was the father of this harebrained, last-minute plan. "Biff, are you sure this is unsafe? We want to kill him, not just scrape him up a bit."

"Don't you worry—I just put a new engine in this baby." To prove his point, Biff gunned the engine powerfully.

The noise fired Beekman's enthusiasm. "Brothers forever!" he yelled. This was gonna be great! In an hour, what's-his-name would be dead, and they would be Mugwumps. And killing him this way meant they wouldn't even have to do extra laundry! Biff slammed the car into gear, and the tires caught with a squeal.

"*Freak*, huh?" The unsuspecting Hart was carefully crafting a tardy riposte for the already absent girl. Then, all the tentacles went taut, and he was yanked off his feet.

Looking back, Beekman saw Hart fly into the air. He shouted with glee as Hart began to bounce along the asphalt behind them. "Let's drag him all the way to New York!"

Watching the New Quad recede at great speed, Hart was quite a bit less celebratory. Physically, he was fine; the snow and ice on the roads had been compacted, and he was gliding over the slick surface effortlessly. But this was exactly what Paula had warned against—he'd probably have to buy a whole new costume, and end up more broke than when he took the job! Hart saw sympathy as the only way out; whatever happens to the suit had better happen to me, too.

265

The CCA Gnomes whooped some more, pounding the dashboard and steering wheel. The Mugwumps—the most secret, most powerful, coolest society ever—was only a short car ride away! They didn't know *why* they wanted to be Wumpsmen, but everybody else seemed to, so it must be cool, right? As they slalomed through Great Littleton's windy streets, Biff and Beekman were suddenly alarmed not to hear any screaming.

Beekman looked back. "He's sliding! The mother's just sliding!" He grabbed Biff's shoulder in the excitement.

"I told you: never touch me when I'm driving!" Biff was a nervous driver.

"I think that son of a bitch is laughing at us!"

Biff saw a road sign and knew what he had to do. "I'm taking him on the turnpike. We'll see who's laughing then."

Moments later, Hart saw the sign too. Maybe this happened to everybody who wore the costume, sort of like a hazing thing for new employees. But the turnpike was going to be full of the general public, people who wouldn't be able to keep college hijinks in the proper perspective. And it would be plowed, so Hart wouldn't glide so much as grind. Hart decided it was time to call for help. Jouncing along, it was harder than hell to dial the phone. Peter picked up.

"This movie *blows*," Peter said. "A bunch of guys are going down in this submarine that looks like a female giant squid, hoping that a real male squid will try to—"

"Shut up for a second. My tentacles got stuck in somebody's car and they're dragging me."

"You crazy college kids."

"Pete, we're headed toward the turnpike."

Peter got a lot more concerned. "On purpose?"

266

"Maybe. I can't talk, I—" Hart hit a pothole painfully and the phone was knocked out of his hands.

"Hart! Hart!" Peter left the building, then hit the street with maximum speed. There was only one road to the turnpike, and Peter blew through the stoplights, thanks to a rotating red light and siren he'd just installed on his chair. He saw the hearse, with Hart attached to the rear, stopped up ahead. Peter poured it on, topping thirty now; he'd never pushed his chair to this kind of speed. He said a silent prayer for the snow tires he'd just developed.

As the hearse accelerated from the stoplight, Biff glanced in the rearview mirror. "We've got company," he said to Beekman. "Go back there and throw shit at him."

Beekman clambered into the back. The cavernous compartment was loaded with empty cans and bottles. Each of these became a deadly missile, hurled with maximum hate (if minimum accuracy) by the tipsy Beekman.

"How you like that?" Beekman said, as Peter weaved to avoid bottle after bottle. "Come and get some, cripple! We're gonna kill you and your buddy!"

Peter avoided most of Beekman's tosses quite easily, but after a lucky shot glanced off his wheel, he decided to quit fooling around. He pressed a button, and a large rotating machine gun folded out into position. Another button, and it began to fire.

"Shit!" Beekman screamed, pulling in his head. (They were blanks, but Beekman didn't know that.) He cowered in the backseat, pulling his battered, soggy cloche down over his ears. "He's crazy!"

Now it was Biff's turn to weave and dodge, and that, combined with the snowy road, made him slow down. Peter was able to get three feet from Hart—then his battery gave out.

Hart, meanwhile, had been watching this whole engagement with enjoyment—what else could he do? He was mildly alarmed to hear Beekman's declaration, and wondered what he could've done to deserve such a fatwa. He didn't wonder too much, however; ever since he'd gotten to Stutts, things just seemed to happen to him. More puzzling was Peter's abrupt dropping back. Oh, well—Peter would come through, he always did.

Peter himself was less sure. Stopped, he dialed Tabitha's number on his cell phone. He couldn't move; the chair's battery read two percent, just enough to keep the heater going. Not expecting a high-speed chase, Peter had left the house without charging up, and at nighttime, the solar panels were useless.

Tabitha answered. "Thank God you called, Peter. I'm on the other line with my great-great-grandmother, and she just called Hart a garlic-eater!"

"Well, the garlic-eater's getting dragged behind a car."

"He's what? Is this one of your stupid pranks?"

"They're not stupid, they're attempts to make people see our shared reality in a different—forget it, just get over to the Great Littleton entrance to the Benedict Arnold Expressway as fast as you can!"

"How will I tell which car it is?" Tabitha caught herself. "Sorry, stupid question."

"Hurry!" Peter hung up.

These kids today, Tabitha thought. She clicked over to her great-great-grandmother and tossed out a lie. "Gotta go eat, Gran—that was the hospital with my takeout." Truncating her ancient relation's sermon on the benefits of fresh food, the perky bloodsucker went into action. Mistifying, Tabitha billowed out the window and into the night air.

"Cool car." She saw Biff's hearse zipping through a quiet, residential neighborhood toward the expressway. Throughout her centuries of education, Tabitha had picked up a little on the workings of a car. Riding currents down to the street, she insinuated herself under the hearse's hood and into its carburetor. Blocking the oxygen, Tabitha-as-mist slowly strangled the engine.

"God-fucking-damn it!" Biff shouted as the engine died. "I just put a new engine in this thing!" Another semester of derision bloomed in Biff's mind as the car rolled to a stop.

Beekman turned on his pal. "Man, your cars suck," he said.

Biff twisted the ignition key again and again. Finally he gave up and began to cry quietly, head against the wheel.

Tabitha seeped out from under the hood and reconfigured herself.

"Something's on the roof!" Beekman yelled.

Standing atop the hearse, Tabitha took out the whistle she wore around her neck and blew a silent note. Suddenly, a wave of rats—Tabitha's ribbon-clad brood, plus hundreds of hangers-on looking for fun—poured out of a nearby storm drain. They scrambled all over the car.

Beekman screamed. The rodents squirted furrily into the back compartment, forcing themselves through the gap in the window made by Hart's tentacles. Beekman scrabbled at the door handle.

"Where are you going?" Biff asked. "What about 'Brothers forever'?"

"Screw that!" As the first rat began exploring his pants cuff, Beekman got the door open and skittered out into the night. Tabitha leaned over—Biff saw her head hanging upside down, looking at him from the passenger side. Their eyes met; she crooked her finger.

"Me?" Biff asked stupidly. He exited the car meekly.

Tabitha leapt to the ground. "What's the big idea dragging my boyfriend around?"

"We were just having fun . . ." Biff said. Then Tabitha turned her vampire mojo on him, and the truth sprang out of Biff like iron filings to a magnet. "We were trying to kill him."

"Why?"

"Everybody in Comma Comma Apostrophe is doing it."

"Young man, peer pressure is no reason to kill somebody," Tabitha said. "Why is 'everybody'"—she crooked her fingers to denote quote marks—"trying to kill a poor freshman?"

"Trip's dad said whoever kills what's-his-name gets into Mugwumps."

"Oh, *those* idiots," Tabitha said, rolling her eyes. "All right. Get out of here," Tabitha said, releasing Biff from her power.

"Can I have my car back?"

Tabitha fixed Biff with a look, giving him a glimpse of his own mortality. Biff wet himself a little, then ran, disappearing into a backyard.

Tabitha opened the rear window and unpinned the tentacles of Hart's costume. Then she got in the car, turned it around, and picked up Hart, who by this time was standing on the side of the road, tapping on the battery pack of his head sign, trying to get it to light up again.

He slid into the passenger seat. "Thanks, Tab."

"Don't mention it," she said.

"Look, there's Peter." They stopped and loaded his chair into the back of the hearse.

"Hart, you're right," Peter said with a smirk. "Your new job *is* a drag."

CHAPTER FIFTEEN

IT WAS an awkward moment—telling somebody they're marked for death always is—but Hart took Tabitha's news surprisingly well. There were three reasons for this. First, the people trying to kill him were not ninjas, or even Mafia types. They were a bunch of beer-addled low-normals simply marking time before shuffling off to predictably disastrous careers on Wall Street.[63]

Second, Hart knew he was going to get kicked out of Stutts in May anyway. The bursar was content to let him rack up $75,000 worth of debt for the current semester, but after that, the game was over. In that twilight time before he dropped off to sleep, when all his worries came to the surface, Hart knew he should cut his losses. The smart thing to do was to leave school, go back home, and get a job slinging smoothies at the Great

---

[63] CCA brothers proudly claimed responsibility for the 1929 stock market crash. Whenever Hart tried to explain that there was nothing great about the Great Depression, and that was just a figure of speech, Trip accused him of "just being jealous."

American National Mall. But he just *couldn't*—he loved his life at Stutts too much. Getting killed by some mope from CCA would at least save him from a life of customer service.

Third—and most important—he and Tabitha had just had mind-shattering sex. "If you're undead, I don't *want* to be alive," Hart slurred. "You're an evil genius. You're like the Madame Curie of sex."

"I can't believe you're taking this so calmly," Tabitha said. (She always came back to the world more quickly than he did.) "I would be totally upset if I were you—and could die. It's just so *rude*."

"Don't move," Hart said alarmed. Then he caught himself. "Whoops. Sorry, my eyes were playing—I thought there was a squirrel in the bed, but it's just your . . ." He flopped back on the bed. Hart's brain felt like a tiny bb rolling around happily in his skull. "Why couldn't they have killed me before February?" he asked blithely. "That's just cruel." Hart was right: if T.S. Eliot had been fortunate enough to go to Stutts (he got wait-listed), he would've let April off the hook. February in Great Littleton was twenty-eight days' worth of raw, slushy, miserable hell.

"Tell me about it," Tabitha said, slipping into her underclothes. She'd lived through more of them than anyone. "Thank God for the parties." Over the centuries, Stutts students had learned to pack the month full of social gatherings, otherwise vast swaths of the campus would extinguish themselves. February passed in a ritualized haze of alcohol.

"Are there any more of those crackers around?" Tabitha kept a stash of human food for Hart's visits.

She tossed him a box. "Here's what is going to happen," Tabitha said, taking charge. "Twenty-four hour bodyguard duty. *Cuckoo* staffers take the daytimes, I'll take the nights."

"Don't you think that's a little excessive?" Hart asked, mouth full. "It's CCA—the only way they could kill me is if I became violently allergic to morons."

She threw Hart his shirt. "Why not be on the safe side? How many guys have a girlfriend who's immortal?"

"And *immoral*," Hart kidded. Then: "You're not indestructible, are you?"

"Why? Are you thinking of cheating on me?"

"God, no. What about sunlight?"

"Survivable. My moisturizer has sunscreen in it."

"A stake through the heart?"

Tabitha tapped her left breast. It made a stiff, metallic sound. "Kevlar sportsbra. It also keeps me from smuggling raisins."

Hart nodded. Women were fascinating: they had a lot more things to think about, even more so if they were vampires. "Don't the Twins get sweaty?"

"Tell that to the Van Helsing Society," Tabitha said, pulling a pink cable-knit sweater over her head. "Anyway, I'm not the one that has to watch out, it's you, Squinty."

"I hate it when you call me that," Hart said. "I can't help it."

"I don't want you to help it," Tabitha said. "I think it's cute."

The Stutts University bursar did not think Hart was cute. After the third letter demanding $75,000, Hart sent in his first month's earnings at the museum. The bursar scrawled, "Are you kidding?" across the envelope and sent it back.

"That's really obnoxious," Hart said, stuffing the correspondence back into its envelope. The smell of ramen noodles was beginning to make him sick, but Hart tried to keep in mind one of the few pieces of real wisdom his dad had ever imparted: "Life is like tee-ball: swing hard, then start running—good things will happen." Instead of giving up and going home, Hart kept ahead in his classes and worked hard at the museum. He'd find a way to pay for it somehow.

Hart was now sleeping at the University Museum, too. Apparently some mummy had exploded—humidity? Barometric pressure? Nobody knew exactly why. Hart moved into the empty sarcophagus, and after filling the bottom with packing peanuts, the pink granite box was a surprisingly cozy place to bunk. Hart's major difficulty was waking up in the mornings. The Plexiglas lid muffled most of the sound, and after Hart slept through his fourth class, he reluctantly bought an alarm clock. There was also a minor difficulty in that Hart had to make sure nobody saw him getting in and out of the tomb, but as long as he got rolling at a reasonable hour, things were fine.

One morning, however, Hart's alarm went off as a group of third graders were taking a tour of the Egyptian wing. The children were quite shocked to hear the sounds of the local "morning zoo" radio program emanating from inside a 5,000-year-old sarcophagus. When Hart sat up and gave his head a vigorous scratch, the kids screamed and scattered. Hart thought he was dead meat, but by the time the guard had come to investigate, he had sneaked under one of Sir Walter Raleigh's beds.

That was the closest he'd ever come to capture, and after that, Hart was a lot more careful. He slept with headphones connected to the radio. His living arrangements weren't perfect, but they were free, and Hart was determined to save every penny.

"What's $75,000 divided by nine dollars an hour?" he asked Peter as they trudged out of the post office and into an exuberant sleet storm.

"I'd rather not say."

Hart did the math himself. "I would have to work eight thousand, three hundred and thirty-three hours and twenty minutes this semester to pay my bill."

"Don't forget FICA."

"Let's say ten thousand hours," Hart said. "That's a nice, round, totally unreachable number."

"Cheer up," Peter said. "Where there's life, there's hope."

"And late fees," Hart said.

With every day that passed, Hart wanted to stay at Stutts more than ever. Surprisingly, it wasn't the grandeur of the place that held him, or the promise of a bright career (which was fading with every day the unpaid tuition bill compounded). It was Hart's friendships—and that glorious, useless thing, *The Cuckoo*—that had captured his heart.

Hart's classes were all right, but Study of Things didn't give you much room for choices—that was part of the winnowing process. S of T was a prestige major, rigorous without being too specialized, the kind of program that could lead to any job you wanted (provided you had the right connections, and let's face it, most Stutts students did). Graduating with a degree in the Study of Things meant that you knew a collection of isolated tidbits, interesting but ultimately useless facts that you didn't have to be taught to forget by your first employer. S of T made you a prime cut of raw material, unsullied by anything the least bit useful.

The combination of high prestige and tolerance for woolly

extemporizing meant that the S of T department was where tenured professors went to die. Every year for decades, these old warriors had been fighting off wave after wave of bright, ambitious, *fantastically irritating* Stutts students, and they were ready for a rest. S of T was that rest. But by the time Hart arrived on campus, all of them were completely burned out, twisted and snappish, like long-teased dogs.

On Mondays and Wednesdays, Hart attended a large lecture given by Professor Jacobs. He was Department Head of S of T—and, thanks to some elective surgery, a disembodied brain in a jar. "A body is a bother," he had famously said as a young instructor. "An imperfect container, distracting and ultimately immaterial." No mere theoretician or idle talker, bit by bit over the course of his life, Jacobs had paid to have himself pared down. He taught Obfuscatory Writing.

Wearing a crown of sensors, a brackish froth sloshing at the top of his clear canister, Jacobs spoke in a computer-generated voice piped directly into the PA system. The apparatus was alarming, repugnant, with Jacobs bobbing there like a bloated cauliflower soaked in salad oil. But after a while people got used to it—some people, anyway; Professor Jacobs always had the cutest graduate assistants on campus.

"Do you think that Jacobs and his assistants . . . ?" Hart whispered to a fellow student during a momentary break in the lecture. (A leggy blonde with a beaker of solution was topping off Jacobs' capsule.)

The other student was scandalized. "You need help! *How?*"

Hart had immense faith in the human sex drive. "Strap-on?" he offered playfully, and they both shuddered.

After Professor Jacobs came lunch, then Professor Wrightwood, who was much more conventional in appearance, but functionally worthless as a conduit of information. Setting fire to a pile of dollar bills would've been cheaper, and more useful, too—at least you could cook a hot dog over it. It was said that the drooling, doddering classicist had risen to the top of his field on the strength of eyewitness information. The indisputable fact was that years of teaching the same material had worn a groove in Wrightwood's brain far too deep for him to ever leap out of. Each lecture began differently, but at some point returned to the topic, The Roman Legion: Could it Win Today?

It was awful to sit through this pointless meander, loaded with spurious examples and invective against "modernophilia" again and again. More awfull still was the tongue-lashing Wrightwood dished out to anyone who suggested that anything was amiss. "Who's teaching this class? Would you like to come up and give the lecture?" Professor Wrightwood would bark, as the student attempted to crunch himself into a fist-size ball of mortification. "Is there *anyone else* who'd like to give an opinion about my lecture? Anyone . . . ? All right then. Now, legion versus aircraft carrier—an interesting question . . ."

Hart's Tuesdays and Thursdays were a bit easier to take. First thing in the morning—10:30—Hart had Professor Cook, who peppered her talks with so many foreign words and phrases that the university gave a foreign language credit.

After lunch, there was Professor Hickey, a broguey, mildew-smelling Irish import whose only real claim to fame was a desire to replace all the grass on campus with pool-table felt. Older students swore that slipping a few antigrass cracks into your essay was a sure route to an A. "But be smart. You just don't come out and say it—he'll think you're pandering. You've got to be sneaky, allusive, like only you and he know the truth."

Such expert-level brownnosing was at the heart of the Stutts experience.

Hart had only one class on Fridays, but it was intense, a small seminar taught by the most profoundly clenched member of the faculty, Professor Abingdon. Thursdays were commonly considered the start of the weekend, a fact that deeply offended the professor. His vigorous questioning (Abingdon wielded the Socratic method like a spiked club), and astigmatism-inducing reading assignments were a one-man crusade for the return of the five-day class week.

"He's much nicer after first year," the upperclass students all agreed. "If he's your adviser, you can cook him dinner instead of doing your weekly tutorial." In the meantime, however, Abingdon stalked around the seminar room, yardstick in hand, firing off queries and jolting sleeping students awake by bringing the yardstick down and bellowing "Kwatz!" like a Southern-accented Zen master. Hart actually saw a girl bite her retainer in half.

Hart kept admirably abreast of his schoolwork, getting his *Cuckoo* buddies to ferry him books from the library (rustication gave him a one-hour time limit, as well as disallowing the use of chairs; really no hardship at all, since the last thing he wanted to do was run into Mr. Charivaria). He spent many long nights in his sarcophagus with watery eyes and a fading penlight.

Soon, schoolwork wasn't his only assignment: Ellen had asked him to write a weekly table tent to keep *The Cuckoo*'s heart beating. Reed and Ellen were in their third year, and starting to get ominous whiffs of the post-Stutts world. The fear was creeping into their bones, and would only get worse as graduation drew nearer. Plus, they were tired; Hart and Peter were not. Not only was a weekly column a way to work out

Hart's still growing abilities and thus ensure that there would be someone to edit *The Cuckoo* after Reed and Ellen went "over the top,"[64] it was also a way to remain viable. *The Cuckoo* could slap one of Hart's columns onto a sheet of paper, Xerox it five hundred times for cheap, then table-tent to their heart's content. Advancement-crazed *Spec* minions scooped them all up eventually, but it was better than nothing.

It was tough to find the time; more than once, Hart wondered if spending his precious college years—four practice laps before Real Life—on *The Cuckoo* wasn't something he'd regret later. He'd made it to Stutts, but what would happen at the next shakeout? Would he have to slink back home, as the rest of his class smoothly merged into the fast track of their choice? With everybody so focused on getting ahead, it was hard not to wonder if they were right. But whenever time got tight—which was nearly every week—Hart remembered that *The Cuckoo* had stood by him when the rest of the campus hadn't. For that, he was more than willing to "sail the high C's" in his classes. Let sleep—and his future—be damned. But the strain of taking classes, pounding out the column, ignoring his ballooning tuition bill, and hoping nobody would kill him eventually began to wear Hart down.

"You don't look so good," Peter said. "Are you sure Tabitha isn't taking little nips? You know, when you're asleep?"

"Sleep?" Hart chuckled bitterly, not looking up. He was skimming an assignment. "Sleep is for the weak," he slurred.

"*The Cuckoo* should do something. A benefit. How much more do you have to pay the university?"

---

[64] This had been Stutts slang for graduation since World War I, and should give you an idea of how they felt about it.

"Seventy-three thousand, nine hundred and fifty-three dollars," Hart intoned, trying to say the words without thinking about them. Whenever he did, he threw up a little into his mouth. "*The Cuckoo* can't even pay its own bills."

Peter got a mad gleam in his eye. "I think we should do a show."

"Like, a play? The *Spec* would shut it down."

"Then it's one-night only! An event," Peter said. "I know Reed wants to do a musical revue. He's always talking about it."

Hart closed his reading packet; clearly Peter wasn't going to let this go. "I've never heard him."

"It's only when he's really drunk. He's a ham paralyzed by stage fright," Peter said. "I'm gonna call him."

"Wait—" Hart was embarrassed at anything happening as a result of his gross financial need, but Peter was determined to follow this spangled caravan of thought wherever it led. And Hart was too groggy to put up a fight.

Peter started speaking rapidly, "Reed, I think *The Cuckoo* should do a revue to raise money for Hart's tuition . . . I thought you'd be interested . . . Uh-huh . . . Uh-huh . . ." Peter covered the phone and said to Hart, "He thinks it should be erotic."

This jolted Hart from his stupor. "We should get the actors to be naked."

Peter nodded. Stutts students got naked constantly; it was a way of easing one's libido without actually having sex. "Hart thinks the actors should be naked."

"I was just kidding," Hart whispered.

Peter paid no attention. "And the best thing is—besides seeing the cutest people on campus naked—is that the *Spec* can't

280

steal it! . . . Right, we'll make the ticket prices really high. One night only, that'll make it even more exclusive. Can you book a theater, and I'll get working on a poster: 'A Night of Singing, Satire, and Your Classmates Naked!' . . . Great. Call Ellen, will you? If she gives you any static, tell him that this is prime back-of-the-*Times* stuff . . . Right. Bye."

Peter hung up the phone. "He's really excited."

"But—"

"No buts, it's already in motion," Peter said. "Reed says he'll bring material to the meeting tonight."

"All right," Reed said, "this one's called, 'Lesbians Until Graduation.' The scene opens with a junior named Susan sitting in her common room listening to something warbly. Her roommate Teresa walks in, dejected. 'Another terrible date?' Susan asks. "Yeah," Teresa says, helping herself to some box wine. Then, the duet starts:

TERESA

Men are smelly, and rude!

SUSAN

Obnoxious, and crude!

TERESA

Morally reprehensible!

SUSAN

Completely indefensible!

TERESA

And if you meet a nice one, he'll . . .

SUSAN

. . . be a homosexual!'"

"Wow," Hart said. "You've been waiting all your life to write this, haven't you?"

Reed smiled and continued reading from the sheaf of pages. "Now Teresa says,

TERESA
I'm tired of searching for companionship.

SUSAN
Are you ready to [yells] 'Abandon Ship!'?

Reed was really getting into it. "Then the orchestra swells—"

Ellen choked on her Coke. "*Orchestra?*"

"Okay, okay, somebody plays something on the keyboard, and Susan sings,

SUSAN
Why not join the sisterhood?
I'll treat you better than any mister would.

TERESA
I admit, cunnilingus is appealing . . .
But do you think it would hurt my dad's feelings . . . ?

"Susan pushes her advantage—we might have to get some choreography for this . . ."

"*Choreography?*" Ellen sputtered.

"Okay, fine, we'll do it ourselves," Reed said, playing the thwarted artist.

SUSAN
Do you get queasy thinking of penetration?

282

Slip over to mutual masturbation.
Sisterhood is powerful! Join the celebration!

TERESA

I'll be a lesbian—until graduation!

SUSAN

[miming a full belly]
No pregnancy!

TERESA

[lifting up her pants legs]
No shaving!

SUSAN

[turns around and slaps her ass]
No keeping thin!

TERESA

[wags her tongue through her split fingers]
But plenty of mis-be-hav-ing!

"That's mind-blowingly crude, but somehow, it works," Tabitha said.

"Thanks. Now," Reed said, "with a blast of female choir and a single spotlight, a women's studies professor enters. Tabitha, you read this part."

Tabitha took the page and read. "The rest of the stage is dark, as she speaks:

WOMEN'S STUDIES PROF

Hetero sex
Is an outmoded text
With disastrous effects.

But if she rejects
What I call
(crooks fingers for quotes)
"rape-as-sex"
She could be a female Malcolm X!'"

Reed exhaled. ". . . and that's all I've got so far on that one," he said.

They all clapped. "Wow," Peter said, smiling. "Shockingly competent."

"Right," Ellen said. "Got anything else?"

"Yeah," Reed said, to everybody's amazement. "I'm working on a short calypso number." Reed cleared his throat and sang.

Careersexuality!
I'm choking with virginity, I wanna rub against the nearest tree.
But my future is key to me; I'm still deciding what I want to be!
If I sleep with you, what will everybody think of me?
I better keep my options free, and keep things masturbatory.

Now, the chorus:

Some say it's a waste
To remain devoutly chaste
But I'm the quickest rat that's ever raced
And someday, I will run this place!
My corner office will be graced
With one intern perched upon my face,

And another clamped around my waist!
Until then, I'm careersexual!
So am I! So am I! So am I!

It was a memorable meeting, with everyone shouting out ideas and adding lines. Other songs were discussed: a fifties doo-wop number called "He's Got Da Crabs"; "Monogamy is Provincial" a la Cole Porter; and even a faux Italian madrigal entitled "*Il mio amante non può trovare la mia clitoris.*" To soften the show's edge, Tabitha came up with a rap number about preteen sublimation called "I Like Ponies."

It was the happiest kind of meeting—the ideas were good and came easily, and everything seemed to write itself. The staff decided to strike while the iron was hot, and do it before spring break; after that, the year devolved into a frenzy of worry (over passing finals, or getting a job). Before they broke up, the staff divided up the tasks: Ellen would handle getting the permissions, advertising for cast, and handle all the money. Reed would finish the songs, and he would work with Tabitha on the tunes, getting help from a professor he knew in the music department who owed him money. (Reed was a *Name That Tune* shark.)

"What should I do?" Hart asked.

"You're doing enough with the columns," Ellen said. "But if you have an idea—this goes for anybody—write it down. It's only five weeks to spring break, which means the show goes up in a month. Can we do it?"

"Yes!" everybody yelled.

"Okay, but *should* we do it?"

"*Hell*, yes!" Peter and Reed bellowed louder than the rest

combined. The tipping point—that moment in every *Cuckoo* meeting where the dulling effects of fatigue and alcohol overtook the buzz of creativity—had been reached, and Ellen brought the proceedings to a close.

CHAPTER SIXTEEN

MANY CONSIDERED it evidence of a benevolent God that there was no female equivalent to Comma Comma Apostrophe. The Wymyn's Cyntyr only got rowdy one day a year, on the anniversary of the Great Littleton witch trials. Women had been attending Stutts only for a few decades, and they simply hadn't developed the sense of entitlement necessary to trash the place.[65]

The leading females-only group on campus was something called Sophia. Sophia had started out as a group of wives and daughters of Stutts' high holies—administrators, tenured profs, big local donors. Expanding to include the occasional female professor, it had existed for more than 150 years as a sort of kinder, gentler Mugwumps. A Mugwumps where the lust for unlimited power had been replaced by a love of tasteful decorating. Student chapters had sprouted at all the nearby women's colleges, and when Stutts finally welcomed undergrads with

---

[65] Also, public urination is a more complicated proposition.

ovaries, a chapter of Sophia was consecrated at the place where it had been born.

The Stutts chapter of Sophia was grand indeed. Unlike the rest of the campus, its sanctum was classical, not high colonic. The ambience could not have been more different than the ragged and collapsing CCA building next door; tall columns supported a portico shading a well-maintained drive. Each window showed glimpses of a genteel, antique-filled interior, a bit fussy but immaculately maintained. There was no half-burnt furniture on Sophia's lawn—in fact no blade of grass was out of place. This juxtaposition with CCA's tumbledown premises made the brothers consider Sophia women as uptight, humorless, and repressed.[66]

Hart, no friend to CCA, had nevertheless absorbed this opinion, and so was surprised to see an invitation to Sophia's annual Casino Night on Tabitha's coffinside nighttable.

"You're in Sophia?" Hart marveled. "You, the girl who introduced the 'therapeutic personal massager' to turn-of-the-century Stutts?"

Tabitha made a face Hart was coming to know quite well. "I knew I shouldn't have told you that," she said. "The Sophia girls are great. I've been a member for a hundred and seventeen years."

"They're okay with you being a vampire? They've always struck me as a little" —Hart chose his word carefully— "starchy."

"Well, they're the daughters of the Daughters of the

---

[66] There was a rumor that Sophia had the largest water bills in the entire state; which grew into the rumor that the club had a waterslide in the basement; which grew into the rumor that Sophia held massive nude water parties. Members were always running outside to chase boys crouched in the building's shrubbery trying to catch a glimpse of the supposed parties. The fact that they didn't want weirdos leering at them was claimed as yet more evidence of their supposed frigidity.

American Revolution, for God and General Washington's sake," Tabitha said. "They're great fun, they just keep it to themselves. They like outsiders like me; it makes them feel rebellious. Would you like to go? I get a free ticket for myself and a guest. And I should make an appearance, as the oldest living member."

"I can't dance," Hart said, suddenly feeling shy.

"There's not much of that—mostly gambling."

"I don't have any money, either."

"It's not for real, ninny. They give you some play money in exchange for your ticket. Depending on how much you redeem at the end of the night, you get prizes." Tabitha bounced closer to him on the futon-coffin. "Come on, Casino Night's fun. Plus, it's for charity: they raise money for Project Polish."

"What's Project Polish?"

"A charity that goes into the ghetto and teaches children how to use the right fork," Tabitha said.

"You gotta be kidding . . ."

Tabitha hit him with a pillow.

Two weeks later, Hart was decked out in a sweet vintage tuxedo borrowed from The House of Old. (Chauncey let him have it on the condition that he let people know it was for sale.) Tabitha looked ravishing in a pale pink dress that set off her red hair. Her beauty was accentuated by the finest jewelry that decades of unwitting alumni donors could provide.

Hart felt a pleasant tingle as they walked into the building. For once, his life was exceeding expectations, and he didn't much care whether that long black shape in the corner was an anaconda or a dropped umbrella. Sophia's front hall was ablaze with chandeliers and mirrors; the womblike inner rooms promised rich Oriental carpets, gleaming brass, mellow paneling, and mallard prints. Hart was finally being accepted into the very bosom of Mother Stutts, and he liked it.

This feeling fled immediately, as a clot of chumps from CCA oozed in behind them.

"I didn't know CCA guys had that kind of money," he said, watching them shell out a hundred bucks a head.

"They don't," Tabitha said. "Look at the cheapo beer they're drinking." Each brother clutched a can of Putz Ice, the brew that made Great Littleton infamous.

Hart wouldn't have been surprised to learn that Trip Darling had paid for them—three hit teams of two people each. "It's funny how they never do anything alone, have you noticed that?"

"They were probably waiting for you to show up," Tabitha said. "I'll be right next to you all night, but be alert, okay?"

"I will," Hart said. "It won't be hard to pick them out." Each CCA brother's tuxedo was louder and more "fun" than the last. Tabitha laughed.

They dumped their coats and began to mingle, another essential part of a Stutts education. Hart felt like he was in a movie—everyone was dressed to the nines. Waiters were circulating with trays of champagne and canapés, and a string quartet in the corner sawed away diligently, adding a whiff of Mozart to the room. Hart suddenly realized that a passerby might actually mistake them all for adults. Apprehensive, he downed a glass of punch.

A stately young woman in a formal gown glided up to them.

"Margaret," Tabitha said. The two women hugged lightly. "Lovely job, as usual."

"Thank you, Tab. I was hoping you'd make it. Still as young as ever, I see."

"It's my diet." They laughed. "This is my boyfriend. Hart Fox, this is Margaret Draper, current MP."

Hart shook her hand. "What's an MP?"

"Mainly a lot of work," Margaret quipped. "The Latin title roughly translates to 'Maximum Priestess,' but we use MP instead. People already think we're made of marble." Margaret smiled. She looked solid and honest, the kind of woman who belonged on the prow of a ship. "I coordinate all the committees," Margaret continued, "the social committee, the building committee, the Old Girl committee, the community outreach committee, the library committee . . . How is somebody supposed to apply to law school under such conditions, I ask you?"

"I knew you'd be MP as soon as I met you," Tabitha said. "You had that Machiavellian look."

Margaret laughed again. She was guilty as charged, but like most members of Sophia, she had learned to conceal her competence—when one is destined to marry inside a specific, quite small class, it doesn't pay to be too intimidating.

They sauntered past the blackjack table, where a young man in a blue, frilly tuxedo and mirrored sunglasses was complaining loudly to the dealer. "Wait," he slurred. His hair had been blow-dried into a seventies frizz, and he'd clearly been laying down a base of booze for hours. "I thought if I got twenty-one, you were s'posed t'take yer top off."

"I told you, those aren't the rules," the dealer said calmly. She and Margaret exchanged a glance.

"But wait! Listen! Listen—I said, 'If I get twenty-one, you gotta flash me,' 'member? 'Member I said that? An' then I said, 'If you don't say anything, then you automatically agree,' 'member?"

"Is there a problem, sir?" Margaret said.

"No, but there's gonna be! I beat her fair and square, and now I get to see her—dammit!" He dropped his beer. As it glugged out onto the carpet, he fished a fresh Putz Ice out of his jacket.

Margaret's smile froze a little. "You must think you're next door, Paul. Why don't I refund your ticket, and you can—"

"Get lost, you tight-assed bitch." Paul popped the top and began to shotgun the beer.

As Paul gulped, Margaret sprang into action. Unhooking her necklace, she whirled it around her head, then cracked it like a whip. The heirloom pearls wrapped around Paul's crooked arm. She gave a mighty pull and he sprawled toward her, spilling more frothy, noxious beer onto the carpet. She grabbed the off-balance drunk and expertly twisted his arm behind his back.

Subdued, glasses hanging askew, the drunk gave a small belch of defeat. The crowd clapped politely.

"Come with me. We'll send your group a bill for the carpet." Passing Hart and Tabitha, Margaret shot them a smile and mumbled, *"That's* an MP," shaking her head. Hart saw Paul try to grab a deviled egg from a waiter carrying a tray. Margaret slapped his hand.

"The house always wins," Hart chuckled.

In the commotion, neither Hart nor Tabitha had noticed the young man with the madras cummerbund sidling next to the massive grandmother clock behind them. Seeing that everybody was watching Paul's ejection, the man gave the clock a heave.

Tabitha spotted it toppling straight for Hart and shoved him out of the way. She mistified, and the clock passed through

292

her harmlessly. She then recondensed beside her date, as the clock fell with an enormous crash.

Margaret came rushing back in. After checking to see that everyone was all right, she deputized some Sophia members to haul away the pieces.

"Did you see who pushed it?" Margaret asked. "CCA man, obviously. Miserable bastards—grandmother clocks don't move on their own."

"I hope it wasn't an antique," Hart said.

"No, no, it's just a reproduction. We store all the valuables when we know the neighbors are coming over."

"Shouldn't we tell her about the plot?" Hart asked Tabitha, after Margaret had gone. He wouldn't mind having somebody so unflappable looking out for him.

"No," Tabitha said, watching her eject another malcontent. "Poor Margaret has enough to worry about tonight."

Hart stood at the baccarat table, shaking a pair of dice.

"This is a card game," the dealer said.

"I was making a joke," he lied, throwing the dice over his shoulder. "Hit me, pass the shoe, whatever," Hart said, then won the hand. He felt like James Bond—suave, lucky, irresistible.

Actually, the feeling was of being aimed at. Twenty feet away, a CCA brother was standing behind a potted palm, drawing a bead with a sharpened butter knife. The frat boy spoke in a menacing singsong as he aimed. "Enjoy the last sweet moments of life, upstart! Now you must prepare to die. . . . You have been fortunate so far, upstart, but now you have met The Assassin. . . . A trained, professional killer, a harvester of men for money . . ."

"Why are you talking like that?" asked the brother standing next to him, eating a canape. "Who's 'The Assassin'?"

"Dude, you are *totally* breaking my concentration!" the first brother said, exasperated. "You're the lookout, I'm the assassin, that's what we agreed . . ."

"So, I can call myself 'The Lookout'?" the second brother said. "That's not cool. How about 'The All-Seeing Eye'?"

"Sure, fine, whatever," the first brother said. "Crap, now I gotta get loose all over again." He sort of jiggled his arms and rolled his head around. "Be the knife," he said to himself. "You *are* the knife."

"You *are* the retard," the lookout grumbled. "Hurry up and throw it, spaz."

Pumping the butter knife at Hart like an oversized dart, the thrower cleared his throat and returned to his special I-am-a-trained-killer voice. "I must aim well, for this is no ordinary weapon, upstart. This butter knife once belonged to the renowned Nazi Hermann Goering. . . ."

"Bullshit!"

"Look, if you're not gonna *participate*, why don't you just go?"

"I am participating. I'm participating by saying that you're full of crap."

The thrower stopped pumping the knife. He gingerly held the blade and showed the butt end to his pal. "See? Right there, 'H.G.'"

"Lemme see." The lookout pulled the knife toward him.

"*Ow!* Shit, dude, you cut my effing hand!"

"Looks like somebody scratched the letters in with a screwdriver or something." He handed the knife back. "No way that's a real Kraut blade."

"I don't care, okay? Just shut up for a second so I can kill this dude." The assassin tried to throw, but the butter knife was too slippery. Drops of blood were hitting the carpet. "Shit, man! You cut my throwing hand!" he said bitterly. "You did that on purpose!"

"Give it," the lookout said impatiently, "I'll throw it."

"No, you don't know how . . . Fine," the assassin said, handing over the knife. "Wait, CSI will find my blood and think I did it."

"Forget it, I'm throwing it. Scoot over so I can be behind the plant, too."

There was a commotion emerging at the baccarat table. Hart was on a roll.

Just as the lookout was about to release the knife, Margaret glided up next to them.

"Having fun?" she asked.

"We weren't doing anything," the CCA boys chorused. The lookout whipped the knife behind his back, in the process slicing a large hole in his sleeve and pricking himself in the ass.

"*Ow!* Damn, dude! It's cursed!"

"It is not! I got it off eBay! They couldn't sell it if—"

"What? What's cursed?" Margaret asked.

The CCA brothers stopped glaring at each other. The lookout said the first thing that came to his mind. "The punch . . ."

"The punch is cursed?"

"Sorry," the ex-assassin said. "My friend is really drunk. Two cups of punch—what secret ingredient did you put in that mess, baby?" He wrapped his arm around Margaret chummily, staining her dress with his blood. "You ladies are *crazy!*"

"Uh . . . Grapefruit juice?" Margaret offered.

"Right on! High five!" the ex-assassin said, forgetting

about his wound. They slapped, and he roared with pain. "SON OF A—!" Then, remembering the deception, he squeaked. "He's allergic to grapefruit!"

"Really? Is he going to be okay?" Margaret asked. "There's a nurse on duty."

"Oh, sure. He *likes* being allergic." He elbowed his partner. The lookout chimed in. "Yeah. Love it."

"Okay, but if you change your mind . . ." Margaret, puzzled, walked away.

"Thanks, shithead," the lookout said. "She probably thinks I'm some sort of freak."

"Shut up and throw it, if you're not scared. Pussy."

"*You're* the pussy!" The lookout said.

"Only pussies need to aim that much."

"I don't need to aim at all!" the lookout said, looking away as he threw.

"I win *again*!" Hart hollered. "Maybe I should drop out and go to Las V—"

The knuckling butter knife sailed over Hart's head, breaking through a window behind him. There was a small metal bonking sound, then from the yard below, they heard a man shout, "Dude! Whoever did that: that was definitely uncool!"

The crowd around the baccarat table turned to look at the throwers. The potted palm was pitifully transparent.

"I'm not with him," the ex-assassin said lamely, pointing at the lookout standing next to him. Blood dripped from the pointing hand. "It's the grapefruit—it deranges him."

"Is everybody okay?" the lookout called. "Sorry, our mistake, Hart—we thought you were a friend of ours."

". . . who likes to have knives thrown at him," the ex-assassin added.

Tabitha put down her drink and started walking toward them with a definite purpose. They ran.

"Weird," Hart said, then prepared for the next hand.

With Tabitha gone, the next plan slid into position. A man in a suit carrying a tray came up to Hart and offered him a deviled egg.

"Oh, no thanks," Hart said, rubbing his stomach. The champagne had made him jokey. "During break I ate over forty of those in one twenty-four-hour period. Now, I can't even smell a deviled egg without feeling a little urpy."

"I guarantee that these are better," the man said with a foreign accent. "There's only one left, as you can see." This one had been dusted with rat poison.

"It's got hair on it," Hart said. Not being an actual waiter, the CCA brother had dropped the egg on the floor more than once.

"But sir—" The man's accent was strange, Hart thought—almost intermittent.

Another man walked up. "I'll take it," he said, reaching for the lone egg. He turned to Hart. "If you don't mind—?"

"He *does* mind!" the waiter said, slapping the man's hand. "This is for him! He was first!"

"I don't want it," Hart said, trying to defuse an awkward situation. "But if you see the girl with the rumaki tray—"

"No!" The waiter's eyes burned with intensity. He grabbed the egg and leapt at Hart. "Eat this, you jerk!"

"That egg must be *really good*!" the second man said. "Give it to me!" The two men grappled. The waiter finally broke free, and he and the egg lover circled each other warily.

"I'm giving it to him!" the waiter said, pointing at Hart.

"Really, I don't want it," Hart said. He'd been raised to be polite.

"You see? You see?" crowed the egg lover. "Hand it over."

The crowd realized that something strange was going on; for the waiter (none other than Brother Nipples) all hope of a clean getaway was gone.

"Quit standing there and get us more hors d'oeuvres," somebody shouted.

Nipples looked at the door—the crowd blocked it; then he looked at the window. It slid open and a man with long hair and a hooded Mexican sweatshirt stuck his head through: "Which one of you dudes threw this?" he said, with the throaty drawl of the recreational pot smoker. The knife was stuck in a large orange gourd he'd been using as a bong. "I demand an apology, *and* a new gourd."

Seeing that there was no escape, Nipples opened his mouth wide and popped the egg in. He chewed, and chewed, waiting to sink into the arms of death.

He didn't.[67] Now everyone was looking at him.

"Too much paprika!" Nipples yelled angrily, then scuttled off, tearing off his false mustache.

Tabitha and Margaret reappeared at Hart's elbow. "What happened?" Tabitha asked.

"I'm not sure," Hart admitted.

"Margaret, there's a stain on the back of your dress."

---

[67] The poisoned egg had been prepared by CCA's much abused cook, a local woman named Patchet. Mrs. Patchet had grown tired of CCA brothers breaking into her spice cabinet and randomly smoking the contents, so she had switched the bottles for every ingredient. Paprika was in the rat poison box, the pepper had been switched with the thyme. The brothers were too drunk to taste the difference.

Tabitha scraped it with her fingernail and licked it. "Yum."

"Oh, foo! This dress was my grandmother's," Margaret fumed, then grabbed a glass of champagne from a passing tray. "I need a drink."

CHAPTER SEVENTEEN

A STUDENT stood naked on the dusty, tape-speckled stage of the Cummerbund Little Theater. He had the physique of a Greek god. Unfortunately, that God was Bacchus.

"Thanks," Reed said, cutting him off mid-song.

"I'm going on a diet," the student said.

"We'll let you know," Reed sighed.

"If it's about the back hair, I can . . ."

"*Next!*" There was no time for sentimentality. Every hour that passed was an hour closer to opening night. The fact that it would surely be closing night, too—their only shot to make some money for Hart's rapidly ballooning tuition—made haste even more essential.

Over the past week, all of Stutts' dramatic community had paraded in front of Reed's appraising eyes. Slowly, out of this mass of bruised egos and bared flesh, a cast for *The Cuckoo*'s first-ever erotic revue began to take shape.

Tabitha had been camped out in the back row all afternoon. "He wasn't bad," she whispered, stuffing another handful of popcorn in her mouth.

"You liked *him?*" Hart asked, mildly offended because the kid looked nothing like him. "I bet he wouldn't have gone out and gotten you popcorn."

Tabitha shrugged. "Speaking of, the popcorn's a little wet."

"It's raining," Hart said. Winter and spring were engaged in their annual life-and-death struggle to see who could produce the worst weather.

Reed walked up the aisle and sat down next to them. "How's it going?" Hart asked.

"Excellently!" Reed said, rubbing his hands together. "Stutts is bursting with hidden talent. We might have to add a chorus."

"Are we going to make it?" Tabitha said.

"Yes," Reed said. "I was worried about the sets"—Peter had submitted a bunch of incredibly suggestive, Georgia O'Keeffe–like sketches—"but we decided to go with a blank stage."

"Good," Tabitha said. "Nothing to distract you from the *real* scenery."

"What's the latest word from Ellen on the money?" Hart asked.

"Since we can only plan on one performance before we get shut down, we've decided to make it by invitation only."

"Smart," Hart said. Nobody ever lost money playing to a Stutts student's elitism. "How many invitations are you going to send out?"

"Not too many," Reed answered. "Just twenty or so. Ellen's worried we'll get 'bug bombed' again." Two years ago, the *Spec* had used insecticide bombs to clear out a last-ditch *Cuckoo* bake sale.

"How's that going to make any money?" Tabitha asked. "How much are you planning to charge per ticket?

Reed smiled. "Nothing."

"That's insane!" Tabitha said. Hart was puzzled, too.

"No, no, it'll work perfectly," Reed said. "But we've all got to be absolutely silent about it, okay?"

"O-kay . . ." Hart said. After all, Ellen and Reed were upperclassmen. They knew what they were doing—right? And since he was the beneficiary of all this work, shutting up and going along seemed only polite.

"I don't think you guys know what you're doing," Tabitha said.

Reed smiled again, even bigger than before. "Trust me."

For the next two weeks, Hart and Tabitha wondered what Ellen and Reed were planning. When they tired of lobbing absurd possibilities back and forth, they bothered Peter.

Peter's release from set design had unleashed a dangerous amount of time in his schedule. Rather typically, he had decided to turn Tabitha's inherited hearse into a *Cuckoo*mobile. "It's going to be amphibious," he shouted. He was under the Buick, doing something loud to the undercarriage.

"Don't you have schoolwork?" Hart shouted at Peter's feet.

"No time," Peter said in between bursts of tightening or untightening or something. "Gotta get it ready for the May Regatta."

"Oh, right," Hart remembered the Stutts Navy. Did any of these people ever study? Why was *he* the one always in trouble?

In coveralls liberally smeared with grease, transmission fluid, and his own blood (scraped knuckles), Peter slid from under the car. All of his tools were located six inches off the floor so that he could scoot around on his creeper. Peter put down the drill, grabbed a wrench, and disappeared again.

"Do you know what Ellen and Reed are planning?" Hart said.

"'Fraid not," Peter said. "I bet it's gonna be good—could you hand me that periscope?"

The night of the show, Hart, Peter, and Tabitha arrived early and went backstage. It was a madhouse. When they walked up, Reed was standing in front of the male lead, fixing something on the codpiece of his costume.

Hart spoke. "Reed, I know you're busy, but we just wanted to stop by and say break a—"

"Try it now."

The actor pulled a tassel and his entire costume fell off. He was hung like a beast of burden.

"My *goodness*," Tabitha said. The boys were struck dumb.

The trio stumbled out to their seats, trying not to bump into anything too personal. As Tabitha told Hart an anecdote involving her first date with Charlie Chaplin, Peter counted the crowd. "There's nobody here," he said with alarm. Out of the twenty invitations, only four people had turned up.

"It's too close to midterms," Hart said glumly.

"I wish I had called the Children of the Night," Tabitha said. "We could've packed the house."

"Children of the Night?" Hart asked.

"It's a publicity service for the vampire community," Tabitha said. "Every town over a certain size has a CotN squad. They post handbills, do grafitti, clue all the other vampires in to parties and stuff. Sometimes shops have sales just for us."

"Sales for vampires?" Peter said.

"We buy stuff, too, Peter. After all, this is America."

"But how does a vampire make money?"

"Investments," Tabitha said. "Charlie called me his 'little capitalist bloodsucker.'"

Hart laughed, then looked around—still only four other people. He felt the weight of his debt start to crush him again. "Well, it was a nice idea," he mumbled to no one in particular.

The lights went down. Peter activated his chair-mounted video camera. "Selling this is what the Internet was made for," he whispered.

Someone played a sprightly tune on the piano as the curtain rose. There the cast stood, dressed normally. With confidence (and a bit of overacting) they began to sing the opening number. At the final crescendo, each pulled a tassel, and their costumes fell off. Even the piano player was naked—and he stood up to prove it.

Within seconds, Hart, Peter, and Tabitha heard excited whispers all around them, and the chirps of cell phones being activated. By the end of the first sketch, they could hear a rowdy crowd gathering around the ticket window outside, demanding to be let in. They heard Ellen's voice rising above the hubbub. "There's not gonna be enough seats, folks, so we're going to do this auction-style. Do I hear fifty dollars?"

Staring at the stage, but listening to the auction, Hart and his friends felt mounting glee. Finally, they heard Ellen shout, "Sold, for one thousand dollars!"

Hart sprang out of his seat with a barely suppressed whoop. "Tab, let's go see if Ellen needs any help with the money." He rubbed his hands in a caricature of greed.

People were beginning to stream inside. Tabitha and Hart fought their way into the lobby, where Ellen was taking cash and processing credit cards as fast as she could.

"Thank God you're here!" she said. Closing a metal cash

box crammed past capacity, she gave it to Hart. "Take this and put it somewhere safe. Tab, you stay with me and we'll fill this bag." There was a grocery bag at her feet, where she was now dumping cash. Tab was tearing tickets as fast as she could.

As the strains of "Old Abe Lincoln's Thighs" wafted through the heavy curtains separating the ticket area from the seating, a student wearing glasses and a rumpled green raincoat pushed his way in from the outside. Hart recognized him as Miles Monaghan, the *Spec* staffer who snapped pictures of him hanging from the scaffold, and later ID'd him as The Mad Pisser.

"Excuse me, folks," Monaghan said, taking off his rain-soaked hat and shaking it. It sprayed several people. He paid no attention. "I'm from the *Daily Spectacle*. I got here as fast as I could. This show is obscene."

"We know, asshole," a woman barked. "That's why we're here."

"I'm very sorry to hear that," Monaghan continued pompously. "The campus police are coming over to shut down this piece of filth."

If the *Spec* editor thought this would convince people to disperse, he was wrong. In fact, the competition for tickets grew even fiercer as the mob of students realized that they might miss out on seeing some of the hottest students on campus naked.

Monaghan took his trusty camera out of his pocket. "People, don't force me to use this. It would be a shame to derail any future political careers."

An immense senior—a wrestler sprayed by Monaghan's hat—reached over and swiped the camera. Monaghan beat on him with tiny, useless fists. "You'll get this back later, punk," the man-mountain said.

"*Go*, Hart!" Ellen yelled.

Hart walked toward the door, but the room was packed and his progress was slow. Monaghan was still exhorting the crowd to come to its senses. "Don't you have studying to do?" the editor pleaded.

"Kiss my ass!"

"We wanna stay!"

"But you don't have to stay!" Monaghan said. "The whole story will be in tomorrow's *Spec*!"

"Kiss my ass twice!"

As Hart passed, the frustrated editor made a grab for the cash box. "Gimme that!" Meanwhile, the campus cops had arrived.

Thinking quickly, Hart yelled, "Officer, arrest this man! He just tried to steal this money from me."

"Did anybody else see it?" the officer asked.

"Yeah!" the crowd chorused boisterously.

"No, no, *no*!" Monaghan cried, rain dripping from his glasses and bow tie. "*I* was the person who called you! They're the pornographers—arrest them!" He was taken away thrashing and protesting vociferously.

Thanks to the crush of people, the show wasn't shut down until well into the second act. Reed even convinced the cops to let them do a truncated finale.

"You know, for kids who study all the time," Peter heard a cop say, "they've got some nice muscle tone."

After the show was over, Reed had sent the cast and crew off to a prearranged champagne dinner at Der Rathskeller (paid for with the first two inches of cash from Ellen's paper bag). Then, he and Ellen had gone to *The Cuckoo* offices. By the time they'd arrived, Hart had taken off his socks and shoes, and had his feet resting in a bucket of bills. "There wasn't enough for a full bath," he said, "so I decided on a footbath instead."

"Well, let us top that off for you," Ellen said, pouring the bag of bills over Hart's head.

As large as the haul was—more than nineteen thousand dollars—it wasn't anywhere near what Hart needed.

"As I see it, we have two options," Ellen said at the group's next meeting, a boozier-than-usual dinner at the C&E. "One, we can give whatever's left after tonight to Hart. This is a nice gesture, but useless." There was general, slightly thick-tongued concurrence around the table. "Or," Ellen continued, "we can take this money and invest it in a bigger project, one that might be able to raise the whole amount."

Reed was unsure. "That seems risky to me," he said.

"In this case, nineteen thousand dollars is the same as nothing," Ellen said. "And whatever happens, we'll always have our memories. Shall we vote?" They all had to stare at Reed for a moment, but eventually it was unanimous; they would take the profits from the revue and . . . do what?

As they brainstormed, Hart knocked over his soda. He grabbed a trodden-on copy of the *Spec* from beneath the table. As he sopped up the soda, he caught a glimpse of the front page. "Semester in Hell," the headline screamed above a picture of none other than Trip Darling. "One man's encounter with the tide of underclass overachievers that are ripping apart the social fabric of Stutts University."

Hart couldn't resist; he peeled the wet paper off the table and began reading Trip's editorial. It was charmingly titled "Let's Put the 'Status' Back in Status Quo."

"Last semester," the article began, "I entered Stutts as a freshman. Words cannot describe how geeked I was to be here. For my entire life, I'd heard about Stutts from Dad and

Grandpa, my uncles, several cousins, and lots of family friends. They told me about the hallowed traditions of partying and going to bars, plus how the campus cops would never arrest you, no matter how illegal you were acting. It sounded like a magical place of magic. The first night I was here, I saw some guys throwing a girl's laundry into a tree, and I knew: these were going to be the best years of my life.

"One morning, recovering from a night of hallowed traditions, I heard a knock on the door. 'Who is it?'"

"'It is I, Mr. X.,' the voice said. 'We went to high school together—I just got here and have no friends. Everyone hates me, because I do not belong here. Could you teach me how to be cool?'"

Hart read with a rising gorge. For another 500 words—a gargantuan length by the *Spec*'s subliterate standards—Trip described a series of totally fraudulent adventures with "Mr. X." "It was sad to see how everybody thought he was totally lame," Trip wrote, "but sadder how he was totally clueless about it." Through trips to classes, football games, and exclusive CCA-only parties, Trip attempted to mold Mr. X into Stutts-worthy material. He failed—and yet Mr. X refused to leave.

"It's cool if somebody isn't born with a lot of opportunities," the column continued, "but why do people like that have to ruin things for everybody else? Ask yourself this question: why does every poor neighborhood look like crap? It's like some disease or something. If you want to keep where you are *nice*, you have to keep them away.

"For centuries, people like Mr. X were kept safely away from special places like Stutts, and that's why they were special. But today's Mr. X is determined to be inappropriately successful. He will stop at nothing, using sympathy and standardized tests to go anywhere, even if he's not welcome. . . ."

"What's wrong?" Peter asked Hart. "You look like you just swallowed a bug."

"I know what we're going to do," Hart said, biting off the words. "We're going to parody *Daily Money*."

"I don't know," Reed said. "Seems a bit . . . dry."

"It's national, it's got the largest daily circulation in the United States, it's never been spoofed before—it's a big, fat, sitting duck," Hart said.

Peter chimed in. "It's also black and white, which makes it easier to design and cheaper to print. We ought to keep that in mind, if we want to do something in time for April Fools'."

Ellen looked half sozzled, half thoughtful. "It has the biggest circ in the country?"

"Yeah! And Trip Darling is the publisher's son," Hart said. "I absolutely *loathe* the guy."

"Ah," Peter said. "The dynamic meathead returns."

Hart's personal animus swayed Reed. "If Hart hates them so much, I think we should do it. After all, we are doing it to raise his tuition."

Tabitha saw her opportunity to push it over the edge. "If we do it right, we could make a lot more than that," she said.

Ellen thought some more, then took one of her multivitamins, followed by a swig of beer. Hart could swear he could see the gears turning in Ellen's head: would this get publicity? Would it get the right kind of publicity? Pinch Day was coming up—was she dooming herself somehow? Finally Ellen said, "What the hell—we'll do it."

"All right!" Hart said jubilantly.

"But I'm laying it on you, Hart. Reed and I are busy during spring break," Ellen said. "It's your balls on the chopping block. Make it funny."

CHAPTER EIGHTEEN

SOON it was March, and college students everywhere were ogling topless bikini contests, licking whipped cream off strangers' pudenda, and generally enjoying spring break as God (or at least the beer commercials) intended. But Hart wasn't; he was wracking his whimpering brains for jokes. And while Hart pleaded with/raged at the gods of humor, Peter designed their spoof. This precision-crazed task required long, bleary hours of fine motor control and not one single *Girls Gone Wild.*

"This sucks," Hart said as he walked into *The Cuckoo* offices. He brushed cold pellets of rain off his shoulders. Great Littleton held on to winter like somebody determined to win a bet.

Peter grunted and handed Hart a printout of a page. "Need two more hysterical paragraphs," he said.

"I'm not feeling funny today," Hart said. "Can't you just repeat every twentieth word or something?" Since both Reed and Ellen were engaged in internships (prestigious, copier-intensive) down in New York, it fell to Hart to be the parody's main brain. He would think of jokes on the spot, to use up any empty spaces in the layout.

"How is it outside?" Peter asked. "Still pissy?"

"Yeah," Hart said, cracking open a soda. Caffeine helped.

"This sucks."

"That's my line," Hart said. The original plan was to stay at school and do the work there. But within forty-eight hours after President Whitbread declared spring break,[68] the campus was devoid of life—save for the fretting, scurrying mass of seniors finishing the big paper or project that every major required. Add to this the fretting, scurrying mass of graduate students worrying about how to extricate themselves from a torment of their own creation, and the fretting, scurrying mass of faculty desperately trying to do some publishable research before "the tanned barbarians" returned. So it was no wonder that Peter abruptly turned to Hart and asked, "You wanna go to my parents' house and work on it there, instead?"

"Sure," Hart said. "At least it won't be raining there." Great Littleton sat in a bowl-shaped depression that held in clouds. "Let me call Tabitha."

"You two go, I'll stay here," Tabitha said. She was worn down from protecting Hart and had her own schoolwork to catch up on, all take-home midterms in lieu of the ones everybody else took in the daytime—it was amazing what a doctor's

---

[68] There was a nice ceremony on New Quad, where the president fired a cannon pointing directly upwards. This ritual had announced spring break at Stutts for over 200 years. For the first 150 or so, the students were the ones with the cannon; the supposed object was to catch the cannonball in the barrel, but students often took the opportunity to point it at buildings or people they didn't like. Since World War II, the ball had been replaced with blanks, and the president fired the cannon personally. It wasn't nearly as much fun, and Mr. Darling (along with a lot of other alums) were agitating for a return to the good old highly lethal days.

note (and fear of a discrimination suit) could do. "I'm drowning in work," she said. "And let's face it, sweetie, when we're together, neither of us gets much rest."

Hart felt a pang—in various places. He would miss Tab over the next few days—all of her, of course, but certain parts especially.

When Hart and Peter got to the train station, Peter rolled directly to the ticket window.

A shade snapped up and a woman spoke through the hole in the Plexiglas. "Can I help you?" she said sharply.

"My name is Peter Armbruster. There's a private car waiting in the yard."

The agent's frown melted into an ingratiating smile. "Already attached, Mr. Armbruster. Platform ten, west end."

Hart was suddenly struck by all the things money could buy, and wanted some. He tended to forget about money, except when reminded by situations like this one. Hart suspected that this forgetfulness would keep him from ever getting too rich. Should he change his priorities? It must be fun to treat a private railroad car like it was nothing special. Or maybe it really *felt* like nothing special to Peter. That wouldn't be too fun.

"It's the family biz," Peter said. "My great-great-grandfather Augustus built supra-Pullmans for the robber barons."

"My great-great-grandpa probably shoveled the coal," Hart said.

"And here we are, equals," Peter kidded. "I've read a little bit about old Augie—our kind of guy."

"Did he go to Stutts?"

"No way! He was a rough character—third-grade

education, swore constantly, no manners whatsoever. One time, he blew his nose on Mrs. Astor's favorite scarf," Peter said with relish. "But he was a mechanical genius, and knew it, too. Augie had quite a scam going; he'd spend ten bucks on damask or fifty on mahogany, and slap ten times that onto the price." Peter laughed. "Augie loved screwing the robber barons so much, he became one himself!"

Once they left the yard and got away from Great Littleton, the view from the large windows improved dramatically. For one thing, it stopped drizzling. The farther away they got, the mellower and more pleasant the afternoon became. "Look," Hart said, pulling aside a velvet curtain. "Fishing boats."

"Wave," Peter said. Some battered boats were coming in for the evening. Hart thought about the presumably battered people in them, and how he must look, rocketing past in a private railroad car.[69]

Hart must've worn a guilty expression, because Peter said, "They didn't do anything special just for us. This car's always sitting in the yard, waiting for the next plane-phobic celebrity . . ."

"Or the next Armbruster," Hart teased.

"I ain't complainin'," Peter said. He rolled over to a cleverly hidden rolltop compartment and opened it. Hart got a rich whiff of cedar and tobacco. "Cigar?" Peter said. "Unless dad's off his game, they should be pretty good." They both lit up and watched the countryside roll by. Hart got a little nauseous, but since this was the high life, he was determined to get used to it.

---

[69] Stutts students always assumed, generally incorrectly, that they were the center of attention. For the record, the fishermen didn't notice. They had gotten a good haul, and Monday was three-for-one Budweiser night at Davy Jones'.

* * *

Peter's house was nice—in Hart's opinion, palatial—but they didn't stay long. Since he was company, it was hard for Hart to relax enough to be funny, and Peter had forgotten how much he hated being there himself. So they bought a lot of junk food, got the private car hooked up again, and wrote the whole spoof while being pulled around and around New England. When Hart and Peter pulled into Great Littleton station, they were smelly, unshaven, and hallucinating from lack of sleep, but the parody was done.

"Is it funny?" Hart asked Reed, once everybody had returned, and gathered in *The Cuckoo* office.

"I think so . . ." Reed said, "when it's in English."

Ellen looked concerned. "If you had a serious drug problem, you'd tell us, right?"

"Just caffeine," Peter said. By the end, he had been eating roasted coffee beans right out of a fifty-pound sack.

"Now I have to do all the work I should've done during break," Hart said, hefting a backpack full of books onto his shoulder. "Some vacation," he said, and walked out.

Two days later, Ellen was on the phone making the final arrangements before they delivered it to the printer. "So: You'll deliver one hundred thousand four-page parodies to us next Wednesday. How many boxes is that?" Ellen suddenly got a look like someone had just filled her pants with tapioca. "A thousand boxes? *Really?* . . . Uh, can I call you right back?" She hung up her cell phone and walked over to Reed, who was reading that morning's newspaper and coming up with little ideas. They would stick them into the parody somewhere, to make it more timely.

"They're going to deliver one hundred thousand copies to us next Wednesday," Ellen said quietly.

"Great," Reed said. "So?"

"So, what are we going to do with them?"

Now it was Reed's turn for that filled-pants look. "I thought you had distribution all worked out."

"I forgot," Ellen said. "I've had a busy week." Ellen had missed the magazine's Wednesday meeting for the first time ever. She said she had a dinner she couldn't miss, but wouldn't say what it was for or with whom.

"Folks!" Reed said loudly, "Ellen's screwed up distribution. Does anybody have any last-minute, project-saving ideas?"

"Do you mean that we're about to pay nineteen grand for a bunch of newsprint nobody else is going to see or pay for?" Peter asked. "Don't say yes."

"Yes."

Nobody needed to say the f-word out loud. It was implied.

They all started to think. Hart's brain went into overdrive and—amazingly—an idea came. "Why don't we wrap them around copies of the real newspaper?"

"Give me more on that," Ellen said, grateful for any way out.

"It's simple—each of us goes to one of the *Daily Money* newspaper boxes around campus. We buy a copy. Once that little door is open, we take each paper and wrap the four-page parody around it. People pick up the paper and don't even know our parody is there until it's too late."

"I always knew you were a sneaky bastard," Reed said admiringly. "And it's not *totally* illegal, either."

"Interesting," Ellen said. "How many copies a day does the *Daily Money* send to Great Littleton? A thousand? What about

315

the rest of our run?" The room was silent for a moment. "Peter, what are you thinking about?" Ellen asked.

"I'm wondering whether ninety-nine thousand four-page parodies will fit in this office," he admitted.

Tabitha dug her cell phone out of her purse and started dialing. "Honestly," she said. "What would you all do without me?"

"Who are you calling?" Hart asked.

"Children of the Night . . . Hi," Tabitha said, her voice suddenly warm. "I have something I need to get out on April first . . . That's right, April Fools'. Ten largest cities in the country."

Her fellow staffers gasped—all they'd talked about doing was Great Littleton and maybe New York, plus a few sprinkled around Keasby, just to show the jokers down there who was boss.

Tab continued, "No, you'll laugh. It's a spoof of a newspaper; I need teams to go into newspaper boxes and wrap them around the real thing . . . One hundred thousand . . . I know, it's short notice, something fell through." Tabitha put her hand over the phone. "He says they can't do a job that big any sooner than April fifteenth, is that okay?"

Ellen was crestfallen. "Damn. Are you—"

"Yes!" Reed said.

"April fifteenth is fine," Tabitha said. "Where should we deliver the copies? . . . Ten cities, ten thousand copies each city, one week in advance . . . Okay, hold on, I'm writing this down . . ."

CHAPTER NINETEEN

STUTTS UNIVERSITY looks like it's part of the United States, but the campus is really its own little country, a secular-humanist Vatican City. This is never more obvious than on April fifteenth, the day when Americans pay their income taxes, and four thousand Stutts students run naked around the Old Quad to celebrate spring. Stutts students have a folk belief of trying to will warm weather into being by showing bare flesh. It never works.

Ellen had just finished her post-streak shower when a roommate stuck her head into the bathroom. The roommate spoke the words every Stutts student longs to hear: "It's the *New York Times*. They want to talk to you."

Ellen screamed—but she didn't have time to get nervous: This call was followed by one from the *Los Angeles Times*. And when she was talking to CNN, somebody from *Good Morning Seattle* called. This continued until well after lunch.

Hart's day, on the other hand, was completely uneventful. He knew that the parody had been dropped, and thousands of people were (at least theoretically) reading things he had written—but he didn't feel any different. It took more than a 100,000-copy spoof to cause a ripple at Stutts. The only time the outside world really made its presence felt was when the stock market took a tumble and all those trust funds shivered.

Hart liked this about Stutts. It helped him keep things in perspective—a bizarre perspective, but perspective nonetheless. It was only after he bumped into Peter on the New Quad that Hart realized big things were afoot.

"Watch out!" Hart said. "Sorry. I thought that stick was a snake."

"Have you heard?" Peter asked.

"Probably not," Hart said. "I've been in class all morning." As a rusticant, he was prohibited from taking part in the mass airing of genitalia.

"Reed and Ellen have been interviewed by a bunch of newspapers, and the local news wants us all for an interview this afternoon!"

Hart suddenly realized his life might actually be happening. "Where?"

"In *The Cuckoo* office."

"Are you sure it doesn't still smell like sex?"

"That might help my image," Peter said jubilantly. "How quickly can you and Tab get to work?"

After the interview, Ellen, Reed, Hart, Tabitha, and Peter were useless for the rest of the day. They skipped class in favor of anxiously counting the minutes until the 5:00 broadcast.

"He said it would be the last segment of the show," Reed said, "but I think we should watch the whole thing, just to be sure we don't miss it."

Ellen agreed. "Shall we watch it at the C&E?" As the magazine's office-in-exile during the bad times, and unofficial clubhouse the rest of the time, the Cause & Effect was the natural choice.

They arrived five minutes early, to stake out the best bar stools for viewing. "Hey, Dennis, gimme a Boarsbollocks, and turn on channel four," Peter said.

"We don't receive American television," Dennis said. When the students began to squawk, the bartender puffed himself up and said defiantly, "English pub, English telly!"

"Yeah!" a grad student said in a brogue thick enough to cut peat. "Turn on the football!"

"Dennis, be reasonable. It's just for thirty minutes," Ellen said. "We're gonna be on TV."

"Payback is a bitch, Colonial."

Hart went for broke. "I guess we're gonna have to go to O'Binge's . . ."

"Don't make us do it, Dennis!" Peter pleaded. "Don't make me chug this!" he said, lifting his nearly full pint.

But Dennis wasn't budging, and every second that ticked by increased the stakes for the Good Eggs. Peter thumped his empty glass on the table, and they all ran out.

O'Binge's was a grim, squat slur against Irish people everywhere. The staff was surly and crude, the patrons, sloppy and combative. The food was inedible, the ambience frankly toxic. Everything, from the peeling floor to the uncomfortable bar stools to the earsplitting, poorly stocked jukebox to the omnipresent leprechaun art, was covered with a sticky, ancient emulsion equal parts beer and cigarette smoke. O'Binge's was a bad time at high prices. On the other hand, it had local TV. And they didn't card.

Except today. "ID's," the bartender growled. Florid-faced, with the furious eyes and puffy menace of the committed alcoholic, he was surely somebody's least favorite uncle. Everybody fished out their wallets and handed over what they had. Hart gave his fake ID from high school, a fishing license from American Samoa.

The bartender flipped it back at Hart. "Not even close."

Ellen made a last-ditch attempt. "Listen, we don't wanna drink, we just wanna watch the television—we're gonna be on the news."

"*That*'s a new one," the waitress said. She was a bottle-blond with bright pink talons and a non-specific grudge against humanity.

The bartender frowned. No drinking meant no money. "All right, but you each gotta order something to eat." O'Binge's food came from shady outfits a cut or two below the Stutts dining halls. It was still nominally "institutional," but too low quality to be served by any institutions with significant assets to protect.

The staff perused the menu with a rising sense of dread. "Tab, that diet of yours is looking better and better," Peter said.

As the broadcast played on, the students tried not to look at the food being ritually tortured in the bar's grimy microwave. The bartender put the plates in front of them, then walked away to discipline another patron.

Hart poked at his enchilada fearfully. "I think there's a dead fly embedded in this. Look—there by the dried cheese."

"Watch," Reed said, taking a big forkful of macaroni. It went from fork to mouth, then from mouth to napkin, then from napkin to lap, and lap to floor. This process not only kept the food from entering their digestive tracts, it also stuck it to

O'Binge's—assuming anybody would notice. As the minutes ticked by, the Good Eggs got more and more excited. Eventually they became prone to contextless whoops.

"Simmer down," the waitress said crossly, flicking Reed's ear with her diamond-studded fake fingernail. "This is a family place."

"Which, Gambino or Corleone?" Hart quipped.

It was 5:29. Now or never. Ellen and Reed had their arms around each other, bouncing up and down on their bar stools. "We're gonna be on TV! We're gonna be on TV!"

"And finally, as everybody knows, it's Tax Day . . ." the anchorman said.

"Don't remind me," his pretty blond co-anchor read off the teleprompter.

Hart could barely contain his excitement. Was there anything sweeter than being a rebel, *and* winning the Stutts rat race at the same time? They were gonna be famous—his parents would be so proud.

"Fortunately, somebody in Great Littleton is doing their bit to give us all a laugh . . ."

"Trip Darling, eat your heart out!" Hart yelled.

"C'mon, baby! Bring it! Bring the love!" Peter hollered.

The broadcast showed a clip of a batty-looking woman in a tutu and wings. "Yes," the anchorman said, "it's the Tax Fairy. This afternoon, weary filers at the main post office were greeted by Agnes Biddel, aka the Tax Fairy."

"I like that wand," the co-anchor said.

"And the green eye shade. The fairy handed out candy and jokes to all . . ."

The Cuckoo screamed as one—their story had been spiked!

". . . I think she's great," a postal worker said.

"I think she SUCKS!" Peter said, grabbing a chicken finger off Hart's plate and whipping it at the screen.

"That's it," the bartender said, "you're outta here!" He grabbed a bat.

"You're goddamn right I'm out of here!" Peter started wheeling toward the door.

"Hit him! Hit him!" came a few blurred voices from the dank back booths.

"He's in an effing wheelchair!" Reed said to them.

"Then hit *him*! Hit the guy who just talked!"

"Come on, everybody—let's go," Ellen said, slapping some money on the sticky bar. "Back to the C&E. Drinks are on me."

Dejected, the Good Eggs shuffled out.

The bartender spat a curse at the swinging door. "Stutts punks," he said (he'd been valedictorian at Keasbey). He flipped the channel, pausing for a second on CNN.

"Boo! No more news!" a drunk yelled. The bartender kept it on CNN, out of spite.

". . . Now, from the 'Too Good to Be True Department,' a group of college students from Stutts University have pulled a fast one all over the country, wrapping copies of a leading financial newspaper with a parody of their own creation. The lead story? 'President Authorizes Moratorium on Income Tax.' If only, right?"

A harried commuter appeared on the screen. "It totally got me this morning. Everybody in the office was talking about it . . ."

"I even called up my accountant," a smiling businesswoman said.

"But not everybody thinks the students' spoof is all fun and games. A spokesman for Burlington Darling, the

322

publisher of the real *Daily Money*, called the parody 'an irresponsible attack. He said the students' spoof 'did irreparable harm to our paper's century-long reputation for trust and accuracy' and that he was, quote, 'investigating legal options.' Luckily for the students, the IRS is looking at their fun a bit more kindly, offering an extra day's grace period for anyone who was taken in by the spoof."

"So I guess a lot of last-minute filers owe the kids some thanks, eh Dallas?"

"Right, Kitty. That's it from us. For Kitty O'Shea, I'm Dallas Wheatley . . ."

"What did you find out?" Burlington Darling said into the speakerphone. He was seething, jamming a pen into a squeezable Earth stress-reliever. "Can we sue the little bastards?"

"Not for parodying us, no," the lawyer said.

There was a knot of rage moving slowly up from Burlington's guts. "But they're injuring our brand! It's my right as an American to sue!"

"The law comes down on their side," the lawyer said. "They're not taking anything away from the paper, they're adding something to it."

"So we can get 'em for breaking into the boxes?"

"No," the lawyer said. "They didn't break into any of them. They must've paid for a paper, then . . ."

"But that's our proprietary distribution channel! Those boxes are private property!" Darling said. "If we can find out who put the spoofs in there without our permission . . ." The knot of rage reached Mr. Darling's mouth. "Son of a *bitch*! I *hate* goddamn freedom of speech—who the *fuck* came up with that idea?"

The lawyer waited for Darling to calm down. He didn't like telling his biggest client bad news. "I thought of that, so I got some of our representatives in each city to get copies of the parody, then I got 'em dusted for fingerprints."

"And?"

The lawyer paused again. "I don't know how to tell you this, but—you can't sue any of these people."

Darling, really savage, grabbed the handset and shouted, "I can sue any asshole I want, shit-for brains! Who was it?"

"They're all . . . deceased," the lawyer said. "The ones that the police had fingerprints for, were all dead. I assume the rest of them were dead, too."

"How the hell could that be?"

The lawyer didn't say anything, waiting for Darling to put it together.

"They must've killed them after they distributed the copies, to prevent us from suing!" Darling said. His mind reeled—this guy Hart and his pals were rougher than he'd ever realized.

"The only ones distributed by warm bodies were in Great Littleton," the lawyer said. "The kids on the magazine did those. We got their fingerprints from the university. So you could sue them . . . but as your lawyer, I would advise against it."

"Why not? *Somebody* should get sued! That's just good business."

"Think about it, Burlington," the lawyer said. "You, the publisher of *Daily Money*, governor-elect of Michigan, taking on a bunch of kids at your old college? It wouldn't look good."

"I don't care! I'll win—I'll spend whatever it takes."

"Maybe you will, and maybe you won't, but you'll

definitely make them famous . . . and a lot of money."

This brought Darling up short. His mole in the Stutts bursar's office had just left him a delightful message, saying that Hart Fox was less than a week away from defaulting on his tuition payments and getting kicked out. If *Daily Money* sued them all, sales of the parody would skyrocket, and Hart might make enough to stay in school. On the other hand, if things fizzled out naturally, and Hart had to come home, *Governor* Darling could make his life an even bigger hell . . . but quietly.

"Okay, you win, goddamn it," Darling snarled, and slammed the phone down.

After a long evening that featured not one but several cycles of intoxication and sobering up (first Peter would buy them shots, then Ellen would buy them spirulina and wheatgrass detoxification smoothies), the staff went their separate ways. Near the end of the evening, there had been much maudlin commiseration regarding Hart's fate. Ridiculous plans were put forth on how they were going to get him reenrolled, "maybe only after a semester." Hart saw it for the wishful cheering-up that it was. Without the power of television, there was simply no way that *The Cuckoo* could sell enough to pay Hart's humongous bill.

"Well," Hart said as he and Tabitha wobbily escorted Peter back to Dacron, "I hope people liked the parody. That's the important thing."

"Yeah," Peter said. They passed an all-night copy shop. "Hey," Peter said, "do you think they have Internet access?"

"Peter—" Tabitha said, surprisingly sharply.

"I'll just be a second," he said. "Wait out here."

"Remember your promise!" Tabitha said.

"Yeah, 'never drink and surf'!" Peter joked, and rolled into the shop.

"What promise?" Hart asked.

"It's nothing," Tabitha said. Hart's buzz swiftly deadened his curiosity. Tabitha looked especially pretty late at night, almost luminescent. This made sense: it was, after all, her element.

Peter reemerged with a big smile on his face. "Well, I don't know what happened, but something must've," he said to Tabitha.

"All over?" Tabitha asked.

Peter nodded. "You should see the numbers."

"Numbers for what? What are you talking about?" Hart demanded.

Peter opened his mouth, looked at Tabitha, then closed it. "I, uh, started a blog," he said. "G'night."

"Why does everybody care so much whether I take finals or not?" Hart said a few days later. "It's a buttload of work, and I'm going to get booted, what could it possibly matter?"

"It's the principle of the thing," Reed said. "You owe it to yourself."

"Oh yeah, Mr. Straight-and-Narrow,'" Hart said. "Are you going to take yours naked again?"

"Come on, Hart," Peter kidded. "Misery loves—in fact, in this case, it insists on—company."

Tabitha took the logical route. "You've done the classes. You might as well finish."

Hart felt ganged-up on. "Fine!" he said crossly. They didn't understand; it was a no-win situation. If Hart did poorly, he'd feel like shit, but if he did well, he'd feel even worse, since he couldn't come back. But the truth was that he didn't have anything better to do (besides hang out in the office counting *Cuckoo* subscription orders that were trickling in through the mail), so he studied.

One afternoon Hart was taking a break from cramming for his Things of Ancient Greece exam, lolling in a leather chair in his favorite corner of the Dacron College library. He knew the library was out-of-bounds, but what could they do, expel him with two days to go? Wood paneled and powerfully soporific, the college library was the heart of Dacron, and Hart wanted to make sure he remembered every detail. A pleasant breeze came in from the Old Quad; after gorging on the honeysuckle bush below, a fat bee trundled through the open window. Hart was trying to count the dust motes in a sunbeam when his cell phone rang.

"Hello," Hart said contentedly.

It was Burlington Darling. "Listen, you prick, if you think that you and your little friends are going to bait me into making you famous, think again."

"Hi, Mr. Darling," Hart said cheerily. "I'm still not dead yet, no thanks to—"

"Shut up, punk," Darling said. "And don't interrupt. I don't want to spend a second longer talking to you than I have to. I don't know how you survived, but I'm calling off the fraternity. If you say anything to anyone about it, I will sue you, and your idiot mother, and that slut you hang out with, there's something weird about her—"

"For what?" Hart said. "We haven't done anything to you. You hired me, then you fired me, then you tried to kill me . . ."

"People like me don't *have* to have a reason," Mr. Darling said, "not for people like you. My spies tell me that you're getting kicked out," he said. "You know what that means? You're coming back here . . . where I'm king. Every time you go for a drive, you'll get a ticket, Fox, and they might find a little something in your glove compartment, too. You'll get to know all your state troopers very well . . . And forget going to college in-state . . .

"I could get rid of you, but I want you to live and be miserable for a long, long time. And someday, when you're in the gutter somewhere and Trip is president, you can think to yourself, 'I never, ever should've fucked with Burlington Darling.'"

Hart had heard enough. There was nothing he could do about any of this, but he didn't have to listen to it. He remembered a juicy tidbit Peter had recently found in an old issue of the magazine. "Thanks for calling"—Hart paused—"Mr. Sniffle-Britches."

Hart's use of Darling's Mugwumps nickname (he'd bawled during the initiation) enraged the mogul. "I'm not finished with you! Don't you hang up on me! I'll—" Hart hung up.

It was a long time before Hart could concentrate on ancient Greece again. What did the personal habits of Pericles matter if the rest of his life was going to suck?

CHAPTER TWENTY

THE DAY AFTER the last exam was Ebekenezer Stutts Day. The staunchly Puritanical, more than slightly insane founder of the college would've had a stroke if he'd ever seen the Mardi Gras–like celebrating that went on in his name. However, that year somebody must've approved: the day was Great Littleton's rarest type, cloudless and perfect. It cheered Hart up.

The poor sucker needed it. Not only was Hart going back home tomorrow—for good—he was going back to an entire state governed by his arch nemesis. As he emptied his closets, Hart tried not to think of all the unpleasant things Governor Sniffle-Britches was doubtless cooking up. Did boardinghouses need permits? Could he be arrested for breathing?

"If I were you, I would blow the whistle on him," Tabitha said. They hadn't slept much last night; Hart was missing her already. Tabitha was less emotional. Hart figured that once you broke 150 years, lost love didn't hurt as much. History proved there would always be somebody else.

"Well, I'm not you," Hart said testily. "I can die, for one

thing." He had a stray thought flitting around his brain—should he ask Tabitha to bite him? Then Mr. Darling couldn't do anything too awful to him. He could protect his mom, if necessary. And he could come back and live with Tabitha forever. Several times throughout the morning, he was right on the verge of asking her, then lost his nerve. How did you bring something like that up? And what if she said no?

Hart was taking everything extra slow today, so that he might remember it better later. Tabitha caught him smelling her pillow.

"We have to leave," Tabitha said, adjusting the burkalike outfit she wore in direct sunlight. It helped somewhat, but she still felt rather sautéed. "Peter said the boat's launching at noon sharp."

Stutts Day was also the day of the May Regatta. Thanks to all the stuff *The Cuckoo* had done in the second semester—Hart's table tents, the erotic revue, and the parody—Ellen and Reed had gotten a lot of other student groups to enter a craft.

"It used to be an actual race," Ellen said, as they all waited at the makeshift slip north of downtown. "But Reed and I figured that we should take it slowly—a parade this year, a race next year—if nobody gets killed or anything."

"I wouldn't want to fall in," Hart said. The Turbid was the consistency of chocolate syrup, and smelled like dead seagulls. Occasionally fish broke the surface, not to catch a bug, but to call for help.

Peter was bringing the hearse in from the garage. Nobody had seen the finished project. "Do you think it'll work?" Tabitha asked.

"If anybody can make a '38 Buick float, it's Peter," Reed said. Just then, Peter's creation lumbered into view, and the

Cuckoo staff broke into applause. It was miraculous; the original vehicle was there, but it had been transformed: Peter had bought an immense number of reflective fishing lures, "spoons," and had covered the entire craft with them. So instead of being black, the vehicle sparkled in the sun like a thousand-faceted diamond. A massive cuckoo, wings outstretched, sat atop the roof. The body of the hearse was designed to go below the waterline, with the windows acting as portholes to view the murky depths. The driver sat in the usual spot, protected from the elements, directing the car by two stereoptical periscopes, mounted where the bird's eyes would be.

"I've converted the motor so that it's electric. Completely silent," Peter said. "But she'll be able to make ramming speed, if that ever becomes necessary."

"What's it run on?" Hart asked.

"High-fructose corn syrup," Peter said.

Right on cue, Reed cracked open a Coke.

"Hey, easy on the fuel, gas-guzzler," Ellen teased, then turned to Peter. "Are you going to patent it?"

"Oh, I don't know," Peter said. "That kinda takes the fun out of it, don't you think?" They all piled into the Buick. Peter had modified the front seat to accommodate his chair. Slowly, he edged the car onto the slip and down to the water. Minute by minute, the crowd of boats was gathering. Meanwhile, a bunch of students on both sides of the bank were watching to see what would happen to this odd contraption, silently hoping—like crowds everywhere—for something awful and spectacular.

Peter felt it. "Everybody check the seals on the doors, please," he said. "Make sure they're shut good and tight."

"What happens if a seal goes?" Hart asked.

"It's not going to," Peter said firmly.

"Yeah, but what if one did?"

"We'd probably all drown, so let's not talk about it." The car was filled with nervous laughter, and a dark surmise popped into Hart's brain: could some CCA guys have sabotaged the hearse? Some night they could be *sure* that Peter wouldn't be in the garage? Say, the night the parody came out? He decided not to share that worry.

"Here we go," Peter said, and shifted the car into drive. They eased into the murky, thick water of the Turbid. As the rest of them marveled at the pollution-perverted aquatic life, Peter pulled away from the slip and into the middle of the sanitary canal. Hart realized he'd been holding his breath.

The seals held, the engine was working, the periscopes were clear. "Where are the torpedoes?" Reed asked.

"On the next version," Peter said. "I ran out of time." Once the aqua-hearse was in position at the head of the line, all that was left was to wait for the other campus crafts to fall in behind it.

"I'm going upstairs," Reed said. Everyone but Tabitha followed.

"Aren't you coming?" Hart asked.

"No, I'm going to stay down here with Peter," she said.

"You're nice to spend my last day at Stutts with me," Hart said. "I know how daylight must—well, I don't know, but I can imagine . . ." His heart gave a mammoth squeeze and Hart realized how much he was going to miss her. He probably loved her, but not having anything to compare it to, he couldn't be sure. If being miserable at the thought of not having her around was any indication . . . What was he going to do? "I'll stay down here with you, I think."

332

"No," Tabitha said, with surprising firmness. "Go upstairs with the others." Hart hesitated, so Tabitha pushed harder. "You need to get in as many last looks as you can." She presented her cheek; Hart kissed it and climbed upstairs.

The sun was hot, and Reed had broken out more Cokes from a cooler/auxiliary fuel tank built into the bird's flank. "Amazing, just amazing," he kept saying. Peter really had thought of everything. There was even a bottle opener. There was even a perfect place near the bow, above the *Cuckoo*'s head, for Hart to sit and feel the spray.

"You're going to get sick," Ellen said. "That water's teeming with bacteria."

"You call it cholera, I call it a souvenir," Hart said.

"Really, it's making me nauseous just to look at you," Ellen said. "Oh, God, some just got in your mouth!" She ran downstairs.

Out of kindness, Hart moved back. He was sitting on the back bench with Reed, having a fine time. They were topping off the engine, "one drink for me, one drink for the boat," and watching a line of ramshackle crafts bump and squabble behind them.

Reed had just suggested betting on which one would sink first, when Ellen emerged from below, and came over.

"So what do we do when—note I did not say 'if', but 'when'—somebody sinks?"

"Hope it's the *Spec*," Ellen said.

"They didn't deign to join us, did they? I don't see Harry Sproul's solid-gold yacht . . ."

Ellen and Reed exchanged a look. "Hart," Reed said, "I think you know how much we all appreciated your work this year . . ."

"Well, I appreciate how hard you guys tried to help me out," Hart said. "That was totally beyond the call. If either of you are ever passing through the Midwest—which you won't be, but still—"

Ellen pulled an envelope out of the pocket of her Bermuda shorts. "We all got together and . . . well, we wanted to give you something to remember us by." She handed the envelope to Hart.

"Oh, you guys didn't have to . . ." Hart opened the envelope, expecting to find a card. Instead, he found a page of newsprint, folded up several times, around a piece of paper. "What the hell . . . ?" Hart unfolded the page; it was from their *Daily Money* parody.

"Look on the back," Reed said. It was an ad for a collection of Hart's columns for the weekly table tent, bound into a book, with a Web address for ordering.

Hart was really touched—they had mocked up an ad for him! "Aw, guys, this is so great! I'll take this home and frame it. And someday, when I sell something for real, I'll remember . . . What are you guys smiling about?"

"Look at the other piece of paper," Reed said.

Hart unfolded it. It was a printout of *The Cuckoo*'s online bank account. He glanced at the number at the bottom.

"One hundred and twelve thousand dollars?" Hart said hoarsely. "Is this a joke?"

"No joke. It's sitting in the bank even as we speak," Ellen said. "That's no fake ad—we really ran it. Everywhere except Great Littleton. We wanted to surprise you."

Hart's head was swimming. "Do you mean to tell me that people actually ordered the book?"

"And subscriptions to the magazine, too," Reed said.

Hart didn't know what to say, so Ellen kept filling him in.

"We had no idea it would work, but after the story on CNN . . ." Ellen said. "We never thought we'd get so many orders—and the more you print, the cheaper it gets. So all of a sudden we're sitting on quite a pile."

"And it's still growing," Reed said. "There've been twenty-five more orders today. Now, if Burlington Darling would just sue us . . . " They all laughed.

The reality hit Hart all at once; he thought he might get seasick. "I don't have to leave."

"Not unless you want to," Reed said. "I've been itching to tell you ever since we saw the numbers climbing, but Ellen convinced me not to."

"We wanted it to be a surprise, plus we didn't want you to be disappointed if we couldn't make enough."

"Did you tell him?" Peter yelled from below. "How's he taking it?"

"I think he's going to throw up!" Reed shouted.

Jubilation reigned on the shining bird as it carved through the water at the head of the line. The campus, spread out on either side before them, for once looked approximately like it did in the brochure. Crowds waved from the banks, and any children who threw rocks were promptly shoved into the water by representatives of the university (who denied doing it).

Reed saw a boat under full sail approaching from the opposite direction. "What's that?"

"That, my friend, is a Carthaginian marijuana barge," Hart said.

"You just made that up,"

"No, really," Hart said. "The ancient Carthaginians traded pot."

"And they say Study of Things is a useless major," Reed joked.

"Ahoy, *Cuckoo!*" a man on the Carthaginian ship said through a bullhorn.

"Points for the nautical lingo," Hart said.

"Please stop, so we can pull alongside your craft!"

"I think we're being boarded by the reverse-DEA," Reed said.

"Is there a Pirate Club at Stutts?" Hart asked.

"Shit, I didn't bring my wallet," Reed said. "They'll have to be satisfied with Coke."

Ellen looked strangely tense. She called down to Peter. "Stop the boat, Peter."

The boats behind the *Cuckoo* all began to chatter with complaint. Someone called from behind, "Why are we stopping? I have to pee!"

"Yeah, Ellen—why are we stopping?" Hart asked, but Ellen didn't answer.

The Carthaginians had reached them, coasting to a stop so that they floated alongside. The man who had used the bullhorn—not a student, but an adult—grabbed Ellen's arm and pinched it hard, so that it left a mark. Then he said in a voice loud enough for all the boats around to hear, "Ellen Pokorny: accept or reject?"

"Oh, you have *got* to be kidding," Peter said loudly from below. "Stupid Mugwumps always—" Tabitha shushed him.

Ellen wavered. She looked at Reed, then at Hart.

"*Accept or reject?*" the man repeated. "I cannot ask again."

It seemed like an hour passed. Hart didn't know what he wanted Ellen to say.

"A-accept," Ellen said.

"Then you must come with us," the adult said.

Ellen took off her Grand Marshal's hat and gave it to Hart. "Here," she said, turning away. "I'll see you guys later." She climbed down on to the Carthaginian ship. Hart saw a look pass between Ellen and Reed before Ellen turned away, but he had no idea what it meant.

Most of the student body and even some of the town was arrayed along the banks. The boisterous hijinks of the earlier part of the day had mellowed into many perfect parties. Some people tossed Frisbees across the Turbid. Others barbecued ineptly. Music was everywhere, frequently interrupted by a splash and a cheer as another person was tossed into the slow-moving, fudge-colored river.

"I'm glad Ellen wasn't here to see that," Hart said to himself. The day was ending, and Hart was worn out. It wasn't just his reversal of fortune, or Ellen and Reed's departure, or being out on the water for five hours, but all these combined to make him bone tired. With a late night ahead of him—he still had some packing to do before his flight back home tomorrow—he decided to ask Peter to let him off right after sunset.

Hart suddenly had an idea. Grabbing the banner from under the seat, he unfolded it and hooked the eyelets through the supports Pete had put in for the future awning. The wool was slightly wet, and old, and smelled rather funky. But it would do.

"Tab," Hart called down, "could you come up here?"

"Is the sun down?" his vampire-girlfriend asked.

"Almost," Hart said. "Just come up here."

"But I—"

"Trust me, Tab, it'll be okay."

Tabitha walked up the stairs; Hart took her hand. "Madame," he said, leading her to the back bench, where the mildewy, stained banner blocked the rays of the fading sun.

Tabitha turned to Hart and smiled, then slid under the banner. "You're sweet."

"I do what I can," Hart said. "Sorry about the smell."

The craft got in an especially good place to see the sunset, where Hart and Tabitha could peer between two buildings to the horizon.

"This is nice," Tabitha said, as the boat rocked gently at anchor. "Are you sure you're going to be okay back home?"

"Oh, yeah," Hart said, sounding more confident than he felt. "I don't see what Governor Sniffles can do to me, as long as I stay off the roads."

"I would still feel better if you were staying here," Tabitha said.

The last bit of sun disappeared. "And that's all she wrote," Hart said. "I'd like to take this opportunity to—" He leaned over, kissing Tabitha and groping her shamelessly.

"Don't," Tabitha said, then pointed at a window. There was a person in it; in fact, every window on either side of the Turbid was occupied.

Hart was unfazed. "Let 'em watch. We'll show 'em how it's done."

"Hart Fox, I *will* throw you overboard. . . . Oh, look!" Little sheets of paper—pages—trickled down from a window to their left. This fistful was followed by another, and another. Students in other windows up and down the river joined in, until the air was filled with paper, white and ghostly in the moonlight, fluttering down to the water below. "I didn't think anybody still did this!" Tabitha bubbled. "It's a tradition called

338

'Drowning Euclid.' Graduating seniors rip out the pages of all their books from the last four years, and toss them into the water."

Hart laughed. "I guess this is what a ticker-tape parade feels like . . . And me not even a Wumpsman."

"Not yet," Tabitha said.

Hart laughed nervously—it was bad form (and probably bad luck) to even mention the possibility of being pinched. He thought of Ellen, spirited away earlier that afternoon. Peter, naturally, had begun to weave her into his conspiracy theories. Reed took it more personally, predicting that the *Cuckoo* would lose her in favor of her glamorous new spook friends. Hart had defended Ellen. It was her choice, he said; if she was happy, then he was happy. Peter had accused him of sucking up to increase his chances of being pinched in two years. Hart laughed—he was just glad to be coming back.

Hart felt a sudden rush of pleasure—he'd survived! He'd been able to hack the classes. He'd withstood the slings and arrows of outrageous Darlings. He'd cobbled together a collection of like-minded weirdos. Hell, he even had a girlfriend (though God knew how long that would last). Stutts wasn't the heaven he had expected, but it was his, goddammit, and seeing its flaws up close made him love the place even more. For once in his life, Hart belonged.

Suddenly something splashed on the deck in front of them. Then they heard raucous laughter.

"Water balloons!" Tabitha said, pointing. A group of color-coordinated lunkheads were clustered on the edge of CCA's roof. Each held a candy-colored globe of hate.

Hart sniffed, and smelled an odor he was all too familiar with. "Not water balloons," he said sadly. "*Piss* balloons."

"Oh, how awful!" Another one came in, hitting the side of the craft.

The pair scrambled downstairs. At the top step, Hart turned and saw Trip Darling hefting the biggest balloon of all, a monster at least a foot long; it must've taken a day of hydration to fill. He heaved it, missing badly.

"You haven't won, Fox!" Trip yelled. "Sophomore year's going to be even worse. I guarantee it!"